CRASH LANDING!

She heard MacAran mutter from the controls, "Here goes nothing. This is about as good as we're going to get." He raised his voice. "All right, back there! Brace for landing! Crash positions!"

She bent over obediently, taking the approved tuck and covering the back of her neck with her hands. She felt them strike hard, rebound, and come down again; the crash restraints deployed, nets holding them in their fetal curls. Cushions billowed up from beneath the seat under Ysaye, and she heard the *beeping* of a dozen different alarms. They bounced, struck, and rebounded yet again. Ysaye was beyond fear now; she was paralyzed. Nothing in her training or her experience had prepared her for this.

I'm going to die, she thought dumbly. Thought moved sluggishly through the thick sea of fear that flooded her. The hull cracked sickeningly on the next bounce and Ysaye thought she heard the rending of metal.

That was when she mercifully blacked out.

She came to with freezing cold air and snow blowing into her face. . . .

A Reader's Guide to DARKOVER

THE FOUNDING:
A "lost ship" of Terran origin, in the pre-Empire colonizing days, lands on a planet with a dim red star, later to be called Darkover.
>   DARKOVER LANDFALL

THE AGES OF CHAOS:
1,000 years after the original landfall settlement, society has returned to the feudal level. The Darkovans, their Terran technology renounced or forgotten, have turned instead to free-wheeling, out-of-control matrix technology, psi powers and terrible psi weapons. The populace lives under the domination of the Towers and a tyrannical breeding program to staff the Towers with unnaturally powerful, inbred gifts of *laran*.
>   STORMQUEEN!
>   HAWKMISTRESS!

THE HUNDRED KINGDOMS:
An age of war and strife retaining many of the decimating and disastrous effects of the Ages of Chaos. The lands which are later to become the Seven Domains are divided by continuous border conflicts into a multitude of small, belligerent kingdoms, named for convenience "The Hundred Kingdoms." The close of this era is heralded by the adoption of the Compact, instituted by Varzil the Good. A landmark and turning point in the history of Darkover, the Compact bans all distance weapons, making it a matter of honor that one who seeks to kill must himself face equal risk of death.
>   TWO TO CONQUER
>   THE HEIRS OF HAMMERFELL

THE RENUNCIATES:

During the Ages of Chaos and the time of the Hundred Kingdoms, there were two orders of women who set themselves apart from the patriarchal nature of Darkovan feudal society: the priestesses of Avarra, and the warriors of the Sisterhood of the Sword. Eventually these two independent groups merged to form the powerful and legally chartered Order of Renunciates or Free Amazons, a guild of women bound only by oath as a sisterhood of mutual responsibility. Their primary allegiance is to each other rather than to family, clan, caste or any man save a temporary employer. Alone among Darkovan women, they are exempt from the usual legal restrictions and protections. Their reason for existence is to provide the women of Darkover an alternative to their socially restrictive lives.

THE SHATTERED CHAIN
THENDARA HOUSE
CITY OF SORCERY

AGAINST THE TERRANS
—THE FIRST AGE (Recontact):

After the Hastur Wars, the Hundred Kingdoms are consolidated into the Seven Domains, and ruled by a hereditary aristocracy of seven families, called the Comyn, allegedly descended from the legendary Hastur, Lord of Light. It is during this era that the Terran Empire, really a form of confederacy, rediscovers Darkover, which they know as the fourth planet of the Cottman star system. The fact that Darkover is a lost colony of the Empire is not easily or readily acknowledged by Darkovans and their Comyn overlords.

REDISCOVERY/(with Mercedes Lackey)
THE SPELL SWORD
THE FORBIDDEN TOWER
STAR OF DANGER
*WINDS OF DARKOVER

AGAINST THE TERRANS
—THE SECOND AGE (After the Comyn):

With the initial shock of recontact beginning to wear off, and the Terran spaceport a permanent establishment on the outskirts of the city of Thendara, the younger and less traditional elements of Darkovan society begin the first real exchange of knowledge with the Terrans—learning Terran science and technology and teaching Darkovan matrix technology in turn. Eventually Regis Hastur, the young Comyn lord most active in these exchanges, becomes Regent in a provisional government allied to the Terrans. Darkover is once again reunited with its founding Empire.

    THE BLOODY SUN
    HERITAGE OF HASTUR
  *THE PLANET SAVERS
    SHARRA'S EXILE
  *WORLD WRECKERS
  *RETURN TO DARKOVER

THE DARKOVER ANTHOLOGIES:

These volumes of stories edited by Marion Zimmer Bradley, strive to "fill in the blanks" of Darkovan history, and elaborate on the eras, tales and characters which have captured readers' imaginations.

    THE KEEPER'S PRICE
    SWORD OF CHAOS
    FREE AMAZONS OF DARKOVER
    THE OTHER SIDE OF THE MIRROR
    RED SUN OF DARKOVER
    FOUR MOONS OF DARKOVER
    DOMAINS OF DARKOVER
    RENUNCIATES OF DARKOVER
    LERONI OF DARKOVER
    TOWERS OF DARKOVER
    MARION ZIMMER BRADLEY'S DARKOVER
    SNOWS OF DARKOVER

(*forthcoming)

REDISCOVERY

A NOVEL OF DARKOVER

MARION ZIMMER BRADLEY

AND

MERCEDES LACKEY

D A W B O O K S , I N C .

DONALD A. WOLLHEIM, FOUNDER

375 Hudson Street, New York, NY 10014

ELIZABETH R. WOLLHEIM

SHEILA E. GILBERT

PUBLISHERS

First paperback printing, June 1994

1 2 3 4 5 6 7 8 9

DAW TRADEMARK REGISTERED
U.S. PAT. OFF. AND FOREIGN COUNTRIES
—MARCA REGISTRADA
HECHO EN U.S.A.

PRINTED IN THE U.S.A.

REDISCOVERY

A NOVEL OF DARKOVER

CHAPTER
1

"Ysaye? Are you up there?" Elizabeth Mackintosh poked her head cautiously into the shaft that held the computer core. She was a small, slight woman, not exactly pretty, but with a gentle yet intense liveliness about her that made "prettiness" inconsequential. She had thick, dark hair and blue eyes, lovely and clear, and a voice that sounded, as it echoed the length of the shaft, as if she were singing. She didn't much care for the computers at the best of times, and the narrow shaft that held their working components made her positively claustrophobic. Once she had told Ysaye that the warm gloom, dotted with tiny red working-lights, made her feel as if she were surrounded by a sphere of red-eyed demons. Ysaye had chuckled, thinking she was joking, but it was true.

"I'll be done in a minute," Ysaye Barnett called down. "Just let me get this last board back in." She replaced the board she had been working on and pushed her fingertips lightly against the panel to start her tall body moving down the tube. In the low gravity of the core, it didn't take much of a push. The gravity, and her speed, increased as she neared the end of the shaft, and she landed carefully on bent knees next to Elizabeth at the base. Gravity in the main computer room was .8 standard; and, as usual, Elizabeth had a death grip on the rail that ran down the center of the room. Variations in gravity made Elizabeth nervous; she lived for the day when the ship found a planet she could settle on. Sometimes she wondered why she had ever gone to space— but then she remembered what overpopulated, noisy, techno-addicted Terra was like and knew she could never go back. Only the very wealthy could afford room and privacy on Terra. Back there, light-years behind them, she'd never even be able to afford the privacy of a tiny cubicle like her shipboard quarters on the miniscule salary of a cultural anthropologist.

Ysaye, on the other hand, seemed made for life on shipboard. Changing gravity zones was a game to her —rather like a grown-up version of hopscotch. Her black, wiry hair was braided in cornrows, which kept it out of her face, the equipment she worked with, and the ventilation ducts. She kept her quarters so tidy that the room could pull negative Gs and nothing would fall out of place; she knew the ship's schedules, procedures, and emergency drills forward and backward. The junior ensigns claimed that every piece of data in the computer was duplicated in Ysaye's head and could be retrieved just as quickly from either place.

One ensign who worked third watch even insisted that the computer woke up at night and cried for her. Ysaye had informed him with a twinkle in her bright brown eyes that he needed to be careful of his tendency to anthropomorphize. Not that she didn't talk to the computer herself, of course; but she did try never to do so when anyone might overhear her. After all, she had a reputation as a scientist to maintain.

"Well, that should take care of our little glitch," Ysaye said happily. Nothing pleased her more than finding the answer to a puzzle, and this one had plagued the techs for days, an intermittent Loss-Of-Signal from the robot probe that preceded the ship by about a day. "I told them it was in our hardware and not the probe's.

And I'm going to have *someone's* hide for not running regular tests to check for that sort of thing."

"Any more news on our new planet?" David Lorne, Elizabeth's fiancé, entered the computer room and walked carefully along the rail to join the women. Elizabeth automatically held out her hand; he took it just as automatically. Like a phototropic response, Ysaye thought. David was like Elizabeth's sun, and sometimes it seemed that without him she might wilt and fade.

"No name," Ysaye replied, slipping automatically into reference librarian mode, and keying commands into the console. "Even the star's only in the unabridged. Cottman's Star. Six planets, the record says, but," she pulled up a diagram on the console screen, "our latest scan data makes it seven. Three little rockies, four big fuzzies. The fourth out from the sun is habitable or at least on the edge of being habitable. It's low on dense metals, but it wouldn't be the first planet settled that's short on metals. Plenty of oxygen, though."

"Is that the one with the four moons? Sounds so exotic—like there would be a lot of material for a ballad there," Elizabeth said.

"Well, *everything* sounds to you like there would be material for a ballad," Ysaye pointed out affectionately.

"And why not?" Elizabeth replied with complete seriousness. Ysaye shook her head. Elizabeth had a habit of relating everything to some ballad or other. Granted, folk music was her hobby, and anthropology her specialty; and granted that an awful lot of primitive history was contained in songs and ballads, but still. . . . There was a limit, at least as far as Ysaye was concerned. The time Elizabeth had tried to compare Ysaye's tendency to disappear for days when tracing a computer glitch to the abduction of Thomas the Rhymer by the Queen of Elfland . . . well, it had taken Ysaye weeks to quell all the nonsense about elves and fairies living in the core.

"Any people?" David asked. "Or rather, any signs of sentients?" For both Elizabeth and David that was the big question. It didn't matter much to Ysaye one way or the other; she was ship's crew. But David and Elizabeth wanted to marry and raise a family, and they couldn't do that on shipboard. Children couldn't even travel on a ship—not if they wanted to grow up with anything resembling a human skeleton. Immature bodies were much more delicate and fragile than the planet bound could imagine. They still had time; all three of them had joined the Service right out of the university and were only in their late twenties. Theoretically, sooner or later there would be a planet suitable for either colonization or Empire Contact where the contact and explorations teams could set up shop and stay put for twenty years or more. But after three years of nothing but rockballs, Elizabeth, at least, was getting anxious.

"You're both telepaths," Ysaye teased; "you tell me." It was how they had originally met, as experimental subjects in the parapsychology lab in the university. Unfortunately, the instruments hadn't been set up to measure love at first sight, or they might have had some very interesting data. Ysaye had been the technician working that day, and had dutifully noted down everything else the machines measured. She had never told anyone about the other effects that she saw—or thought she saw. After all, "seeing auras" was such a subjective experience.

Elizabeth was not at all reticent about her "gift"— even if she was a little defensive about it. David just shrugged it off; if people didn't believe him, that was their problem, not his. If really pressed, Ysaye would admit to having some intuition, or the occasional hunch.

Other than that, she preferred not to talk about it. "Things invisible to see" and the knowledge she had from no discernible source were something she used but didn't bandy about.

She had always been something of a loner, and her "talent" had made her lean even farther in that direction. She had learned as a child how to convey the things that she "knew" in the form of questions to the people around her; a child wasn't supposed to correct adults in *her* family, probably because any child was presumed to know less than any adult. But it was very hard for Ysaye to hide what she knew, and so she had chosen solitude instead, as a better sort of "hiding place."

She had carefully concealed her intelligence as well behind a mask of childish innocence and spent every possible moment with her computer. This had not been as difficult for her as it might have been for another child; her parents had enrolled her in computer instruction—"home schooling," it was called—instead of sending her to public school. They considered the values taught in Earth's schools irreligious—and sadly lacking in ethics, morals—any differentiation of right from wrong, a subject Ysaye's mother felt particularly strongly about. Ysaye could *still* hear her mother in the back of her mind sometimes, whenever someone around her indulged in sliding ethics and fuzzy logic.

"I'm not that strong a telepath," Elizabeth replied, quite seriously, although Ysaye had been joking. "And besides I *want* there to be people, so I'm too biased. You don't have any emotional stake in this; what do you think, Ysaye? Are there people there?"

Neither her parents nor the computers Ysaye worked with had ever considered "I don't know" to be an acceptable answer. If you didn't know off the top of your head, you got more data. Almost as a reflex, Ysaye cast her mind toward the planet and got an answer, all without conscious volition or words.

The planet was inhabited; suddenly she knew that. But she couldn't explain how she knew, or prove it, so she temporized. "We'll find out soon enough," she said. "I hope for your sake that it is—though I'd miss you if you left the ship. We need *something* besides a ball of stone and dust; people are starting to get a little bit stir-crazy."

Little behavioral quirks had threatened to turn into full-blown neuroses in the past couple of months. Ysaye had been somewhat insulated from it all, living as much with her beloved computers as she did—but she'd certainly noticed it. Everyone was looking for some kind of an escape from the other members of the two crews. Even lifelong friends—or lovers—were beginning to get on each others' nerves.

"Anyhow, it probably means a few months down," David said cheerfully, "even if it doesn't turn out to be inhabited. Plenty of work for us both, Elizabeth, in our secondaries, if not our specialties." David Lorne was a linguist *and* xenocartographer, Elizabeth an anthropologist *and* meteorologist. Everyone aboard the ship had two or three jobs—except for Ysaye and the computer, who did quite a bit of almost everything.

"I'm ready for that," Elizabeth said. "I'm ready for some *room*. A place where I'm not always bumping into someone. All this travel isn't getting us anywhere."

"That sounds kind of funny," David said teasingly, "especially when you consider all the light-years we've put on this ship."

"I don't mean literally," she replied, making a face at him, "and you know it as well as I do. *Metaphorically* speaking, we're standing still, however many light-years we've traveled. I mean, as far as we're concerned, we might just as well have been confined to a single building in Dallas or San Francisco for the past three years. I'm *tired* of studying textbooks and computer simulations. I want to study something real again."

"Well, I could stand to be employed again," he admitted, with a lopsided grin. "All this space travel makes me feel like I might as well be supercargo. It'll be good to get back to work."

There was nothing unusual about David Lorne except his astonishingly clear eyes and a way he had of looking very straight at anyone he spoke to. He was a remarkably serious young man, already balding and looking somewhat older than his twenty-seven years, but with a subtle and unique sense of humor which he shared with Elizabeth more than anyone else.

"What do you really want to find down there, David?" she asked, feeling suddenly very sober.

"A planet I can make my life's work; some interesting stuff I can really get my teeth into," he answered, with equal seriousness. "A place you and I can make our own; isn't that what we both want? So we can settle down, have a couple of kids who'll grow up to be natives of this world—whatever it turns out to be."

"I'll certainly be glad enough to get down to a planetary surface, *any* surface," she agreed. "I'm so tired of feeling superfluous. Nothing much for you and me to do in space except give concerts for the crew." Elizabeth didn't just collect and study ballads, she performed them as well. She had an extensive repertoire and played and sang beautifully, so she was much in demand for impromptu recitals in the Rec Room as well as the regularly scheduled concerts.

"Well, there are certainly enough people to appreciate them," Ysaye laughed. "And we do have our reputation to maintain; they say we're the only ship in the fleet where the Captain chose his chief engineer because he could play the oboe."

Elizabeth chuckled. Captain Enoch Gibbons' eccentricities were known throughout the Empire's fleet. Anyone on *his* crew, ship's personnel or otherwise, was, of course, chosen for his skills, but Captain Gibbons always seemed to find skilled crewmembers who just happened to have a passion for music. When challenged over the matter of the engineer, he had allegedly argued that good starship engineers were turned out wholesale by the military colleges; but good oboe players, on the contrary, were rather rare—the oboe having been characterized popularly as "the ill woodwind nobody blows good." Captain Gibbons was also an opera buff, and if anyone on board did not have a fair knowledge of the Italian, German, and French languages, it was not from lack of exposure to at least some of their vocabulary. Not a bad thing, really, Ysaye reflected, when month followed month without planetfall. Not like having a ship full of amateur athletes going crazy trying to keep fit—or one full of inveterate games players who might turn competition into quarreling. At least on Gibbons' crew, the personnel could find a harmony in music that they might otherwise lack as the strain increased with the length of the voyage.

"Nothing wrong with giving concerts, either," David told her. "You're a fine singer, and you're doing your part to keep us all from chewing our nails from boredom."

"Good enough," Elizabeth agreed diffidently. "No opera singer though."

"Since I don't really care for opera that much, I don't mind," he said. "And I doubt if there are many of the crew who do, except for the Captain. Although I admit that anyone who actually hates it won't last long on this ship."

"Like your friend Lieutenant Evans?" Elizabeth inquired, with a wrinkle of her nose. She didn't like Evans; his manner put her off, although David liked him well enough. There was something vaguely disturbing about the Lieutenant, although Ysaye had once said dismissively, "Oh, don't worry about Evans; he has a great career as a used aircar salesman ahead of him." Somehow Elizabeth could not see him that cavalierly.

"I don't know about that," David protested. "Yes, he makes rude comments about opera, certainly, but that's just his style. He talks like that about nearly everything." He shook his head. "Anyhow, what on earth are we talking about music for, with a new planet to explore in a few days?"

"Because your new planet is a maybe, and it's *days* away from us, and the crew concert is a certainty, I suppose," Elizabeth answered with a sigh. "It's hard to think of anything but the routine we've had when it'll be days before we can even get close enough to get some decent pictures of the place. I promised my department I'd give them the low-down on the new planet, as soon as there was anything to tell; but if there isn't, I'd better go. I'm due on duty."

"All right, then, love," he agreed, kissing her quickly. "See you later."

David and Elizabeth left for their respective posts, and Ysaye turned back to her console. But instead of keying in anything which could only be answered by "insufficient data," she sat quietly, pondering the puzzle of the inhabited planet.

Who, or what, could those inhabitants be? Perhaps indigenous pre-space peoples, in which case there would probably be no sign of civilization visible from orbit, at least not without a lot of clear sky for their optical telescopes to peer down through.

It *could* even be a lost colony, one of those founded from one of the pre-Empire Lost Ships. That would be fascinating, although Ysaye hadn't heard of any of them out this far.

Yet, she told herself. Just because no one had found one—well, that could be because no one had been looking in the right place.

One had been found only last year, and some of the really old Lost Ships seemed to have gone amazingly far, the ones launched a couple of thousand years ago, before the Terrans had learned how to set up a ship for tracking. Ships lost after that were picked up within a couple of years. So if there *was* a Lost Ship colony here, it would certainly be one of the very early ones, on its own since long before the Empire.

On the other hand, even if her hunch was wrong and the place was uninhabited—not that she really thought it was, but until she had hard evidence it was a good idea to consider all possibilities—it was a good location for a transfer point spaceport, right near where the spiral arms of the galaxy joined, give or take a billion miles or so. So as long as it was habitable, if David and Elizabeth were willing to exercise their secondary specialties instead of their primaries, there would be work enough here for them for a lifetime, provided the Powers That Were decreed that such a spaceport should be built here.

The chime for shift change sounded just as the chief technician for the next watch came in, striding easily across the gravity-gradient to the console terminal. Ysaye logged out, he logged in, and she left the computer room.

As she went down the corridor she found herself stretching aching muscles, and realized that her shoulders, arms, and hands were cramped and stiff. Obviously she had spent more time curled up over finicky little adjustments in the core than she had realized. She decided to wander around for a bit before going to her quarters.

As she passed the door marked "Port Viewer" she decided to stop in. "Come to have a look at our new system?" the young man there inquired as she entered. He was one of the ship's scientific crew, Ysaye knew, so he wouldn't stay on the planet unless they decided to set up a spaceport here. His current job was to survey the planet as much as possible before they landed on it—and right now all their information was coming from the probe. "Thanks for finding the glitch, Ysaye, it was driving us all crazy," he continued. "Or rather, crazier."

She shook her head dismissively. "Nothing special," she said diffidently. "If I hadn't found it, someone else would have."

The young man gave her a skeptical look, but didn't comment. "I suppose you know there's at least one habitable," he continued, "the fourth. The fifth maybe, but that's stretching it a bit—the fifth is mostly frozen; ice caps all year, and the year's five Standard years long. Four is just barely habitable though: pretty rough climate, but carbon-based life-forms could live there. No major unfrozen seas, one continent. I wouldn't want to live there, and I doubt you would either; it's cold as Dante's hell. But it's definitely within limits."

"Not bad, Haldane," Ysaye said—then grinned. "Rehearsing for your report to the captain?"

"You guessed it," John Haldane replied cheerfully. "Oh—did I mention that it has four moons, each a different color?"

She shook her head at him, and made a *tsk*-ing sound. "No, you forgot them; you need to organize your material better. Isn't four moons a record for a planet this small?"

He nodded, half of his attention on his console.

"You may be right; if a planet has more than that, it's usually a big fuzzy, and the moons are planetlike. Like Jupiter in the old solar system. I forget how many moons they finally decided it had; seemed to capture every bit of flotsam that came anywhere near it. But there were at least eleven major ones."

Ysaye peered down at the screen. The object of all their perusal was singularly unprepossessing at this range. "Four moons. Hmm. Wonder how it managed that?"

Haldane shrugged. "Who knows? That's not my specialty. I think Bettmar's World has five, but there is a limit: mass of the combined moons must be less than that of the planet for a habitable. Usually less than a fifth its combined weight. Also there is a limit to size; too small and they escape the primary and become asteroids." He gestured at the view. "The white one there is just about at the lower limit for size."

"Elizabeth was saying something about how much material there would be for ballads on a world with four moons," Ysaye told him.

Haldane adjusted the focus, and the white moon all but leapt out of the screen at them. "At a guess, I'd say they must do strange things to the natives' mythology, if there are any natives, that is. With four moons, I'd say the concept of monotheism wouldn't have much chance of occurring! They must look like something from the surface of the planet—all different colors. I've never seen anything like it before. Definitely anomalous."

Ysaye narrowed her eyes and tried to make out more details of the planet itself, but it was a cloud-sheathed enigma. "Are they really different colors, or is it just some effect of the sun that makes them look that way?"

Haldane shook his head. "Your guess is as good as mine; I never saw anything like—oh, I said that. I know one thing though," he added. "I'll bet that no matter how advanced the natives are, they still play a substantial part in whatever religion there may be down there. Moons always do."

"Do you know if we're going to land on any of them?" Ysaye asked.

"Probably we'll want a weather station on one of them," he said. "That would be the first step in any case. And if it's a pre-space aboriginal culture, that's about all we can do, observe the weather. We wouldn't be allowed to affect anything they do; primitive people have to be left to evolve in their own way."

"If there's any kind of culture down there, just landing on the planet would affect them," Ysaye pointed out.

"True," Haldane said blithely, "but anything we do before we make an official evaluation of them doesn't count. My God! Look at that!" He broke off suddenly, fussing with his instruments. "No, I can't focus any closer, damn it—the clouds down there are something awful."

"What is it?" Ysaye leaned over his shoulder for a closer look. "Signs of life? A beacon saying 'We're here, come and get us'?" When he didn't answer, she added flippantly, "A giant alien advertisement sign?"

"Nothing so definite," Haldane replied, "Great Wall of China effect—but that was a deliberately created structure. I suspect this one is a natural formation."

"Like what?" she asked. "What kind of formation would be big enough to see from this far away? The probe isn't even in orbit yet!"

"A glacier," he said. "Something bigger than any glacier in any of Terra's ice ages. One which goes halfway round the world. A wall around the world."

A wall around the world? That certainly caught her imagination. "Who could have built it?"

"No one; it's a natural phenomenon," he said positively.

"A natural formation?" she replied skeptically.

"Why not?" he retorted. "Earth's Great Wall can be seen, under proper magnification, from the moon. There was even some debate about whether the Great Wall of China was made that way on purpose, and then the society that built it dwindled down to pretechnical—or do I mean post-technical?"

"Whichever you mean," Ysaye said repressively, "I wouldn't advise you to run that particular theory past the Captain. Haven't you heard his standard speech about 'the pseudoscience of psychoceramics'?"

"Several times," Haldane admitted, wincing. "All right, then: while I am *assuming* this glacier is natural, given the hideous climate down there, I can't be *certain* whether this glacier is natural, made by resident Intelligent Beings, or left over from a previous or visiting society of IBs. For all I know, it could be the equivalent of a school science project for the proverbial bug-eyed monster. Or even an art project."

"All right, enough theories," Ysaye laughed. "Any signs of travel on any of the moons?"

He shook his head. "Nothing obvious. Nothing the probe can pinpoint, anyway. We left footprints and assorted garbage on ours, but it's too soon to tell about this one. If we really search, we might find a stray beer can or so, and that's proof of a sort. Ah, look! The clouds are clearing!"

He fussed with the instruments until the glacier was neatly centered in the viewer. "At least this will serve for a landing marker, although the terrain there might be fairly rough and mountainous. There's a higher oxygen content than normal, so the hyper-Himalayas there would still be climbable, believe it or not. If you like that sort of thing. Personally, I think if God had wanted us to climb mountains, He'd have given us hooves and pitons instead of hands and feet."

"Climbable by what?" Ysaye asked dubiously. "Do you think the planet's inhabited?"

Haldane shrugged. "Can't tell from here. Unless it's heavily industrialized, we couldn't see anything from out here anyway, and it doesn't seem to be industrialized. If we find it's inhabited, we may have to set up a weather station on one of the moons and go home without disturbing them."

"And if they're a Lost Colony?" *Why did I ask that?* she wondered. She had already dismissed the idea once, yet here it was again, cropping up and making her feel vaguely disturbed.

"I don't know," he said uncertainly. "There are no real rules for dealing with Lost Colonies. Every time we've run into one, the situation has been different. They're us—and yet, they're not us, if you get my meaning."

"Not really," Ysaye replied. "What are the odds, though?"

Haldane shook his head. "It's really unlikely; but I understand there are a couple of ships that are still unaccounted for. It's funny to think if it is, we'll only be legends to them. Or maybe a religion—my, I wonder how *that* would mix in with four moons! Would we be gods returning, I wonder, or something horrible out of the Utter Night?"

"Probably gods. If, against all odds, this were a Lost Colony, it would make Elizabeth happy," Ysaye pointed out. "Legends are her business, and in a sense religion is, too."

John Haldane laughed. "I can see it now: you and Elizabeth can be the goddesses, one black and one white." He bowed to her, clasping his hands across his chest. "Oh, great Sky-Goddess of Night, hear the prayers of your humble servant! You'd never want to come back to the ship, you'd have hundreds of nubile young men literally worshiping at your feet!"

Ysaye laughed, too, shaking her head. "You're incorrigible, Haldane. I assure you; the only divinity I care for is the kind made with sugar and covered with lots of chocolate."

CHAPTER 2

The banner-bearer saw the Tower first, where it reared isolated and lonely, a structure of brown unfinished stone. It rose high above the plain and the little village that huddled at its feet, as if seeking protection beneath the Tower's skirts. It was nearing evening and the great red sun hung low on the horizon, sinking visibly. Already three of the four moons hung in the sky, nearly invisible behind the clouds of a late spring rain that had just begun to mist down upon the riders, nothing more than pale blurs of slightly brighter cloud amid the gloom. The clouds were heavy, but at this season the rain did not turn to snow, at least.

There were eight guardsmen including the banner-bearer, all mounted on the finest of riding animals, and the Hastur banner went before them, noble blue and silver with its device of the silver tree and its motto. *Permanedal*—"I shall remain." Behind them rode Lorill Hastur, his sister, the lady Leonie Hastur, and Melissa Di Asturien, the lady's companion and chaperone—although at the advanced age of sixteen, Melissa was hardly much of a chaperone, and since she bored Leonie entirely, she wasn't much of a companion either. Both women were swathed in long riding-veils. Fine though the riding-beasts were, they moved slowly, wearily, for the caravan had been on the road since sunrise.

Lorill signaled them to halt. With the Tower already

in sight, it was hard to stop, even though they all knew that their goal was still several hours' journey away. Distances here on the plain were often deceptive.

From long habit, Lorill Hastur left the decision of whether to camp or go on to his sister.

"We could camp here," he said, waving at a clearing sheltered by budding trees beside the roadside and ignoring the mist that beaded up on his eyelashes. "If it begins to rain hard, we would have to stop anyway; I can't see any reason to try to push ahead in a rainstorm and risk laming our beasts."

"I could ride all night," Leonie protested, "and I hate to stop in sight of the Tower. But—"

She paused for a moment, thinking. If they continued to ride in the rain, they would arrive at the Tower sodden, chilled, and exhausted. It was a night of four moons—and her last night of freedom. Perhaps it would not be such a bad thing, to spend it in the open. . . .

"And where will we stay?" Melissa asked, with a frown that betokened immediate rejection of Leonie's idea. "In tents?"

"Derik tells me that there is a good inn in the next village," Lorill said. "I suppose he is thinking of their beer, though, and not the accommodations."

Leonie chuckled, for Derik's capacity had become a standing joke with them all on this journey.

"He drinks like a monk at Midwinter," she laughed. "But he is sober enough on the road. I suppose we should not grudge him his beer—"

"I don't wish to ride all through the night, at least," Melissa put in querulously, with an odd combination of whine and her usual simper.

Leonie tensed with irritation and held back a snappish reply; but Lorill only said good-naturedly, "Well, I don't suppose *you* are thinking of the beer."

"Not at all," Melissa replied, with a pout, "only of

a warm fire. There is no reason to suffer in a tent when we may *have* that warm fire with a little more riding."

Suffer in a tent? In the style of tents a Hastur entourage carried with them, Leonie thought a night in a tent was hardly suffering, although it might be a bit chillier than Melissa preferred—but Melissa was given to complaints and delicate allusions to her fragile health. And, without a doubt, once Melissa was warmed through, there would be complaints about the food, the smoke-filled room, and squeals of fear at the sight of any pests. Leonie much preferred a night in a tent, though it might be a trifle cold and damp, to a night spent in a vermin-infested inn. The tent, at least, was a known quantity; the quality of the inn ahead a matter of speculation.

And there was that one other consideration. . . .

Leonie's beast stirred restlessly, as she said, with a wistful sigh, calculated to coax her brother into indulging her, "It will be a night of four moons—"

"But you will not be able to see them," Lorill pointed out with inescapable logic. "They are hidden by clouds; you might as well enjoy the fireside. The inn will at least be heated and dry."

"The inn *may* well be as leaky as a Dry Towner's promises, and with a legion of mice and fleas. But I will have the rest of my life for firesides," Leonie protested. "I will have the rest of my life for seeing only the world within four walls! And a night of four moons does not come so often that I care to miss it!"

She glanced scornfully at Melissa, wishing the young woman anywhere except riding as her chaperone. For that matter, she could quite readily have done without the guardsmen and banner-bearer as well. If truth were known, she would rather have ridden alone with Lorill. The Hastur twins had always been close, and she could see no danger in such a brief journey together—he was her *twin*, after all, he was hardly going to offer her any insult!

But both her high rank and the present fashion in manners did not approve of young ladies riding even in the company of their brothers without ladylike escort and chaperonage, guards and the proper entourage. According to Darkovan custom, Lorill had been formally declared a man on their fifteenth birthday; and Leonie was now considered a young woman, not a child. She was rather hoydenish still and very strong-willed, but of absolutely unblemished reputation—

Which a long ride with no chaperones could conceivably damage.

Bother custom, she thought rebelliously. If Lorill could not be thought to provide enough protection, she was not above protecting herself, after all! Lorill was medium height for a man, but Leonie, at almost the same height, was unusually tall for a woman. That very height should give no few men pause to think.

She was striking in other ways as well. Like all the Hastur women, and most of the men, she was fair of face with brilliant copper-colored hair, hair that was currently bound into a crown of braids over her forehead. Even more than Lorill, she bore the strong stamp of the Hastur kindred. *Comyn*; that was branded into every inch of her. Comyn and Hastur—the combination should make even the boldest outlaw think twice about interfering with her. Should she come to any harm, the search for her attackers would be unrelenting, and the vengeance exacted terrible.

Leonie was also remarkably beautiful—a fact of which she was very much aware—and had for the last three years been the toast of the court. Between the courtiers and her would-be suitors, Leonie had been very much the petted and spoiled darling of her set. Their father was one of King Stefan's major advisers, and it was well-known that at one point even the widowed King Stefan Elhalyn himself had sought Leonie's hand in marriage. That had made her more popular yet, if such a thing were possible, as even those outside her age-group sought her attention, with an eye to the day when she might be Queen.

But Leonie had shown no mind to marry. She had another goal in mind entirely, and not even the prospect of a crown could distract her from it, for a queen's power was limited to what her lord and king granted her. Leonie wanted no such limitations on herself. Lorill did not have to suffer them, so why should she? Were they not twins, and born equal, except for sex?

From early girlhood Leonie had wanted to seek a place in one of the Towers, where she would devote herself lifelong to the calling of a *leronis*. This would give her a place substantially above, both politically and socially, that of any female aristocrat, and power equal to Lorill's.

And if she achieved her secret goal and became the Keeper of Arilinn Tower, she would have power greater than her twin's, at least as long as their father lived. For the Keeper of Arilinn held a Council seat in her own right, and took the orders of no man except the King himself.

There was no difficulty in finding a Tower that would accept her. It was widely known that the lady Leonie was richly endowed with the Hastur *laran*. Yet now that the moment was at hand, Leonie had become acutely and painfully aware that this chosen path of hers would separate her from her family and loved ones, for Leonie would be isolated from her kindred during the period of her training in the Tower. At this moment, whatever she might become, she was only a young girl facing separation from her brother and all her kinfolk. It was a daunting prospect, even for Leonie.

"I will have the rest of my life to sit by the fire," she repeated, staring vaguely up at the darkening sky. "On a night of four moons—"

"Which, unfortunately, or perhaps fortunately, you cannot see," Lorill teased. "You know what they say about things that happen under the four moons."

She ignored him. "I do not want to be locked away inside a building tonight!" she said stubbornly. "Do you think a *chieri* might come and ravish me in my tent without you and the guardsmen noticing? Or would Dry Towners suddenly spring up from the Plain and carry me away?"

"Oh! Scandalous, Leonie! For shame!" Lady Melissa remonstrated, covering her mouth with her hand, as if she had been hideously shocked by such a silly idea.

Perhaps she was simply shocked by the notion that Leonie had dared to joke about such things as abduction and ravishment.

Leonie had gotten quite enough of Melissa's crotchets and vapors, and she was heartily weary of them. "Oh, do be quiet Melissa," she snapped. "Already at sixteen you are an old maid! And a fussy one at that!"

Lorill just grinned. "I take it that means you don't want to go to the inn? Well, Derik can do without his beer for once!" He shook his head. "At least we can set up the tents before the real rain begins. But you are the most unnatural girl I ever knew," he teased, "wanting to camp out instead of going to a good inn!"

"I want to be under the stars," she repeated. "It is my last night outside the Tower, and I want to spend it under the stars."

"What, in this rain?" he asked, laughing. "Stars? You might just as well have a wooden roof over you, for all that you'll see them."

"It won't rain all night," she said positively.

"It doesn't look to me as though it will stop before morning." Lorill shrugged, giving in. "But we shall do as you wish, Leonie. It is your last night before entering the Tower, after all."

Leonie sat her saddle easily, her reins loose, her beast calm, waiting for Lorill to arrange the camp. She was a good rider—and at any rate, her *chervine* was far too weary to bolt.

He gave the order for the tents to be pitched, and Leonie ignored the faint grumbles and occasional resentful glances that were cast her way as well. The guardsmen should be glad enough to stop, and a night spent in a stable—which was all the shelter a retainer would likely get in a tiny inn—was no better than one in a tent. It might well be colder, in fact—in a stable they would not be permitted a fire. Once they settled into their own tents, they might well recall this.

While the guardsmen were unfurling the canvas structures, Lorill dismounted, helping Leonie down from her riding-beast, and into the dubious shelter beneath a tree. Melissa followed, sniffing loudly, pretending to a chill Leonie doubted she truly felt. Melissa just wanted someone to feel sorry for her—as always. Why her father had chosen Melissa as her companion, Leonie had no notion. Perhaps it was that Melissa was so *very* prim, there was no chance whatsoever that Leonie could be tempted into mischief, as she might have been with a livelier friend.

The rain grew heavier as the guardsmen struggled with the bulky canvas, and Leonie's riding mantle was less protection by the moment. She felt a touch of dampness along her shoulders, and more than dampness at the hem—and Melissa's sniffles had gone from theatrical to genuine. For a moment she regretted her stubborn decision—but only for a moment. This was her last night in relative freedom; not until she wore the crimson robes of a Keeper would she ever have this much liberty again. She was resolved to savor it.

The moment the tents were erected, the young Hastur lord gave orders for a fire to be lighted, and for braziers to be carried into the tents to warm them. He guided Leonie through the thickening darkness to hers, holding her hand to keep her from falling when the sodden hem of her cloak wrapped around her ankles and threatened to trip her.

"Here we are, then. I still think you'd be more comfortable in the inn in the village, and I know perfectly well Melissa would be," he sighed patiently, "but here is your bed under the stars—not that you'll see much of either stars or moons this night. I can't imagine where you get these notions, Leonie. Do they spring from some logic that only you can see, or simply from a desire to see us all bend to your will?"

Leonie divested herself of her wet cloak, flung herself into a nest of pillows, and lay gazing up at her brother. Candlelight from the lantern hanging on the center pole of the tent revealed his handsome face clearly. It gave Leonie the unsettling feeling of seeing herself looking back down at her. "I think often upon the moons," she said without preamble. "What do you think they might be?"

If the abrupt change of subject startled him, he gave no sign. "My tutor tells me that, regardless of the old legends about *chieri* marrying into the Domains, the moons are no more than immense pieces of rock circling our world," Lorill said. "Dead, deserted, airless, cold, and lifeless."

She thought that over for a moment. This did not match with the recent uneasy feeling she had been experiencing. "And do you believe this, Lorill?"

"I do not know." Lorill shrugged, as if the matter were of no importance. Perhaps, to him, it was not. "I am not a romantic like you, *chiya*. I see no reason to doubt it; I don't really care much what they are. They cannot affect us, after all, nor can we affect them."

"I do care about them." Leonie frowned suddenly. This was the only time she might have to talk with her brother in person about her premonitions. It might not be the best time—but there would be no opportunity once she was inside Dalereuth. "I feel that something is coming upon us from the moons—that our lives may never be the same." She turned on her back and stared at the tent ceiling, as if she could look through it and the clouds above to see the moons. "Truly, Lorill, don't you feel that something very important is about to happen?"

"Not really," he said, yawning. "Nothing but sleep. You are a woman, Leonie; you feel the influence of moons, perhaps it is no more than that. Even though it is raining and you can't see it, Liriel still pulls at you. Everyone knows how sensitive women are to the moons—and how dramatic their influence can be."

Leonie knew the truth of Lorill's words. "With the present conjunction," she pointed out, "they *all* pull at me. I wish the sky were clear tonight. But quite apart from that, I feel—"

"Come, Leonie, don't go all mystical on me." Lorill interrupted, seeming somewhat worried. "Next, I'll think you've turned into Melissa, all vapors and nonsense, and you will be having visions of Evanda and Avarra!"

"No," she said. "You may tease, Lorill, and you may doubt as you like. But I say something is coming to us—some great change in our lives—and nothing will ever be the same again. I mean that for all of us, not just you and me."

She spoke with such conviction that Lorill looked sharply at her, and stopped his teasing. He nodded, quite soberly. "You are a *leronis*, sister, Tower-trained or no. If you say something is going to happen, well, it may be that you are gifted with foreknowledge. Do you have any notion what this great event will be?"

The vagueness of her feeling gave her a headache. "I wish I did, Lorill," she replied, uncertain and unhappy. "I know only that it has to do with the moons; nothing more than that. I feel it; I could swear to it. Sometimes I do not even know if I want to go to Dalereuth anymore in view of the days which are coming now."

"What do you mean?" he asked, startled. As well he might be. Leonie had never let any consideration stand in the way of her desire to go to a Tower before this. She had ridden roughshod over anyone who had suggested she might choose some other course for her future. She had refused even the hand of the King, all in her quest to become a *leronis*.

"I wish that I could tell you," she said, knitting her brows, trying to concentrate. "If I were a fully-trained *leronis*, not just a novice . . ." her voice trailed off, as if the words which could describe what she knew eluded her. But it was not the words that she lacked, it was the ability to narrow her foreboding down to anything more than *feelings*, something as evanescent as the morning fog, and as hard to catch.

Lorill stood for a moment, looking pensive. "Whatever it may be, I wish I could share your foreknowledge. But you know what they told me when I received my matrix," his left hand absentmindedly fingered the silk bag at his throat, "that with twins, one has rather more, and the other rather less than the usual share of *laran*. I need not tell you how it is divided between the two of us. No doubt you will use yours better than I do mine."

Leonie knew what he meant. It was just as well that

Lorrill had the weaker *laran*, for in these days, even though there was peace in the countryside, no profession so withdrawn from life as that of matrix worker would be allowed to any Hastur male unless he were something as redundant as a seventh son. It was inevitable that Lorill would take his place at court beside their father, and whether or not he cared for that notion was of little matter. In her way, Leonie would experience far more freedom than he would, once she was fully-trained. She would have her choice of where she went, and only the strength of her *laran* would limit her in her quest for the ultimate prize—the post of Keeper.

"What is it that you *see*, sister?" he asked in a low voice, dark with apprehension.

"No more than I told you." Leonie sighed, turning back to face him. "Danger, and change, and opportunity coming to us—from the moons. Isn't that enough?"

"I could hardly take that to our father, or to the Council," Lorill shook his head. "If I go to them with nothing more than a vague premonition, and talk about the moons, they will think I have been drinking like—what was it you said about Derik?—like a monk at Midwinter."

"True enough," she sighed. "But what can I do?"

"If you had more information for me—" he suggested delicately. He should *not* have hinted that an untrained girl go seeking further enlightenment, with no supervision. Especially not a Hastur, with the Hastur Gift being what it was—the power of the living matrix. If Leonie had *that* in full measure, she would not need a matrix crystal to find herself in trouble from which only a Keeper could extract her. But Leonie was accustomed to doing things her own way—and Lorill was used to her remarkable ability to do just about anything she set her mind to.

Leonie frowned, but in distress rather than disapproval. "I will try," she said, after a moment. "I'll do the best I can. Maybe I can yet *see* something more definite—something that we can use to convince Father."

As Lorill left her to her solitary meditations, Leonie extinguished her lantern but did not undress, listening instead to the sounds of the camp about her, patiently waiting for the last guardsman to settle into his bedroll.

She did not have long to wait. Virtually everyone was so weary from the chill and rain that they were glad to seek the warmth of blankets. As soon as it seemed as though all had retired for the night, save the one guard prowling the perimeter of the camp in his soggy cape, Leonie got up and went to the entrance of her tent.

She peered out cautiously, turning her attention to the sky. The clouds lay heavy and dripping above, showing little inclination to move until they had dropped all of the rain they carried. But Leonie knew from years of experience that clouds were always moving, it was merely a matter of which way and how fast. It had only been within the last year or so that she had been able to put her observations to actual use.

She watched carefully until she could tell the direction of movement, the direction that would tell her which way the wind was blowing at the height of the clouds. Past experience had shown her that it was not always the same direction as the wind on the ground. Once she knew the right path, she reached out with her mind and nudged the heavy clouds in that direction, pushing them along like a shepherd with a flock of fat, lazy sheep, until they were out of her way and she could see the sky. The four moons floated high above the tents, all at the full, each a different color. They were beautiful—but they were silent and enigmatic as ever.

Leonie tied the entrance flaps open and sat on one of her pillows, trying to touch something within her that would give her vague premonitions some form or substance.

All that earned her was a growing sleeplessness.

She sat at the entrance to her tent and stared up at them for several hours, trying to focus her *laran* on what she could see with her physical eyes, the round shapes of the four moons—trying to focus her mind on what she knew was coming, trying to focus on the terrible apprehension she felt.

Trying to find the answers she sensed that she would need—and soon.

CHAPTER 3

A ring of little domes, like an untidy nest of mush-
rooms, had sprouted on the surface of the largest
of the moons. Around the domes, space-suited personnel and machines worked to make the installation self-
supporting and self-maintaining.

Inside the largest of the domes, Ysaye sat before a
computer terminal, watching on the screen as the
brightly painted, toylike satellite fired a last retro and
slid elegantly into orbit.

"Well, that's number one—the first mapping and
weather satellite," David commented happily, looking
over her shoulder. "Now Elizabeth and I can really go
to work. That's a remarkably sophisticated piece of
machinery, according to her."

"Sophisticated in what way?" Ysaye asked. "The
onboard computers aren't all that special."

She wanted to keep him talking; she was aware of
the hiss of air in the ventilation system in a way she had
never been on the ship. She just didn't feel entirely
confident with nothing between herself and vacuum but
a thin skin of flexible membrane.

David seemed willing to oblige her. "It's the ob-
servational equipment, the optics, that are special.
I hear that this Terra Mark XXIV has high enough
resolution to see a lighted match on the night side.
At fifty thousand meters, I've been told the ones in

geosynch orbit over Terra would let you read the license plate on a car parked in the Ambassadorial Parking Lot in Nigeria. I assume this one can do the same."

"That's if they have cars and parking lots," commented Elizabeth, coming up behind him. "And Embassies. Of course if they don't, I suppose we can help them to build some—"

He turned with a smile and answered, "Well, to see the numbers on a street sign. Or whatever they use down there for streets and signs. Hello, love! Are you here to start the weather observations?"

"You guessed it," she replied. "If you've got first watch for Mapping and Exploring, we're going to be able to work together." She looked around her, at the bank of monitors showing the ships' crew working outside. "Do you think the people here ever reached their moons?"

"If they did, they didn't leave as much as a stray film wrapping or food tube," he said, "at least not that we've seen so far. Personally, I tend to doubt it; there're no real signs of technology that we'd recognize as such—no big lighted areas at night that might be a city, and no radio signals at all."

Ysaye shook her head. "As the techs keep reminding me, we don't even know yet if there's sentient life down there at all, and we won't till the cameras on the satellite get working."

Elizabeth frowned at the blank monitors that represented incoming pictures from the satellite. "I'm not sure we'd know even then, Ysaye. There is heavy cloud cover down there. If there are sentients, and they aren't too advanced, we could easily miss them."

"I can't see how," David replied. "With that kind of resolution, all we need to have is a break in the clouds and we should be able to see a monkey—or whatever else they have that fills that particular ecological niche," he added quickly, "moving through the branches of that forest down there."

"Only the top branches," Elizabeth argued. "And only if the cloud cover *does* break *and* the camera is pointed in the right direction!"

"Surely sooner or later it will be," David said, with a dismissive shrug. "And sooner or later the clouds have to break. But even if there *are* IBs down there, we're not going to pick up anything much smaller than a lighted city until we get most of the weather satellite network going. Any idea how long that will take, Ysaye?"

"Hours," Ysaye said tiredly. "Good thing it's mostly automated. All I have to do is baby-sit it."

"You look awfully tired, Ysaye," said Elizabeth, with concern in her blue eyes. "How long have you been working, anyway? Or should I say—overworking?"

Ysaye shrugged helplessly. "I don't know. I've lost track again."

"Does that translate to 'I hooked my brain up to the computer three days ago and I haven't taken a break since'?" David teased.

"Something like that," Ysaye admitted with a weary chuckle. "That, and—well, you two know I don't like sleeping in a strange bed. I couldn't get any sleep, so I just kept working."

"Why don't you lie down over there for a bit and try again?" Elizabeth suggested, indicating the pile of padded computer blankets in the corner. "Even you admit this whole process is automatic, and David and I will be here to let you know if anything goes wrong. Nobody else is likely to come in here for hours; everyone but us and the construction crew is still on the ship. It should be nice and quiet."

"That won't last long," David warned. "There's nothing to equal the stampede off-ship, as soon as security passes the air and gives the all-clear. That'll happen here, too, as soon as security is happy about the domes being stabilized. Not that there's any fresh air here, but at least the domes are a change from the ship."

"Yes," Ysaye murmured, "the gravity's lower." She walked over to the blankets and flopped loosely down onto them. "I think I'll take your suggestion, Elizabeth; right now I probably could sleep anywhere—and possibly right through nearly anything. Nudge me if anything interesting happens."

"Will do," Elizabeth said cheerfully. "You definitely need a break before they put you to work in the library, looking up obscure papers on moon formations for the Captain. One of the techs told me that this four-moon system was driving him to distraction!"

David, who had been watching the monitors showing the work going on outside the dome said suddenly, "Hey, looks like they're setting up the Recreational Dome—unless it's the Living Quarters. It's a big one, anyway."

"No, I'm sure it's not the Living Quarters. I heard the First Officer say we'll wait for the first party checking out the planet to come back with a report before they do that," Elizabeth said. "We might be able to just set up down there, especially if there *aren't* any IBs. Why put up another full-size dome and make air for it when there's plenty of perfectly good natural air down on the surface there—"

"Good point—though I still wouldn't bet against IBs," he agreed. Ysaye, lying quietly with her eyes closed, heard the scratch of a chair across the floor. She didn't need to look to know that David had appropriated both her chair and the terminal. Her guess was confirmed when his voice continued from there, a little to the right of her. "One thing the planet won't be short on is fresh air—and even if there are IBs, no planet yet has figured out a way to sell the air. You may get that on orbital colonies, or colonies on airless worlds, but natural air is still the one thing that's free, everywhere."

"Don't let the authorities hear you say that," Elizabeth teased, "or they'll figure out a way to meter it, and charge us for breathing."

"What do you think a head tax is?" he asked, laughing.

She joined in the laughter. There was silence for a long while, as Ysaye half-dozed, then Elizabeth, noticing a change on the screen, asked, "What's happening now?"

"The system's setting up the satellite's instrument package," he replied. "It ought to be just about ready, and then we'll start getting some initial meteorological data. Ysaye was right about one thing; there's a lot of cloud cover down there. I'm going to have to really work to get some decent maps done."

"Well, at least I'll have plenty to do for a while," she exclaimed, laughing. "Good! I admit it; I'm a weather junkie."

"Probably just as well, since it's your assigned job," he teased. "And we've been in space so damn long—"

"Nothing but simulations to keep me from going stir-crazy," she sighed. "I am so *tired* of computer models—"

"Well, I suppose they keep us in practice, but they sure aren't the real thing" he agreed. "Look, the computer's finished the remote tests. Looks like everything is ready to set up." He keyed in the "go" entry. The screen started scrolling through the incoming data too fast to read, but neither of them were worried, since it was all being stored for later perusal. The printer slurped in a piece of paper and delivered the first of the weather maps, as a second monitor built up a detailed view of the planet below them, with Dopplered radar showing wind-flows and cloud-density.

He scanned the map, which showed essentially the same thing, translated into numbers. "Looks like you've got a storm building in the mountains," he said. "We can watch it; it ought to hit later tonight. Looks like it will be a big one. The next couple of orbit swings will pick it up."

"Give." Elizabeth tweaked the paper out of his hand. "Goodness, those are complex patterns down there! Lots of storms. I pity the natives; probably the people on the surface don't know half as much about their weather as we already do, and wish they did."

"Then we'll have something to give them," said David, turning away from the screen. "Weren't you supposed to give a concert to celebrate getting the domes set up or something?"

"With Captain Gibbons in charge?" Elizabeth laughed. "It's a certainty. He's ordered one to celebrate just about everything else. Folk songs this time, I think, which means the burden of performance will fall on me, but not until I get the local weather patterns established. Now that I finally have some real work to do, celebrations will just have to wait! Though Ysaye *was* talking about some new instrument sounds she's got out of the orchestra synthesizer that she wants to show off; she told me she's hooked up a flute to it and transposed the wave forms so they come out in the bass register. Maybe she can give her own concert."

"Hmm." He was studying the monitor intently. "Well, there's no hope for it; I'm going to need the full net in place to get any level of detail at all. There's just too much cloud cover, and so much snow on the ground that I'm not sure my topographical reads are going to be even close to correct."

Elizabeth patted his shoulder sympathetically. "I wish I could help," she replied.

"Well, I might just as well go to the concert," he said with a shrug. "There won't be anything I can do until we get all the satellites in place. At least it'll give me something to think about, especially if she's really got a new sound," he continued. "Though so many people have been playing around with synthesizers, and to me they all sound exactly alike anyhow."

"Not all that much," she protested absently, her attention all on the next weather map. She chewed a hangnail as she frowned over something on the paper she either didn't like, or didn't understand.

Rendered temporarily useless by the same weather that held Elizabeth fascinated, David continued the discussion. "Well, when you come right down to it," David said, "an electronic tone is an electronic tone, and there's not that much difference between electronic sounds, or what you can do with them."

"I don't agree," Elizabeth answered, though she didn't look up from her work. They were both used to carrying on conversations that had nothing whatsoever to do with what they were doing. "With the sounds we've programmed in—"

"Sounds," he said firmly. "Not music."

"You're thinking like a prehistoric," she teased, glancing up at him for a moment and wrinkling her nose. "I don't accept that much difference between them. You think you have to bang on something, or blow into it, or scrape on it, to make music. What's sacred about that?"

"You modern musicians!" he said resignedly. "Any

kind of noise, clatter, disharmony—a fine example of folk musician *you* are! I'm surprised they don't take away your card in the Authenticity Union!"

"Folk musicians wouldn't put up with a union," she told him. "And I think we've had this argument before." She laughed, and went back to her maps, making notations and calling up more data from her terminal, seeming happier than she had in months. "You've got to admit that randomness—"

"I haven't got to admit anything," he said, laughing. "I have a perfect right, if I want to, to say no real music has been written since Hardesty—or for that matter since Handel. What came afterward was not, by my definition, music at all. Just noise. Don't they even teach the elementary tone-row any more?"

"Haven't you got *any* work to do?" she asked. At his shrug at the cloud-covered globe in the monitor, she sighed. "Well, I learned it. Granted, it was a small private college, but you'll be happy to know that Juilliard still requires knowledge of the major and minor scales for admission."

"Hooray! The next thing you know, they'll be expecting people to learn a simple ground bass," murmured David.

"Next thing you know, someone might expect a cartographer to earn his salary!"

"I would if I could," he pointed out. "There's nothing I can do right now that the computer isn't doing better."

"Well, I've got work to do, lots of it, and I'm not going to argue anymore" she said. "You're just one of those primitivists who refuse to accept compositions for electronics, like art schools that insist for graduation, before they submit any modern art, a candidate must submit a male or female nude, a still life, and a landscape done in classical style."

"There's nothing wrong with that," David said, "at least the artist can't graduate without learning to draw, or hide a lack of talent under a haze of art-babble and angst."

"Drawing isn't everything, even in art," she said, "but I'll leave that argument to someone else. I haven't time to go through the whole theory of art right now." She cleared her throat pointedly, but David did not take the hint.

"Well," he said, with a creak that told Ysaye he had settled back in the chair, "I'd enjoy music much more if every modern composer had to submit a song in the style of Schubert, a chorale in the style of Bach, a sonata, and a classical symphony before doing anything more modern, and I think most audiences would agree with me. Your modern symphonies are losing their audience because they deliberately write music no one wants to listen to; they're competing with the past. Of course, in folk music—"

Ysaye drifted off to sleep to the sound of their amiable bickering about music. Or rather, David's monologue; Elizabeth made nothing more than absentminded noises as she got involved in her work. It occurred to her, in a vague sort of way, that David's harping on music was symptomatic of the mild craziness that had infected everyone. *Too much idle time; not enough real work to occupy our minds . . . nonessentials are getting to seem as important as the job we're supposed to do. . . .*

She woke to the printer's swoosh as it produced a new map and David's startled exclamation.

"What is it, David?" Ysaye asked, sitting up and rubbing her eyes. "Is something malfunctioning?"

"Something's wrong here—and maybe it's another glitch with the computer," he told her. "Remember that big storm I said was building on these plains here?" He tossed her the earlier map.

Ysaye frowned at it; it looked perfectly normal to her, at least, it looked like the storm patterns she'd seen in simulations. The clouds formed the usual swirls of a storm in a satellite photo; she had seen the same pattern on dozens of worlds and thousands of simulation runs. "What's wrong with it?"

"Nothing," he said. "But it isn't there now. It just vanished."

Ysaye shook her head. "Computer glitches don't erase storms. You've misread the map, that's all. You probably need a nap, too."

"Look for yourself," he said, handing over the new map.

Ysaye glanced first at the time on it; she had been asleep for a little over two hours. Elizabeth came to sit on the blanket beside her and look on.

"He's right," Elizabeth said, tapping the map with her finger, "see that low pressure area right there? The low's still there, but the clouds are gone. There's no sign of a storm; no rain, no snow—nothing."

"Maybe on this planet, a low doesn't mean a storm," David said uncertainly.

"There's nothing else it *could* mean," Elizabeth said, looking extremely puzzled, "unless this planet is completely unique in the Galaxy. Maybe all those mountains change things—or that monster glacier. Or all the snow." But she sounded doubtful.

"Anything is possible," Ysaye replied.

"True. Still, I wonder where that storm went. We'll wait and see whether the low's on the next weather map." She shrugged. "Well, at least I'll have something to report. 'Lost: one storm.' It is rather a big thing to mislay."

"God help me. Don't say that. You know regulations; we'll probably have to set up a special lost and found bureau for missing weather patterns," David joked. "I can see it now. Reports in triplicate, and entries on the notes of every meeting. Lost: one tropical depression, two hurricanes. . . ." He pretended to tear out his hair.

"That's ridiculous—" Elizabeth giggled.

"Well, you certainly seem to have mislaid this one," he pointed out.

"I didn't lose it," Elizabeth said indignantly. "My job is to report and predict the weather, not make it. Maybe it's a computer malfunction. Maybe the computer reported a low where there really wasn't one, and the storm clouds were just—just an odd formation in dispersal. Or else the storm was all set up to come roaring down out of wherever these storms roar down out of, and something made it just—go away."

Ysaye crawled over to the terminal, pulled off the cover, and starting running diagnostics. "Maybe," she said absently, "someone down there has solved that old problem: 'Everybody talks about the weather and nobody does anything about it.' "

She paused for a moment, as her own words struck an odd chord within her. *Did I just dream something about that?* She tried to remember, but the dream, whatever it had been, was gone.

David looked down at her soberly.

"You think so?"

Ysaye shrugged. "We've said it before; anything is possible. Including natives who have technology that doesn't match anything *we* think of as technology."

David frowned at the now-blank screen. "Well, if someone *did* change the weather—whoever it might be, if he has that kind of power, I'd like to meet him—or her, or them." He paused for a moment, as if he was having second thoughts.

"Or, then again," he said softly, "maybe I wouldn't."

CHAPTER 4

In the garden of the Dalereuth Tower, three young girls walked together; two of them closely, as if they were best friends, and the third a little apart. All three bore the red hair and the strong aristocratic stamp in their features of the Comyn, the hereditary autarchy of the Domains. Comyn is what the scions of the seven families were styled; and they were looked upon with awe and envy, for each family bore a special Gift, or power of *laran*. Not every member of the Comyn had this Gift in strength—or even had it at all—for their blood was thinner these days, and the powers seemed to be dying out. Towers that had once sent messages and even messengers across vast distances now stood dark and empty. That was what made these three girls so precious—both to their Families, and to the Tower.

Melora and Rohana Aillard, aged ten and twelve, were cousins, but were as alike as sisters; the third girl was Leonie Hastur, a little taller, a little fairer, a little older than the others. And very much more conscious of her rank and the strength of her *laran*. Her pride was evident in even the way she carried herself, head high, and not with eyes cast downward with the maidenly modesty that society preferred.

At this time, late in the day, the younger girls in the Tower were allowed to gather in the gardens, weather permitting, to play games and amuse themselves as they wished. Leonie considered herself much too old for such nonsense as games, but it was a chance to escape the walls of the Tower, at least for a little while.

"I'll push you in the swing, Rohana," said Melora, who was delicately made and the smallest of the three. "It's not raining yet. I want to stay out as long as we can."

"Give it time," Rohana replied, with a sigh. "It always seems to rain at night here in this season. The best we can hope for is that it doesn't start until after we go in."

"It won't rain tonight," said Leonie very positively, and with a sly smile. "I want to see the moons, even if they are separating from conjunction; it is very important to me."

She did not say why it was important to her, nor did the other two girls bother to ask. After even so short an acquaintance, they knew that Leonie would never tell.

"And I suppose," responded Rohana Aillard, almost mockingly, "the weather will cooperate and stay clear just because you want it to. I should have known, of course. Even the weather must listen when a Hastur speaks."

"It usually does," Leonie remarked, as if Rohana's veiled mockery meant nothing to her. "If you don't want the swing, Rohana, I do."

"No, it's my turn first," Rohana said, climbing into the swing and setting it in motion, and giving up on her attempt to ruffle Leonie's temper. "They should have two swings—"

"Or three, but how often do they have more than one person here young enough to be interested?" sighed Melora. She turned to Leonie, with innocent cheer. "I am glad to have you here with us, Leonie; everyone else here is so old and staid."

"Fiora's not old," Rohana protested, out of a vague feeling of loyalty to the Keeper.

"She might as well be," Leonie said dismissively. "She acts as if she were a hundred years old, and stuffier than any old grandfather. When she welcomed me here, she gave me a dreadful long speech, and reminded me that I was now a *leronis*, and must always represent the best of what the Comyn stand for." Leonie sniffed disdainfully. "As if I would not! I am, after all, a Hastur. I have been taught my duty since I first left the cradle!"

"And you are already more of a *leronis* and a better telepath than most of us will be even after training, I suspect," said Rohana, with a hint of resignation. Her eyes sharpened with curiosity, and she forgot her earlier attempts to prick Leonie's temper. "Tell me, Leonie, do you have the Hastur Gift?"

Leonie did not—quite—preen. "Yes, I think so."

"Which means you can do, *without* a matrix, more than the rest of us can *with* one," said Rohana, awed. "Tell us, if that is true, why do they send you to a Tower at all?"

Leonie's lovely, arrogant face became very serious. *Laran* powers—her own in particular—were something she never took lightly or frivolously. "Ever since I was a child," she said, "people have told me that an untrained telepath is a danger to herself and to everyone around her. And it is true—truer for me, perhaps, than for anyone else in the Domains. When I was tested, the *leronis* found that I have some of the older *laran* Gifts, which have been known to become—" she hesitated, choosing the proper word, "—*unmanageable*— at least, without proper training."

Rohana shuddered, and so did Melora. Every child knew what could happen when a Gift ran out of control.

Along with tales of ghosts, tales of *laran* run wild enlivened many a winter hearth—and caused many a child's nightmares.

Leonie waited a moment, to gain the full impact of her words. Power, however it came, immediately brought respect. Already she had gained that respect —or at least, caution—she saw it in their faces. Good. Now there would be no more unsubtle verbal jabs.

She shrugged, descending a little from the pinnacle of mystery she had placed herself upon. "Also, I am a woman," she continued, "and for women, to become a *leronis* is the only way to escape being married off at the earliest possible moment to some half-witted young fellow and having six or seven of his half-witted children."

"Surely they're not all half-witted," protested Rohana, who cherished ambitions of her own in the bridal market.

"No, only nine-tenths of them," Leonie countered, "and what, do you think, are your chances of getting someone from the other tenth?"

Melora said peaceably, "Well, you have certainly chosen the best way to put it off for a year or two."

"For more than that," said Leonie, in a tone that brooked no argument. "I know what I want; I have known it for as long as I can remember. I shall not marry *any* man, and I fully intend to have a Council seat."

"For that, you would have to be Keeper at Arilinn," laughed Rohana, as if she found the idea preposterous, despite Leonie's self-assurance.

"Precisely," Leonie replied, lifting her head and looking a little down her nose at the younger girl, and smiling the smile that hid secrets.

Rohana sighed with exasperation. "And are you so

sure you can do that? Have you foreknowledge as well?
Does everything always go as you expect it to go?"

"Almost everything," said Leonie, with an ineffable
air of arrogance, "I have found that I am very seldom
wrong. And Fiora has told me I have the talent to be
trained as a Keeper, so I think that the outcome is likely
enough that even my brother could bet upon it and take
home his winnings."

Her assurance finally annoyed the usually sweet-
spirited Melora. "Oh, you'll probably end by marrying,
just like the rest of us," she said crossly.

"No, I won't marry," Leonie looked at Melora
strangely, in a way that made her feel very uneasy. As
if Leonie were looking through her, rather than at her.
"And neither will you," Leonie said, in an oddly flat
voice.

"And I?" asked Rohana flippantly.

"Yes, you'll marry," remarked Leonie, still in that
strange, flat, thin voice. "But you'll have a Council seat
as well." She frowned, not at Rohana, but at something
only she could see. "I don't understand how, but I know
it will happen. . . ."

Her voice trailed off, and she continued to stare,
frowning.

Rohana tried to shrug off the chill which suddenly
seemed to descend on the girls. She turned on Leonie
in anger, "Are you now a fortune-teller in the mar-
ketplace, then? Or perhaps you'd care to take on the
gray robe of a priestess of Avarra, and go about pro-
claiming doom! Old Martina, who was my mother's
maid, was given to prophesying now and again, and she
could prophesy snow at midwinter as well as anyone
else."

She might have said more, but the faint sound of a
footfall interrupted her. The girls broke off, letting the

swing, forgotten, return to its resting state. Someone else had entered the garden.

More than just "someone." The figure approaching them was striking enough to have warranted anyone's attention even if they did not know her or the significance of her crimson draperies; Fiora, the Keeper of Dalereuth, was an albino, tall and strange-looking, with white hair, and pale, all but sightless, eyes. She came unerringly down the path nevertheless. In her crimson draperies she looked insubstantial, but still had a curious air of presence and a dignity that owed nothing to the haughtiness of high birth.

She did not ask who was there, but simply said, "Leonie."

"I am here, Lady Mistress," Leonie said, raising her head though the other two girls kept theirs slightly bowed. She looked directly into Fiora's pale pink eyes, even though it made her feel—odd. To drop her eyes would have been a confession that she was cowed by the Keeper, and she would never admit to that.

Fiora knew what lay behind that faintly insolent gaze, and wished that the girl had sense to match her pride. "I must speak with you; shall I send the others away?"

"I cannot imagine what you could have to say to me that they could not hear," Leonie said. The faint emphasis on "you" made Fiora bristle, knowing that the girl had intended a slight.

But if she responded, she would be playing Leonie's game, and that she would not do.

"If you wish, then," Fiora said evenly, "although I would not have spoken to reprove you in front of the others without your consent. I understand you think yourself responsible for the unusual weather we have been having for the last few days." She put a faint emphasis of her own on the word "think," as if to imply that the girl was either lying or fantasizing.

"Why, so I am," Leonie said blithely. "What of it? I wished to see the moons; something is about to come to us, and I feel it is from the moons."

"That is interesting, child," Fiora replied, with a hint of condescension, "and especially interesting that of all of the trained *leroni* and all of the matrix workers, with all of their Gifts and powers, you alone, untrained, unpracticed, have been given such foreknowledge."

Leonie's chin shot out, and her mouth tightened, but Fiora did not give her a chance to retort. "Whether it be so or not," said the albino, "and whether or not the weather is truly answering to you, because there is a possibility that the latter, at least, is true, I am here to tell you that you may not do so. Are you aware what may befall us all if you meddle with the weather as if it were a plaything, child?" This time the emphasis was on "child," implying that Leonie had given no more thought to her actions than a little one reaching for a pretty-colored ball or feather.

"If you mean a Ghost Wind," snapped Leonie, "I assure you that I am not as careless as that!"

Then, as Fiora continued to gaze at her reprovingly, she realized what was probably bothering the Keeper. "Oh, the farmers," she said dismissively. "I am not given to worrying about them."

"A pity you have not taken all those lessons in the duty of a Hastur and a Comyn as seriously as you have the lessons in your own *importance*. The farmers need the rain," Fiora pointed out, "and we rely on the farmers for our food. When the crops are wilted and dead in the fields for lack of water, it will be too late for anything, even the most powerful Gift in the Domains, to put the situation right."

Leonie stared at the Keeper as if she could not quite believe her own ears, but Fiora was not finished.

"And quite aside from that," she continued, "one of the first things which you, or anyone else, must learn here, is that is that no *leronis* may ever do anything to disturb the balance of nature for her own convenience. Sometimes, after consulting with others, when we decide that the good outweighs the possible harm, we do indeed change a dangerous pattern, such as when we give rain for forest fire."

"I have done that," Leonie interrupted. "I have a Gift for it. I was brought up on tales of Dorilys of Rockraven, and I think I have a little of her Gift, the Gift of weather control, and I assure you that I am not given to *playing* with it." She smiled again, that superior smile that made Fiora want to shake some humility into her. Had the Keeper been anything other than what she was, Fiora might well have done so. "You need not worry," Leonie continued airily, as if it were no great matter. "I shall restore the rain, if you wish it."

"It is not simply a matter of what I wish," Fiora said, rather sharply. "You must learn to follow what is ordained and what must be in the way of nature. Did your stories tell you what finally befell Dorilys of Rockraven?"

"She lost control of her Gift and killed with it, and, since she could not be killed, her kinsmen sent her to sleep behind shields at Hali," Leonie said, with a dismissive shrug, as if she were certain, with the foolish arrogance of the young, that such a thing could never happen to *her*. "For all I know, she's still there. That is why my family wants me properly trained."

"Precisely." Fiora replied. "Remember this, Leonie. Such a fate could easily be yours, if you continue to abuse your powers as if they were superior sorts of toys. And a far sadder fate could be yours if you boast of powers you do not have, and are found wanting. No one looks more a fool than the *leronis* who calls upon a demon to be answered by a mouse."

So saying, she turned and walked away through the gardens, the brush of her trailing draperies making a whispery sound against the grass. The two younger girls looked at one another with shock. A reproof from Fiora was rare, and never had she spoken to either of them with such harshness.

Leonie, however, was simply angry. True, she had said herself that she did not want the other girls to be sent away, but never in her life had anyone dared to speak to her like this. It infuriated her.

But worse, far worse, were the unspoken insults; the things that Fiora had not said, but had thought, all too clearly.

"So," Leonie said, simmering with barely-suppressed anger, "she does not believe in my Gifts; she thinks that I am boasting of what I cannot do."

"Leonie, she did not say that," Rohana protested, frightened.

"She did not have to say it aloud," Leonie replied. "Do you think I hear only what is *said* to me? Do you? If so, what are we doing in the Tower, any of us?" She stared angrily at the door where Fiora had reentered the Tower itself. "Well, she will see."

"What are you going to do, Leonie?" whispered Melora, her eyes wide, and her voice unsteady. Leonie took some comfort in that; if the Keeper did not believe, she had at least convinced her fellow students that she had powers to be reckoned with.

"Oh, she shall have a storm, if she wants one, and when it is over—" Leonie was too much aware of her own dignity to snarl, but she clenched her hands into fists, and made her mouth into a thin, tight line. "Oh,

I can hear it already; *Oh, Leonie, you must not*. As if *she* were one to tell me what I must do or not do!"

"But she is the Keeper—" Rohana protested weakly.

Leonie tossed her hair with an arrogant gesture of disdain, as if the title *Keeper* meant nothing to her. "Then she might as well learn it first as last; I do what I will, here or anywhere. And she shall learn it. This battle is not of my making, but I will not be denied."

CHAPTER 5

There were more people crowded into the little weather dome on the moon than it was technically supposed to hold. Ysaye held the command seat behind the computer console, with David and Elizabeth hanging over her shoulders, and half a dozen men and women crowded behind them. Silence reigned as the computer created another image on the screen from the data being uploaded from their satellite, and David drew a long breath of surprise and wonder.

"Holy smoke!" he exclaimed softly. Ysaye did not recognize the reference, and ignored it as meaningless except for the obvious context of astonishment.

She had at least managed to ascertain that there was no hardware glitch in either the computer or the satellite, no bug in the software, and no joker playing games on the ship, transmitting phony data by the simple expedient of sending someone with a real, optical telescope and camera outside the dome to take *pictures* of the weather patterns on the planet below. And while those pictures were crude when compared with what the satellite was sending, they proved one thing: the data was real. The weather on Cottman IV was *not* behaving normally.

"Look at this," David said as he passed Elizabeth the latest weather map the printer had finished. She studied the sheet of paper with puzzlement creasing her brow.

"Where did *that* storm come from?" she asked. "First, there are two storms that disappear, and now there is a storm that springs up out of nowhere! Something down there is doing very strange things to the weather."

"What sort of strange things?" asked a voice from the back. "We've just safety-approved the atmosphere for a landing party, don't tell me we're running into problems now!" Commander Matt Britton, Head of the Sciences Section, had just arrived, and crowded as the room was, those between him and the console moved out of the way to let him squeeze through.

Elizabeth handed him her series of weather maps in chronological order. "Look for yourself, sir," she said. "First a pair of storms disappear into nowhere; then we get a rainstorm with no accompanying weather pattern." Elizabeth shook her head. "No low pressure zone, no proper storm pattern, nothing. Just rain."

The Head of Section studied the maps with no sign of any emotion on his face. "Any theories on what is causing this?" Britton asked, after a moment.

"Nothing so far," Elizabeth admitted. "We've been watching this for over forty-eight hours now, and I'm afraid we're getting a bit punchy. The best theory we've come up with yet is that there's a wizard, or something like that; someone down there with magical powers over the weather." She shook her head.

Now the Head did show some emotion as he looked up from under a pair of heavy eyebrows at the meteorologist. Strong disapproval. "Are you seriously proposing that as a theory, Mackintosh?" Britton asked. "That sort of nonsense is all very well in one of your folk songs, but this is a scientific expedition, and I'll thank you to remember that, fatigued or not."

Elizabeth was taken aback by her superior's cold disapproval, and the response from the back of the crowd that followed Britton's reproof did not help her self-confidence any. "Oh, Elizabeth, come off it!" Lieutenant Ryan Evans, one of the younger botanists, said disgustedly.

Elizabeth flushed and, catching sight of Evans, she averted her eyes. He was a friend of David's, but she had never been able to like him much. He was a good-looking young man and knew it; he was quite tall and took psychological advantage of his extra inches to cow people—particularly women—at every opportunity. She had never seen him wear anything other than the gray uniform of Colonization services, despite the custom of wearing "civilian" clothing when off-duty. Strongly built, he kept his physique in top shape in the gym, and used it as a tool of intimidation or seduction, whichever applied. He sounded almost angry about what Elizabeth had said, but then he frequently did; he was a scoffer by nature.

Perversely, though, the look of scorn on his face and the near-insult he had thrown at her made her a little angry—angry enough at least to stand up for her explanation which had actually been given half humorously, half desperately. She turned to Britton, ignoring Evans.

"Well, it's kind of an out-there sort of theory, sir," she temporized, "but we haven't been able to come up with anything else that explains what's going on down there, and neither has the computer. We weren't talking about fairy-tale magic, but something else entirely, and 'wizard' was just the name we were using to describe the kind of person we were postulating. Theoretically, someone with psychic powers could do all that, dispersing weather systems and reforming them again, and it *would* seem like magic to anyone without them."

Evans responded as if she had spoken directly to him. "Even if we did get saddled with that inane experimental program for psychic abilities you people were playing around with, I still haven't seen any conclusive proof that there are any such things—much less that someone could steer storms around with them."

Elizabeth bit her tongue to keep from snapping, and kept her attention fixed on Britton. After all, Evans was nothing to her; he didn't work in her division, he wasn't her superior, and his approval or disapproval didn't matter at all.

Britton shook his head. "I have to agree with Evans," he said, sounding a bit regretful. "I haven't seen any conclusive proof that 'psychic powers' exist. Everything you and David have done could have been explained in other ways. And I can't see any reason to think that 'psychic powers' are in play here."

"Perhaps not," she agreed, "but, sir, you have to admit that there does seem to be something pretty unusual going on here. Wizards aren't any more unlikely than anything else, at this point." She frowned. "I have a hunch that when we find out whatever the truth may be, we'll wish it were something as simple as a wizard."

"Jesus!" Evans muttered—but Britton quelled him with a look. He *was* under Britton's authority, and he knew better than to continue after a look like that.

"Well," Britton said, turning back to Elizabeth, "I trust that when you have a somewhat more viable theory—or some proof that your 'wizard' exists—you will inform me." His tone was less caustic, but just as patronizingly sarcastic as Evans', and Elizabeth almost flinched.

Ysaye winced quietly. This was not the first time Elizabeth had been criticized for her leaps of intuition, which were completely independent of logic, but sometimes gave astonishingly good results. In a more mellow mood, Commander Britton would not be giving her such a hard time about it. At the moment, however, he was obviously *not* in a mellow mood.

Ysaye thought she knew why. The surveillance satellites were performing precisely as advertised, and they had marvelously detailed analyses of the chemical makeup of the environment, but although the air was nearly perfect—more so than they had dared hope for, the planet itself was not cooperating. Thick, dense cloud cover and omnipresent storms prevented seeing all but the most cursory of details about the IBs below. There *were* IBs, that much was obvious from the few tantalizing glimpses of structures that the satellites had been granted, but the inhabitants themselves were still a mystery. The few facts known were that they built individual and grouped structures that included what might be cities, and that they cultivated the land. The rest was a mystery—for on the few occasions that the clouds *had* parted to reveal the terrain below, either the inhabitants themselves were not making an appearance, or the tree cover was too dense to see through, or the famous cameras, that could record a license plate in Nairobi, were pointed in the wrong direction and gazing down on yet another cloud-covered expanse.

Small wonder Britton was not in a particularly good mood.

Ysaye threw herself into the breach and changed the subject.

"Any idea yet, sir, when we will be going down to the planet?" she asked. That they would be sending an expedition down was now a certainty, given the way that the Minions of Murphy's Law had been plaguing them. It appeared that the only way to actually find out anything would be to go in person. A dangerously primitive but proven technique.

"A couple of hours," said Britton. "The captain says

we're sending one of the reconnaissance shuttles down, and landing in this area here," he pointed it out on the computer screen, one briefly and blessedly free of clouds. "It's fairly close to the range of mountains, and covered with snow, but it's a plateau, as nearly as Cartography can figure out."

Britton paused to aim another disapproving glance at David, who simply shrugged, and nodded at the screen, as if to say, "I did my best with what I had."

"It seems to me as arbitrary as most decisions," Evans said. "Surely, there must be more hospitable areas."

Ysaye knew as the figurative emotional temperature dropped a few degrees that Evans had, at last, overstepped his bounds. She hoped he'd get more than a reprimand. . . .

"I don't pretend to be in on all administrative thinking, or to understand what makes our superior officers decide what courses to take," Britton said coldly. "But this is not a democracy; this is a ship, and I obey my superiors without complaint. Anyone who has different notions can feel free to step outside the dome and contemplate them for a moment." Evans paled, and Britton smiled grimly. "I'm told that is the Captain's preferred way of handling those with mutinous notions."

Ysaye applauded silently. Evans was an inspired xenobotanist, but he was not particularly popular with his shipmates. Britton would have been well within his rights to take the matter farther . . . and she rather hoped that he would.

Unfortunately, that was not to be. Britton seemed content when Evans nodded stiffly, his lips compressed into a thin line. "This area was chosen for isolation, both from the resident IBs and from anything we might damage when landing. Since we have not been able to gather any reasonable amount of data about the natives,

it was judged prudent not to approach them too directly.
But since we have no idea how they might regard damage to their agricultural property, it also seemed prudent to avoid all cultivated areas; we're not likely to
burn up anything landing here, or crush anything, or
otherwise damage terrain. Unless, of course, they cultivate snow, which does not seem terribly likely. Unfortunately, to fill all necessary criteria, we end up
landing in a relatively inhospitable area."

"There are a lot of factors involved," one of the
bystanders agreed.

"Who's on the first shuttle?" another one asked.

"It's not official yet," Britton said, "but since there
are IBs, the first load down is going to have to have the
full complement of contact specialists, even though we
don't intend to make first contact yet, not until after
we've had a chance to observe the IBs for a while. You
know how it is—" he shrugged expressively "—plan
not to make first contact, and the natives are likely to
come strolling up within minutes of the landing, wanting
to know who the new neighbors are, and whether or
not they should roll out the red carpet or declare some
sort of Holy War."

Someone laughed nervously.

"At any rate, they're going to want people with
qualifications in xenobiology, xenopsychology, anthropology, linguistics, and all the appropriate expertise, to
go with the first wave."

Meanwhile, the computer had been redrawing the
screen again, and something different caught Ysaye's
eye. "Wait, something's going on down there," Ysaye
said.

Everyone broke formation and waited while the
computer delivered another of the weather maps.

David reached down and handed it to Elizabeth.

"This is your department, Elizabeth. Anything new and interesting?"

"Not that I can see, just that same storm—though that's quite enough. I see what Ysaye saw now, it's growing rapidly; I'm glad I'm not down there in it," she said. "It looks to me as if there's enough wind shear in those thunderheads to rip the wings right off conventional aircraft. Perfectly clear air at the proposed landing site on that plateau, however. As long as that holds, we're okay for a landing." She passed the weather chart to Commander Britton.

He scanned it, and said, "According to the earlier scans, the biggest city on the planet appears to be somewhere in that valley." He put his finger down on a patch of heavy cloud under which, theoretically, the city lay. "Not that you can tell from this map."

"Not all that far from your freak weather either," Ysaye noted, feeling just a little smug. "If there were such things as wizards, I would think they would be found in areas of high population."

"Then why are we landing way the hell out in the mountains?" Evans asked.

"My," Ysaye said, grateful for the chance to get several jabs in at him. "Weren't you paying *any* attention, Lieutenant? Our superior officer just carefully explained that this is *not* a first contact mission, and why." She smiled sweetly. "If I recall correctly, sir, you stated very clearly that we wanted to observe the natives without being observed, since we are unable to make those observations from orbit. And you also stated that we were landing in what appeared to be something of a wasteland, to avoid doing damage to anything the natives considered valuable."

Evans smoldered.

"Less chance of setting a town or crops on fire, and upsetting the natives," a young officer agreed gleefully.

"And if they're pre-industrial, you can stay longer and study them before you have to pack up and go away again. Say, Evans, where *were* you when they gave us all those pre-contact, contact, and post-contact lectures? Sleeping one off?"

Snickers from around the room made Evans flush. "That's the way they figure it, anyhow," said David, mildly, interfering before his associate could do or say something irredeemably stupid. "I hope I'll get to go down soon. We're always wanting some new languages for the linguistic analysis computer."

Evans glared about and saw no sympathetic faces except for David's. He gritted his teeth, gathered what was left of his dignity, and stalked off down the tube toward another dome. Robbed of further entertainment, the rest soon followed. And as the area slowly cleared, Ysaye settled down with the series of weather maps.

Even though she had sense enough to keep her mouth shut on the subject of "psychic powers" in front of Commander Britton, she still had the feeling that, on some level, she knew what was happening—and that Elizabeth's "wizard" theory wasn't as far off as it sounded.

CHAPTER
6

The sky was so heavily overcast that it might just as well have been twilight, not some time near midday. The garden paths were muddy, for the rain had been so heavy that it had washed much of the gravel into low spots. The trees sagged under their burden of rain-soaked leaves, and the few flowers that had survived the deluge intact drooped dispiritedly on their battered stems. The rest dripped water from their remaining petals. The garden was full of storm wrack: broken branches, leaves, flower petals.

Leonie walked slowly through the battered gardens of the Tower, surveying her handiwork. The rain had been so very heavy that there were other tasks with higher priority—such as rescuing the fish who had been flooded out of their ornamental pond—and the gardeners had not yet gotten around to cleaning up. Even the swing dangled limply by one of its ropes, untouched, unmended.

Leonie stared at it and felt nothing but despair. *Isn't there anything for an adult to do out here?* she couldn't help but wonder.

Apparently not; not like the gardens at her own family's estate, or the Castle at Thendara. There were mazes to solve, fountains to watch, cozy grottoes to curl up in, singly or—not. Nothing of the sort here. Nothing but an orderly little patch of trees and flowers, and not

even particularly rare flowers, either. She turned and
went back inside, restless and at loose ends.

She prowled the lower floors of the Tower, finding
them strangely silent and empty. The Tower might as
well have been deserted, for all the company she found.
Not even servants.

She knew how few people truly populated Dalereuth, compared to how many it *could* hold. Was this
what those Towers that had been closed were like, so
silent, brooding? If she were to walk into one, would
she have the same odd feeling of being watched, even
though she knew there was no one there?

After a time she found a deserted room filled with
musical instruments. Finally—an occupation for *adult*
hands! Leonie took down a *rryl* of carved and varnished
rosewood, running her hands lovingly across the metal
strings. After a moment she began to play an old folk
ballad, improvising a bridge of notes, followed by a
spray of odd harmonies. Playing, her restlessness dis-
solved, and she entered a kind of waking trance, so that
when Fiora entered some hours later, Leonie saw with
astonishment that the day was so far advanced that a
low-hanging sun pierced the clouds, glowing huge and
red. She was startled to see Fiora apparently looking
at her intently.

"I did not know you played so well," Fiora said,
and the admiration in her voice surprised Leonie. She
had not thought that anything she could do would impress the Keeper. A pity it was something as minor as
music. "Where did you learn?" Fiora asked.

"I have had music masters since I was very small,"
Leonie said, and shrugged. "It was simply a part of my
education. I preferred it to tedious embroidery."

"Do you know how lucky you are?" asked Fiora, a
trace of envy coloring her words. "My father was poor,
so I had no such teaching till I came here. And when

music teaching is delayed until so late in life it can never be learned properly. If I spent all of my waking hours in practice, I should never be as good as you are now, should I live to be a hundred."

"I suppose not," murmured Leonie in surprise. "I never thought about it. I enjoyed learning new songs, but I used to run away from my governess because I did not want to practice. I used to say there was nothing she could make me do if I did not want to do it."

Fiora smiled, very faintly. "I can well believe that," she said.

Leonie almost laughed, and caught it at the last moment. "But I soon learned to love music for its own sake, and then I practiced enough to please her—though I never even finished the first sampler she set me. I suppose it is still in my work basket, if the moths have not gotten to it."

"Yes," said Fiora, "I suppose that it would be very hard to make you do anything you did not want to do. Perhaps we should be glad that you want this training so much."

Leonie raised her chin haughtily. "That was always a foregone conclusion," said Leonie. "Ever since I was a little girl I have known that, soon or late, I would come to a Tower. I have powerful *laran*. It must be trained; it was only a question of to which Tower I would go."

She had made it sound almost as if *she* had been the one making the choice, not the Keepers of the still-functioning Towers. As if the Tower were being honored by *her* presence, and not as if she were the one honored by being accepted. Fiora hesitated. It was a new experience for her to feel small and unremarkable; but she supposed that with a daughter of the Hasturs in her charge she would have to get used to that. Finally, telling herself that as Keeper of Dalereuth she need not feel inferior to anyone, and certainly not to this proud daughter of Comyn, she asked, "Did you never think —as so many girls do—of marriage?"

"Never," said Leonie firmly. "Not even when I was very small. I always knew I could marry anyone I chose, but there was no one I wished to marry. There was for me no one who could equal my own twin brother in any way; so whomever I chose, *if* I chose, would of course be someone below me in rank. I did not want to marry someone I could never think equal to myself, so I came here." She did not speak of the King's proposal; while rank had never entered into her decision in his case, there were other considerations which had. Personal ones, and to those Fiora hardly needed to be privy.

"I suppose," Fiora murmured, with only a little irony, "we here are the lucky ones, then." In an odd way, she meant this; if Leonie had chosen otherwise, a very powerful telepath might have gone untrained, and one of the oldest proverbs in the Domains was that an untrained telepath was a menace to herself and everyone about her. Dorilys the Stormqueen was only one of a hundred examples of how easily that proverb could be proven true.

Leonie chose to misunderstand. "I suppose I am fortunate you could make a place for me here," she said, her own inflection of irony a great deal heavier than Fiora's. "I had intended at first to go to Arilinn —where the daughters of the Comyn mostly go."

There was no mistaking her meaning; she *should* have gone to Arilinn. She still resented the fact that she had been denied a place there. It was obvious that Dalereuth was a poor second by comparison.

"Yes," said Fiora, after a moment, "when we heard of you, and that you were to be trained as a *leronis*, we had expected that you would choose to go to Arilinn."

She saw at once how that could be misunderstood—as Leonie seemed to be willfully intent on doing—and continued quickly.

"I do not mean," she said, tilting her head a little to the side, "that we are not glad to have you here. But—there were two of you to train. It is different, when there are siblings who need training at the same time."

She hesitated. It was traditional to separate those in training from their families, but Fiora did not think that Leonie could be separated successfully from anyone she did not choose to be divided from. Certainly the bond with her twin would be difficult to shut out, even with Leonie's full cooperation—which they wouldn't likely have, and the great physical distance between here and Arilinn. Training her was going to be a major problem, one way or another, with difficulty being added by the girl's own arrogance. Yet the proper training of this haughty child would be a considerable credit to Fiora—or to any Keeper who could accomplish it. Of one thing there was no doubt: the girl's considerable talent. She would make a *leronis* to be reckoned with.

Even now, the child sat toying with the harp as if the conversation were at an end, and Fiora's continued presence of no consequence. Although she had never been on the receiving end of one before, the Keeper thought wryly that she knew a royal dismissal when she saw one! Fiora thought about the problems Leonie posed for several minutes, while Leonie idly strummed the *rryl*, and finally decided to be completely, even brutally, honest. Perhaps that would shake Leonie's confidence enough that she might—just possibly—listen to the opinions and desires of someone besides herself.

Fiora took a steadying, calming breath, and said,

"Of course, it is a given that if you can be properly trained you will be a great credit to all of us," Fiora paused to be sure she had Leonie's full attention, "but I am not at all certain that you can be properly trained." While Leonie sat speechless, she added, "And I think that any other Keeper in the Domains would tell you the same thing. Perhaps that was one reason why you were sent here, where we have only two other young girls in training, and may spend more time in dealing with you."

Leonie, dumbfounded, stared at the Keeper. Fiora was not certain she could be trained? Nobody had ever expressed qualms about her ability as a *leronis* before! Yet Fiora seemed entirely serious, and quite calm, as if it were a matter of casual fact.

Perhaps—perhaps it was. The thought was daunting. Perhaps she *had* been sent into "exile" at quiet Dalereuth because Arilinn judged her to be too much of a risk! Leonie could sense lies, easily enough—and Fiora was not lying, nor was she making things up to frighten her charge. She was entirely serious.

But Leonie was determined not to be frightened or intimidated; instead, she asked in a subdued, cautious voice, "Why should that be?"

The otherworldly eyes seemed to regard her steadily. "Because of your pride, Leonie. Because you are so *certain* of your importance in the world, and that nothing you desire will ever be withheld from you. I can tell even now that you have great potential, and you may well have the Hastur Gift. But the training in a Tower, especially the training to be a Keeper, to which you claim to aspire, is long and difficult. And tedious. You will have to sacrifice much, and the gain is not all that certain." She sighed, and Leonie stirred uncomfortably. "I do *not* know if you can endure it. You have never had to sacrifice anything; I do not know that you are capable of self-sacrifice to the extent needed. By your own account, you have never done anything you didn't want to do, you have never attempted anything perilous, and you have never failed at anything. Perhaps that lack of failure is due less to your abilities, and more to the fact that you will not attempt things that are not easy for you, and abandon anything that bores you."

Leonie started to open her mouth to protest, and shut it again when she realized that, cruel as those words were, they were also entirely true. She felt even more uncomfortable; Fiora seemed to be able to see right through her in a way that no one else ever had—except, sometimes, Lorill—and it seemed as if what Fiora found in the core of her soul was little to her liking, and rather petty.

Fiora continued, perfectly calmly, as if entirely unaware of the discomfort she was causing her newest pupil. "You have never even started to test the limits of your ability in anything. This training here might be your first experience of failure, and I do not know how well you would endure that. Not well at all, I would suspect."

Leonie blinked slightly, shaken and utterly deflated. It was an entirely new experience for her, and one that she did not at all like. "Do you think that I would fail, then, Fiora? Or give up as soon as the learning became difficult?"

Fiora shrugged slightly, as if it did not much matter to her. "No one can ever know that except you. I can tell you, though, no matter how great your Gift, that your success is not assured. You will never know if you can succeed unless you are willing to push the limits of your body and your mind, to risk failure; and I do not know why you would be willing to do that when you have never done it before. And when, just by walking back through the gates of the Tower, you could have everything you gave up—servants, pretty things, rank, prestige, admiration, and a crowd of sycophants fawning at your feet."

That stung, worse than any physical slap. "Is there any way that I can assure myself success?" Leonie asked, a little desperately.

"Not beyond all doubt, no," said Fiora, and chuckled, as if she had found the question quite amusing. "*No one* can do that. Are you looking for a way to cheat, or an easy answer? The ten simple steps to become a Keeper? The quick, correct answers, all at once?"

Leonie hung her head and bit her lip. That was, of course, exactly what she had been hoping for when she blurted out that particularly stupid question. Now she wished she had kept silent.

Fiora sensed a weakening, and pressed home her advantage. "I do think that if you are willing to work hard at it, you have the potential to accomplish almost anything. But you *must* want it enough, enough to work hard and diligently at it," she qualified. "What I do not know is whether you have the ability to do *that*, especially when the learning is tedious and requires so much that must be sacrificed. Do you know why Keepers wear the crimson robes?"

Leonie shook her head dumbly, surprised at the odd question, and forgetful for the moment that Fiora could not see her.

"It is not to mark them out as special," Fiora said, as if she *had* seen the gesture. "Nor to mark them for great respect. It is to mark them as *dangerous*, Leonie. It is dangerous, deadly dangerous, to touch a Keeper in the circle. Look here—"

She held out her pale hands, which Leonie now saw were covered with tiny scars, like burn marks, as if she had let a shower of sparks fall upon her and burn her flesh.

"It is so dangerous to others that a Keeper is taught *never* to allow a touch, in the circle, or out of it. And *that* is how we are taught. Through pain, Leonie. I do not think you have felt much pain in your lifetime. I am not certain you can endure even a little of it. And *these* are only the smallest part of the training, the *least* of the sacrifice."

Leonie sat thinking that over; in all of her daydreaming, she had thought only of the power of a Keeper, and not what it cost to reach that power. Her father had said, more than once, "Great power demands an equal sacrifice," and she had never really known what that meant. Now she had seen a little—only a little—and for the first time, it occurred to her to wonder just how false her daydreams had been. *They* had not involved giving anything up.

How much had the other Keepers sacrificed for their power? And why would they? At length she said, "Tell me how you came here, Fiora."

Fiora had not actually pried into the girl's thoughts—that was unmannerly, without invitation—but certain things and certain feelings had spilled over, and much could be inferred from them. Leonie was thinking, instead of assuming. That was a start, so she said quietly, "I was festival-born. My mother, who was very young, was married off to a small farmer in the valley. When I was about five years old, I had an illness which damaged my sight, and they knew that sooner or later I would be blind. My father wished to marry me off quickly, so that my prospective husband would not know how bad a bargain he was getting; but my mother's sister told a *leronis* about the illness and about my resemblance to the Comyn. She thought to test me for *laran*. I was gifted, and so I came here. I was gifted enough, patient enough, and willing to endure enough, that I was eventually made Keeper."

"You came only as a second choice?" Leonie said, clearly surprised. "I should think anyone who would choose to be a *leronis* should wish for it above all things."

"True, at first it was only a second choice," said Fiora. "But when I had been here for a time, I came to see how petty and meaningless my life would have been otherwise. I would have been no more than a woman like my mother, producing child after child, laboring in house and field, and if I had been very, very lucky, I would have had a husband who chose to be kind to me. Where a *leronis* has the power to do much good—to heal, to bring the proper weather, to ward from fire and storm. I realized that if I had truly been given a choice I would have chosen this. Above all else." She nodded, then continued. "But few are they who have the luxury of choice. I would not change my life now to be Queen in the Domains, but there are no few women among the Comyn themselves who are not as bound by the wills of their families as I was by the will of my father."

Leonie bit her lip at Fiora's choice of words. She would not have changed her life to be Queen? She said in a low voice, "I think," *no, I know*, she thought, remembering that she *had* had that choice and rejected it, "that I would not change such a life to be Queen either."

"You are fortunate, then," said Fiora. "You are one of those who has been given the luxury of choice, and the choice has been to grasp for your own dream. The question is, if the dream proves to be the naked edge of a blade, have you still the courage and the will, not only to grasp, but to hold it and keep it? If you do,

I think I can honestly say that if you want it above all things, there will be very little you cannot do."

"Do you really think so?" Leonie asked, looking to Fiora's face for an assurance and good-will she suddenly craved as she had never craved it before.

Fiora nodded firmly. "I do."

"I want it," Leonie said, very softly, "and I would risk anything for it. Even—as you said—failure." She smiled shakily, again forgetting that Fiora could not see it. "I will try not to *think* of failure, but I am willing to risk it. More—if I fail, I am willing to try, again and again, until I succeed."

"If you approach it in that spirit," said Fiora, with a smile of her own. "I do not think you need to *fear* failure. You will certainly experience it—as every Keeper has, in order to learn—but you need not fear it."

"Thank you, *vai leronis*," Leonie said, with painful humility.

As she turned to go, Fiora asked, "Did you, then, give us this rain?"

She bit her lip; that question would have caused an angry outburst on her part an hour ago. "Should I not have done it, by your rules?"

"I hope a day will come when you can answer that question for yourself," Fiora said, and she was almost laughing, "but when that day comes, you will be the only person to whom you must answer for your actions. And I think you will find your own self to be a harder taskmaster than I." She laughed again, a real laugh this time, and said, "It is also likely that no one—no one else, that is—would believe you if you claimed to have done it. Perhaps not even another Keeper. So in effect we start from this moment, Leonie."

Leonie breathed deeply as Fiora left the room. Her restlessness and sense of foreboding was back with her again, and after a moment she gave up all thought of turning again to the *rryl* she had abandoned.

It was now late evening; the last traces of crimson had faded from the sky, and the nightly rain had begun to fall in a slow, steady stream; utterly unlike the violent thunderstorm Leonie had called. In spite of the dreary sound of rain dripping onto leaves, roof, and puddles, Leonie felt no impulse to tamper with it. It was not the rain which disturbed her.

She had no sense that anything in the rain, or for that matter anything about the weather, disturbed her; the sense of disturbance was centered elsewhere.

She went up, after a time, to the room which had been allotted to her, a spacious and airy chamber on the third floor. Compared to her rooms in Castle Hastur, or her section of the suite of Hastur rooms at Thendara, it was bare and poor; but the novelty of being in an entirely new place had not yet worn off. Besides, once she tired of it the way it was, she knew that she could furnish it later in any way she chose. She mused for a time about how she might furnish it, trying to distract herself from the sobering conversation with Fiora and the sense of unease that still pursued her.

Perhaps she should decorate her rooms with hangings of crimson silk? No, there would be enough of crimson in her life if she became a Keeper, and at the moment she was resolved to settle for nothing less. Perhaps a blue and green shot silk she had seen in the markets as they passed through Temora. That was a color she had never seen before, a real triumph of the weaver's art, and it would bring a lightness to these rooms, a sense of living in the sky.

Around her the Tower slept. She was conscious of the little girls sleeping, of a solitary watcher at the relays which carried messages across the face of the world, from Domain to Domain in an eyeblink. At this hour it was rather unlikely any messages would be coming through, and yet there must always be one vigilant worker there at all times in case of emergency. She was conscious of Fiora preparing, as she moved through her eternal darkness, for sleep. How strange that would be—never to know day from night, except by the actions of others. . . .

She found herself aware, as she contemplated the Keeper, that she had made a friend. It was not an unpleasant thought, that she had made a friend where at first there had been only hostility. Fiora was on her side, now—and though there would be difficulties in achieving her goal, Fiora would not be compounding those difficulties.

She lay down, placing herself into a light trance state rather than preparing to sleep. She was anxious to know the cause of her sense of foreboding, and found herself exploring it, trying to sense the direction it came from, even as she was able to sense changes in the weather. She could see, as she drifted in the overworld, the weather patterns that she knew as well as she knew the strings of the *rryl* and what they would do; she scanned them, almost by habit, as she had done all her life. But the source of her unease was nothing to do with the weather.

She sensed a storm, normal for this time of year; someone would be caught in it, but that was nothing new. People were caught in storms all the time, and were prepared to deal with them. Even here at Dalereuth, they did not concern themselves with the fate of a herdsman or so, who could not foresee the weather. No herdsman would survive long without making provisions to deal with being caught in several storms in the year.

She passed on, traveling with the speed of thought, unaware of location, becoming somewhat disoriented.

After a while, as the disorientation continued, she considered returning to her body; she was beginning to tire. Then without any sense of interval, she became aware of a woman.

Or rather, of the *sense* of a woman. Leonie could not see her; at this level sight meant nothing. It was the music about her which had brought the contact. Leonie was accustomed to thinking in musical terms, and she first became aware of the instrument the woman held in her hands. It was a flute—or at least it felt like one—but it did not sound like any flute Leonie had ever heard; for the sound was bass; deep and rich, a bass timbre, but unmistakably the sound and feel of a flute.

The music caught her and held her—although at a deeper level, she knew that she was not *caught* as such, intrigued rather, and she could pull away any time she wished to. But at the moment, she had no such wish.

She followed the threading music as its webs of melody stretched through the darkness, enchanted by the unusual sound, feeling the curious vibration through some hitherto unexplored sense, at one with the unknown musician.

A woman, she reminded herself. She knew without a doubt, through some curious empathy that it was a woman, but the instrument that so fascinated her was no instrument that she had ever played, or even thought of playing.

She lost herself in the sound—so easy just to listen, and drift—

She knew she had passed from trance into true sleep, for when she opened her eyes, the rain was over, and patterns made by the moonlight on the walls of the chamber gave the room a strange and otherworldly appearance, and midnight—she could tell from the angle

of the three moons visible from the window—was far
past. The sound of the flute was gone, even from her
mind; perhaps it was its absence which had wakened
her. Had she been dreaming? No, for the memory of
strangely-altered flute song was no dream, but as substantial as any sound she had ever heard. She could
have played on the instrument, recreating the unfamiliar melodies—if only it had been there. But she
could not recapture it.

CHAPTER
7

The shuttle was on its way down, and Ysaye was still trying to figure out what *she* was doing on it. She still wasn't sure how it had happened. Now that they had penetrated the upper atmosphere there was a heavy rime of frost on the windows, so there was nothing much to see.

There was certainly more than enough to feel. Ysaye found herself wondering if there was supposed to be this much turbulence; she was strapped tightly into her seat, but the small craft was buffeted around by the unexpectedly heavy winds, and she was grateful that Ralph MacAran, the Second Officer, at the controls of the shuttle, was their best atmospheric pilot. Judging by the expressions of the rest of the crew on this first landing, she wasn't the only one. The atmosphere of this planet was giving them a pretty heavy introduction to its climate.

"Is this—normal?" she finally asked, leaning forward so that MacAran could hear her.

"Well—candidly, no. This is really heavy weather, and we're hardly down into it yet. But then, with all these mountains, we never expected it would be a fine holiday resort," said the young man at the controls.

Ysaye hoped that he was as confident as he sounded. As Second Officer (the Captain could not leave the ship, nor could the First Officer), Commander MacAran was the ranking officer present, and if there were some kind of emergency, *he* would be the one in charge of the party. Younger than most of his "charges," he was a sturdy, thick-set young man in his middle twenties, with the build of a professional wrestler, and thick, curling blond hair. Normally, Ysaye would never even have considered questioning his competence and experience. Right now, though, he looked terribly young. . . .

And he was looking younger and less confident by the moment. "My God," he muttered, fighting with the controls. "I thought the weather maps showed this as an area of relative calm! The wind shear here is absolute hell. Hang on tight, everybody!"

The shuttle bucked, then dropped like a stone, pulling negative gees for a moment and throwing them all against their restraints. Elizabeth's pale face and clenched teeth showed her fear, and behind Ysaye, someone gave a muffled yelp.

When the shuttle settled for a moment, Ysaye checked to make sure her straps were still properly fastened. Everyone knew that the first landing was the most dangerous moment on a new planet, with everything unknown and strange. Even when you got to the ground, the only thing you could ever take for granted was that you could take nothing for granted. You might, for instance, come down in a field, on an unexplored world, of carnivores—giant saurians, perhaps—who would think you looked just right for a light lunch. On the other hand you might, according to a fallacious story current in the Empire, land on a nearly microscopic, or at any rate, Lilliputian race of beings, and wipe out a whole city's worth of the little things. Ysaye was not precisely certain of the origin of *that* one, but she suspected some prank-minded student of early Atomic

Age literature, who had been rooting around in the old annals of "pulp scientifiction" stories. It was too much like a rumor that had circulated before that one, of a giant who had appeared on one of the colony worlds, continuously shrinking, who had claimed that he was the victim of an experiment gone wrong, and that our galaxy was nothing more than a molecule in *his* universe, with the stars being the nuclei of the atoms of that molecule. The giant supposedly shrank to human, then mouse, then bacterial size, before vanishing altogether. That particular tale had actually shown up on the news nets before being traced to an inventive graduate student at New Duke University.

The shuttle bucked and dropped again, then yawed alarmingly before MacAran was able to bring it back under control. His mouth was set in a thin, tight line, and Ysaye did not think he was likely to answer any more questions at the moment. She tried to tell herself that, all things considered, bad weather and other physical hazards of landing were the least of their worries, rather more to be expected than not. The first contact shuttle ships were always staffed with scientists, people carefully trained to anticipate emergencies and improvise solutions to any problems.

Her attempts at consoling herself did not help. Ysaye was the only one of the seven on the shuttle who had no hands-on experience of new planets. She still didn't quite understand why she had been assigned to this team. The rest were obvious: MacAran for his piloting and command skills, Commander Britton to coordinate the scientific data gathering, Lieutenant Evans for xenobotany, Dr. Aurora Lakshman for xenobiology (and as a doctor to treat any of the survey team who might be injured or ill), and Elizabeth and David for both their technical skills and their linguistic and anthropological backgrounds. In spite of their precautions they might run into some of the local inhabitants, although that was not the purpose of this first mission.

All those specialists—so what was *she* doing here? She did not have a single skill that could replace or even augment any of theirs. All she knew were computers —and right now, she wished she were back among them. . . .

Ysaye tried to tell herself not to worry; there was no rational reason to be nervous about the assignment, even if it was new to her. There must have been a reason for her inclusion; perhaps one of the others had some specialized computer-driven equipment that he or she simply didn't fully understand yet—although, if that were the case, shouldn't Ysaye have been told already, so that she could look it up and find out something about it first? Surely they didn't expect her to get complicated equipment up and running by—by intuition!

She looked across the aisle at Elizabeth, who was rubbing at the frosted window, as if eager for a look at the new world. Well, MacAran had the shuttle under better control now; there hadn't been any of those alarming drops for at least five minutes. Even though the shuttle was still shuddering and sideslipping—

The world below would almost certainly be Elizabeth's home for many years—unless the natives were so primitive that Empire authority felt it best the world should be Closed, she and David would remain behind when the ship moved on, making linguistic and anthropological records for the Empire. If the new world was to be fully Opened for trade, even more people would be staying. Someone from the ship would be appointed temporary Coordinator; they would set up a Terran enclave, and Elizabeth and David would certainly be married there. After all, they had been waiting more than a year for a planet where they could settle down and raise a family.

Ysaye stared at the lavender sky and at the jagged line of mountain scenery just visible through the frost. She was thankful that she was not responsible for flying over them. She knew enough of flying to realize that this kind of terrain was extremely hazardous. Terrain. What a strange word to apply to the country below them, which was not terrestrial at all. Being around David, who had been schooled extensively in linguistics, had made her sensitive to such nuances.

For a moment, she felt a moment of—premonitory sadness. If *this* was the world Elizabeth and David had been waiting for, they would stay here, and she, as ships' crew, would move on. She would never see them again—

And even if this was not "their" world, there would be changes. It was inevitable. The experiences they would have on the new world's soil would change her friends, and perhaps even Ysaye herself, if she spent much time on the planet's surface. No one completely escaped this kind of determinism.

And at the same time, their being here would change the planet and its people; they would bring some of their humanity here, no matter how they tried not to affect what they found. Humans did that; it was a part of their heritage. Humans modified their surroundings, however they tried not to. There had been a recurrent fad in humanity that "biology is not destiny." Ysaye's standard rebuttal to that was "show me a vegetarian lion." Anyone who seriously believed that men and women were not, at the very least, an aggregation of biological impulses was just begging the question. There was certainly more to it; but that was the bottom line.

Ysaye had so successfully calmed herself with philosophical meanderings that when MacAran hit the next wave of turbulence, it took her completely by surprise.

Wind shear—Ysaye thought that was what the pilot had said rocked them earlier—slammed them again, and the little ship plunged like a stone, then tilted wildly. Ysaye caught Elizabeth's eyes across the aisle and saw that her friend's mouth was again set in a grimace, her face pale, as she grabbed convulsively at the arms of her seat. Ysaye told herself sternly not to panic. Surely this wouldn't keep up all the way down. This was not Elizabeth's first planet; she and David had been to four others before this, but they had been rockballs with little or no atmosphere, so Ysaye didn't think Elizabeth was accustomed to this kind of landing either. It wouldn't do to panic on the basis of Elizabeth's reaction; she was just as much a tyro at this part of the journey as Ysaye.

"It's going to get worse before it's better," warned MacAran grimly. "The wind blows down off the ice cap, with nothing to break it. Then when it hits these mountains, we get all these back drafts, cross currents, and the wind shear." He grunted as another buck and drop threw him against his restraints. "Maybe we should have tried to come in on the desert north of here; we have cameras good enough to avoid any civilization."

"So why didn't we?" Evans asked. Ysaye wanted to strangle him. Here they were, fighting to stay aloft —and that idiot was trying to start an argument!

"The satellite report clearly indicated this location as a prime landing site," MacAran said. "The plateau we're aiming for certainly looks better from space than it does from here!" This time it was a roll to the right that interrupted him, and he fought to get the shuttle back on its proper course. When he resumed talking,

Ysaye got the feeling that he was babbling, saying whatever came into his head. To calm his passengers and reassure them?

If so, she thought, *I'm not reassured!*

"I'm not surprised we see no trace of aviation; anyone who tried to build a primitive aircraft here—" he broke off and struggled for a moment with the controls. "No, if the climate is all like this, I wouldn't expect aviation to be a science they'd develop very soon. Maybe on the plains to the south, but not here in the mountains."

"But we can land here," Commander Britton said. It sounded to Ysaye like a question, although it was not phrased as such; she wondered, was the Commander about to order MacAran to break off and return to the ship?

"I'm doing my best," MacAran said, "but this place has hit a new low for flying conditions."

That did *not* sound good to Ysaye.

"I'll be glad when we get on the ground," the Commander muttered.

If we get on the ground, Ysaye thought. Suddenly she realized that her fears were *not* groundless, nor were they overreaction; he was examining all possibilities to get them out of deadly peril. She swallowed, but the lump in her throat would not go away, and her mouth was paper dry. His manner made it pretty obvious that this was far more dangerous than it had sounded on board ship.

This was not what I bargained for, when I signed on with the Space Service.

They had plunged into clouds, thick and seemingly bottomless, a few moments ago; now, as the ship rolled and yawed like an amusement-park thrill ride, they came out below clouds, and Ysaye saw an endless vista of evergreen trees of some kind, lined with black scars from old forest-fires. As they continued downward, still bucking and yawing, she knew MacAran was searching desperately for ground level enough to set the shuttle down. She knew that atmospheric craft were usually landed facing into the wind, but they were not meant to fly into a gale like this. And as if the wind weren't enough—a moment later, the vista below was obscured by a pall of snow as thick as the clouds had been.

She could only hope that MacAran's instruments were working, and working well.

The search for the optimum landing space must be balanced against the shuttle's remaining power; if he delayed too long—there would be no power left for a landing. And an unpowered landing, here, now—

Balance this against the dangers of the landing area—which had not looked particularly good when Ysaye had glimpsed it.

The snow cleared for a moment; Ysaye craned her neck, ignoring the way the shuttle was throwing her against her straps, and caught a glimpse of his enhanced IR/UV imager; it, at least, had not been affected by the snow. And there was evidently enough ambient heat for the IR scan to work. "Beyond the trees," MacAran said jerkily, "that clearing. We'll set down there. Going to have to try anyhow. Not much choice."

"Look!" Elizabeth said suddenly. She was still glued to her window, and apparently she had seen something, the first evidence of the native IBs she had seen with her own eyes. "A *castle*."

"Can't be," David said. "Not exactly. Remember how the French, landing among the Iroquois, christened their fortress cities of wood *chateaux*, and ended up naming three or four cities 'Castletown.' "

Ysaye stared at them aghast. Only David and Elizabeth, Ysaye thought, would argue the fine points of linguistics in the face of an imminent crash landing.

"Elizabeth!" she squawked. "I hardly think—"

Elizabeth turned a face toward her that was so white it looked green, and her expression was as strained as Ysaye's. "I didn't think praying would do much for morale," she replied, her voice trembling.

She heard MacAran mutter from the controls, "Here goes nothing. This is about as good as we're going to get." He raised his voice. "All right, back there! Brace for landing! Crash positions!"

She bent over obediently, taking the approved tuck and covering the back of her neck with her hands. She felt them strike hard, rebound, and come down again; the crash restraints deployed, nets holding them in their fetal curls. Cushions billowed up from beneath the seat under Ysaye, and she heard the *beeping* of a dozen different alarms. They bounced, struck, and rebounded yet again. Ysaye was beyond fear now; she was paralyzed. Nothing in her training or her experience had prepared her for this.

I'm going to die, she thought dumbly. Thought moved sluggishly through the thick sea of fear that flooded her. The hull cracked sickeningly on the next bounce and Ysaye thought she heard the rending of metal.

That was when she mercifully blacked out.

She came to with freezing cold air and snow blowing into her face. The hull had split open in several places, and she could not believe for a moment that she was still alive. She was not certain how long she had been unconscious, but the cushions had shrunk to flat, fluttering ghosts, and the nets had retracted. They were down, if not quite in one piece. She found herself remembering the old saying that "any landing you walked away from was a good one."

"Is anyone hurt?" MacAran called, and there was a chorus of ragged "no's" and "just bumps and bruises." MacAran, his hands visibly trembling, tore loose his restraining straps and stood up. "Sound off!" he ordered, "I want to hear everyone's name!"

Ysaye took a ragged breath, and responded first— then Evans coughed and replied, followed by all the rest, Commander Britton last. Satisfied that his charges were neither dead nor badly injured, MacAran turned and climbed toward the door, which he had to wrench open. The rest freed themselves, then crowded behind him, eager to get themselves out of what was no longer a safe or sheltering vehicle.

"Are you all sure you're all right? Is anyone injured?" Dr. Lakshman asked; she had automatically grabbed her medical kit and was clutching it to her chest as she peered through the falling snow. A chorus of shaky denials answered her.

MacAran bent to look beneath the shuttle. "We may all be okay, but the landing gear sure isn't," he said. "And let's not even talk about the holes in her hide." He looked at the shuttle and shook his head. "I sure never expected to be the one to make the actual test of those crash protections—"

"You did fine, son," Commander Britton said, putting a fatherly hand on MacAran's shoulder. "I don't think anyone could have managed a better landing in conditions like this."

MacAran straightened, and took a deep breath, gathering his authority around him. "Well, crash procedures say you should all get your gear while I break out the survival equipment. So go in there one at a time and get what you can. Take your time. We're not going anywhere soon, that's for sure."

Dr. Lakshman grimly surveyed the snow blowing freely through what was left of the shuttle's cabin.

"We'll have to go somewhere," she said. "In this weather, we won't last long if we don't find better shelter."

Ysaye shivered, and not just from cold; she felt a chill of new fear. Out of one peril and into another. Had they come all this way only to freeze to death?

CHAPTER
8

N^{o!} Leonie started up out of deep sleep, sitting bolt upright and staring into the darkness.

She had fallen, from a great and terrible height— she had hit the ground at a dizzying speed—

She still trembled with fear, and her head rang with the impact.

Except that there hadn't been an impact. She was here, safe in her bed, in her suite in the Tower.

She held one icy hand against the side of her head, and blinked into the darkness. A dream—or was it?

A dream of falling . . . one that left her trembling with the shock of a real blow.

Slowly her mind began to work again as she struggled back to reality. All her life she had heard that, if in a falling dream you stayed asleep and dreamed of striking the ground, you would not wake, but die in your sleep. She was obviously not dead, yet she had definitely struck something hard.

There was still a feeling of real collision, although —she had also heard that the will of a powerful enough telepath could transform illusion into reality. Which lent a certain verisimilitude to the tale of dying from a dream fall.

She shivered, her head aching. Had it been a dream, or could it have been an earthquake, that had given her the illusion of falling in sleep and triggered the nightmare?

No, it could *not* have been an earthquake; she realized that as soon as the thought occurred. The Tower around her was altogether quiet. Without even thinking about it, reflexively, her mind scanned the Tower residents. Fiora slept quietly, and the little girls slept in Melora's room, curled up together like kittens. Only the single young woman in the relays was awake, and she was so far from ordinary consciousness that she might as well have been on one of the faraway moons. The room around Leonie was cool and quiet, a wind from outside barely ruffling the curtains. Yet the sense of disaster persisted, the feeling that somehow, she had struck hard against something.

As her shivering stopped, and she began to analyze her vague memories, strange and alien phrases rang in her mind.

Landing gear's gone . . . we're not going anywhere. . . .

But what was "landing gear," and why would she want to go anywhere?

And now that her own fear was ebbing, why was she filled with this sense of confusion? Why was her mind filled with a feeling of failure?

This was Dalereuth, not the mountains—there would be no snow here for some time—so why were her memories plagued with the impression of bitter, punishing winds, against which she must somehow battle for survival?

Wind shear. Another alien phrase. What was that? And why did it fill her with such a sense of panic?

As she sought to wrest meaning from these unfamiliar words, she realized suddenly that they were not in a language *she* knew, and that somehow she had sensed their meaning without knowing precisely how they were spoken.

That simple fact gave her a grasp on a portion of the truth, and the beginning of understanding; the thoughts, perhaps even the falling and the impact, were not her own. Somehow she had picked them up from someone else.

Leonie relaxed a trifle. As a telepath, although she was not yet formally trained, she was more or less accustomed to thoughts creeping into her mind from unexpected sources. In fact, she was so used to thinking of the meaning of what was being said that she all too seldom thought at all about the actual form of words.

For a moment only, she felt calmed by the solution to her puzzle. But then she thought again: she had *not understood the words*. Foreign thoughts, couched in words she did not understand—that frightened her all over again.

"What is happening to me?" she asked aloud, clutching her bedclothes to her throat.

She recalled the night before she arrived at the Tower, and her feeling, while watching the four moons, of impending peril.

Something threatens us; something is coming to us; it is coming to us from the moons.

She did not know what she had meant by it then; she did not know now, but she *did* know that something threatened her world, her whole way of living.

She closed her eyes, and tried to isolate her sense of foreboding. She could identify only an unfamiliar snow-covered landscape which might as well be one of those same moons she feared.

But there is no air on the moon. . . .

Leonie had never known that the moons were worlds until her brother had told her—but this was different. She had never pictured the moons as worlds, had never thought about it. But now she knew it, as a fact, from that same unknown source, and the *knowing* frightened her.

No air—people could not live there. Why should the moons be a source of peril? And how could they be linked with *this?*

For a telepath of Leonie's skill, learning often came with little or no effort, as she assimilated the thoughts of those around her. She acquired things from obscure sources and frequently the origin of those things never became clear to her; that was nothing new. There was no reason why something so familiar should frighten her now.

But it did; it was the unknown nature of the information, and not the unknown source, that frightened her. She had somehow picked up a link with an—an—*alien* mind.

That was not the least of it. She continued to analyze her fear. That was when she knew; the moons and this thought-source *were* linked. Something about the source of these strange thoughts threatened her; not her alone, but the very existence of all she knew and cherished.

She lay down, composing herself as if for sleep, but instead of sleeping, she tried to focus on the unknown source of the threat. In the darkness, she trembled, afraid to brave the overworld. But where else could she seek a danger coming from the moons?

Danger from the moons—a danger that came with thoughts she could hear, if not understand. It made no sense, even to her. Until recently she had believed that the moons were no more than lamps hung in the sky, a benevolent provision of the Gods to light the night. Now she knew them for what they were, as certainly as she knew the geography of her own Domain; barren, lifeless, airless balls of rock. Yet somehow capable of sustaining some kind of life—

She calmed herself, and firmed her will to her quest. Then, with a thought, she was out of her body, entering that strange realm she had essayed only a time or two before, and then, not for long. The overworld, as she imagined it and therefore now saw it, was a flat, featureless, formless gray plain, without landmarks—

No, behind her the Tower rose, not quite Dalereuth as she knew it, but still recognizable. It was smaller, without distinguishing marks, and seemed to be shrouded in a haze that obscured details; probably, she thought, because she had never really looked at the Tower clearly from the outside, and she saw it here as she conceptualized it. Far away, but not nearly as far away as it truly was, a second Tower rose, which she knew to be Arilinn. This was her first real demonstration to herself that in this space, thought was real, and everything would appear as she believed it to be.

Was this why she had been warned always to think positively?

Does this mean that here there can be no dangers unless I believe in them? she asked herself.

No, that would be too simplistic, too naive; but it did mean that a fearless attitude could keep her from inventing dangers for herself.

She stretched, noting with a touch of surprise that in this environment she was physically—if that word could apply here—different than she was in her ordinary world. For one thing, she seemed older, and filled with a poise that she had often attempted to simulate, with varying degrees of success.

This must mean that this older, adult version of herself was her true self. It need not trouble her when she pretended to be more like this—after all, she was only pretending to be more like her best self.

And wasn't that what most teachers and mentors wanted?

Her long hair, glowing bright red, and usually braided neatly, hung loose and wild nearly to her waist, as if she were some kind of heroine from an ancient tale. Perhaps—some great *leronis* from the Ages of Chaos—

But she was here on a matter of urgency, not to admire this fairy-tale self; no sooner did her mind fashion this thought, then she was off and away, skimming like wind through the overworld, searching for the source of her unexplained fears. In these realms she could move very nearly at the speed of thought; she passed over the plains she had traversed on the way here, traveling in a few seconds the miles it had taken her and Lorill nearly three weeks to travel by road. In the distance she saw Castle Hastur, at the edge of the Hellers, and she thought of Lorill. She wondered if her twin brother, possibly dreaming himself, would join her in her travels. It was terribly lonely here; she wished fervently that he would, hoping that her wishes would have some force here to bring him to her.

But she did not see him, and she went on alone.

There were other travelers in the overworld this night: silent forms, wandering aimlessly or on unexplained business, drifting past her. None of them spoke to or approached Leonie, and she wondered if they even saw her. Were they dreaming or seeking something in this astral world?

Whether they saw her or not, it really mattered very little, for they were none of her concern tonight. It would be far too easy to be distracted here, and perhaps become lost; she focused herself and her will on whatever had wakened her, and found herself among mountains, and conscious, more than anything else, of icy winds.

She realized that she was perceiving wind and cold through someone else's mind, for here in the overworld, there was neither wind nor weather.

But whose mind?

She did not know; it was wholly unfamiliar. It was human, not catman or the half-legendary *chieri*, but there was more of an alien quality about this mind than she was accustomed to. And one thing was absolutely certain; it was no one and nothing she had ever touched before.

Abruptly she was conscious of the cessation of wind; it was still roaring outside, but she was protected from it. She became aware that she was inside a little shelter, a rude sort of dwelling.

Then she recognized it, although the mind she was watching did not, as one of the travel shelters abounding in the mountains. It was crammed, filled almost to capacity, with human beings.

In this weather? Why would such a large party go out into this storm? She groped after more clues as to the identity of her contact, trying to reach for anything that might help.

Sight came to her then, and with astonishment she found herself looking at men and women who were dressed in bizarre and highly unfamiliar garments. Both men and *women* wore heavy rough trousers and jackets, of some kind of strange and oddly slick fabric. But the garments were not all that was strange about them. Some of the faces were like enough to her own to have been distant kin, though few were as fair-skinned as she, but some of the men and women had skins of *dark brown*. They looked as if they had rubbed some kind of dye over themselves, but why would anyone do that?

Were they even human, she wondered?

The mind linked with hers dismissed the question with incredulity; *yes, certainly we're all human*.

But the dark-skinned ones seemed to Leonie completely unlike any men or women she had ever seen. She was so completely astonished that she almost fled back at once to her body, and to the security and familiarity of the Tower. But her surprise and interest— not to say curiosity—triumphed, and Leonie remained, watching silently—for in this situation she could neither be seen nor make herself known, except perhaps by *laran*, to the strangers.

"We may be here for quite a while," someone was saying. "The landing gear is shot, and those holes in her hull aren't going to make her terribly spaceworthy. I'm afraid we're stuck here until the ship can send another shuttle down with parts and equipment for repairs—or just send down a crew to take her apart and destroy what can't be salvaged, and bring us back. Since no one was hurt, we'll do what useful work we can before rescue; it will probably be at least a day before a shuttle can be landed safely."

"More like a week," someone muttered. "That's a killer storm out there."

Leonie felt the fear that statement caused in her contact-mind. And also got the impression from the woman that this talk of "useful things to be done" was just make-work, designed to keep these people from panic, or from the troubles that could arise when so many people were confined in so small a space for a long time.

"There are a lot of very basic things that can be done," one of the men said, "soil assays, water samples—"

"It's the people that I want to find out about," said a woman. "There seems to be an extremely sophisticated civilization here. Perhaps if the shuttle can't land, and we can find some of them, they can help us—"

"You're jumping to conclusions, Elizabeth," a man snapped, and, even then, Leonie disliked him just from his tone of voice. "You can't make judgments on the basis of a single structure. And who in his right mind would live up *here*, anyway? Even if we can get to that stone heap of yours, we won't find out anything!"

"Sophisticated, I said, not technological," the woman called Elizabeth protested. "There's a difference."

"There's a good deal that can be surmised even on the basis of one building," said the man standing next to Elizabeth. "Houses don't build themselves; and if that—well, I'll use your word, Evans—structure that we saw isn't a house, it's something very much like it. And it's an entire building, intact. Considering what archeologists have discovered from a few scraps in a garbage heap that's been abandoned for millennia, I'd say there's quite a bit to be learned from a whole building."

Especially when there are still people in it. Leonie heard the thought, but apparently no one else did, for the debate continued unchanged. And she caught another thought from her "host"—that this kind of senseless bickering over nothing was exactly what she and the man who had spoken of "useful work" had feared. *Cabin fever* was the term her host used, and *post-trauma stress syndrome.* Whatever in Zandru's coldest hell *that* meant.

"A castle, I'd say," Elizabeth said, with something her host recognized as a hint of hysteria, "or something serving the same purpose—"

"Oh, now that's interesting; just what purpose does a 'castle' serve?" Evans said, almost jeering, and trying obviously to provoke some kind of outburst, but Elizabeth answered quite seriously.

She's concentrating on trivia to keep from falling apart, her host thought. Then, fearfully, *If only I could do that. I ought to try. . . .*

"It could be the residence of an important personage, or a place for a garrison of soldiers, a fortified place. . . ."

"You're anthropomorphising," Leonie heard someone say. Leonie recognized the word, from the memory of the mind through which she was hearing it. *A common fallacy*, her host thought, *the habit of attributing human motives or purpose to inanimate or nonhuman things*.

But how else, Leonie wondered, could one think about anything, except in human terms, if one was human? Nonhuman thoughts were forever unknowable; one could only make analogies from the human. Even if one had the Gift of telepathy with nonhumans, there was never any understanding of their thoughts, only their feelings and emotions.

"I say, if it walks like a duck, smells like a duck and quacks, the chances are pretty overwhelming that it is either a duck or something like a duck," said another man. "The chances are it's a structure for humanoid use; it's on the right physical scale. If it's not built by and for humans as we know them, the chances are that it was constructed *for* something like humans."

The voices rose again in a babble she could not sort out, and Leonie took the opportunity to find out where she was. The overworld was without landmarks, but she could see, far off outside the shelter, the rising structure of Castle Aldaran, with the old Tower which still formed a part of the castle.

The Tower—

That reminded her of Dalereuth, and suddenly she

was sick of the strange and half-incomprehensible thoughts of these mad people. She wanted things she recognized, thoughts she could understand—

Then she was back in her body in Dalereuth.

She lay there for a moment, simply gathering her thoughts. Then she realized that her responsibility was by no means at an end.

Somehow I must get a message to Aldaran; there is a strange group of people there, lost in the storm.

Perhaps she might come to regret this, but at the moment it seemed unthinkable that a group of men and women, no matter how strange, should be left at the mercy of the storms of the High Hellers.

There was no one to ask for advice, even if she had been inclined to ask for it. So Leonie set in motion the pattern for all that followed.

She sat up in bed and reached for the fur robe which lay there. Then she stopped; she was always being accused of not thinking, but simply acting; and so she paused to think how she would do this.

After a moment she got out of her bed, thrust her feet into fur-lined house boots, and went out into the halls of the Tower, and up the stairs which led to the relay chamber.

A young girl in a blue technician's robe reclined there in a chair, drowsily watching a large screen of what looked like gleaming black glass. As Leonie came in, she roused slightly and asked, "Leonie? At this hour? What do you want? Are you ill?"

"No," said Leonie, stopping to think about what she really did want. "Carlina, I have been out in the overworld, and there are strangers—"

"The overworld? But you are not trained—I think we must speak to Fiora," said Carlina. "I have no authority—"

Leonie repressed impatience. She was apparently

more concerned about the fact that Leonie had been out in the overworld—untrained—than the fact that great urgency must have driven her there!

"—oh, Fiora, there you are," she finished, with a sigh of relief, as the door opened, and Fiora, very pale in her crimson robes, came in. "I hope we did not disturb you."

"No," Fiora said, turning her blind face toward them. "But I always hear if something moves in the Tower at an unaccustomed hour. Leonie, what ails you? Why are you not in your bed? It is very late—or perhaps I should say very early—to be here like this. And in your night-wear—"

She spoke as if to a small child and Leonie repressed her annoyance, for there was more at stake here than being treated like a child. The more she thought about it, the more important those strange people became. They were important to—to something.

And in truth, they did not seem capable of taking care of themselves through a brutal Hellers storm. Someone must see to them.

She said, as seriously and soberly as she could manage, "Yes, I knew you were the one to be told, but I did not know if you should be wakened. I have been in the overworld, Fiora, and I have seen something—"

She paused, overcome with the apparent impossibility of saying just what she had seen. Fiora sensed her hesitation and spoke a little irritably.

"Well, and so what have you seen, and what can we do about it?" she asked. "I assume that you came up here because you felt we can and should be doing something."

The annoyance in her voice robbed Leonie of the last of her caution.

She thinks I have had a nightmare, and not that I have done what I said—

"Fiora, I felt that there was some sort of peril, or danger; I hunted for the source and I saw strangers," Leonie said. "Strangers, lost in a shelter near Aldaran, at the mercy of the weather."

Fiora's interest rose a little. "Are they anyone you know, or anyone you have ever seen before?"

"No, and no," Leonie answered, shaking her head, then as another thought occurred, qualified, "I think perhaps I have been in contact with one of them before, through her music—a very strange instrument—"

Fiora dismissed that with a wave of her hand. "And these people are lost in a storm?" Fiora asked. "You are certain? Near Aldaran?"

Carlina said humbly, "She may be correct. I have heard on the relay from Tramontana that a fearful storm is raging between Aldaran and Caer Donn."

Fiora pondered that. "If there are strangers caught in it, we must send them succor of some kind." She turned to Leonie. "You are certain of this? You would swear on your family honor that this is no childish nightmare?"

Leonie nodded. "They seem very—foreign," she added. "I really do not think they are capable of caring for themselves in a banshee-storm, Fiora. They seemed as—" she groped for words "—as helpless as a rabbit-horn in the desert."

Carlina responded to Fiora's nod of permission to act. "I will communicate at once with the Keeper in the Aldaran Tower and warn everyone to be on the alert for these strangers."

But Fiora had another question. "You said they were foreign. Are they intruders, invaders?"

She moved to stand before the screen, while Leonie said, "Not invaders, no. I felt they were lost, strangers, and that they had no intention of intrusion or invasion."

"Well, I will trust your instinct," said Fiora. "Your alertness may well have saved lives this night, and so I will not ask you why you were out in the overworld, Leonie."

For some reason this made Leonie angry. What did Fiora think? That Leonie was a wholly unlessoned child, that the overworld was a strange place to her, or dangerous?

Was she to do nothing without Fiora's assent?

But she put aside her pride, remembering the bargain they had made, "I am sorry; I knew I was to try nothing without your knowledge, but truly, I thought this no harm. I—I suppose I was missing my home, so far away, and my brother Lorill—"

She looked so miserable that Fiora said mildly, "No harm done, Leonie. Another time, don't go out unaccompanied; you know so little of the dangers of the overworld. Now I will speak to the Keeper at Aldaran through the relays." She took up her place before the great screen.

After a time Leonie heard her say—for though she did not speak aloud, Leonie could read her easily, *Marisa? One of our novices here has been adventuring in the overworld and has seen strangers in the storm you have there. Is it still snowing?*

Yes, we have had eleven inches since it began and it shows no sign of stopping within the next day or so, came Marisa's answer. *I do not think I would be willing to go out in such a storm, even in the overworld.*

Well, Leonie is young and quite fearless, Fiora said, and in spite of her reproof, Leonie thought there was a note of pride in Fiora's unspoken voice. *She is a daughter of the Hasturs, who has the ambition to become a Keeper.*

Well, I will see to sending out a rescue party, as soon

as the snow quiets, responded Marisa. *And I will let you know about them—if they are there at all.*

Oh, if Leonie says they are there, they are there right enough, said Fiora. *I know her better than to think she would do this as a prank. And she is old enough to know the difference between a nightmare and a true seeing.* She turned away from the screen, and back to the younger women. Once again, Leonie was struck by how easily and surely Fiora moved, though she moved in eternal darkness.

"You have the relays, Carlina. Destry will be coming to relieve you in an hour or two, I believe?"

"Yes, Fiora," Carlina replied, nodding.

Fiora paused, turning her face toward Leonie, and said, "So much for that. We cannot get any answer until it stops snowing a little and they can send out a rescue party from Aldaran. For the moment, Leonie, come with me. Tell me about these strangers, and what possessed you to do such a thing. Whenever you go out of your body, you should be monitored—did that never occur to you?"

She did not sound angry—only tired and a little worried. It was not a reproof as such. Leonie could not think of anything to say except, "No, *domna*."

Fiora sighed. "What am I going to do about you, Leonie? You have so much talent, but you are so foolhardy!" she said, almost in despair. "You do not think these people are intruders or invaders, and yet you said they are foreign; tell me, what do you think they are, then?"

Leonie bit her lip, torn between confiding in her Keeper and sounding like a fool. "I know it sounds ridiculous; but I think that these people are from—the moons. And before that—from beyond even the moons."

She had expected Fiora to break out into laughter

and would almost have welcomed having someone ridicule her fears. *Chieri*, or Dry Towners, or even someone from beyond the Wall Around the World would be less frightening than these people with their alien thoughts. Instead Fiora looked grave.

"You would have no way of knowing this," she said, after a moment of hesitation, "but there was once a tale that—before even the days of the Gods—our own people had come here from another world. It is just an old tale, but what you say makes me remember it."

Leonie raised her head in mingled relief and alarm. "Then what I say is not utter folly? I know that there is no air on the moons and that no one could live there," she said. "I felt such a fool when I said it."

"No," Fiora said, soberly. "Whatever it may be, I do not think it is folly. Whether welcoming them be foolish or not—well, that we will not know until these strangers are found. And that will be some time yet. Now go back to bed, Leonie, or if you are not sleepy," Fiora added so quickly that Leonie wondered if the older woman was reading her thoughts, "then go and lie down and rest, or study, if you wish." After a moment she added, "Whatever comes of this, I promise I will tell you, as soon as I know myself."

CHAPTER
9

Finally, after what seemed like an eternity of howling winds and quarreling colleagues, the snow had stopped. The shelter seemed a little more spacious since about half of those confined inside had rushed *outside* as soon as the winds died. Ysaye had remained indoors, huddled beside the fire, trying not to sneeze when the chimney failed to pull out all the smoke. She was afraid that she would never get the smoke smell out of her hair; she *knew* that she was never going to be warm again for as long as she lived. David had told her when he came back inside a few moments ago that it was much warmer now than it had been during the storm. Even though she had to admit that she could hear the drips of the melting snow plopping into the high drifts beneath the eaves of the building, Ysaye was not impressed by this so-called "warming trend." Barely above freezing was still too damned cold. She hoped that the ship would send someone down to retrieve them soon. If this was what planetary exploration was like, she was going to go hide in the core of the computer and never come out again.

Not that this building, which appeared to be some kind of emergency shelter for people caught out in storms like this, wasn't interesting in its own way. Working on Commander Britton's suggestion, Elizabeth had enthusiastically catalogued every single item in it as soon as they got themselves organized, and then she and David had discussed the implications of each one as they huddled together under the emergency blankets they had salvaged from the ruined shuttle. But Ysaye would much rather have been learning all this from the database, and not at first hand. Actually, she would much rather not have had to learn about it at all.

To Ysaye's mind, most of the assumptions that could be drawn from the place were pretty obvious. She was sure that all of the rest shared her sincere thankfulness that whoever had built the place felt the cold the way they did. This shelter had been built as solidly as low tech would permit, and there was plenty of firewood stored near a primitive hearth. That argued either altruism, as Elizabeth held—or a more practical streak, the knowledge that anyone could be caught by such a storm at any time, and it behooved the inhabitants of this place to erect such shelters on the grounds of "enlightened self-interest."

Evans had been the worst during their enforced confinement, and his absence had begun to ease the tension headache Ysaye had been enduring that was an added insult to the mild concussion she had suffered in the crash. Evidently he found being confined in close quarters with other people for long stretches of time almost as unbearable as Ysaye found his grumbling about it, and the tension headache was due entirely to her increasing irritation with him. As soon as the snow stopped, Commander Britton had suggested that Evans go out to the shed, which appeared to be intended for some sort of riding or pack animals, and begin his analysis of the plants used for fodder that were stored there. The ensuing silence was almost as comforting as a nice cup of hot chocolate would have been.

Dr. Lakshman had lowered herself to sit beside

Ysaye on the floor near the fire. "Peace and quiet at last," she sighed. "How's your concussion doing?"

"I think I've just about lost the concussion headache," Ysaye replied, "And if certain people manage to stay outside, the tension headache may go away, too."

Aurora Lakshman shook her head. "I am trying very hard not to think how little I would care if certain people fell off a cliff," she said wryly. "This shelter is just not big enough to hold Evans *and* his ego."

"Aurora," Ysaye pointed out, "there are still six people in here—and I think whoever built this shelter was thinking of either fewer people or smaller people."

"Or people who didn't gripe as much," Aurora said. "If Evans had said one more word about the quality of the emergency rations in the shuttle, I think I might actually have hit him."

"I'll admit they weren't the best thing I've ever tasted," Ysaye agreed, "but they aren't any worse than the food they served us in training, especially those survival rations when we went out into the desert!"

"Actually, I think they're a slight improvement," Aurora said. "And the moaning and complaining when we had to use the stuff stored *here!* I was ready to strangle him! His scientific analysis of—whatever they are—was first rate, but we could certainly have done without his personal opinion of their palatability."

"Or the comparisons to what they tasted like." Ysaye made a face. "I thought little boys were supposed to grow out of trying to make people sick once they hit adolescence!"

Aurora chuckled. "At least he's good with his analysis techniques. I'm glad they turned out to be something we could eat, or we'd have been in even worse shape after our own supplies ran out." She grimaced. "I'm not at all happy with how under-supplied the shuttle is for an emergency like this. Granted, we didn't expect to spend this long down here, but this situation could easily have been a lot worse than it is, in which case we would be losing personnel by now." She looked carefully at Ysaye, who was wrapped in two of the emergency blankets. "How are you doing besides the headaches, Ysaye?"

Ysaye shrugged and tried to look unconcerned. "I'm cold, like everyone else, I imagine. Except for Evans, who obviously has no nerves, or he'd be getting on his own by now."

"It's true that we're all cold," Aurora said, "but you're the one least physically suited to this environment. MacAran, and our lovebirds over there," she indicated David and Elizabeth, "are descended from people who adapted to live in a cold climate, while your ancestors evolved in Africa."

"Everybody on Terra is descended from people who lived in Africa," Ysaye reminded her. "They proved that way back in the twentieth century."

"True," Aurora conceded the point. "But your ancestors stayed there longer than the ones who became Caucasians. And you have very little surplus body fat, which is what insulates the human body in cold weather. You're so conscientious about your exercise program on the ship—except when you get involved in a particularly interesting project, of course—"

"You know me too well," Ysaye laughed.

Aurora smiled back. "It's hard to keep secrets from your doctor. You're all right, though?"

"As long as no one asks me to go hiking out in the snowdrifts," Ysaye told her. "One step outside that door, and I'll freeze in place."

Aurora nodded, chuckling. "Good. As long as you're all right, the rest of us should be, too. Think of it as a variation on the canary in the coal mine."

"Well, I'm qualified for that," Ysaye agreed. "And at least in this cold weather I don't have to worry about hay fever—or any allergies from blooming vegetation. Just the dust allergy from the straw, and irritation from the smoke. And the medication I brought with me is still holding out."

The doctor looked suddenly concerned. "That's right, I'd forgotten about your allergies."

"No reason for you to remember them under normal conditions," Ysaye said lightly. "There's nothing on the ship that bothers me, and I don't volunteer for landing parties. I don't know why I'm on this one, and frankly, it's an honor I could have done without."

Aurora grinned. "I hate to say this to a scientist of your reputation, but I hear the Captain had a hunch."

Ysaye's jaw dropped. "Captain Gibbons dropped me into this mess on a *hunch?*" she said indignantly. She took a deep breath and let it out. "When we get back, I just may program the computer to 'lose' all the opera recordings for a few months. Well, at least that explains why I couldn't come up with a logical reason for my inclusion in this festive little gathering."

"Such as it is," Commander Britton said, joining them.

"Well, we do have a campfire," Ysaye said, with a wry smile.

"Too bad we forgot the marshmallows," Aurora added lightly. "I'll have to add them to the list of suggested supplies for the next time somebody crashes a shuttle in a blizzard."

MacAran winced, and Ysaye felt a surge of sympathy for him. The pilot was taking his failure very badly. "Actually, under the circumstances, it was a very good landing," Ysaye pointed out gently. "After all, we're alive—although with this headache, I'm not sure I want to be!"

"Thank you for the kind words," MacAran said, making no attempt to sound anything but bitter. "Will you testify at my hearing?"

Ysaye shook her head. "You know perfectly well that they'll want all of us to testify, and I don't think that anyone here is going to find fault with you. I know that I'll tell the Captain that it wasn't your fault and that you did a superb job of landing under nearly impossible conditions." She grinned, and tried to make a joke to lighten his gloomy expression. "Maybe then he won't take the shuttle replacement out of your pay."

"Right," Elizabeth put in, playing along with the joke, "blame it on the weather briefing and he'll take it out of *my* pay."

The door opened suddenly and Evans bounced in. "What an adaptation! You aren't going to believe this! Some of the trees here seem to encase their fruits by thickening their skins into special pods against the snow, and cast the pods off when it gets warmer, so their growing season isn't interrupted!"

He looked as happy as a child with a new toy, which was certainly an improvement over his behavior during the storm. Ysaye could understand his reaction; this discovery would be a fine base for a scholarly paper which would bring him prestige in the community of xenobotany. It wasn't often that anyone in the Service had the opportunity for the kind of research paper that would stun academic circles; when it came right down to it, most research on xenobotany was done at the cellular level and below, and someone like Evans was simply not going to have the time or opportunity to do that kind of research. He was a field xenobotanist; it was his job to decide whether given plants were harmful, neutral, or beneficial to humans. It was not his job to conduct research outside of that sphere—and to be perfectly catty, Ysaye was not certain that he wanted to take the time away from his personal (reliably rumored) explorations of recreational pharmaceuticals to do that kind of research.

He pulled Commander Britton aside and began an enthusiastic report delivered in speech so rapid that Ysaye could barely follow it and soon stopped trying.

There came a pounding on the door, and everyone looked up in surprise. Personnel had been drifting back into the shelter for the last hour, but no one had felt the need to knock—that would have been ridiculous. . . .

A split-second later, they looked at one another, counting noses. Ysaye was no different from the rest; and came to the same conclusion. Everyone was already inside, so that meant whoever was knocking—

or *whatever* was knocking—

A pall of fear fell over the group. For a moment, no one could move.

Then, suddenly, before anyone could stop him, Commander MacAran stepped forward and opened the door.

To Ysaye's astonishment—and relief, for however interesting really different aliens would be, in their current situation she would rather have beings with whom she could communicate—the men on the doorstep looked completely human. No claws, no fangs—unless they had something hidden under their clothing, they looked to Ysaye as if they were "human to the ninety-ninth percentile."

There were four of them, tall, fair-haired, and clothed in several layers of heavy clothing: loose breeches, cloaks that hung to mid-thigh, high boots. They wore their hair long, and some of them were bearded, which looked strange to Ysaye, since nobody on board wore a beard.

MacAran began with Standard speech, and, when

that unsurprisingly failed, tried to explain by signs that they had been marooned here by the crash of the shuttle craft, but evidently he was not getting the message across.

Did they have the concept of flight here? Ysaye wondered. She could see no way that anyone could develop aircraft in this type of terrain, and with weather like that last blizzard.

The leader of the strange men made signs that seemed to Ysaye to indicate that even worse weather was on the way. He finished by gesturing to them to follow him.

MacAran glanced back at the rest of them.

Commander Britton nodded—dubiously, but nodded. Elizabeth and David made motions of immediate agreement. The doctor pursed her lips and looked at the strangers sharply, then added her own agreement.

Evans looked impatient as *he* nodded. Not surprising, Ysaye thought. He was always ready to try and find "angles" on something, and he had been all too ready to swoop down out of the sky and exploit this world, even before they knew about the inhabitants. Right now he was probably looking these natives over and deciding the quickest way to take advantage of them.

Ysaye was the lone holdout; she just did not want to go with these people, whoever, whatever they were. She didn't think they were ill-intentioned—but she had the oddest feeling of warning about them. As if, somehow, something was trying to tell her that if she went with them, she would be walking into danger she couldn't even imagine.

MacAran gave her a sharp look, but the consensus was already in. He nodded acquiescence, and they all gathered up their belongings and followed the strangers outside.

One of the natives led them to a narrow, deeply beaten path in the snow, not quite a road, but the nearest thing to it that could be made in the snow without heavy machinery. The Terrans followed, perforce in single file, with the rest of the natives bringing up the rear.

As she trudged along the path, Ysaye remained bundled in her blankets, squinting against the glare of sun on the snow. The air was cold enough that her breath steamed, but growing warmer by the moment. Buds and even leaves seemed to be springing out of dormant wood on the trees, some of them emerging as Ysaye watched, as if she were watching a motion-study of leaf development. It looked as if Evans were right—that the leaves and buds had been "stored" for the cold weather. Although it looked to her as if the "pods" simply folded back along the stem, rather than being shed altogether. That would make more sense, really; so that the pods could be reused rather than being lost with each storm and thaw.

Ysaye was fascinated. And she could see how such an evolutionary development was logical here. If the storm they had survived was typical of the kind of weather on this planet, some kind of accommodation would have to be made. If the trees and shrubs had to shed their foliage every time there was snow, they'd never survive. If the lower plants died every time the temperature dropped below freezing, they would never form seeds. They must have had something like antifreeze in their veins, besides the waxy outer coat, the protective pods, and the tropic response to dark and cold. A fascinating adaptation altogether.

They went up a long hill, following the path in the snow and down into a little valley. Then they came to what seemed to be a village: a cluster of dark, one- and two-storied wooden buildings; impossible to tell whether they were dwellings, animal housing, or both. But beyond them, partway up another slope was the building they had seen from the shuttle, the one Elizabeth had dubbed a "castle."

More than imposing to the Terrans, it was constructed of gray stone, and loomed over the village as if it brooded protectively over the buildings and inhabitants. It was multistoried and multitowered, and almost as far beyond the tech level of the shelter as one of the domes on the moon was beyond it. This castle of Elizabeth's was surely the most impressive thing they had yet seen on the planet! Ysaye's expectations took an abrupt upward turn. Any culture that could produce a structure like this one had to be well organized and at least sophisticated enough to have some engineering and mathematics. She tried not to think of the other possible implications—that any culture that would produce a structure like this one, so obviously meant for defensive purposes, must have something it needed to defend against.

The native led them through a formidable set of gates and doors, and into the shadows inside.

They paused for a moment in a kind of anteroom. The men conferred among themselves, and one went off by himself. Ysaye studied what little furniture was in the room with them; mostly benches and tables of heavy, functional wood. Odd to think that here wood was so common that houses were built of it, when back on Terra it was so expensive that one of those benches would represent a year of Ysaye's salary.

Finally a woman appeared and indicated that Ysaye, Elizabeth, and Aurora should follow her.

Were they trying to split up the party?

Ysaye shot an alarmed look at Commander Britton, who shook his head at her. "Go along with what they want," he said to the three women. "I don't think anyone intends any harm at the moment. And you've all been trained in elementary hand-to-hand anyhow; you should be safe enough. It doesn't look to me as if these people would ever expect a woman to be combat trained."

Ysaye bit her lip nervously, but she truly didn't have much choice. The three women followed the native upstairs to a spacious room, longer and wider than the shelter with obviously human furniture; stools, a chair or two, dressers and some low tables, with benches along one of the walls that held a fireplace. There was another woman there, apparently some sort of attendant, who produced clothing for them from the heavy dressers that stood along one wall. The first woman indicated that they should follow the attendant's directions, then left. Ysaye was a little nervous, but they were three to the attendant's one; if anything went wrong, surely they could overpower one somewhat primitive woman. The clothing was suitable for the kind of weather here and the inefficient heating; a fire was burning on the hearth, but it could not be said to be heating the room much. After a long moment of hesitation, while the woman made encouraging noises at them, the three Terrans shed their wet uniforms and donned the native gear. It was either that, or risk catching something.

Ysaye was glad of the long heavy skirts and petticoats, although she felt a bit foolish when the attendant had to show her how to put them on. There were layers of inner skirts and camisoles of flannel, covered by blouses, and outer skirts of wool in various tartan patterns. Ysaye, accustomed to the tunic and trousers of her uniform, wondered how she was going to be able to move dressed like this.

Well, at least they were warm, and she knew that women had worn skirts like this for centuries on Terra.

In fact, when she looked at Elizabeth, it was oddly like seeing a portrait from an old biography come to life. Elizabeth looked quite at home in this costume. It still seemed a bit odd to Ysaye to base garments on the sex of the wearer, rather than on what the wearer expected to do while wearing them, but she supposed it must make sense to these people.

The attendant gave them a scented lotion and indicated that it should be rubbed onto hands, feet, and face. Aurora examined it carefully as she rubbed it onto her hands. "It seems to be some sort of chapped skin or frostbite palliative; I'll bet they use it here a lot. It would probably be good for burns, too." She looked at the open fireplace at the end of the room. "And burns probably are fairly common here."

The woman who had brought them upstairs reappeared and signaled them to follow her back downstairs, to an even larger chamber, where tables had been laid with plates of cold sliced meats, bread of some sort, thick and heavy, and pitchers of some kind of hot drink. Groups of natives sat eating at the tables, sparing them curious glances as they came in.

"Can we eat this stuff?" Ysaye said doubtfully.

Aurora shrugged. "We could eat the rations in the shelter. This is the same sort of thing, only fresh—fresh meat instead of dry, fresh-baked bread instead of that trail-bread. I don't know what the drink is, but if it isn't alcoholic and doesn't trigger an allergic reaction, I'd say you're safe."

Ysaye sat with the others at a long wooden table, and cautiously tried the drink, taking a little on her tongue and waiting for the warning tingle that would indicate she was violently allergic to it. After a minute, when she didn't seem to be reacting to it, she tried a few more sips, fairly sure now that even if it made her sick after a while, it wouldn't send her into shock and kill her before she could get help.

The drink turned out to be very similar to hot chocolate, but somewhat more bitter than Ysaye was used to. There was also something that was obviously beer, but Ysaye decided, after one cautious sip, that she liked it even less than Terran beer, which she considered fit only for washing hair. The mugs were tall and had faces carved on one side, and Ysaye realized that either the carvings were intended to face away from the drinker, or—

Aurora, on her right, had apparently noticed the same thing. "Look around the tables, Ysaye," she murmured quietly. "The people here are almost all left-handed."

"You're right," Ysaye replied. "Tell Elizabeth to be careful what she does with her elbow—it won't win us any points if she jabs it into her neighbor's ribs."

"I wish we could talk to them," Aurora said. "I'd love to know about their medical supplies."

Ysaye stared cautiously at the thick sandwich she had put together, hoping that all the ingredients were as innocuous as they appeared. "It would be a lot better to be able to send a message to the ship." She looked around at the natives, surreptitiously. "They look as though they could be of Terran ancestry, but apparently they don't speak Standard."

"There were about a half-dozen ships that went off before there *was* a Standard language," Elizabeth said, listening intently to the buzz of conversation in the hall. "I know bits of some of the old languages, and I'm not sure, but I think I'm picking up a word or two here and there."

"Now that you mention it," Ysaye said, a little surprised. "I know what you mean. It feels like trying to identify a piece of music you haven't heard before by a composer whose style you know well."

"Maybe it really is a colony from a Lost Ship," Elizabeth said excitedly. "I wonder where it could have been from. Any ideas?"

"I think we can safely rule out the one from Zaire," Ysaye replied dryly. "They're staring at me and at Commander Britton as if they'd never seen dark skin before. And there's not a one of them who doesn't look like Northern European stock. That should narrow it down quite a bit—once I can get back to the computer and check the old ship lists!"

"But if they're Terran stock, shouldn't we be able to understand more of what they're saying?" Aurora asked. "After all, language can't have changed that much!"

"You don't think so?" Elizabeth chuckled. "I hate to disillusion you."

"But—" Aurora protested, "there are medical terms that haven't changed in millennia!"

"If they're one of the really early ships," Ysaye said, "they could have had over two thousand years for the language to change." She glanced over at Elizabeth, who nodded encouragingly. She continued. "That's plenty of time for a language to diverge. Look at the difference between Old English and Middle English—and only a few centuries separated them, on a very small island."

"Which, if I recall correctly," Elizabeth said, "was being intermittently invaded by foreigners."

That brought up another thought to all three of them. The obviously defensive nature of this structure could mean that these people were under attack fairly often. If that were so, were *they* under suspicion of being enemies?

"If they consider us invaders," Aurora pointed out,

indicating a new group of people entering the hall, "they're certainly treating us well. Giving us clothing, food, and even including us in their mealtime entertainment."

Elizabeth turned to look. "Minstrels!" she said, in mingled pleasure and speculation. "Oh, I can't wait to hear what their music is like! If they *are* from a Lost Ship, there might be something I can recognize—songs stay intact longer than the original languages. I hope they sing."

Ysaye looked curiously at the instruments the musicians were carrying. There were some that looked rather like a cross between guitar and a lute, though the number of strings varied from four to fourteen. When the number of strings exceeded fourteen, they seemed to change to something strung like a harp but held across the player's lap.

After several minutes of rather pleasant-sounding tuning, they began to sing. They hadn't even reached the first chorus when Elizabeth gasped. "That's a form of Gaelic," she exclaimed, "and I know that song!"

"You know that song?" It was Evans who asked, coming up to the women, looking curiously at Elizabeth. The men had finally made their own appearance, and they had been garbed like the natives as well.

But it was Ysaye who answered. "Not only does she know it, she's sung it. I've heard her."

Elizabeth added, "This means they *are* one of the Lost Colonies, they *must* be. I even think I know which one!"

Evans looked at her skeptically. "How do you know that?"

Elizabeth was not to be put off by him this time. "I had relatives on the ship; it's an old family tradition—and a mystery. They went out before the modern ships—back when we hardly had navigational systems at all. Any little thing could throw them off course: a gravitic storm, for instance, which today would be nothing at all. As far as I know there was only one colony which was Gaelic-speaking; it was manned by something called the New Hebrides Commune. Terra lost contact with them, and logged them as lost. They were mostly Neo-Luddites, and they had—"

"Hold on," interrupted Evans, "Slow down. What in the world—any world—were neo-whatever-you-callems?"

"Well, the original Luddites were radicals who went around smashing textile mills and power looms because they believed they were going to put so many hand weavers out of work," Elizabeth explained. "In general, Neo-Luddite was a name given to anybody who was generally, politically, against too much technology—or whatever they happened to think was too much—or who wanted less technology than the governments did." She shrugged. "Kind of a catch-all term that covers quite a few of the early colonies."

Evans laughed; a short, sharp bark. "That would include an awful lot of people even these days."

There was something about that laugh that Ysaye didn't like, but Elizabeth didn't seem to notice anything. "Well this lot were in general all artsy-craftsy and primitivist; so they were welcomed joyously by the Colony Authority of that day because they usually were willing to live without modern conveniences for a couple of years—and in fact rather enjoyed the idea."

Evans grinned. "I can imagine. What luck for them! Too bad no one told them how many of those ships tended to get lost."

Elizabeth went on, "My own ancestry is Scottish—that's how I came to hear about them. It was a kind of romantic, sad story in my family, the 'lost ones.' They thought they would be able to recreate the Scotland

and Ireland of the ancient days, before 'the English contamination.' Everyone was supposed to speak Gaelic fluently. When I joined the Space Service—well, that's neither here or there. But I do know a lot of old Gaelic folk songs. Gaelic as a language has died out back on Terra. And if these people preserved their language, a lot of the songs that have died out on Earth may have been preserved here. In fact, probably were," she exclaimed. "What an incredible opportunity!"

"Yeah, lots of work for you, and David, if you're right," Evans said. "Recreating the language from living speakers—and with the new surge of interest in ancient music—"

"But I never thought anything on this world would turn out to be within my own field of expertise," Elizabeth said happily. "Now, I guess the thing to do is to tell the Captain—"

"Have to wait until we can get in touch with him," Evans reminded her. "Do you speak whatever that language was?"

"Gaelic? No, I only know a few words—whatever is in the songs I know," she said ruefully. "But now that we know they're from a Lost Ship, there are a lot of assumptions we can make. And most human languages, including a lot of the dead ones, are in the ship's computer. So once we get back to the ship and the corticator, we won't have any trouble communicating with them."

Ysaye was unable to restrain her disbelief. "Won't have any trouble? Really, Elizabeth. After we just discussed how easily a language can change?"

"Of course," Elizabeth amended hastily, "the language will have evolved; there will be a lot of new words for new situations." She went on hesitantly, "But at least we'll have the basics, and can begin our work without having to start from scratch. We know where they come from, and basically that they're of Terran origin—whether we can tell them, or not."

"But why wouldn't we be able to tell them?" asked Evans. "Does it have to be done by rank, or something?"

"Of course not." Elizabeth looked at him in surprise. "It's a matter of culture shock. Just look at it from their point of view. Here you are, a planet without even space travel, and we come along and tell them they were just, well, seeded here by an interstellar society. That they're *us*. They have probably forgotten that entirely. They probably even have some variation of the old theory of origin from the Gods."

Evans sneered. "Superstitious religious drivel."

Elizabeth shrugged again, and now that she was out of her area of expertise, Ysaye could tell she was feeling on uncertain ground with Evans. "Maybe by your standards, but what else would they have to go on, after two thousand years of isolation? Especially if their ship actually crashed. There are ways of telling them who and what they are that don't come across in a way that would offend or shock them. That's what xenopsychology can do, one of the things it's all about."

"I think we would do better to wait for a xenopsych," Ysaye said, with a frown for Evans and a cautionary shake of her head for her friend. Elizabeth looked all too ready to try to take things into her own, inexpert hands. "That's their specialty."

"Well, I've had some xenopsychology," Aurora said, "but I'd rather wait for a professional xenopsych. We don't really have one on this crew. On the ship—maybe Doctor Montray."

"I'm not sure we are going to be able to wait," said Elizabeth, "when we know who they are and we *don't* know when the ship is going to be able to send anyone down—"

Elizabeth shook her head and turned away from them. She listened to the musicians for a moment, but when they paused at the end of a tune, she suddenly stood and with a look of determination, began to sing the words of the ancient folk song she had known so long, in a high clear voice.

> *"Why should I*
> *Sit and sigh,*
> *Pullin' bracken, pullin' bracken—*
> *Why should I*
> *Sit and sigh*
> *All alone and weary,"*

The harper, who had just begun another melody, broke off in mid-chord; he got up and came toward Elizabeth in astonishment. He addressed her in what sounded like a flood of Gaelic, very swift and all unintelligible. Elizabeth made signs to him that she did not understand, that she could only understand the words to the song. After a minute she began another ancient song; this one she could not sing in Gaelic, but only in English. After a moment, however, the harper picked up the melody and began to play with her. There were little differences, but after a moment they adjusted to them, reaching the refrain together.

"What is that song?" Aurora asked. "I've heard you sing it fairly often."

"The one I don't know the Gaelic words to? It's called 'The Meeting of the Waters' and is supposed to be the oldest English or Irish melody in existence. It goes back to at least the twelfth century, several centuries before Terra got into space." She smiled. "At least we have real proof that they *are* the New Hebrides colony. No one else would ever have known that one."

"It goes back more than several centuries before

space flight," Ysaye said. "Eight hundred years before Terrans even walked on the moon."

Elizabeth took up another song, this one in Gaelic, and that, too, was picked up by one of the lute players. Among them, there seemed one or two who knew more music than the others, but all of them were crowding now around Elizabeth, eager for more.

Commander Britton spoke up behind them. "Good thinking Elizabeth! You seem to have found a way to communicate with them, even if you don't speak the language—"

"Nobody alive speaks Gaelic; not anybody I know of who's gone into space anyhow. Maybe a few old professors of language at the top universities might know some of it," Elizabeth said. "As soon as we have access to the computer, that will be remedied; we'll have tapes and the corticator. Someone, probably David, will be speaking Gaelic like a native within a couple of hours. Or maybe half a dozen of us."

"I should hope so," Britton said. "That has to be our number one priority, getting a way to communicate with these people. Although it was an excellent way to lessen potential hostility, we can't just stand here swapping folk songs all night and all day. I think—"

He broke off, so they were never to learn what he thought.

"Stay professional, everyone," Britton said in an undertone. "Here's somebody important coming."

The great doors of the room opened, and a tall man came into the room. He seemed to be in early middle age; his red hair was starting to go gray, but his eyes, also gray, were keen, and his clothes, though similar to those of the rest, were finer of cut and material than the others'. He spoke for a moment with the harper who had first played the song which Elizabeth had recognized, then advanced toward them and bowed.

"Whoever you may be," he said, in poorly inflected but understandable Terran Standard, "be welcome, you who bring music to my hall. I am Kermiac of Aldaran. I do not know from where you come and you seem to have sprung from the loins of no Domain I have ever heard of. Tell me, do you come from beyond the Wall Around the World, or do you come here from the Fairy Kingdom?"

CHAPTER
10

The storm had been a powerful one; so powerful that within a day it had traversed the Hellers and had brought a fair load of snow to drop down upon the rest of the Domains. For a while, as the winds wailed about Leonie's windows, she had the oddest fancy that it had sought *her* out, to take revenge upon her for snatching the strangers out of its grasp. Now, though, it was over, and the garden of Dalereuth Tower was ankle-deep in melting snow and mud, the flowers re-emerging from their snow-pods.

Fiora, urged by her promise, went looking for her arrogant protégée, following the faint traces of her surface-mind to the garden.

Leonie had wandered into the garden, although it was not a particularly pleasant place to be at the moment. This time the weather had been none of her making, and true to her promise she had not meddled with it. It had been a disturbing experience, actually—the feeling of wanting to change something and knowing she could not, dared not touch it. Now she came to the garden, not to look at her own handiwork, but at what she could have prevented, if she had been permitted. She was idly stirring the ropes of the swing, when Fiora, fastidiously shaking snow off her shoes, found her.

"I thought you would want to know," the Keeper

said, "that the search party sent from Aldaran has found your strangers."

Leonie turned to Fiora with a face full of interest. "Was no more said than that?" she demanded.

Fiora smiled at her, as if amused by her curiosity. "They are a party of about a half-dozen men and women who had taken refuge in the old travel shelter between Aderes and Alaskerd. They must be from very far away; but they seemed harmless enough. The technician at the relay said that they knew some of the oldest mountain songs."

That little only whetted Leonie's appetite for more information. "Why do you say they must be from very far away?"

"I am not sure; that is what the messenger said to me," Fiora replied, and her brow creased for a moment with puzzlement, for that *was* a very odd thing to have said. "They are quite odd, however; let me think, for she told me some other things that would confirm her words." She paused to think. "Ah, she said that they seem to know nothing of our customs. They speak neither *casta* nor *cahuenga*, for all that they know several mountain songs, so perhaps that is why the messenger said that they were from far away. Or perhaps it is because of *their* customs and costumes. Some of the women might be Renunciates or something like it, for they wore breeches and some of them, earrings; yet they were in the company of the men, so whatever they are, they are not ordinary Chartered Renunciates." She shook her head over what she had remembered from the message. "I must agree with the matrix worker who told me of them. They are certainly people of strange aspect. I know no more than that."

Leonie rubbed her temple, then murmured without thinking, "I feel sure they are from the moons."

Fiora shook her head. "I know that you said that

the night you learned of them—and you have been quite correct in all else—but Leonie, that stretches the bounds of believability. How can that be? You know perfectly well that nothing human can live on the moons."

Although she had not intended Fiora to overhear her words, Leonie felt impelled to defend them. "I do not know how," said Leonie stubbornly, "but I feel it."

"Well, that's as may be," Fiora said, with a faint suggestion that she was humoring Leonie by not arguing with her. Leonie frowned a little but held her tongue. "I must admit to you that what I have been told does not match any peoples I have ever heard of. Not even Dry Towners or wild mountain folk speak languages no one can understand—nor do they act and dress as these folk do."

"Then they might as *well* be from the moons," Leonie retorted, "And we know of no other peoples they might be! They are surely not *chieri*—so where is it you think they may come from?"

Fiora shrugged. "I myself feel they may well be from some land beyond the mountains, where we thought was only frozen waste. Perhaps they have even come from beyond the Wall Around the World. Or perhaps the ancient mountain tales of fairy folk are true after all, and they come from the fairy realms. Whatever they may be does not matter to us; they have been welcomed by a party from Aldaran Tower, and perhaps by Lord and Lady Aldaran themselves. We do not know who or what they are, nor do I think it right to indulge idle curiosity about these strangers. If it is of any concern to us, we will know soon enough." She paused a moment, then continued, as if reluctantly, "As a Hastur, *you* should know well enough that there is little love lost between Aldaran and the rest of the Domains. It may be that Lord Kermiac of Aldaran will take any inquiries poorly. It might be more politic to pretend that these strangers are ordinary travelers, until those of Aldaran choose to tell us otherwise."

"As you wish," Leonie said, secretly promising herself that she would communicate as soon as possible with Lorill and ask him, or perhaps her father, Lord Hastur, to journey to Aldaran and investigate. This made no sense at all. If there were people *that* odd now in the hands of Lord Aldaran, shouldn't *someone* be concerned? What was the matter with Fiora? Didn't she have any curiosity, any worries about what these strange people might mean to her?

Well, Leonie had concern enough for both of them. Far from feeling that they would know soon enough, as Fiora said, she felt that at the Tower, they were isolated so much from the regular pattern of Comyn life that they might not find out about these people until too late—

Too late? Whatever had made her think that? And too late for what? Yet there was something ominous about these strangers, however innocent they had seemed to be. As ominous as her feelings of troubles coming from the moons.

Fiora, of course, had picked up some of her thoughts. She looked uneasily at Leonie, blind eyes seeming to stare at and through her protégée. "You are determined to find out about these people, aren't you?"

"I think it my duty," Leonie said doggedly. "Although I am not fully trained, you have said yourself that my *laran* is very strong. It told me that the strangers were in that shelter. It warns me now that there is something about them that is amiss. I do not know what is wrong, but I feel it must be looked into."

Fiora sighed. "You should be content to leave it to us, Leonie. Truly. If there is anything to be done, surely we can deal with it. But would it be of any use to demand that you should stay out of it?''

"Not the slightest," Leonie said, with a faint smile, and thought, *How well Fiora is beginning to know me.* "I am not ashamed of my curiosity! I have been in the right too many times; I see no reason to forget that." *And I am in the right this time, too. Fiora wants me to think first of others—well, I am. No one else seems to worry about these people, so I must. Anything I feel I should know . . . I shall find a way to learn.*

"Leonie," Fiora said reluctantly. "You above all should know that the Comyn Council is not on the best of terms with the Aldaran Domain. We do not know all that they are doing in the Hellers. It is said that they alone do not abide by the Compact. And they seem to think not only that we do not care what they do there, but that we *should* not care, that we have no right to care. They are a dangerous people, up there in the Hellers; scarcely removed from mountain bandits. I must ask you to be cautious."

"Well, then, if I show some interest in their doings, they will know that we do pay heed to what they do," Leonie said. "They will know that we have a perfect right to know what passes in the mountains. They will learn that what they do in their mountain castles is watched and weighed." She raised her chin proudly. "I am a Hastur. You tell me that I must have a care for the people of the Domains—well, I do. It is my duty to care for them, and it seems to me that this is one way to do so."

Fiora sighed and said nothing, more because she did not want to prohibit Leonie and have the girl deliberately disobey than because she did not care. She cared; she cared deeply.

She had not lied to Leonie; the Keeper at Aldaran had made it subtly clear to her, many times, that Lord

Kermiac did not approve of the Council's "meddling." There had been bad blood between the Hellers and the Plains for as long as Dalereuth Tower had been standing, so far as she could tell. There was no record of what had begun the long-standing animosity, although Fiora often wondered if the troubles dated back before Varzil the Good and the Compact. Aldaran alone had never signed the Compact that prevented men from carrying and using weapons that reached beyond swords' length. As a result, although they ceased to use the deadly weapons that had caused the Compact to be forged in the first place, the Lords of the other Domains had from that day forth regarded them as a kind of outlaw Domain. For their part, the Lords of Aldaran kept a proud separation, dealing with the Domains only through go-betweens: traders, Renunciates, and the Tower workers. And that last was somewhat difficult at times, as Aldaran staffed his Tower with his own people, and many of the Comyn who came to work at other Towers could not work with those of Aldaran without a certain animosity rising between them. Since Fiora had become Keeper at Dalereuth, of course, this problem had not arisen. She was not Comyn; she had none of their prejudices. She could and did communicate and work with those of Aldaran as easily as with those of Arilinn. But Leonie . . . one touch of her arrogant thoughts, and the Keeper at Aldaran would shut the relays down entirely rather than have to deal with her. Fiora knew that from experience; she had seen an Ardais precipitate just such an incident at Arilinn. It had taken a great deal of persuasion from the common-born to get Aldaran to reopen to them.

As she went back into the Tower, she wondered if Leonie would indeed prove to be a problem beyond her handling. It was the first time the Keeper of Dalereuth Tower had ever found any problem beyond her.

It was a new sensation to Fiora, and one she did not particularly enjoy. She thought, *I am no more used to uncertainty than Leonie is—and far less used to defeat.*

Perhaps if I keep her occupied—and wear her down. Fiora nodded to herself. *Yes, that may solve the problem. She has wanted to take a full part in the work of the Tower, and she has certainly proved that she has the strength for it. She may be too willful, unskilled, and unpracticed at the moment to work in the circle, but she can certainly do the work in the relays, and free someone with more training for other work. And if she is worked until she is weary . . . well, then, she will fall asleep, and there will be no chance for her to meddle where she may cause harm by her prying.*

For the rest of that day, Leonie had little leisure to think about the strangers. She received a summons as soon as she reentered the Tower; a message that surprised and pleased her. Fiora had decreed that she had all the strength to do her share as a true matrix worker, at least in tasks involving only one. She was to be allowed for the first time to take her turn in the relays, watching and listening for messages sent from the other Towers.

It was tiring and exacting work, with enough of novelty about it to keep her excited. Fiora came by once or twice to observe; Leonie waited for some kind of a response or criticism, but the Keeper only nodded, and went on to another task. Finally, someone came to relieve her; by then she was ravenous and thinking only of food, and so it was long after dark when she had leisure to seek contact with her twin brother.

It crossed her mind, as she lay down upon her bed, that Fiora might have tried to tire her in order to keep her from finding out more about the strangers. She smiled to herself as she relaxed each muscle, slowly, and limbered her mind. If Fiora thought that a watch in the relays was enough to tire Leonie—she had really underestimated her pupil.

She closed her eyes, and reached out with her thoughts for the mind so familiar to her that it might have been an imperfect reflection of her own.

Lorill—

She got a response; an immediate one. It felt as if Lorill was no more than a room or two away. *Is it you, Leonie? Is all well with you and the Tower?*

She allowed amusement to shade her thoughts. *Of course. How not?*

As she opened her mind to him, relaxing into the familiar companionship, Lorill flooded her mind with something like laughter. There was enough of her recent conversation with Fiora still in her surface thoughts to let him know that she was once again working *her* will despite official opposition.

Still up to your old tricks, sister? Or do they not let you get away with them in the Tower? I thought that when you were there—

She sent him laughter of her own. *You thought that perhaps they would break me to harness like a horse, or to chains, like a Dry Town bride? Not a bit, though I cannot say they have not tried. I believe some of them think that with one reprimand I have become a meek maiden or girlchild who will do everything she is told when she is told to do it. But I have learned a little about how to be less rebellious—on the outside, at least.*

Lorill nearly lost contact as he broke up with laughter. *You, Leonie, meek? How little they know you. All your life, you have done what you wanted, sometimes making sure it was I who took the blame—and the punishment.* He settled himself, his mental voice full of irony. *Well, you cannot place any blame on me now;*

you are too far away. Whatever you wish to be done, you must do for yourself—not like that time when—

No, but listen. She firmly broke into the flood of childhood pranks and their shared past. *Have you heard? There are strangers at Aldaran, and I think the Council should know about it. These are very odd people. I have touched their minds, a little, and they are from no land or Domain that I have ever heard of. They speak no language that I recognize, and the little that Aldaran would tell us is that they speak neither* casta *nor* cahuenga. *I think Father should investigate this himself. Aldaran should not have the leisure to pry secrets from these people without the Council knowing of it.*

Lorill sobered immediately. *Leonie, you know Father cannot go to Aldaran; there is bad blood between the Hastur lords and the folk of Aldaran. If he should condescend so far, even by sending a messenger—*

Impatience colored her sending, for she had a great deal of time to think about what should be done while she was idle in the relays. *Oh, I understand that he cannot,* she replied, *but he could send* you, *Lorill—you are not yet old enough nor powerful enough to threaten Lord Aldaran and you are Father's other eyes and ears. Is it not Hastur's sworn duty to know what is going on in the Domains? Should there not be at least one high Comyn lord letting Kermiac of Aldaran know that there are eyes upon his doings? These strangers—*

If he had been with her, she knew he would have thrown up his hands. *Oh, now I see! I am to go and satisfy your curiosity about them. Well, I won't do it. Too long I have had to take the blame for what you did, and agree to what you want. Now I am Heir to Hastur; I shall not take the blame for your mischief any longer. This must end, Leonie.*

She frowned; this was not going as she had thought it would. *Lorill,* she replied placatingly, *you are a man, and as you have said yourself, the Heir to Hastur. The Council will heed you, where they dismiss me. These are unknown people, with unknown reasons that brought them here. They could be dangerous—they could be seeking an ally. Don't you feel that it is necessary to know what they are doing at Aldaran?*

Lorill was unimpressed. *No, I don't. And I am always suspicious when you take that tone with me. I don't see how a mere handful of strange people can be any serious threat to anyone.*

After another half hour of coaxing, the most she could win from him was a grudging promise that if he could get leave from their father—*And it is by no means certain that he can spare me*, Lorill cautioned—he would go to Aldaran and ask Lord Kermiac some tactful questions about his guests. Perhaps try to meet them himself, and give them some notion that there were other Domains beside Aldaran, with their own set of priorities. If he could, indeed, see these strangers, he might be able to convince them that Kermiac of Aldaran was not the only power they needed to reckon with.

And it is likely that they may simply tell me to mind my own business. Even if I am a Hastur—or all the more for that, Lorill cautioned, *I cannot see Lord Aldaran giving an account of his doings to any lowlander, let alone a Hastur. Even one traveling for personal reasons, without the knowledge of the Council. . . .*

He broke off the conversation with a plea of exhaustion and a hasty farewell. And with that Leonie had to be content.

CHAPTER
11

Do you come here from the Fairy Kingdom?
The question struck Ysaye with a jolt; never before had she so felt the reality behind the words "culture shock." She herself was now on the receiving end of such a shock—for although this might well be a Lost Colony, descended from star travelers like herself, the people here might as well have been complete aliens. Descended yes—but likely with no memory of their origin. Not only had records of their Terran history probably been lost, but their origin had obviously become buried in myth. They did not seem to recognize their far-traveled "cousins" even as human beings.

How did one explain space travel and a star-spanning Empire to anyone who apparently believed in fairies? But she might be overreacting. Could these people have turned their tales of space flight into tales of fairies? Is that what the man had really meant?

Perhaps it's just a reaction to Elizabeth's choice of folk songs, she thought hopefully, looking at Elizabeth, who seemed rather nonplussed. *Well, at least this will be a challenge. If she and David want a culture to become their lives' work, I think they've found it. There's probably work enough for a few thousand linguists and anthropologists here.*

With some relief she saw Commander MacAran, who was the ranking officer present, come toward them.

He was no more a xenopsychologist than she was, but he outranked her; she was perfectly content to let him take charge of the situation. At least he had training in diplomacy.

"Have you found a language in common, then?" he asked, looking from Elizabeth to Lord Kermiac with an expression of interest and hope.

"Commander, he *is* speaking Terran Standard," Elizabeth said with puzzlement. "That's better than finding a language in common."

Commander Britton looked at her as if he thought she had gone quite mad. "No, Elizabeth, he is not speaking Terran Standard," Commander Britton said carefully. MacAran's expression said quite clearly that he suspected Elizabeth of taking a knock on the head. "He is speaking, so far as I can tell, a different language from these musicians, but it is definitely not Terran Standard. If I were to guess, I would say that it is closer to some of those songs of yours than the musicians' language—but I'm no expert."

"How is it, then, that I understand him so well?" asked Elizabeth in bewilderment. "I could swear he was speaking Standard."

She looked from Britton to MacAran and back again, her face paling.

"I can answer that," said Kermiac, who had been monitoring this exchange. He smiled slightly, as if she were a child, and his tone was soothing, as if he realized how alarmed she was by this. "You hear my thoughts, of course."

"She hears what?" David had been standing quietly behind Elizabeth for some time, listening with a frown of concentration on his forehead as he attempted to make out some of what the musicians and others were saying. But this statement was unusual enough to provoke a reaction to the content instead of an analysis of the phrasing and word choice. And Ysaye realized then that David understood the man, too.

"I am Comyn, of course, and so something of a telepath," Kermiac continued calmly, as if such a thing were more natural than saying "and so I breathe oxygen," "and it would seem that some of you can understand me, while others cannot. That is simple to explain; those of you who can understand me are also telepaths, although you are—less practiced than I."

Ysaye blinked. Why had she been so certain that he had been about to say, "Although you are ill-trained and clumsy"?

"So," Kermiac said, turning again to Elizabeth, "if you can, tell me from whence you come, and why you have come here?"

Ysaye listening carefully to the actual sounds of the words, realized that he was indeed not speaking in any language known to her; but she understood him perfectly, word for word. She looked at the rest of her party. Elizabeth and David seemed to understand this "Kermiac of Aldaran," whoever he was, but Evans, Aurora, Britton, and MacAran were still looking blank.

Ysaye shivered, and wondered fleetingly if her concussion had been worse than she thought. Was she even now lying in that shelter, and hallucinating all this? But no—she had none of the other symptoms of a severe head injury. . . . It was one thing to watch David and Elizabeth demonstrate telepathy in the lab, but quite another for *her* to hear and understand a total stranger from another world.

And why do I understand him now? I never heard anything so coherent when I was working with David and Elizabeth. Could it have been that I just wasn't listening? She decided to keep her new-found understanding to herself. Bad enough that she could hear this stranger, but worse to find herself the focus of pitying gazes as Elizabeth was.

Elizabeth clearly still did not realize that there was something wrong; she was confused, but not alarmed. Instead, she asked, "Do you all really not understand what he is saying?"

"I can't imagine that you really do," MacAran replied. "It still seems gibberish to me. Maybe you've finally hit on words from one of the languages you sing, and you're picking up what he means that way. What did he say?"

"He told me who he is, and asked who we are, where we are from, and why we have come here. He gave his name as Kermiac of Aldaran," Elizabeth replied. At the sound of his name Kermiac nodded and smiled.

MacAran raised an eyebrow, but only said, "You seem to be our *de facto* interpreter. Speak with him, then. You might start by introducing us; that's usually the appropriate way to begin."

"Even if we have botched our First Contact completely by now," Britton muttered under his breath. Ysaye sympathized with him; nothing had gone according to Procedure and Regulation from the moment they had entered this world's gravity-well. And someone would have a great deal to say to him and MacAran about that, once they contacted the ship.

A First Contact forced by natives coming to rescue us; culture contamination, and amateurs handling the initial overture to the local authority figure. No, the Powers That Be are not going to like this.

Elizabeth nodded, and raised her chin. "Kermiac of Aldaran," she said formally, "I should like to present to you Commander Ralph MacAran, the leader of our party."

"Rafe MacAran?" said Kermiac in surprise. He considered the Commander, while MacAran did a noble

job of not squirming under that direct gaze. Kermiac
continued to speak to Elizabeth as the only one who
could understand him, although he nodded to MacAran
as he did so and had no hesitation about keeping eye
contact with the Commander. "Yes, he does have the
look of the family, a bit. It is a shame that he appears
to be head-blind. Has he none of the *donas* of his family,
then?"

"His family?" Elizabeth blinked, then the real
meaning of what Kermiac had said dawned on her. "Uh,
Commander MacAran, sir, did you have any ancestors
on any of the Lost Ships?"

"I don't know off the top of my head," Commander
MacAran said patiently. "That was at least a thousand
years ago, after all. Is it really relevant at the moment?"

She shook her head. "Well, he seems to think he
knows your family. It might be important. They might
place a heavy emphasis on family and anything the local
MacArans have been up to, you might be held account-
able for—"

"Elizabeth," Ysaye put in quietly, "he also seems
to understand every word you say, and perhaps every
word you hear." She directed a questioning look at
Kermiac, who grinned at her, then turned his attention
back to Elizabeth.

"True enough, *mestra.*" Ysaye was not mistaken;
that was meant as much for her as for Elizabeth. So
Kermiac knew that she understood him, even if Britton
and MacAran hadn't figured it out yet. "What are Lost
Ships?" Kermiac continued. "There is no ocean near
to here."

"*Mestra?*" David jumped on the term. "I wonder if
that's a variant on the old Italian word maestro?" He
turned to Elizabeth excitedly. "Are you sure that what
the musicians were using was Gaelic?"

"Yes!" Elizabeth replied distractedly. She was

clearly completely confused by the conflicting demands on her, and the contradictory things people were asking of her. "I am absolutely positive!"

"Compare linguistic notes later," MacAran said severely. "You are being rude to our host. More than that, Elizabeth, you are our translator. Was he asking you a question, just now, and did you understand him that time, too?"

"Yes, and yes," Elizabeth said, subdued, and looking a little unnerved, as Ysaye sighed in relief, realizing that MacAran had not noticed that the question had been directed to her and not Elizabeth. "He was asking what the Lost Ships were," Elizabeth concluded. "I don't know what to tell him!"

MacAran directed a rather less than thrilled look at Elizabeth, who had been the one to bring up the subject, then glanced at Aurora. "Dr. Lakshman, can you understand him?"

Aurora shook her head helplessly. "No, sir, I'm sorry. Not a bit. I'm inclined to think now that a background in ancient folk songs might be a good thing for a xenopsych to have."

MacAran sighed. "Just great. The only member of our party with xenopsych training can't understand them, and our xenoanthropologist drops one of the most alien concepts we could fling at them into practically the first sentence she utters!"

He looked at Kermiac, who was regarding them with an inquisitive patience, and straightened a little. "Talk to him for me, Elizabeth, but carefully, please. The cat's out of the bag, but we can try not to botch things any further."

Ysaye bit her lip, wanting to say something, and not daring to. She did not want MacAran convinced that she was under delusions—and he had obviously completely ignored the fact that the sentence that had "let the cat out of the bag" had not been in this stranger's babble of Gaelic, but in good Terran Standard. In fact, he was ignoring the fact that Elizabeth was speaking to Kermiac in Terran Standard, and Kermiac understood that as well.

Elizabeth flushed and hung her head at the implied rebuke.

"Try to explain briefly who we really are, and who we think they might be—" MacAran continued, "—since if they are a Lost Colony, they seem to have forgotten the fact. When we get more people down here—if we can land here at all, if these hellish mountains don't completely defeat us—then the Captain can look up this Gaelic-speaking ship of yours and give them—and us—the facts."

Elizabeth bit her lip, and said carefully to Kermiac, "My name is Elizabeth Mackintosh."

She hesitated briefly, wondering what she ought to call him, and then compromised on a simple "sir." "Sir, this is Commander Britton, and this is my friend and companion Ysaye—"

"I have never seen anyone like them," Kermiac stated baldly, staring at Ysaye out of the corner of his eye, as if she were some kind of exhibit. "Are they not human, then? Or do they coat their skin with dark brown paint?"

Shocked, Ysaye realized that the very concept of different human races was unknown to him. Elizabeth bit her lip in consternation, then went gamely on. "Ysaye and Commander Britton are so by birth."

"By birth?" Kermiac shook his head. "There are those who are swarthy of skin in the lower parts of Thendara, but none have ever been born of such a color—"

Elizabeth stared at him. "You have never seen anyone like them? Are there truly no black peoples known to you?"

"Black? People with black skin?" Kermiac seemed unsure as to whether he was confused or Elizabeth was. "Her skin is brown, is it not—or do you call that color black?" He looked from Ysaye to Commander Britton to Aurora, whose skin was a sort of olive-brown. "I thought if anyone was not of our kind they would be nonhumans," said Kermiac, after a moment of consideration. "But if they are your friends they are welcome as yourself and as the head-blind young MacAran yonder." He shook his head, pityingly. "I have great sympathy for his misfortune, in being so without any gift."

Again the word he used for gift was *donas*, and Ysaye could hear David muttering something about the Latin word *donum*, also meaning gift. "I think we're getting a Romance language here," he said to himself, and Ysaye could feel his impatience at being trapped so far from his computers and recording instruments.

Meanwhile Elizabeth completed the rest of the introductions, paused, and added bravely, "We came here from the violet moon which now stands in your sky."

Ysaye waited for the sky to fall, Kermiac to declare them some kind of madmen, heretics, or demons and have them carted away, or MacAran to have a fit of apoplexy.

None of the three happened.

"Wait," said Aldaran firmly. "I will call no man or woman liar who speaks to me mind-to-mind, and I know that you believe what you say, but even I know that the moons are lifeless and airless worlds circling our own. No man can live there. Are you telling me, then, that I am mistaken about the nature of the moons?"

"No. We came here from a world like your own, from another sun, with air like this one," Elizabeth said, and groped for a simple explanation. "We stopped on the moon and set up a dome there to observe the weather before we landed. But I suppose we did not observe it well enough," she concluded forlornly, "since the wind in these mountains led to the crashing of our vehicle."

"Interesting," Kermiac said, though Ysaye could not tell whether he meant that *they* were interesting, or what Elizabeth had told him was interesting. "These mountains are not called the Hellers for nothing, you know; their winds are known to be dangerous. I suppose in this tale of yours, your vehicle is something like a glider, but more complicated." He smiled a little. "As a boy I flew a glider in these hills, and wished someone could manage to invent a heavier-than-air vehicle, as they had in the old days. I assume the tale is that you have done so—where you come from."

"We have indeed," said Elizabeth eagerly. "But you said that you had such things in the old days! That would be years ago, when your ancestors first landed upon this world—"

"Wait," he said. "There is someone else who should hear this, if you do not mind." He looked up and beckoned, and a tall young man with strange, steel-gray eyes came toward them. As he neared them, Ysaye realized that he was not just very tall, but unusually so. He towered above everyone else by a full head, at least. He had a narrow sharp face, unbearded as a boy's, a guarded expression, and an untidy shock of dark hair.

"My good friend and paxman," Kermiac said, "Raymon Kadarin. He knows more about these hills, perhaps, than any other man living. I think he will understand what you have told me and where your vehicle was supposed to have crashed. Now, what were you saying about my forefathers?"

"We believe," Elizabeth began, "that your ancestors, many, many generations ago, did not originate on this world. From the language I heard in your songs, which is now an extinct language to our people, we presume they were on one of our ships. They were sent out to explore, and somehow they ended here, perhaps crashed, but at any rate lost to us. That is what I meant by a Lost Ship; and it means that we are the same kind of people, with a common background."

"I am sure that you must believe what you say," Kermiac answered, very carefully. "I am at least enough of a telepath to know when I am being lied to. You believe what you are saying; whether I can credit it or not is something else again. Your tale of coming from the stars is a difficult one for me to believe; this other, that my forefathers did likewise, is far more difficult. I do not think this is something to be discussed while we stand about at mealtime, *mestra*, and," he paused, looking very uncomfortable, "to tell the truth, I am not accustomed to discussing serious business with women. Perhaps your superior officer . . ." He shook his head. "But no, your superior here is that head-blind young man who spoke before."

Kermiac pursed his lips, as if he was confronting a difficult and delicate problem. "I should of course be unable to do any business with him, since I have no way of communicating with him."

"Don't you ever do business through translators?" Elizabeth asked, her face and voice reflecting the dismay she felt when Kermiac called what she had told him "tales."

Kermiac shrugged. "Not more than once or twice in my lifetime," he replied dryly. "In any case, you are my guests. Refresh yourselves, overcome the fatigue of a journey which at least must have been very long, even if you did not come from one of the stars in the sky.

Perhaps in a few days we can speak rationally of these things.''

It seemed to Ysaye that she heard what he did not say, that it would a great pity if so pleasant-spoken a young lady should prove to be mentally disordered. There were other things, too, but so jumbled she couldn't make any sense of them. He bowed to them and went to get a mug of beer from the sideboard and take a seat at the end of the hall. At his gesture the musicians resumed their performance.

So he does not really believe us, Ysaye thought with well-concealed dismay. *But how can we blame him? I wonder what sort of origin myths they have. Whatever they are, I doubt they match with people claiming to come from the stars.* Another disquieting thing occurred to her. *And he is not accustomed to doing business with women; a pre-equality society. Fascinating, I'm sure, but not very rewarding for us women.*

"There is whiskey over there, too, besides the beer and the herbal stuff, if anyone wants it," said Evans, gesturing with the mug he was holding. "Trust the descendants of Scots, if they really are, to make whiskey wherever in the Galaxy they find themselves. Good whiskey, too." He took a healthy swig of it. "Fine for medicinal use—or better, for conviviality."

"And yet I don't see anyone getting drunk," Aurora commented in a low voice, looking around her. "This seems to be a culture with substantial social restraints. Evans, I suspect we should be careful about how much we drink and how we act; we don't want to give them the idea that Terrans are likely to lose control. Especially if they don't think of themselves as connected to us in any way. The cultures where people don't get drunk in public put a strong value on social control."

Evans grinned, "No fear, I'm not stupid enough to get drunk."

Yet, Ysaye added to herself. She had seen too much of Evans' past behavior to put too much faith in his self control.

Evans continued, blithely ignoring Aurora's skeptical expression. "At least I've got a handle on what I can concentrate on—if these people are from a Lost Ship, it's fairly obvious that whatever they can eat or ingest, the rest of us can, too. So what I'll be doing here is to find out what use they make out of the various plants they have—like the trees I saw with the pods. If they can distill alcohol, they can distill other things, and they've probably got a whole pharmacy of native-made drugs. This planet could be a good source for alkaloids, resins, medicinals, various recreational drugs—"

Aurora made a face. "So as we all expected, you're already planning out how to exploit this situation, and this place."

Evans looked at her as if he could not figure out why she was objecting. "Why not? That's what planets are for, and once we open this place up and show these folks all the things we can sell them, they'll want the maximum number of exports to buy things with."

"There will be plenty of that with the kind of music they have," Elizabeth said, indicating the minstrels who had begun to play again. "The instruments are very sophisticated, even if they are mostly variations on guitars and harps. If they can play them, so can an offworlder."

"But all hand-made," Britton commented. "Not an electronic instrument among them, and there's certainly no sign that they have electricity here. But no brass instruments or even reeds."

"We already knew the planet was metal-poor," Elizabeth protested, obviously feeling a need to say something. "While, as for electronics, if we're going to export recordings, the collectors may simply prefer the sound of natural acoustic instruments. Some people do."

MacAran looked around the hall again, and smiled. "Commander Britton, these people are obviously not going to be making and using synthesizers. I doubt they'd be able to reproduce a vacuum tube, much less anything more sophisticated than that."

Elizabeth's attention had wandered back to the musicians. "I wonder if they play any music for dancing; a society's dances are frequently its society in miniature. Right now, though, I'll study anything they'll show us."

"What about their language, Lorne?" MacAran asked David. "You and Elizabeth seem to be picking it up amazingly quickly. Why is that?"

His jaw got progressively tighter as David tried to explain, as Ysaye had known it would.

"And you really believe all that stuff about telepathy?" MacAran asked.

David seemed bewildered, and Ysaye cursed him for not picking up the hints of this earlier. "How can I disbelieve it, sir? It just happened—and to me."

"Do you think they are entirely human?" Britton asked, suddenly. "Have you noticed that a few of them have six fingers on both hands?"

"That's known to be a common human variation," Aurora answered, obviously glad to have something to contribute. This came within the field of her professional expertise, after all. "Some families of Basques have had it for generations. It's one of the most-studied genetic variations among the original Terrans. A strain of Basque ancestry—and there were a couple of Basques on that lost ship, or a cross with—" she paused, thinking. "It might be a pro-survival evolution in a society where handicrafts and music are highly valued; watch the fingering on that fellow with the big guitar. They don't all have it, though."

"No. That man who's our host—if your translation or so-called 'telepathy' is on track—has only five, but the very tall man who was with him has six. Now I could well believe he's not all human," MacAran said, his eyes seeking out Kadarin where he stood watching the others. "There's a strange look to him, like some kind of wild animal. I'd be interested to get a look at his family tree."

"There's never been a nonhuman race known to be cross-fertile with humans," Aurora said firmly. "It just can't happen. The genes can't be compatible."

"Not yet, you mean," Britton commented. "Wouldn't it be something if we found one."

"And you think telepathy is unlikely?" Elizabeth protested angrily. "You postulate a nonhuman race that could interbreed with humans, and you think *I'm* given to fantasizing? Remember, sir, I was able to talk to our host. Maybe you have a better explanation for how?"

She flushed when Britton stared at her skeptically, then, carefully not answering, he moved away and went to study one of the instruments. Elizabeth followed, taking refuge in her beloved hobby. The musician handed it to her; Elizabeth examined it, struck a note or two and began to play and sing one of the oldest Gaelic folk songs she knew. After a minute the musician, smiling a smile that nearly split his face in two, joined in.

"Universal language," commented Britton. "And there is your answer."

"Not telepathy?" David asked.

"Come on, David. There could be other explanations besides your own personal hobby-horse," Evans said scornfully. "Granted, I don't know all the new electronic devices—"

Suddenly Ysaye felt an enormous revulsion for Evans. She said, "I don't know absolutely all of them either, but I know what happened. And I simply don't think these people are capable of creating electronics that we can't detect! I don't think they're capable of creating electronics at all! What's the matter, do you think they're putting all of this on for us, to trick us into thinking they're low-tech? Don't you believe anything you can't see or hear?"

"Damn little," Evans answered, cynically. "And I wouldn't put tricking us with a low-tech act past them. Look, here's someone new. What's this?"

Ysaye turned toward the entrance, following Evans' gaze. Two ladies, richly dressed, had entered the room. One was a girl who seemed hardly out of her teens, who bore a strong resemblance to Kermiac; the other was much taller than many of the men, with masses of very fair fine hair and large compelling eyes of a most unusual gold color. It struck Ysaye that she looked even less human than Kadarin. They joined Kermiac where he stood, and after a moment he beckoned to the Terrans.

"My lady Felicia," he said, "and her companion, my sister Mariel."

Mariel seemed just an ordinary girl, although her face was both handsome and intelligent. But Ysaye, from her first look at the one he had called Felicia, thought, as MacAran had said about Kadarin, *I'd like to get a look at her family tree*. Felicia was unusually tall and slender almost to emaciation; she had those strange eyes, and six fingers on each of the long slender hands. Even discounting stories of nonhumans, Felicia did not look quite human. There was something eerie, almost birdlike, in the golden eyes.

What are you? Ysaye wondered silently. Those strange eyes were bent on Elizabeth, who was joining in the songs. The musicians were going from song to song now, trying to find some she did not know. Elizabeth was evidently enjoying the game, for the moment forgetting her distress.

Music was a universal language, right enough.

Felicia listened for a time, then went over to the musicians, and stood there, listening and evidently asking Elizabeth something, but obviously not in words. Ysaye felt curious; she was perhaps Elizabeth's best female friend on the ship, and she had shared in the apparent telepathic contact with Kermiac, but she could not "hear" what was going on now. What were they saying to each other? She was too well-mannered to try and join in, and after several minutes, Felicia, her curiosity apparently satisfied for the moment, turned away, and went out of the room.

Elizabeth joined Ysaye, and they went to get themselves a drink at the long table. Ysaye asked, "What did she want?"

Elizabeth was flushed and relaxed-looking, and it seemed to Ysaye as if she fit in *here* better than she ever had on the ship. "Felicia? I think she wanted to make sure that Kermiac hadn't made a pass at either of us. Between ourselves, I wouldn't be surprised if the man's a womanizer; he has all the marks of it. I could tell her honestly Kermiac hadn't said a word to me he couldn't repeat in front of my mother. You might be a lot too exotic for him, but you never can tell. Anyhow, I'd think Felicia is pretty exotic myself, so maybe he has a taste for exotics."

Ysaye laughed; Elizabeth seemed to have forgotten—or dismissed—MacAran and Britton's discounting of her telepathy. Or perhaps she had decided that it didn't matter; that she would continue to play translator as long as they needed her, and let them make up whatever ridiculously convoluted explanation they had to in order to convince themselves that telepathy was not the way Elizabeth was handling the problem. A reasonable attitude; it really *didn't* matter what the Commanders believed, as long as the job got done.

Now, if they could just convince Kermiac that they all weren't escapees from a mental hospital. . . . "Relax, Elizabeth; nobody ever makes passes at me. I don't invite them."

"Or you honestly don't notice them when they happen," Elizabeth teased.

"Whatever," Ysaye said lightly. "I don't play those games. And I shouldn't think he'd say anything offensive anyhow, while he's depending on us for communication. If he bothers you, tell him you're betrothed to David."

Elizabeth's enthusiasm overflowed.

"It's so exciting for David and me, after all these years never knowing if telepathy can be real outside ourselves—"

"To find a world where it's accepted as commonplace. Felicia at least seemed to take it entirely for granted," Ysaye murmured. "Well, if they're reading our minds—maybe we don't need to worry too much about misunderstandings. If they can tell right away what's behind everything we say, it might help communication. There isn't the possibility for mistranslation, at any rate. But it would certainly make diplomacy difficult."

"True enough," Elizabeth said, then her face clouded. "But it's possible that this world will be declared off-limits and closed. After all, it's a pre-industrial culture."

"Can they do that, if it's a Lost Colony and the people are really all Terrans?" Ysaye wondered. "I don't believe there's any precedent for this situation."

"I think they can, if the consensus is that they need protection," Elizabeth said hesitantly. "I don't know of any legal precedent. I don't think there's ever been a case like this before. But Evans is already considering what this planet could be good for; how to exploit it best. Somehow I don't think these people are ready for that."

"I heard him, too, but it's not as if they were simple-minded folk, or a race that wouldn't be capable of defending themselves from something they didn't want," Ysaye said. "There must be some trace of their Terran heritage—and please remember that if they're descended from Scots, there's a strong tradition of shrewd traders and judicial advocates among them, not to mention a good touch of larceny." She smiled at Elizabeth. "Have you appointed yourself their unofficial protector, then?"

"Maybe, if the alternative is to let somebody like Evans have his way with them." Elizabeth frowned unhappily. "David says that at the university Evans majored in botany and minored in recreational pharmacology—and I'm not at all sure he was joking. I hope we can get the personnel from the ship down here soon, though God alone knows what will happen then."

Ysaye shrugged. "Let's just take it one step at a time," she suggested. "We have our hands full with convincing Lord Kermiac that we aren't lunatics, Commander MacAran that you haven't been hallucinating these translations, and Commander Britton that you haven't taken a bump on the head that makes you think you're telepathic."

"But—" Elizabeth protested.

"Never mind that you *are*," Ysaye said, "If he doesn't believe it, he won't trust you. So let him come up with an explanation that satisfies him, and don't argue with him."

"The lie that will work being better than the truth that isn't believed?" Elizabeth replied with a sigh. "All

right. I don't like it, but all right." She looked brood-
ingly at the musicians. "But it doesn't seem right, that
the very basis of our understanding with these people
is mixed with a lie. It just feels—wrong. As if—"

"What?" Ysaye prompted.

"As if something bad was going to come of it,"
Elizabeth said, and shivered.

CHAPTER
12

The day dawned bright and clear, and blessedly free of snow. Ysaye, awake at dawn as usual since their arrival, watched the great red sun coming up behind a line of snow-laden trees from the single, tiny window in the guest room where she—and Elizabeth and Aurora—had spent their nights for more than a week now. A movement at the far edge of the trail caught her eye—a line of riders approaching the castle gates below. They rode under a banner, blue and silver with a device she could not make out. Some of the riders, who so far as she could tell were all men, rode horses, or something so like them she could not tell the difference, while others rode heavy-set antlered beasts not unlike deer.

Ysaye had never seen live horses before; they were a toy for the rich and powerful; she was completely fascinated by them, by the way they moved, their slow, deliberate steps through the snow, hardly faster than a human could walk, and the way their complicated harness was put together. She watched them for a time, wondering how someone could afford so *many* horses —thinking how slow and tedious a long journey would be on something so limited—then coming to her senses, and thinking that of course the attitude toward horses would be different on a world where they were the most commonplace means of transportation. It was beginning to look as if that were the case here. But surely, that first night, Kermiac had spoken of gliders?

Had they truly never invented or preserved the tech of the internal combustion or steam engine? Well, at least that meant the planet's air would be cleaner; and she hadn't smelled anything more noxious than woodsmoke since they had arrived here. As a matter of fact, the air smelt better than Ysaye had ever remembered, somehow more vital and alive. But how could they travel or communicate over any great distance? Or had they some more satisfactory substitute?

She turned away from the window and looked around the chamber which she and her companions had settled into, making conscious analysis of its furnishings and appointments. They had spent quite a bit of time up here, recovering from their ordeal. There were four large beds, in two of which her friends were still asleep; they were hewn of wood, had ropes supporting the mattresses, and the bedclothes all seemed to be hand-made and hand-woven. There were hand-made rugs, large and colorful—for which she was grateful, for the chamber was heated only by what seemed a rather inadequate fire, burning sluggishly in a brick fireplace. There were a couple of wooden, hand-made chests of drawers, and a door that still had smoothed-out chisel marks on it which led to a very cold, but perfectly adequate bathroom. They seemed to have at least retained the notion of "modern" sanitation; the bathroom had something like running water, hot and cold, and facilities for bathing. Ysaye tried to remember what she had read about medieval bathroom facilities; as she recalled, bathing was done so seldom that the facilities were not permanent, and waste disposal was so primitive as to be a bare step above an outhouse. That was certainly not the case here. Though, of course, the Cretans had some "modern" sanitation.

A knock sounded on the door; and a woman entered. Across her arms she bore the Terrans' own clothes, which had evidently been laundered and dried. Ysaye smiled with gratitude and took them from the woman, who in turn, smiled shyly; the uniforms were warm and sweet-smelling. Ysaye was deeply relieved to have her own clothes back after so long in a strange costume, and Aurora, sitting up in bed, exclaimed, "Our uniforms? Oh, wonderful! I'm *so* glad to have my breeches back. I've been feeling quite clumsy in those skirts. A day or two was fine, but the novelty was wearing thin!"

The woman smiled again, ducked her head in a kind of bow, and went away. Aurora got out of bed and began to put the uniform on. "Nice of them to lend us clothes, but I'm just as pleased to have my own back; it's all in what you're used to, I suppose, but I simply didn't feel right. Not myself."

But Elizabeth was putting on the native clothing she had been given by the attendants, and as she caught the questioning look that Ysaye gave her, she shrugged. "I guess they've given us back our clothes because they sense that we're finally rested and ready to resume our normal functions, but I can tell Lord Aldaran is more accustomed to seeing women in these skirts," she said quietly. "Maybe as long as I have to deal with him, I ought to dress in what he considers more suitable. It might make him more comfortable about dealing with me."

"Well, you're an anthropologist and I suppose since you're working as an interpreter, you'd better make sure you don't offend the man," Ysaye said. "But I'll wear what feels right to me, and if he doesn't like it, he can pick someone else to look at." Then she laughed. "Given how oddly he looked at me the first night, I probably seem so strange to him anyway that what I wear doesn't matter. He'd think I was just as peculiar in a skirt, or in a Vainwal dancing-strap, or in space-armor."

A few minutes later when they had finished dressing, there was a tap on their door and another woman entered, bearing a tray laden with breakfast. She built the fire up, and asked by signs if there was anything else they wanted. Ysaye examined the heavily-laden tray and shook her head. There was more than enough there for all of them: bread, made of flour extended with nuts or some similar substance, and very hearty; a large dish of stewed fruit, still warm; something like cheese; and a dish of boiled eggs of some sort, which tasted quite like ordinary hens' eggs, a change from the nut-based porridge they had been given previously.

"So they have birds and they domesticate fowl," Elizabeth remarked. "In fact—since they are evidently a Lost Colony, they might even be successfully breeding the chickens that are part of the livestock each colony carries."

"I saw horses, or at least what looked like horses," Ysaye offered. "A group of men came riding in on them this morning."

"That would cinch it, I would think," Elizabeth replied, nodding. "Human-to-the-Nines would be hard enough to explain; humans and horses could only be explained by having come from Terra in the first place. We could hardly have had a quicker introduction to the level of their society than by being thrown on their hospitality this way."

There was also a pitcher of the bitter-chocolate drink, as there seemed to be at every meal, and Ysaye was surprised at how good it had begun to taste. She was also surprised at how quickly it woke her up; and concluded it must be the native version of coffee—every society, "human" or not, had one.

So they can't be too different from us after all, she thought wryly, *if they "need" their caffeine to wake up in the morning!*

Elizabeth surveyed the impressive quantity of food, and urged Ysaye and Aurora to eat their fill, saying that she had been taught in her xenoanthropology classes that people felt strongly about their food; on strange planets it was as well to eat whatever was set before one. When they had all had as much as they could eat, the first woman appeared and conducted them down the stairs to another large room. Ysaye was not certain if it was the one they had gathered in the first night, or a different one; with sun streaming in the tiny windows, the shape and size of the room looked different, but the furnishings were the same.

Their male crewmates were already waiting there for them, in their uniforms and looking nearly as pleased as the women to have their own clothes back. The men had been staying in a barracks of some kind, leading the Terrans to hypothesize that it must be the custom to maintain standing armies or something of the kind. The place where the men slept could easily hold fifty or sixty.

"Elizabeth, aren't you out of uniform this morning?" inquired Commander Britton. Everyone else was obviously feeling especially chipper to have their familiar, comfortable uniforms on again.

"These clothes seem to fit the climate," Elizabeth answered. "And—well, it just seemed like a good idea to maintain native costume. I haven't seen any women here in anything but a domestic function, so I thought it might be a good idea to continue to conform in outward appearance at least. There were periods on Terra like that, and some of the earlier Lost Colonies had taken up that kind of social structure. I don't want our hosts thinking, even subconsciously, that I don't care about proper behavior in their society."

"You talk as if you were still planning to settle here," Evans said scornfully. "I wouldn't waste time on that right now, if I were in your shoes. Now that we all seem to be back on our feet again, the first thing we have to do is get back to the wreck of the shuttle and use the radio to contact the ship. We need to get a real team down here, since we've had First Contact forced on us. And then we can finally get to work; evaluating what's here, to start with. It's a long time since we've found a new world for opening."

"If we can open this one at all," Elizabeth cautioned. "I tried to tell you that before. The authorities may decide this should be a Closed World for the protection of the natives. The level of their apparent culture—"

"Don't give me that," Evans snapped. "I thought you'd decided this is a Lost Colony—and that means that as Terrans they're entitled to full colony status. It only remains to bring them up to the level of other colonies. It's their right."

"But they're stuck in a pre-industrial society," Elizabeth argued, stubbornly. "If they were aliens, their society would be protected so they could develop in their own way—not in ours. I don't think their world should have to suffer because they have developed a system so far different from the one they left! In fact, if these are descendants from the colonists on the ship I think it is, they left Terra to get away from us—to bring their level of technology *down*, not up! In history, every primitive society which encounters an advanced one is wiped out. And if there are other sapient races of nonhumans here—"

"Now look, the definition of a species is cross-fertility," Evans said. "If there should be an indigenous species here which has interbred with humans, as absurd as *that* seems, legal definitions would make that other species human anyhow. Cross-fertility means Human-to-the-Nines."

"I don't agree with you," Elizabeth said. "I like this society and these people; I don't want to see them wiped out by cultural accident, and this argument we've been having all week is giving me a headache."

Evans looked heavenward, as if for help. "Why do you assume we would wipe them out?" Evans asked, scornfully. "Hell, Elizabeth, you make us sound like pirates! This is Space Service you're talking about; we wrote the book on primitive cultures and culture shock. You're acting like we're worldwreckers; you know there are very strict laws against cultural interference. We are perfectly capable of protecting an existing society—"

He's humoring her, Ysaye realized. *He doesn't mean a word of it. He's decided that this place is a—an orchard full of fruit trees, and he's going to somehow get some of the best and the ripest, and be damned to whoever owns the place.*

And in the next moment she was wondering why suddenly she was so completely certain of his motives and plans.

But she had no chance to explore it further. Evans shut up as Mariel and Felicia came into the room, and the latter came immediately to Elizabeth, smiling in a friendly and encouraging way.

Evans gave Elizabeth a look she could not read and left, rejoining Commander Britton. For that rescue alone, Elizabeth would have gladly welcomed Felicia.

Kermiac has asked me to do what I can to help you, she said to Elizabeth—her words unintelligible, but that unspoken "speech" as clear as the purest Terran Standard. *We would like to know your plans now that you're all back on your feet.*

"Thank you for your offer," Elizabeth said, vocalizing, because trying to speak only with her mind was too difficult. "I must consult with my—ah—superior," she added.

Felicia seemed to approve—and the sidelong glances that the lady gave Aurora and Ysaye convinced Elizabeth that she had done the right thing in continuing to wear the native costume. She beckoned Commander MacAran to her side and said, "The lady says Lord Aldaran wants to know our plans, sir."

"To get in touch with the ship, and bring it down, of course," MacAran said. "Evans is right about that, anyway; the First Contact has been botched so badly now that nothing we do is going to make any real difference. Once the language computer and hypnolearners are functioning, we won't be dependent on you for this form of communication—you can call it telepathy if you're that credulous, but I have other ideas."

"I can't wait," Elizabeth said wearily.

She turned to Felicia, and struggled for words and concepts she thought the woman could grasp. "There is a communication device in our crashed ship; we must get in touch with the others of our kind. They will be concerned about us, and they will probably wish to meet with your lord. There is much that our leader and your lord should discuss."

Felicia nodded, agreeing without having to say anything, her strange eyes full of thoughtful shadows.

Elizabeth turned back to MacAran, "Just what do you think it can be if it isn't telepathy? You can call me credulous if you want to, but what would your explanation be?"

MacAran shrugged. "Evans could be right; they could have some kind of electronic devices monitoring us. Do you know what a PSE is—a psychic stress evaluator? They could have those. Or Commander Britton thinks it's simpler than that. You know all those old folk songs, you and David, and you know what they mean. You could be understanding what they are saying on a subconscious level, and explaining it to yourself as 'telepathy' because your conscious mind insists that you couldn't possibly know the language. Add to that the ability to read body language very accurately, and you have something that looks like telepathy."

Elizabeth shook her head. "I doubt that; devices like a PSE would mean they have a very exact and miniaturized electronic science, and honestly, sir, *none* of us have seen anything to indicate that they have a tech level above the medieval! As for Commander Britton's idea—I may know what songs mean, but that doesn't mean that I know what the individual *words* mean! And that wouldn't explain why they could read me and not you. And specifics—names? How would they or I extract those?"

"There is that—though frankly I think that you are selling your subconscious and your intelligence short. I do have to admit that so far I haven't seen any sign that they have any electronic science at all, miniaturized or not." He sighed. "I'll be glad to turn all of this over to the Captain."

"I don't know what he could do that we can't," she said, "Although it will be a good thing to get the corticators down here, so maybe some of you will start to believe me about the telepathy when you can talk to these people yourselves—"

Movement at the door caught her eye, and she broke off and added, "Oh, here comes someone else. Looks like they've brought in their heavy artillery."

The doors of the hall had opened while they were arguing, and a young man in what looked like a uniform, green and black, drew his sword at the doorway, intoning, "*Dom* Lorill Hastur, Heir of Hastur."

The dramatic entrance caught the attention of everyone, Ysaye included, and she wondered what the arrival of yet another high-ranking native meant. News certainly seemed to travel awfully fast, considering that transportation was supposedly by horseback!

Ysaye caught the telepathic overtones that told her that "Hastur" was not only a name, but a title, and an important one at that. Lorill Hastur, as he strode through the door as if he owned it, proved to be a fairly tall young man, red-haired, strongly built, though neither as tall nor as broad as MacAran. Ysaye recognized the colors of his clothing and realized that he was among those she had seen ride in just after dawn. He looked around the room, came at once to Felicia.

"*Domna*," he said, nodding very slightly, and ignoring Elizabeth. "I have arrived just this morning from Thendara after a tenday's ride. Lord Aldaran has kindly told me that there are people in your keep who are unlike anyone we have ever met. Indeed, it was knowledge of these people which brings me here. You are in charge of these strangers?"

"By the favor of my own lord, *vai dom*," Felicia answered, curtsying deeply, by her speech and manner quite overwhelmed by the young man. "We were told there were those in peril on Aldaran lands by the *leroni* of our Tower. We sought the strangers, and found them marooned by an ice storm in the travel shelter, and were privileged to guide them here, to offer them food and drink and music. As you can see," she cast a sideways glance at the Terrans who had donned their uniforms, "we found them to be very strange indeed. They spoke neither *casta* nor *cahuenga*, Trade-speech nor the speech of the Dry Towns. Then we discovered that some of our oldest songs were known to them—as if by magic. Or perhaps they can read our minds, although Lord Aldaran says that most of them are head-blind. He gave them the hospitality of Aldaran. Should he have done otherwise?"

"By no means," said Lorill soothingly. "It is hospitality to strangers which separates man from the beasts. There is even an old saying to that effect among our people—and for all I know, among yours and these strangers as well. Still we need to know who and what they are and whence they come. And why."

Ysaye found this difficult to follow, since he was using not telepathy, but ordinary speech; she only got the barest sense of it by concentrating very hard, as if she were overhearing things from a distant room—just enough to gather what the conversation was about.

But even Commander MacAran could follow Lorill's curious glances at them, and guess that he was inquiring about the Terrans.

Lorill Hastur looked inquiringly at Elizabeth, and Ysaye wondered if he thought she were a native. To Ysaye's eyes there was nothing to differentiate Elizabeth from the rest of the people in the hall as long as she was silent. She wondered if Elizabeth had fallen prey to the desire to seem one of them, and dissassociate herself from her Terran fellows. Already she seemed almost at home here, and already partisan—and a little abashed about it. There was something of a stigma attached to anyone in Space Services who "went native"; a sense that they were somehow too weak to do their jobs, too easily seduced by primitive ways of life. "The Lotus-Eaters," Ysaye had heard them called. Too ready to forget their own world and life in the dream of a "simpler" existence.

Ysaye hoped that wasn't what was happening to Elizabeth. *Maybe she's just been in space too long*, she thought. *And she always did like underdogs. Maybe that's it; she's just trying to protect something that couldn't possibly stand up to the Evanses of the universe.*

After a whispered consultation with Felicia, Lorill came toward Elizabeth, asking, "Do you speak for these people?"

"Not really," she replied, "I'm actually sort of a go-between. This is my superior."

She turned to MacAran. "Commander MacAran, he wants to speak to you. This is Lorill Hastur, and he seems to be a major VIP around here. From all I can tell, Lord Aldaran has given him leave to speak with us."

Can he really follow what I say? she wondered. Kermiac had been able to—or seemed to—but—

Of course I can. Lorill Hastur's thought was almost complacent. *I have been properly trained. And you are correct; Kermiac of Aldaran would not be inclined to interfere with my wishes.*

Elizabeth swallowed, her throat suddenly dry. "Sir, he can follow what I say to you and vice versa. Go ahead."

Ysaye shook her head a little, for now she seemed to be able to pick up thoughts from her own colleagues! She could hear MacAran thinking, *So now she's convinced that this new fellow can read her mind directly. Nice story, but she believes it, and something's going on. Anyhow, no good arguing now.*

MacAran just cleared his throat, looking uncomfortable. "If he's a local VIP, you might as well tell him about the ship crashing. See if he believes us any more than that Aldaran fellow did."

"Just for fun," Evans added, "see how well he understands when I tell him to go to hell." Commander MacAran glared him to silence.

Felicia sucked in her breath at his temerity, but said nothing, quickly moving away. Ysaye knew what that meant. She, at least, had understood.

Before Elizabeth could repeat the words, or even

decide whether or not she wanted to repeat them, it was already too late. Lorill had plucked the meaning from her mind. His narrow, fine features went tight.

For a moment, Elizabeth was afraid that he was going to do something—what, she had no idea, but a shiver went through her at the look in his eyes.

But instead, he said, "You may tell your foolish countryman that I understood that. I will spare you the embarrassment of repeating it. It is natural enough that the head-blind should wish to test me, if most folk in your land are so half-crippled and lacking in *donas*."

He paused, then added, purely mentally, *I can think of no way to give back his insult without putting you under the obligation to repeat an insult as crude. He cannot understand me at all, and you would be only under the suspicion of having originated it. But when we have some language in common, we will see if the six-fathered bastard has enough courage to repeat his insults to one who can understand them directly.* He smiled silkily. *And perhaps, when he understands the consequences of such insult, when he realizes that I could challenge him to duel with sword or knife, for speaking such words, I am sure he will be very polite. Meanwhile, tell your commander that Aldaran's men will take him to his crashed vehicle and give him access to the communication device. And yes, I believe your tale. I have access to information that Aldaran has not.*

Elizabeth repeated what she could, and MacAran nodded.

"I don't know how you got all that just by staring at the man," MacAran said, "But it looks to me like you got what you say. Thank him."

Elizabeth complied, with relief that a nasty incident had been avoided.

Some of Aldaran's men appeared when their leader summoned them and led MacAran outside; Commander Britton accompanied them, motioning to Evans to stay with the women. Felicia and Lorill Hastur went off in the opposite direction, leaving the Terrans alone.

Evans stared off after Lorill Hastur with his habitual expression of contempt.

"Evans, be careful," Elizabeth warned wearily, feeling certain that Evans would ignore her, but knowing that if she didn't warn him, she would feel guilty if anything happened. "He understood your insults. I'm afraid you've made an enemy. He may look young to you, but he's a man of immense importance among his people, and he has the power to—to call you to account for yourself, if he wants to."

"Oh, sure he heard them," Evans mocked. "If you believe that, you'll believe anything. I don't believe there is anything like telepathy, but I will believe he somehow made you think he has all that power." His sharp glare made Ysaye think that they didn't need an enemy among the natives; they already had one in Evans. "He's just a snobbish kid who wanted to go poke at the strangers to see if he could make them twitch— playing 'chicken.' Once we get things settled, I'll see he finds out who's really in charge around here."

Elizabeth sighed as Evans stalked away. "What's the matter, Liz?" Ysaye asked. *I might as well keep up the pretense that I can't hear what's going on* she thought. *It might be useful.*

"He's insane; you heard him insult the Hastur lord," Elizabeth replied. Ysaye wondered why she had put it in that form, rather than saying Lorill Hastur. "I think he believes I somehow repeated those insults to the man's face. He knows he made the Hastur angry, but he wants to blame it on me."

"Conveniently ignoring the fact that you didn't open your mouth until you translated Lorill Hastur's reply for Commander MacAran," Ysaye pointed out.

"You're right," Elizabeth said in surprise. "I didn't. And Lord Lorill is angry, *really* angry; he called Evans a six-fathered bastard, and suggested he might challenge Evans to some kind of duel if he dared repeat it."

Ysaye considered that. "Interesting insult. Bastard used to be an term of insult in many societies, but what do you suppose six-fathered means?"

"I suspect it's an aspersion on his mother's virtue —or maybe her ancestry," Elizabeth said doubtfully. "I don't think I really want to know; but it was something not very nice, judging by the tone. Anyway, I wouldn't go around gratuitously insulting that man; if they have a code duello here, incorporated as part of their law, the Empire might just uphold it. And the moment Evans set foot on soil that was *theirs*, he would have to obey *their* laws."

"I wouldn't want to go around insulting anybody around here, even if the Empire *doesn't* uphold a dueling-code," said Ysaye. "There was no reason for Evans to pull that kind of stunt; it could have precipitated a serious diplomatic incident. Besides, the people here have been very hospitable to us."

"They certainly have. And there's still the question of how they knew we were there and in trouble," Elizabeth added, thinking about the telepathy issue. "I mean, how else would they know about us without some ability to sense thoughts?"

Doctor Lakshman joined them just at that moment. "Good question," Aurora remarked. "If they found us that way, from here, that implies that somebody has a pretty good range."

"Yes, it does," Ysaye agreed, "as well as raising the question of which of us they can pick up and how much they can tell without our knowing it."

That was not the most comfortable of questions—

and the answers to it were even less comforting. The three women exchanged uneasy glances, as each of them tried to examine their memories for anything that they might have thought could cause them trouble.

"Did they say anything about Kadarin or Felicia?" Aurora asked, changing the subject. "I'm looking forward to an explanation for them."

"And both Felicia and Raymon are old Terran names," David remarked. "What kind of explanation does Evans give for that? Or has he decided that this is a Lost Colony after all?"

"Apparently he has," Elizabeth answered.

"I'd bet a year's pay he'll think of something to explain mind-reading," Ysaye said. "Probably something totally strange. The man may know botany and drugs, but for anything else he's practically useless, if not a downright liability."

"I'll be glad when Captain Gibbons brings the ship down," Aurora said. "If you want the truth, in a way I'm rather glad that the standard First Contact procedures got botched. It makes things so much simpler."

Simpler, perhaps, Ysaye thought soberly, *but by no means easier.*

CHAPTER
13

The mere existence of the wrecked shuttle, concrete, impossible to replicate, and quite solidly *there*, turned Kermiac Aldaran from a skeptic to a fervent believer. The change was quite remarkable, really; he had gone out with his men to see the "craft" of the strangers, possibly quite prepared to find nothing more exotic than a ruined cart or wagon, yet equally prepared for something entirely outlandish. In the case of the former, he would probably have had his guests escorted to more secure quarters, or so Ysaye suspected, quarters in which the local equivalent of psychiatrists could attempt to deal with their delusions. In the case of the latter, she was not certain what he would have done. From her impressions, she suspected he would have treated them as supernatural visitants.

But he got neither cart nor occult phenomena; instead he found himself inspecting something obviously made by the hand of man, but infinitely more complicated than anything his people could produce. And it was a vehicle made entirely of *metal;* he confessed to David that this alone would have convinced him. There was enough metal to be scavenged from the interior alone to supply his armsmen with metal weapons for the next three generations.

That had given them a basis for trade; in return for permission to bring the big ship down, a place to land it, and agreement to open negotiations for a spaceport, Captain Gibbons granted Lord Aldaran salvage rights on any non-tech, unusable equipment in the shuttle, and the shell of the shuttle itself. There was no point in even trying to salvage anything but the electronic equipment from the wreck. MacAran had returned saying that he must have hit his head harder than he'd thought, to say that it was only the landing gear that kept them from taking off. With the huge rents in the side of the craft, there was no way it could have been made spaceworthy.

Aldaran's men swarmed over it, prying off every piece they could with their primitive equipment. That at least convinced Evans that there weren't any "secret electronic devices" spying on the Terrans, for the workers showed neither interest in nor understanding of broken circuitry and electronics except for metal content. They scavenged every bit of copper, however; no bit, however small, was overlooked, convincing MacAran that in terms of the value of the metal, Aldaran had gotten the better of the deal, or thought he had!

One day later, another shuttle landed, bringing with it a crew to cut up the wrecked shuttle and remove the remaining usable equipment. Aldaran's men spent the day hauling away pieces of metal still hot from the torches; by day's end, there was nothing left to show that the shuttle had landed there but the mess in the snow. Even tiny bits of plastic had been picked up and carried off; within two days, Ysaye saw some of the villagers, and even some of the "Comyn" women in Aldaran's castle, wearing carefully set and polished bits of plastic as jewelry.

Two days after that, in a great barren space outside

a village that Lord Aldaran had called *Caer Donn*, Ysaye watched the starship settle down, creating its own null-grav field to drop onto the snow like a huge feather. Everyone from the castle was there, and most of the villagers—and not all their familiarity with the two shuttles kept the castle folk from gaping with the same astonishment as the villagers.

Ysaye was very glad to see it. She was tired to death of being cold, of smoky fires, of the strange food. She was even wearier of the constant threat of allergy attacks. Twice now, she had gone to Aurora for emergency treatment; once, she had required oxygen. One of the effects of her allergies, during an extreme attack, was hypoxia; she had already found herself sitting on the floor of Aurora's makeshift sickbay, dizzy, weak, befuddled, and not quite certain where she was. A dangerous condition to be in. . . .

Even more dangerous; another effect was toxemia, and the potential to literally become allergic to herself. She was glad to be back inside the controlled environment of the ship.

With the help of what she could only conclude was her new power of telepathy, she had learned the rudiments of the language Lord Aldaran spoke, *casta*, and had accompanied Elizabeth as she began making assessments of the level of culture showed in the village of Caer Donn and in the Aldaran castle. But she longed for her computers and her screens, her sensors and her data files. No matter how interesting all this was, she was tired of seeing it at first-hand. She wanted the buffering of her computers between her and this too-real reality.

So far, everything she and Elizabeth had seen indicated that the culture was precisely what they had thought: a preindustrial society, without much manufacturing capability, on a metal-poor world with a fragile economy, and an even more fragile ecology, based mostly upon simple agriculture. Unless someone discovered something here that could be *grown* that was worth exporting, there would be very little these people could offer besides handmade novelties. Of course, there was a fairly brisk, if limited, interstellar trade in such things. Items of wood, leather, fur—art objects— even music and musical instruments—all found their way into the luxury trade. So it might well be that some trade could be established, although, of course, what they really had to offer was their location. The Terran Empire would pay the locals quite well for the privilege of establishing a spaceport here.

She and Elizabeth had seen a blacksmith in the village, a jeweler; a bakery where all the village came to bake their own loaves, combined with a simple cookshop where a man made stews and roasts, with his wife and daughters to wait on the customers; a public bathhouse which Elizabeth believed served the purposes of a social hall and whorehouse (Ysaye hoped it wasn't used for both at the same time, and looked forward to returning to the ship for a hot shower); a tavern; a small, open-air theater which stood dark and deserted, though some people said that acrobats and ballad singers and the like came there at fair time to entertain; a butcher shop; and a seller of simple clothes and leather boots and packaging material such as bags and sacks. Elizabeth had wondered aloud what the influx of Terran style goods and services would do to these people. Ysaye thought she knew; it would spoil them for their own goods. She had only to see a brisk bargaining session over a piece of scavenged plastic sheeting to know how much the locals would come to value Terran goods, whether or not their own officials liked it or approved of it.

And doubtless, Ysaye thought with disgust, when

the inevitable black market arose, Evans would be in the thick of it, if not the originator.

The ship had sent messages back to Terra, and Elizabeth jittered about, waiting for the results. Captain Gibbons and his officers would divide the finders' fee for this world; that was normal procedure. That was not what Elizabeth was worried about; she was concerned with how this new world would be classified.

If the official powers of the Space Service decided there was no reason to restrict the place and to bring it fully into the Terran Empire as an Open world, it would be opened to exploration and various means of exploitation.

But if it was a world to be protected by Closed status, they would all be back on the ship and gone within the month. David and Elizabeth would not even have an opportunity to do the work they found so rewarding, and, of course, it would mean postponing their marriage.

All that, resting on a decision following a hearing by Empire Central.

Ysaye herself could not have cared less if they all packed up and left for the next world, but she knew that Elizabeth cared passionately. The worst part, Ysaye knew, was that Elizabeth was literally torn between wanting the place granted Open and wanting it granted Closed status. If it were to be Opened, she and David could settle down, and devote themselves to a culture that was not only fascinating to them, but one that they actively liked. But if it were Opened, that left this place vulnerable to those like Evans, who saw nothing without calculating how much they could get out of it. A Closed status would protect them from that—but it would mean, not only that Elizabeth and David would have to leave, but that the people themselves would lose the considerable benefits of becoming a member of the Empire.

The second shuttle had been commanded by Captain Gibbons himself. The captain was a small slender man with shaggy hair and wrinkled skin. Ysaye had no idea how old he was; he seemed ageless. She heard that he had begun his career as engineer's mate, because as a small man he could get into places where larger men could not go; at that time there had been no women in the Service, and even now, the ones that chose to go into Engineering were few and far between. Captain Gibbons still knew his way around every nook and corner of the ship, and, it was said that if he could not fix anything aboard, it could not be fixed at all. Certainly, he took an active interest in things mechanical and electrical, and it had been by his own decision that the first shuttle had been declared beyond repair.

Now that the ship had landed, the Captain had fewer duties with regard to it, and more with regard to what the *de facto* First Contact team had learned. Ysaye was not at all surprised when he summoned them to his office for "an informal debriefing."

Ysaye let Elizabeth do most of the talking. She was just happy to be back on shipboard, warm and fresh from a hot shower and wearing a clean uniform. Breathing air that, at last, didn't smell *of* something: smoke, cooking meat, lighting oil, animal waste, sweat.

He took their reports and listened with interest to what Elizabeth said of telepathy.

"Well, Intelligence thought enough of the possibility to put you and David aboard," he said mildly. "We can't entirely rule it out."

But when the Captain approached Evans and asked for his opinion on the subject, he got an entirely different view.

"Oh, come on, Captain; who do these people think they're kidding! Telepathy that works only for some people? I'll just bet," Evans scoffed. "It makes a great excuse for not understanding someone you don't *want* to understand." He took all the sampling devices he could carry and disappeared outside; in fact, he wasn't in the ship much at all anymore. Ysaye got the impression that he was setting up his own little lab outside somewhere—though why he was doing so outside and not in the perfectly good facilities of the ship was still a mystery to her. Still, she admitted, if he wanted to do anything illegal. . . .

Aurora gratefully accepted the various paraphernalia of the language computers and corticators and began working with David to set them up; most within the ship, but some in a room in Kermiac Aldaran's castle, so that certain of the natives, if they chose, could learn Terran Standard. That was one side benefit of having fumbled the First Contact; at this point, things were so badly off-program that it no longer mattered what they showed the natives, or exposed them to.

The man Kadarin—if he was a man—had been the first to volunteer for the strange-looking machines, and the happy result was that they not only had a Terran Standard speaker among the natives, but they had excellent records for the Terrans to learn both *casta* and another language called *cahuenga* that many of the peasants spoke. Once Kadarin had survived his bout with the corticators, he had at once begun to chatter technical terms with Britton and the Captain, and had exerted himself, so MacAran said, to find a site for further ships to land.

No one seemed terribly surprised to learn that he considered Caer Donn the perfect site for more landings. Captain Gibbons concurred. Here, Ysaye realized, if the Terran spaceport could be built at all, it would rise, near to Aldaran's influence. Whether it could rise at all, only time would tell.

At least part of the time, she was sure that the residents of Cottman IV would wish to become a Terran Colony like any other. It seemed so logical—after all, these people *were* Terran, didn't they deserve the benefits of being Terran? Of course Empire Central would have to rule on that one.

The rest of the time, she was afraid that it would turn into a Terran Colony—whether the natives liked it that way or not. Although she found it hard to believe, there *were* people who didn't consider the things the Empire offered to be "benefits." She was troubled sometimes; mostly when she overheard Evans, making plans with Kadarin.

As soon as Kadarin had learned Standard, Evans had drafted him to show him about and help him carry things, and Ysaye noticed that their conversations often changed subject abruptly as other people approached them. Some of the little that she overheard made her distinctly uncomfortable. She did not think that planning for exports was ethical, not before a final report by ecologists, psychologists, and sociologists on the society.

The rules of the Terran Empire itself demanded such a report before any trade was established; but already there seemed to be considerable local enthusiasm for the idea. Plans had at least been discussed for the building of the spaceport, for the employment of local labor, and for supplying some of the spaceship's people with fresh food—which at least would be good for local agriculture and economics, or so Kermiac of Aldaran had given them to understand. And he had hinted at the favors he would like granted, for the concession of having the spaceport on his land.

Ysaye knew that Kermiac wanted weapons, and she

did not know if that was permissible. As she understood the matter, that would be interfering in local politics; always a bad idea, considering what local politics were. She understood that Aldaran was like an independent kingdom, with Lorill Hastur representing another kingdom to the south of here, where the climate was considerably more hospitable. She thought that the standard operating procedure was to examine both societies, and look more thoroughly into the relationships between them, before making any decisions on the sale of even low-tech weapons.

She had finally approached Lorill Hastur about it; obliquely, she thought. Lorill had remained very much in the background of what was going on—always watching, but never interfering, and not often commenting.

But you must realize, Lorill Hastur had commented in that unspoken speech, *that we of the Domains claim overlordship over Aldaran. They do not always admit it, but we are their sovereigns. Anything that Aldaran can do to press his independence from us, he shall.*

If this should be true, it put quite another face on the whole matter, especially on Aldaran's wish for weapons. It was strictly against Empire policy to take sides in purely local struggles, or to adjudicate causes, even if the struggle seemed based on something as meaningless to Terrans as the proverbial struggle in Swift's *Gulliver's Travels* between the Big-endians and the Little-endians. There was a well known Terran Empire proverb: *It is not up to us to determine by which end other peoples shall eat their eggs.* Unfortunately there had been many examples in which this law had been honored more in the breach than the observance.

Ysaye decided the best thing she could do in the situation was to stay out of it, and went to check the computer status logs. To her great relief, no catastrophes appeared to have taken place during her absence.

She returned to her cabin, appreciating the luxury of being able to go back to a truly warm room as she had not been able to do in weeks, and pulled out her music synthesizer keyboard. She set it for harpsichord and played through Bach's *Two-Part Inventions* until her fingers finished thawing out.

The next morning Elizabeth came to her with the news that she and David had decided to go ahead and get married, delaying any children until the planet's status was decided. "We are just tired of waiting," she said. "It doesn't make any sense anymore. I'm not even sure if it matters whether this world is Open or Closed. I'm not even sure why we waited so long in the first place—it seems pretty senseless now. And, Ysaye," she asked, "will you be my maid of honor?"

"Of course," Ysaye replied, hugging her. "Where and when?"

The wedding—for Elizabeth told her that they had spoken both to Captain Gibbons, and to the chaplain, either of whom were empowered to marry ship's personnel anywhere in the Empire, and had decided on the chaplain, who wanted them to wait the traditional three days for "cooling off"—was set for three days in the future. "Three days doesn't matter much when you've been waiting three years," David had said philosophically. Ysaye agreed.

So now, besides their other duties, she and Elizabeth had a wedding to prepare. Not a fancy one, for after all, this was not a bulwark of the Social Registry, it was a survey ship—but nearly everyone on the ship would want to come, and they would be severely disappointed if there weren't some kind of celebration. Most people didn't know Elizabeth well, for she kept to herself a great deal—but David was popular with most of the Ship's personnel.

One more thing, Ysaye thought to herself.

But Elizabeth was happy—and considerably less tense. Finally the waiting was over.

Then came a development she hadn't expected. The natives took an interest in the proceedings. Aldaran—and Felicia—asked a good many questions about their marriage customs, and even offered the use of the Great Hall and the castle servants to help with the celebration. This was an unexpected bonus for Elizabeth's work, for she had begun to see herself as an interface between their two cultures; and she was entirely ready to have the natives participate in this part of her life.

The wedding would be the first event scheduled for the ship's company on the new world, and it seemed fitting that it be a ceremony involving both the Terrans and the natives.

After discussion with David and Ysaye, she accepted Aldaran's invitation for the ceremony to be held in his Great Hall. Now that he and the ship's company had a language in common, he had lost no time in extending any number of invitations, but this was the most practical one to accept—and the one with the least number of metaphorical strings attached. Elizabeth spent her time between planning every detail of the wedding, and categorizing every new facet of the native culture she ran across. And in little bits of spare time, she could be found gleefully cataloguing folk songs and checking them against the library copies, exulting over every shifted half note, every major key that had somehow over the years mutated into minor, checking out lute sounds on the synthesizer, recording new sounds to be synthesized.

When Ysaye asked her why she was spending so much time on cataloging music, she protested that it had everything to do with her major specialty. Folk songs and the changes in them, she insisted, indicated deep rooted changes in the society, and changes in the people's psychology. She pointed out that of the overwhelming number of ancient Gaelic songs which dealt with the sea, hardly a single one had survived into the present native culture, probably because the lifestyle of these people did not include a sea, or anything like one, as they were surrounded by the mountains. She mentioned especially one long-known song about seagulls, which had become a sad love song; the words had somehow mutated from a refrain based on the cries of the gulls to the sad sound of wind in the trees, and the cries of birds of prey. The original words had become, not seagull cries, but the sad refrain: "Where are you now?/ Where does my love wander?"

Ysaye had shrugged. "I hope that Empire Central feels the same way," she had warned, "or you're likely to do very poorly on your next status review."

But somehow she didn't think that mattered much to Elizabeth, at least, not now.

On the morning of the wedding Ysaye stood in the Great Hall, showing the servants where to set up the table which would serve, covered with a length of spotless white polysilk, as an altar. The whole ship's company would be there, and most of Aldaran's people.

When Ysaye had asked why so many of his people—who wouldn't even understand the tongue the ceremony was spoken in—had wanted to attend, he had said, with a sly twinkle in his eye, "Any excuse will do for a festive occasion; a wedding is as good as any, and better than most."

He had made another offer to Elizabeth as well. "I will give you away if there are none of your kinfolk present."

Elizabeth had thanked him and refused, telling him it was not their custom for a bride to be given away by her kinfolk. "Personally," she told Ysaye privately, "though I would never have said so to Lord Aldaran, I find the custom rather degrading, as if one were property, rather than a person. But I know he intended a real honor."

Ysaye remembered that conversation as Lord Aldaran entered and asked her if everything were satisfactory. "Yes, sir," she replied, casting her eyes over the surprising displays, not only of evergreens from the forest, but of real flowers from what she *thought* one of the servants had said was a hothouse. "Everything is beautiful. We are deeply appreciative of your kindness and generosity."

She looked around one final time, checking the details. Perhaps, she thought, he would be doing this again in the near future. The girl Mariel, who had been with Felicia the first night they arrived—was she his daughter? No, she was too old for that, must be his sister, his niece, or his cousin. These days Mariel seemed to be always with Lorill Hastur. Ysaye wondered what was between them; they certainly seemed to spend a lot of time laughing in corners.

Ysaye suppressed a smile as she found an unsought picture in her mind, of Aldaran charging up to young Hastur and demanding, like some patriarch in an old-time drama, to know what his intentions were.

And if he did? What would that arrogant young aristocrat answer? And was any of it her business anyway?

She looked up to find Aldaran staring at her oddly.

"I will speak to Lorill Hastur," he said, his face betraying nothing. Then he turned on his heel and left her standing in the middle of the Hall.

She stared after him, alarmed by the sudden change in his demeanor and his expression. Her hand went to her lips in an unconscious gesture of alarm, as she realized that the change had followed on the heels of her thoughts about the Hastur boy and young Mariel.

Had he followed her thoughts?

And what was he going to do, if he had?

CHAPTER
14

Leonie had gone to sleep exhausted, with no thought for anything *but* sleep. She hadn't even noticed whether her bed was warmed; she didn't even feel her head touching the pillow. Certainly she had no interest tonight in the strangers at Aldaran, not after the workday she had just been through.

Days—or was it a tenday?—ago, Fiora had found her idling her time away in the garden, watching the two younger girls playing on the swing, and had asked her if she had nothing else to do. She had been feeling a little superior to the younger girls, because she had once again been allowed to help in the relays. Fiora's question had come as something of a surprise.

"I do not," Leonie had replied truthfully. Fiora had smiled then, and had asked her sweetly (too sweetly, she thought now), if she, Leonie, considered herself capable of an accelerated form of the teaching usually given a *leronis*. "For you told me you aspired to be a Keeper," Fiora told her. "And it seems we may have need of a new Keeper sooner than we thought. Even if we do not, well, it will do no harm to have someone Keeper-trained and ready to step in where she is needed."

Fiora did not tell her *where* the new Keeper would be needed, nor did she say how soon—and indeed, it was possible for there to be more than one Keeper at a Tower. In fact, it was a desirable state, though one not often achieved these days, when so many of the young women of the Comyn were pulled out of the Towers to make advantageous marriages for their families, to breed more sons and daughters for their caste. Leonie did not think that Fiora meant for her to be under-Keeper to someone else, however. Something about Fiora's thoughts, so carefully guarded, gave her the impression that there was a great deal more going on than Fiora was willing to tell her.

So when Fiora had offered the new teaching, phrasing it as a challenge—then had implied that this might be Leonie's chance to prove herself, not only to Fiora, but to all the workers of all the Towers, Leonie had accepted the challenge.

Leonie had no idea what Fiora had in mind. She had gone from having too little to do, to far too much, all in the space of a single day.

She took a regular watch in the relays now, like any other adult; and she had gone from the same daily lessons to twice the teaching in the use of her abilities of any of her fellow students.

More than twice the teaching; she had *special* lessons, and now she knew for herself just what the Keeper of Dalereuth had meant when she had scolded Leonie that day in the garden. Leonie had endured more pain in the past few days than she had ever had to face in her life. Fiora had taken her in hand and had ruthlessly taught her to monitor properly within the space of a day; from there, she had gone on to the specialized training only a Keeper received. Leonie's hands were already laced with some of the tiny scars Fiora's bore; legacy of learning, in the most striking way possible, when not to touch, and who. The scars on her soul went deeper, though they were invisible.

And Leonie was more determined than ever to wear the crimson robes of a Keeper.

So among other duties, Leonie now routinely monitored while one of the other *leroni* healed. Today she had taken her first patient as a healer. It had been a small thing, a child with a puncture wound gone bad, but she had drained the wound of poison, purged the child's system of fever, and healed it, as she had been instructed, from the deepest point outward. The *leronis* who was her teacher and monitor had praised her deft and sure touch, and had told her that before very long, she could expect not only to be assigned patients to heal without supervision, but to take her place in true surgery.

"We do not often risk it," the woman had said, "but sometimes it must be done, for there are cases where there is no other cure. There is a man in the village who has a bit of a bandit's blade lodged within him that gives him pain and must come out one day; when you are ready, he shall be your first patient."

Leonie had glowed with the praise, though she had been quite ready to take a rest when she was done with the child, and she could not imagine how it would be to perform surgery . . . unless, the more a *leronis* practiced, the easier things became. (Nothing, Fiora said when she asked, is ever *easy*, but it is always possible.)

But Leonie's day was not over; when she had finished with the child, there was another lesson to be dealt with, this one in the still-room. Fiora had decreed three days ago that she should learn everything to do with healing, whether or not it involved *laran*. "A Keeper must know these things," she had said, "or how else can she train others?"

That had made sense to Leonie, who had bowed to her will, and had begun learning the making of herbal medicines and potions. She soon found, somewhat to her own surprise, that this work interested her greatly, for she had an active curiosity and a retentive memory. Her teacher here praised her as being both quick and accurate. Today, this teacher had also said that one day she might be entrusted with surgery, a task usually limited to the most skillful and observant of the technicians.

By the time she had finished her lesson in herbcraft, it was time to take her place in the relays. And when that at last was over, she had no thought at all for anything other than food and sleep. She was never even truly hungry, but Fiora came and pressed food upon her, saying that matrix work dulled the appetite, and she should eat even though she did not care to.

She had quickly discovered that Fiora had been right; devouring every crumb of the sticky fruit and nut bar Fiora had brought her, and going down to the kitchen for a full meal. But the end of that meal found her even wearier, nearly falling into her plate, trying to keep her eyes open. Someone, she did not remember who, helped her to her feet and to her room. Somehow she had undressed on her own—her new robes making it easy, and had fallen into bed, and immediately into deep and dreamless sleep.

So when, some time well past midnight, she woke out of fatigue-sodden sleep and felt the familiar and insistent tug of her twin's thoughts, her initial response was to try and ignore him. But the contact grew ever more insistent, and finally she gave in. She turned over on her back, suppressed a sigh of exasperation, and opened her mind to him. She knew it was Lorill; she knew his "voice" as well as her own.

Around her the Tower was quiet, full of the silence of sleeping minds, minds with nothing to disturb them. Not even the *leronis* minding the relays ruffled the peace about her.

Lorill? Leonie responded grumpily. *Where are you?*

What do you want at this *time of night? I was asleep.*

I am at Aldaran, where else would I be? Didn't you send me there? Lorill seemed to be both amused and disturbed by something.

That only made her temper sour a little farther. What could be so important that it meant he had to call on her in the middle of the night?

Now her sleep had been disturbed and her temper ruffled by a source she would have considered most unlikely: her brother. *And since you sent me here,* he continued, *it follows that you are the one responsible for what has happened.*

That brought her awake. *So what* has *happened? Tell me at once! Are you in trouble? Did the strangers—?* What had he done? Had the people from the moon taken offense at something?

There was no mistaking it; Lorill was full of conflicting emotion—an underlying concern covered by giddy laughter that seemed to her very much out of place. She wondered if he had been indulging overmuch in wine. *Oh, just a grand to-do over Kermiac's sister. These mountain girls are not like those in Carcosa; I suppose I should have known better, but there was no one to tell me.*

A to-do over *Kermiac's* sister? How in the name of Avarra had Lorill gotten involved with her? *Tell you what?* Leonie demanded. That much hadn't changed— Lorill could be so infuriatingly obtuse!

That the girls are flirtatious, Lorill replied carelessly. *She tried her wiles on me, and I admit I did not drive her away with the flat of my sword! Well, I suppose old Domenic must have seen me with her, and so Kermiac came to me, like the outraged father in a very bad play.* He chuckled nervously again. *It would have made you laugh, Leonie, I swear. It took all my control to keep my face straight and my thoughts under a shield.*

What did he want? Leonie asked, not at all amused.
*Trust Lorill to get involved with the single most unsuit-
able girl in all the world*—and *the sister of his host.*

He solemnly asked me my intentions *toward the girl!
As if a Hastur could intend anything toward her but a
bit of fun which she was all too ready to give.* There was
a touch of arrogance about the words which grated on
Leonie; she was not so self-centered that she could not
recognize the same kind of arrogance in her brother
that she herself had displayed on more than one occasion. Reflected back at her, it was like looking into
a mirror and seeing an ugly flaw she had not expected.
Nevertheless, Lorill was her twin . . . in any conflict,
it would be his side that she stood on.

And what did you say to that? she demanded fiercely.
What answer did you give him?

What would you expect me to say? Lorill replied,
with a feeling as if he was shrugging. *I told him politely
that I was simply offering her the admiration she had
asked for. He seemed to feel I should have had some
thought of marrying the girl.*

Marriage—no, not possible. Not with her brother,
the Heir to Hastur.

Lorill obviously felt the same way. *I can't imagine
why, unless it was that marrying was in the air. There
was a wedding here today; a pair of the strange people
who claim to be from somewhere off our world, another
star, they say.*

That took her by surprise yet again. So the strangers
were from the stars! Well, that was near enough to being
from the moons that Leonie felt her powers and the
knowledge that came from them validated, her state-
ments justified. So she had been right about them! And
they married, just as if they were ordinary people . . .
that was almost enough to distract her.

But not for long; she had to learn how much of a

situation Lorill had gotten himself into. And what, exactly, had gone on between him and Kermiac's sister?

What did Aldaran say? she asked.

There was a trace of sullen anger in Lorill's thoughts that hadn't been there before. *Kermiac spoke to me in a way I shall find hard to forgive. At last I asked him, "Do you mean to tell me that your sister is a sheltered virgin?" I meant it as irony, but he took it for a true question. Or else he meant to insult me in a way that I could not reply to. He said to me, "Isn't yours?"*

Leonie could not tell what Kermiac had meant by that, but the insolence of such a question made *her* angry. How dared the man make imputations about her honor? *And?* she prompted. *What did you tell him?*

So I replied, "Yes, but my sister is properly guarded in a Tower, not frisking her skirts at any man who looks at her." He seemed rather pleased by his own cleverness.

Cleverness? Well, it wasn't monumentally stupid, but it wasn't the brightest retort Lorill could have made. Small wonder if Aldaran were angry. Lorill should really have put aside his pride. But who was she to criticize him for *that*. Leonie lost *her* anger; now the argument sounded like no more than two little boys exchanging insults. How had she gotten so much older than her twin in the past few tendays? Or had she always been older than he? *Oh, Lorill, that was most exceptionally stupid. Were you trying to shock him? What did he say and do then?*

Lorill seemed a bit taken aback by that. *He laughed at me, though I could tell he was angry, and he said that any man of honor would know what to do in this matter, since no one had ever breathed a word about Mariel before I arrived. He went on and on about that, how I must have misled her with my lowlander words, turned her head with my rank, and perhaps even used my* laran to influence her. So at last I had to tell him that I was only fifteen, and could not marry anyone without the Council's consent.

There was no heat behind the accusations, but a great deal beneath the last sentence. So that was what had made him angry; having to admit his age when he had been so proud of being sent out on his own like a full adult. But there was also an undertone of smugness there that Leonie did not like; a sense that he was proud of himself for having so quickly and easily found a way to escape an obligation that didn't suit him to admit. He said to me, "Here in the mountains, it is held that if a man is old enough to compromise a good girl, he is old enough to make it right." That made me truly angry, and what could I tell him except that it had never occurred to me from the way she acted that Mariel was a "good girl."

Leonie felt a sudden stillness come over her. There was enough trouble in those few words to have caused bloodshed between the Domains and Aldaran, and Lorill had no idea how lucky he was that Kermiac had not challenged him on the spot. Somehow she had to make him understand that, before he did something that *would* cause Aldaran to challenge him. Why was it that men allowed anger to overpower good sense, especially when women were involved? *Lorill, she is Comyn, and the sister to Aldaran's lord. How could you think such a thing, much less say it?*

He seemed to think that she was indulging in female vaporing. *Sister, I swear to you—oh, see for yourself!* He backed up his words with memories of Mariel which *did* seem to Leonie to be terribly flirtatious—

But that was in the world of the Domains, not the mountains, and she at least could tell that Mariel, who had been raised very differently from herself and her twin, had not meant flirtatiousness. There was a quality of innocence in her smiles and glances, in her gentle speeches, that could not have been counterfeited.

Lorill's tone was now tinged with more of that smugness that Leonie did not care for. *Those mountain girls are shameless, and I had of her no more than she offered.*

Which was, if Lorill's memory served, not much more than to dance with her, surrounded by her kin, and her fingertips to hold, for a few seconds, on the rare occasions when he and the girl were alone. At least Lorill had that much sense, not to treat a lady of Aldaran as a serving-maid to be tumbled.

Leonie now felt torn by conflicting emotions. Part of her reaction was envy of Mariel's freedom, she suspected. During all of her life, she had been a sheltered lowland lady. She had never gone anywhere unchaperoned and without a gaggle of other girls of her age and *their* chaperones. She had never spoken to an unmarried man alone, apart from her brother. To do as Mariel had, to speak with, even dance with, an unwed man—

It was shocking to Leonie; it made her feel both oddly titillated, as when she had heard a nasty bit of gossip, and yet a little uneasy and fearful. And if the mountain girls could do these things, should they not bear the consequences, even if it meant they were misunderstood by someone like Lorill? Wasn't that only fair and right?

She was too confused to respond properly, and said the first thing that came into her mind. *Of course, no woman of Aldaran could hope to marry into our kindred,* she replied, still trying to sort out her conflicting feelings. *You could not have a bride who acted in such a shameless manner, and it might even be that she tried to trap you, I cannot tell. You cannot afford such an entanglement as this, at any rate; so would our father and the Council say.*

No, such an alliance would never be allowed, even if this put them more at odds with the Aldarans—which it was sure to do.

I would not worry overmuch, Lorill said carelessly. *Kermiac told me to keep my distance from his sister, made some comments about my being a child, and stalked off. It may simply have been the wine talking; there was quite a celebration over these star folk and their marrying.*

Leonie relaxed; that could well be the case. Men said things when flush with drink that they would not have at any other time—and often what was spoken beneath the influence of drink was as something done beneath the four moons; ignored, if not forgotten. As long as Kermiac considered Lorill a foolish child, however insulting Lorill himself felt that to be, it would be beneath his pride to challenge Lorill over his foolishness. At any rate, it was done, and all the smiths in Zandru's forges could not mend a broken egg. Whatever would come of this, would come.

But she was now wide awake, and reminded of the reason she had begged for Lorill to go to Aldaran in the first place.

I wish I might see these folk from the moons, she said wistfully.

Lorill snorted. *I cannot believe that you could not contact them if you wished. Your* laran *is stronger than mine, after all.*

I suppose that is true, she admitted, reluctantly. And yet, she felt uneasy about trying any contact with them. She had not been able to do much in the way of *controlling* the contact she'd had with them when they were in the shelter, and she had no guarantee that she would have more control now.

Perhaps later, she said, just as reluctant to confess that to her brother. *For now you must simply be my eyes among them—and make certain that you are not entrapped or compromised by the Aldarans. Remember, it would gratify them a great deal to have one of the Hasturs in their debt—or worse, in their power. It would cause even more trouble to have one of the Hasturs in their family.*

You don't need to remind me, I am fully aware of that, he said quietly. *I am not likely to forget it at any time soon.*

Her thoughts drifted back to the strangers, since Lorill at least seemed aware that he could cause a great deal of harm if he kept playing the fool. *The star folk —can any of them read you like this?*

For some reason, most of them seem to be head-blind, Lorill replied. *One or two of the women and perhaps one of the men are not. I would guess that they have* laran *different from mine, but it is* laran *no less.*

He did not seem particularly enthusiastic about discussing the star folk; Leonie could not tell if that was because he was tired, or because she was not asking the right questions. Or, perhaps, the situation with Kermiac disturbed him more than he was willing to admit, even to her.

Still, she persisted. *How can that be?* she asked. *How can some of them have* laran, *and some not?*

Be sensible, Leonie, he said crossly. *Do all peasants have* laran? *Or even all Comyn? Why should the star folk be any different? Besides, they have contrivances to do things that the Tower-trained do with* laran, *for I have seen some of them. Perhaps they do not need it. Now, I am tired, I should like to sleep.*

And before she could question him further, the contact between them melted away, leaving her awake and frustrated by a hundred thousand unanswered questions.

Questions that Leonie knew she must indeed find out more about, on her own.

She had no opportunity to do so for some time, since now she had been entrusted with more than the ordinary duties in the Tower. Fiora had no intention of easing her work load, it seemed. But in the few times she had to stop and observe, she realized that Fiora herself was just as busy or more so. So Fiora was truly training her to take on a Keeper's responsibilities. That thought alone succeeded in driving away the thought of the strangers.

But at close of day she was once again left alone in her room, and this time she was not so exhausted that she felt the immediate need for sleep.

So, spurred by her half-forgotten curiosity, she *reached out* with her mind, to make contact with one of the star folk. She felt the need at least to find out the truth of their origin. That they had come from the moons was outrageous enough—but from the stars?

She made contact with one almost immediately; that it was one of the star folk she had no doubt, for the mind was crowded with bewildering images of machines, awash with concepts with strange names like *computer*, and *corticator; meteorology* and *astrogation*. She discovered quickly that the girl was the one Lorill had spoken of last night, the one who had been wedded that very day.

Leonie could not keep contact for long, however, for the girl's mind was not only full of those alien words and concepts, but of other things, equally alien to a virginal Keeper candidate.

Perhaps bedtime had not been a good time to try to reach for a contact . . . the girl's mind was full of her love, and of her new relationship with her now-husband; fleshly and sensual images that troubled Leonie, and frightened her a little, too.

For all her "accelerated training," Leonie was not sufficiently experienced to sift through the girl's thoughts for the ones she wanted. Too many other things kept intruding, and it soon became obvious that the girl was waiting—quite eagerly—for her husband to come to bed.

This will never do, she decided, and broke off contact. Better the mind with which she had communicated before, the one of the musical instruments. At least *that* one was more like Leonie's—she had gotten an impression of a kind of Tower or construction over which the virginal woman ruled. Something—white as bone, or ivory. There might be alien concepts there, but there would be no disturbing sexual images.

It was easier to find the woman's mind than she had thought it would be. Leonie seized the thoughts, and used them to bring her closer. And once she had made contact, she found much to challenge and interest her. For one thing, the woman was one of the strange kind; glancing in the mirror, her unknowing host had been revealed as darker of skin than any human Leonie had ever seen.

That was no great matter; Leonie had been reared on tales of the *chieri*, although she had never seen one of the creatures. Ysaye—the name came to her after a little discreet prodding—seemed human enough in her thoughts. Virginal, yes, and likely to remain so—men did not interest her, and neither did women. But to Leonie's delight, she learned that Ysaye *was* a kind of Keeper, a Keeper of knowledge, and her Tower (Ysaye thought of it as an "Ivory Tower") was one of those *machines*, one that stored and brought forth information at a speed that dazzled Leonie. In Ysaye's mind, she found out how much information that was, and the very idea left her gaping. Why, all the libraries in all the world could not hold a tenth of what this *computer* held!

Nor was that all; the computer seemed to be the key to vast stores of other things. It could even play music, as if by magic, without musicians. . . .

So great was Leonie's delight that she came very near to revealing herself to Ysaye.

The woman was selecting music for the computer to play for her to go to sleep by; curious, Leonie lingered, and listened to some of it. She was awed and thrilled by something called *Mozart*, and it seemed to her that the strangers might have a great deal to offer if they could produce music such as that.

As Ysaye relaxed, Leonie examined the random memories that came into her mind: a sun much brighter than her own, and blazing white, a single cold white moon. Shadowy trees over a lake, and the sunset flight of strange, beautiful rose-colored birds, fluttering up from the lake. . . .

The work that Ysaye was doing, the Keeper of her computer-Tower. . . .

To Leonie's surprise, she worked with men on equal terms. Well, perhaps she should not have been surprised, for that was the case in the Towers Leonie knew as well, and so would she when she was a little more experienced. And the wealth of knowledge that had been available to Ysaye was amazing, the more so when she realized how humble Ysaye's descent was. Almost poverty-stricken. And yet, she had been given all this learning, even to instruction in music, the pleasure of the rich, as Fiora had pointed out.

Discovery of Ysaye's origins in poverty destroyed any compunctions Leonie might have had about rummaging through her mind or memory. Even though Leonie had already taken the first of the *laran* oaths given to telepaths—to enter no mind unwilling, and never save to help or heal—to her way of thinking, the oath could hardly apply to one such as Ysaye. The woman was both an alien and not of Leonie's caste.

Besides, she told herself, since Ysaye knew nothing of this searching, no harm was done.

Even if she knew, she'd probably be only too willing, Leonie told herself. *How could she not be? She serves knowledge; and I am learning of her and her people.*

Learning more than enough to be certain that what Lorill had been told was true; these people were from another star. *Terrans*, they called themselves.

Ysaye was falling asleep at this point, and Leonie slipped easily and softly out of contact, resolved to throw her influence with her father and the Council in favor of these star folk. They had a great deal that was useful, and more that was simply desirable.

And Ysaye was more like to Leonie than nearly anyone else she had ever encountered. Perhaps—even more than her twin.

CHAPTER
15

Word came at last from Empire Central. The situation had been debated, and the verdict was in; Cottman IV had been given a status by the Terran Empire, and against all hope, it was one that pleased both Elizabeth and David and Captain Gibbons—though *not* Ryan Evans. Elizabeth Lorne took a certain enjoyment in Evans' sour face when the verdict was posted.

Not Closed—which meant that everyone would have had to wind up projects, collect anything of Terran origin, pack up, reenter the ship, and leave. But not Open either, which would have left the natives and the fragile world at risk of damaging exploitation. Instead, the world had been granted the seldom-used designation of *Restricted*. MacAran had expressed some surprise when he'd seen the status, and so had Britton, who had muttered something about "never in my time. . . ." In fact, it was so seldom used that Elizabeth had not been aware that it even existed, and had to look it up. What she found there made her feel like cheering.

A Restricted world was one with severe limitations on the amount of trade and contact that could be made with the natives. Terrans would be permitted to build a spaceport, *if* the natives agreed, and were prepared to deed them the land. But any and all trade agreements had to be initiated by the natives, were subject to approval by the local native government, and all movement of Terrans outside the spaceport and the Trade City that would be built around it was forbidden except by express permission of the natives.

There would be no unescorted roaming about the countryside. There would be no leeching away of native resources, like hardwood forests, or the few metals this poor planet boasted. There would be no chance for Evans to find something he could purchase cheaply here, and get its weight in credits off planet. Should he find such a thing, some of the fair profit, at least, would go to the native supplier. Granted, the native involved might be as great a schemer as Evans, but at least it would *be* a native, and some of that profit would trickle down to the planet itself in the form of taxes and outlay.

As far as Elizabeth was concerned, it was the best of all possible situations. The restrictions on *her* would be few—or even none at all. She and David were welcome everywhere in Caer Donn and Aldaran's castle and grounds; as a musician she was fairly certain she would be welcome anywhere on the planet. But people like Ryan Evans, who grated on most of the natives, would probably find themselves limited to Terran-held ground. It was extremely doubtful that Evans would find anyone willing to initiate a trade agreement that would not be challenged by the Terran Legate. Perhaps that strange friend of Kermiac's, the one who called himself Raymon Kadarin, would be willing to help him, but Evans' general contempt for most of the natives made it unlikely that anyone else would be his partisan.

Captain Gibbons and the crew, of course, would be getting a larger reward and finder's fee, since the planet could support both limited trade and a spaceport. So the Captain was happy, and Elizabeth had a notion that he might have been the one that had suggested Restricted status in the first place. Though he would have

earned more if the planet had been posted as Open,
Elizabeth knew that Captain Gibbons was too ethical
a man to put credits first.

And meanwhile, as everyone else prepared the
spaceport and settlement, Elizabeth and David could
start that family, long hoped-for, long discussed. . . .

As soon as the status was posted, she had gone to
Aurora to have her contraceptive implant removed.
When the doctor asked whether Elizabeth's plans for
children shouldn't wait until she had adjusted to her
new environment, Elizabeth had replied that she had
already waited three years, and that was long enough!

Besides, once confirmation of the status came, Captain Gibbons went at once to Kermiac and was closeted
with him for half a day, negotiating for the Empire,
while Lorill Hastur cooled his heels, all unaware of what
was transpiring inside the Castle. By the time he
learned, it was too late. Negotiations were complete,
and the new Terran spaceport and Trade City would
rise—on Aldaran lands.

Lord Aldaran gave his permission and deeded over
his property, in return for concessions to which Elizabeth paid scant attention. So far as she was concerned,
the important part was that construction began at once
on the new settlement and the spaceport. As newly-
wedded *and* starting a family (as signaled by the removal
of the implant) she and David were entitled to the first
single-family dwelling scheduled to be built. Elizabeth
had heard what had happened to others who waited
"prudently" to begin their families when a settlement
opened; they got put at the end of the line, and as other
needs of the port and port city came up, their requi-
sitions got lower and lower priority. She even knew of
couples who had been forced to spend the first year
with their new child in a single-room apartment in Mar-

ried quarters! That, she was determined, was not going to happen to her—or to David!

She and David had gone off today to see how far work was progressing on their house. Terran machines supplied the construction materials fabricated from native raw materials, and Terran plans, modified to suit the area, were being used, but it was native workers who were constructing the buildings under Terran supervision. The new settlement was rising on raw ground just outside of Caer Donn. The Terrans had set up the beginnings of a village there, with Married and Single dormitory-style housing for those who would be staying when the ship lifted, and the Lorne house was the first entirely private dwelling. They had already constructed a biology lab, a language lab and school (David Lorne's special project), and several other simple wood frame buildings, which would serve as Empire Headquarters until the usual imposing Government HQ could be constructed. That would be quarried of native stone ("We have no shortage of that," Kermiac had said humorously) once the weather improved and the quarries could be opened again.

The native builders had been supplied by Kermiac of Aldaran; they were glad of the work at this slack season of the year and seemed to have no problems working for the Terrans. The Terrans had agreed to pay them in raw metals and metal tools, and an exchange system had been worked out which seemed to please everyone.

Elizabeth nestled against David's shoulder, and sighed happily. Their new house rose a full three stories, and would easily qualify as a mansion on Terra. Here, it was simply a large house, and the sole concern would be how to heat it all. And for Terran technology, that was scarcely a problem. "We could never have had a house like this back home. Big enough for a dozen children, if we want them."

"Big enough for all your instruments, you mean," David teased. "I've seen that collection you're amassing. And I have no doubt that somewhere you'll find a native craftsman who's willing to try to copy our instruments! Next, I suppose, you'll be wanting a piano!"

She laughed at him. "Of *course* I will, if I can find someone to build it!" she retorted. "They already have harps; what's a piano, after all, but a harp in a sounding-box?"

"You're shameless," he told her.

Kermiac of Aldaran had been pleased to find this work for his people, so much so that no one, not even Elizabeth, could find any reason to think that her fellow Terrans were "exploiting" the native labor force.

"The skilled craftsmen have no work at this season," he had said. "And for the unskilled pool of workers— so many of the small farms in the hills have been run together for raising sheep in the last generation, and there is really no work for many of the farmers. They will be happy for the work, and if you will agree to teach them a trade at the same time. . . ."

It was easy enough for Captain Gibbons to fulfill that promise. By the time these buildings rose, the local labor pool would be well-skilled in everything from brickmaking to wiring. Interesting, that few natives knew anything about brickmaking, here where there were materials for both the bricks and the kilns. Perhaps it was because stone was so plentiful—but once they realized how superior bricks were to stone, the natives who had been trained to make them would find the demand high.

The natives knew what materials were available; they could advise the engineers designing the sewage system for this particular climate. The tools with which they were paid were in painfully short supply at Aldaran, and if the rest of the world was as metal-poor as this northernmost Domain, were probably in short supply everywhere else as well.

Gold seemed to be rare, but oddly enough, little valued or used except in dental work and some ornamental inlay-work. Sometimes it was alloyed with silver, the old alloy called by the Egyptians "electrum," and used in ceremonial knives and vessels. Otherwise it was deemed too soft to be of use, for it bent too easily and would not take an edge. Silver had a higher value, for it was harder, though it tarnished. Some smaller coins were made of it, and jewelry and inlay-work.

Most of the local money was made of copper, and much of the jewelry. Copper money was either made of large coins, or necklaces of carefully weighed links that could be bent open and handed over to a merchant.

Iron was in short supply, and steel nonexistent except for the weapons of Kermiac's private soldiers. What iron the common folk had seemed to be kept mostly for shoeing horses.

Simple iron and steel tools represented the real portable wealth of the natives. David had seen an old horseshoe that had been found by the roadside when they cleared land for the port, a bit of a scrap almost consumed by rust, salvaged and treated as a Terran might have treated a similar find made of platinum or some other rare and precious metal.

The village blacksmith had told them that metals were a little more plentiful in the lowlands. Elizabeth had not entirely understood how they were mined, but gathered that the process was infinitely difficult—and oddly, he had said that it was more difficult now than in his grandfather's time. Many things that the Terrans would have assumed to be made of metal were made of hardened wood, ceramic, or some alternative material.

She also gathered that things had been simpler in the longago days; that *laran*, which was what the native called telepathy, had made things possible then that were not now. She had to wonder how much of that was simply a "Once there was a Golden Age" type legend, and how much was actually based in fact.

She knew what Evans would have said: *it was all tall tales*.

David left her to contemplate their new home; he had people to process at the language lab. Not all the natives were as accommodating as Kadarin; their language had to be captured the hard way, a phrase here, a word there, and they were sometimes a little afraid of David's machines. He often had to coax them just to get a few words or a story out of them.

She wandered around the house site, staying out of the workers' way. Here would be the kitchen; there, the music room. The next room had no purpose at the moment, but it was large and would catch the sun during most of the winter; perhaps she should revive the old concept of a "solar," that room where a lady spent most of the days of the winter . . . she had a dreamy image of herself, playing a lap-harp in the sun, a sleeping baby in a cradle beside her.

The next room would be David's office; they had decided that many of the natives would find a room in a house less threatening than a lab in the HQ building. Kadarin had helped him plan it, making it look as much like a room in a moderately prosperous house in Caer Donn as possible.

As if thinking of him had called him, she raised her head to see Kadarin approaching.

"Where have you been?" she asked curiously, after greeting him.

He indicated the building which had been given over to Terran Intelligence with a wave of his hand. "An interesting proposition," he said. "Your captain wishes to know more about this world; he has offered to employ me."

She raised her eyebrows. "As an—ah—"

"As an agent," Kadarin said smoothly. "He wants to employ me to go beyond Carthon and bring him information about the Dry Towners."

She poked at a bit of stone with her toe. "Why you?" she asked.

"Easy enough," he told her. "I am one of the few people in these hills willing to go beyond the Kadarin River and into the Dry Towns to see what is happening there. He has pledged to give me instruction in your map-making techniques, so that I may map out all that territory."

"This doesn't bother you?" she asked carefully, stepping over a pile of two-by-fours.

He shrugged. "Not at all. I know a good many of the Dry Town languages. I have a few friends there, and because of my height and coloring, I can pass there as a Dry Towner. There are few enough even of your folk that may do that, but naturally, none of you are suited to the task."

She eyed him speculatively. There was little enough that she or any of the other Terrans knew about him; that he was Kermiac Aldaran's friend, and was more tolerant of Evans than any of the other natives was the beginning and the end of it. "Are you of Dry Town blood?" she asked bluntly.

He turned and gave her a speculative look. Whatever he saw there in her face must have assured him of something. He smiled, slightly.

"No," he replied. "I was—let us say, that I am a

kind of foundling, although I knew my people. They preferred that I take myself elsewhere."

His voice, so toneless, still conveyed an edge of bitterness to her. "Who are your people?" she persisted boldly, remembering some of what Ysaye had said about his appearance, and what that might imply.

He smiled at her presumption. "Well, in these hills, because of my age and my coloring, it would be obvious that certain of my people are of the old fair folk of the hills—the *chieri*—the folk Kermiac thought you had come from. So, of course, being no one's relative, I am the obvious choice for an errand to the Dry Towns. And later, perhaps, I may go down into the Domains, near Thendara, as an envoy from both Kermiac and your Captain."

Elizabeth licked her lips; that was not the plan she'd heard before the wedding. "I thought Lorill Hastur was to be sent back to the Domains for Kermiac. That is the country south of here, correct?"

"It is. But Lorill is not currently in good odor." Kadarin grinned. "Kermiac has quarreled with Lorill Hastur. He found Lorill playing at such games with his sister Mariel as would do the girl's reputation no good. Innocent enough by your standards, I expect, and to tell the truth, I think the boy meant no harm. He is, after all, very young, and he is not accustomed to the free manners of girls here in the mountains. Maidens of good family are chaperoned every moment until they are wedded, down in the Domains."

Elizabeth shook her head. "I expect we must shock you."

"Me?" Kadarin chuckled, mockingly, as if he had secrets in his own past that made the Terrans seem tame. "I don't shock easily. And Kermiac takes you as you seem, for mountain folk are used to freer ways.

But, oh, the Domains-folk would find you *most* peculiar and, frankly, quite appalling."

His smile was genuine and unstrained, and invited her to share the joke. She chuckled.

"Well, Kermiac is not giving Lorill a further chance to play with Mariel's heart; at the moment, he is nothing more than an exciting stranger, but he is taking no chances. So Lorill is going back to his homeland to-morrow, alone, and with no word from Aldaran. Kermiac will be trusting the boy with no errands. There is no point in making your envoy one who doesn't even have good sense about a young girl."

"That's probably true," Elizabeth agreed. They walked away from the house site, picking their way through piles of construction materials, some of which, like greenboard, polyester insulation, and composite board, had never before been seen on this world. Nothing could make more trouble in such a civilization as this one than trifling with their protected women. She had studied hundreds of such societies, and that constant never changed. Nor was there ever any lack of young men such as Lorill, eager to find women of whom to take advantage.

"Do you leave at once for the Dry Towns?" she asked. And as she asked that, she realized that she would miss him. He was the only one of the natives who had been truly friendly, except for Kermiac Aldaran himself. All the rest had regarded the Terrans as benefactors, but warily, and had kept their own, cautious distance.

"Not at once; I shall be here for some time yet, assisting your husband and—others," he said. "Captain Gibbons has also promised me a journey in one of your craft. He has said I may go to the—the place you have made on the moon Liriel. I wish to see your—" he hesitated, for there was no word in the native language for "weather station," and finally he had to say it in Terran Standard.

"You've really picked up our language amazingly fast," she said, complimenting him. "And more than the language, you've gotten the concepts. That's astonishing."

This was unusual for a native of a planet with such a low tech level as this; not unknown, but definitely not usual, either.

It also might mean something else, on the Terran side. She and David had already discussed the origin of the natives as part of the crew and passengers of the Lost Ship with Kadarin. He had seemed to accept it as he accepted everything else the Terrans told him, calmly, as one more fact. He had warned them, however, that his fellow natives would be very resistant to the idea.

"Is Captain Gibbons accepting the natives here as full Terrans?" she asked. "If he's offering you a job as an agent and promising trips to our off-planet installations, it seems to imply that."

Kadarin gave her a peculiar look. "I really don't know what your Captain thinks about that," he said, "I haven't asked him. It doesn't much concern me, after all."

Elizabeth didn't miss the hint, and it was fairly obvious to her, although she was too polite to mention it, that whatever Kadarin was, he was unlikely to be an ordinary Terran human.

And whatever strange blood flowed in his veins, it was evidently shared by Felicia.

Kadarin smiled, and his eyes narrowed as he seemed to follow her thoughts. Although, given that Kermiac could speak mind-to-mind with her, perhaps that was exactly what he had done.

"I sense curiosity in you," he said. "I am not wholly

sure of my heritage. I was fathered by one of the woods folk, the *chieri*, and my mother was at least half that blood. I do not know much about her, and I do not know how old I am, but it has been hinted that my mother was a friend and relative of Kermiac's grandmother. I was a kind of foundling—no, not as you are thinking, the babe in the basket—I was older than that when I was left among the humans."

He said that as if he did not consider himself to be a human—and once again, he followed her thoughts.

"I could not remain with the *chieri*, or so I was told," he said, and again, there was that trace of bitterness. "Because I was not wholly of their kind, there were traits from my human blood that were—not acceptable. A certain level of uncontrolled aggression, they said. A certain—instability, by their rather exalted standards. And I am wholly male; they find that to be rather limiting, and inclined to warp one's behavior in ways they cannot accept."

To be "wholly male" was not acceptable? What kind of creatures were these *chieri*, some kind of hermaphrodite? "They sound as if they have rather unrealistic standards," she said dryly. "But—Kermiac's *grandmother* was the friend of your mother?"

He looked as if he were in his late thirties at most, about David's age. She couldn't help but stare.

"Indeed," he replied wryly. "I am much older than I look. I almost wish now I had kept track of the years. But there is no retracing last year's snow." He sighed heavily. "And the years went by very quickly when I was young, and among the *chieri* there is no attempt to keep count of them. Then suddenly, I was—no longer wanted. I did or said something, I do not know what it was, and I was thrust back among my mother's people, and too bewildered to keep track of time."

I can imagine, Elizabeth thought, a little angrily.

Poor man; rejection and culture shock all at once. How could anyone do that to a child?

"Then the time came when my mother's people knew that I was more *chieri* than human, and they would have sent me back to the woods. There were some who wished to rid Aldaran Domain of me, and tried—" Kadarin said, half to himself, and Elizabeth wondered just *how* they had tried to get rid of the young man. "But Aldaran's father would have none of it, for Kermiac had grown fond of me, and Aldaran's mother had lost two other children and clung to Kermiac and would not risk anything that might harm him. So I was reared here, treated as alien, almost as Kermiac's pet. Subject to—trouble, if I left the area of Caer Donn. Now I feel more accepted by your people than either of my own. Can you understand that?"

Elizabeth nodded, her mouth compressed with anger at these insular people. "Quite well, actually," she said. "You were named for the river, then?"

"Oh, no, not really," Kadarin said, and grinned, but it was a grin with no humor in it. "Custom in these hills is to call anyone whose father is unknown a 'son of the river.' I simply made that custom into a kind of badge no one can ignore."

And he thinks himself more like us than like one of his own kind, Elizabeth thought. *I am not surprised. His life thus far must have been impossibly hard.*

"I think I have some notion of—of your feelings," she said aloud. "I suppose that we must seem more compatible with you than either your father or your mother's people."

And there was no question but that someone like Kadarin would be of enormous use to the Terrans. Alienated from his own folk, eager to find a home among people who did not immediately reject him— oh, yes, if Captain Gibbons had any notion of Kadarin's background, he would have been quick to see what a good agent the man could be. The intangibles—like a sense of belonging—were often vastly more important to a thinking being than the tangibles, like genetics.

"I hate to ask," she said hesitantly, "But you know by now that I'm insatiably curious. What are the woods people like? Who and what are they, really?"

He shook his head, gently mocking her curiosity. "Ah, that's a fine question. No one among the humans really knows, and I was too young to know myself when I was with them. In earlier times than this, it is said, they came often from their dwellings within the great forests. But now, since there has been much more logging in the woods near the human places, they have withdrawn into deeper forests and into the secret places of the mountains, and have less and less contact with men. I cannot remember when I last saw one whom I *knew* to be one . . . surely, it was when I was still a child." He pondered that, his face thoughtful. "Felicia is also of that blood; that much I know. Old Darriell —one of Aldaran's father's paxmen, they say—got her on one of the *chieri* women and a year later, so I remember, a babe lay at the forest's edge near his house. Darriell had no other children, and took her gladly. Felicia fit into this society in a way I cannot. I think Felicia's first child is of Aldaran blood; may even be Kermiac's own. But she is a half-blood, and I am somewhat less than that; I remain restless. She has enough human in her to be quite content here."

"She looks like you," Elizabeth observed. "I thought perhaps you were kin."

Kadarin shrugged, and laughed. "You are not the first to think so. We have known each other long enough to think each of the other as sister and brother. Neither of us, after all, has other kinfolk."

Interesting. Elizabeth had rather assumed that Felicia was Aldaran's mistress, although the woman gave herself no great airs. Lady Aldaran was not often seen; Elizabeth had the feeling that she was not of robust health. She had seen Felicia's little dark-haired daughter, with the same strange, golden eyes as her mother.

The idea of Felicia being a kind of official mistress didn't shock her; that sort of arrangement was common enough in Terra's past, when the marriage was one of dynasty and power, and the wife did not much mind where her husband took his pleasures. Even in some of the old Terran folk songs, there were instances of wife and mistress getting along—though not often. Probably because one or the other trying to kill her rival made a better song.

"So Felicia is more or less your nearest kin?" she asked.

"More or less," Kadarin replied. "She has never thought of herself as anything but of *chieri* blood though she was not raised among them. I think she is truly more human than I am. Strangeness can be very wearying. I know who and what I am, but not what my true relatives, my kinfolk, are. Of my families, I know only that they did not want me. I suppose that should be all I need to know about them." The bitterness in his voice was very strong now. "To know you would never have been born except for a Ghost Wind—"

"A Ghost Wind?" she asked, puzzled. "What have ghosts to do with anything?"

"You've mentioned that before," said Evans from behind her, startling her into jumping a little. "Something about the pollen from those flowers."

Kadarin nodded. "Yes, the ones that I showed you. *Kireseth*. The plant in bloom is called *cleindori* and releases the pollen, and the wind picks it up and carries it off—the pollen brings—a form of—of madness, perhaps. In any case, it causes strange behaviors among men and animals. Among other things, it causes both men and beasts to mate out of season, passionately, without regard for niceties such as privacy." He shrugged at Elizabeth. "The cause, you see, of both Felicia's birth and mine. The plant is made into medicines for some illnesses, by fractionating and distillation. One of the products is known and shunned as an aphrodisiac. Another is more useful, for it has a special effect upon telepaths. That drug is called *kirian*, and it is used sometimes in the Towers and in testing of the young."

Evans took in this information eagerly. "Now there's something I'd like to check out. If the stuff's a true aphrodisiac, it would be worth a fortune. There's people on Vainwal who'd kill to get their hands on it. Not just impotent old men, either. Madams, for instance . . . what a help that would be in training!"

Elizabeth's shock must have registered on her face, for he grinned at her in a particularly nasty way. "I knew there had to be something on this godforsaken cold rock that would be worth shipping out! Don't look so shattered, Lizzie, the people here have seen plenty of things they'd be willing to trade that pollen for. I bet before long they'll think of more things they'd like from the Empire."

She frowned, and he laughed at her. "Elizabeth, I thought being married to David would cure you of being such a prude! There's nothing saying we can't sell drugs to places where there's not an interdict on them!"

"No," Elizabeth protested, "Only basic ethics and morality."

"I might have expected that from you, I guess," Evans replied sarcastically. "God knows you're the biggest Puritan on the ship except her Holy Highness the Vestal Virgin Ysaye; you're two of a kind, and I'm not surprised you're friends. I'm a bit more broad-minded than that. If there are people who are willing to enjoy themselves and call it legal and moral, it's legal and moral enough for me.''

"What about addiction?" she persisted. "What about places where they use these drugs to keep people enslaved?''

"That's their problem, not mine," Evans replied carelessly. "They got themselves into trouble, that's their lookout.''

"I happen not to agree with you," Elizabeth said hotly, "And what's more, neither will Captain Gibbons.''

Ryan Evans flushed with anger. "I don't give a damn about what Gibbons' personal morals are; he has no right to impose them on me. Neither do you, and that's the *law*, Lizzie. If you people want to go live in a self-restricted colony, you've got the right, but you can't take the crew in there with you, or impose your standards on anyone else. So I export a recreational drug, and an aphrodisiac. Big deal. So someone misuses it; that's their problem, karma, or whatever you want to call it. Not mine. And I might as well be the one to get their money, since somebody will, no matter what.''

He turned and headed for the HQ Building. Elizabeth rubbed the back of her neck, and looked at Kadarin, who only shrugged, and followed him.

But what else did she expect him to do? Kadarin was Evans' friend—and this was, in the abstract, a private dispute about morals. She should not have expected Kadarin to support her, particularly not if he had already agreed to be Evans' business partner in this venture.

But she was very troubled as she went to find David.

CHAPTER 16

When Leonie came down the stairs from the relay chamber, Fiora called softly to her from the little room at the foot of the staircase.

Leonie had never been in this room before, but it was a comfortable place, well-shielded by thick stone walls, lit and warmed by a tiny fireplace. There was no window, but then, she supposed, Fiora would have little need of one. Here, she would literally be at the heart of Dalereuth Tower.

"Leonie," Fiora said, when the girl entered her room, "What would you think if I said you were to leave us here at Dalereuth?"

Leonie took the seat she indicated, on a bench softened and cushioned by a thick sheepskin. Many possibilities went through Leonie's mind, but some of them were unlikely. She did not think that she had displeased Fiora—she was not being *sent* away. She did not think that Fiora knew anything about her contact with the star woman's mind, and if she did, she could not know the details. She did not think that Fiora knew Leonie's part in having her twin sent to Aldaran in the first place. And it was not likely that Fiora had, at this late date, taken exception to Leonie's assertion that the strangers had come from off their world.

So it did not seem likely that Leonie herself was in trouble. At least, not yet.

The first question in her mind was—where was she being sent?

"Arilinn has asked for you," Fiora said, answering the thought before she could voice it. "You remember, I told you that we cannot have siblings in the same Tower? Well, events have speeded what we would have needed to do anyway. Your brother is being sent here to be trained, and so you must go elsewhere. The Keeper at Arilinn has been tracking your progress and would very much like you to go there. I have given you the early training, and you have excelled; now you are ready to go somewhere where you can be trained in the proper isolation."

Leonie blinked, surprised. Not only the *where* of where she was being sent surprised her, but the *why*. She had not thought that the Keeper of the most prominent Tower in the Domains would have been monitoring her progress, not after Fiora's repeated assertions that she was still a bare beginner in Keeper training. "The Keeper of Arilinn said that to you, and talked about me?"

"Yes," Fiora said, simply. "She has taken a great interest in you since I put you on such intensive training; she has been advising me at my request on what I should be doing with you. She told me to make things as difficult for you as I possibly could. She said that you would either break beneath the strain—or make a really remarkable Keeper. You have come very late to the training, after all, and there was some doubt that you would get this far. But you have done remarkably, and now she wants you at Arilinn."

Leonie thought that over, carefully, for all that was implied, but not stated. "The best Keepers are trained at Arilinn, are they not?"

"They are," Fiora told her, nodding. "I was there

for five years until I was needed at Dalereuth. Only the very best go to Arilinn for training."

And only the best remain there to be Keepers, she thought, but did not say. *She* knew what was in Marelie of Arilinn's mind, though she would never reveal it to Leonie, lest the girl's already formidable pride become unbearable. Marelie had it in mind to train Leonie as *her* own successor. The Keeper of Arilinn Tower; the height of any Keeper's ambition. And Leonie was certainly ambitious. Power the equivalent of any Comyn lord, and a seat in the Council in her own right would be hers if she succeeded.

"And if I wanted to stay here?" Leonie asked. "If I thought it might be better to remain with the same teacher I started with?"

Fiora considered that, her hands folded carefully in her lap. An interesting question, and one she thought almost too perceptive from the girl. She wondered if it indicated fear of the unknown, or a certain laziness, or simply a reluctance to change. Or was it just idle curiosity, to see what other options were available? "I would be the first to tell you that I am not the best teacher for you. I am not at all certain I could keep you challenged enough to bring out your full potential. But if that were what you truly wished, perhaps your brother would simply be sent to Neskaya instead."

Leonie shook her head. "No, I do want to go to Arilinn. I simply wanted to know, Fiora. I have a great deal more respect for you now than when I came here. You have been just, and more than fair, even when I was being terribly obnoxious. I did not want you to think I was ungrateful. But I—oh, I *do* want to go to Arilinn!"

Fiora raised her sightless eyes and smiled. So, it *was* only curiosity. Just as well, for the girl would have a great deal of work, pain, and sacrifice ahead of her.

"Thank you, Leonie. I think you will do very, very well at Arilinn. In fact, I think that you will make a most remarkable Keeper. How soon can you be ready to go?"

Leonie rose eagerly. She wished she were there now! "As soon as you like."

Fiora picked at the wool of the sheepskin on her own bench, feeling the curly fibers in her sensitive fingers. "You must say your last farewells to the younger girls, for after this you will not be allowed to see any friends or any kin until your training is almost complete—perhaps for years."

"I shall be sorry to say good-bye to you, Fiora," Leonie looked down at her hands.

Fiora smiled again, warmly. "Thank you for saying so, Leonie; I shall miss you as well, my dear. You have kept *me* well-challenged, I assure you! But you are too gifted—and too valuable to us in the Towers—to be spoiled by having any but the best of teachers." She stroked the folds of her robe, smoothing out imaginary wrinkles. "You will leave at daybreak under guard from Arilinn, and travel with them. The Keeper at Arilinn is Marelie—she is one of your kinswomen, even though you have never met her; she is a Hastur, too. She will personally see to your education as a Keeper. I must warn you that this training will be even harder than you think; she is by nature stricter than I, and she feels that at your age, you should already have been in isolation for at least four years. You will have a great deal to make up, and it will certainly be very hard for you. I remember my own training very vividly, and I came to it at the proper age. I cannot imagine what Marelie has in store for you."

"Truly, Fiora, it does not matter," the young girl replied, with a firmness that did not exactly match her years or her occasional impulsiveness. "This is what I have wanted for so long—I—I hardly know what to say."

Fiora smiled to herself, realizing that she had succeeded in shocking Leonie to speechlessness, perhaps for the first time in the girl's life.

Yes, well, she will be even more speechless when Marelie takes charge of her. I doubt that the Keeper of Arilinn will think well of anyone meddling with the weather without permission in her Tower. And I doubt she will be amused by it, or by Leonie's audaciousness in venturing into the overworld unwatched.

"There is no reason for you to say anything," Fiora replied firmly. "But I must warn you, too. You have been treated very gently until now, and perhaps wrongly allowed to indulge your whims. That will end. We are all under orders in this, I as much as you. The day will come when—like all Keepers—you will be responsible only to your own conscience. But for now you must do as you are told. Marelie is a hard taskmistress and will brook no disobedience. You must obey not only the spirit of what she tells you, but the letter as well. There must be no impromptu trying of your *laran* powers; no excursions into the overworld or unordered weather-working. And I doubt you could cozen her in any way." Fiora allowed a hint of a smile. "After all, since she is also a Hastur, she was probably much like you as a girl. It is most likely that she knows all your little tricks. At any rate, it is out of my hands; the Comyn Council has been informed and has backed her request with their order, which is what I would have told you if you had been reluctant to go. You would have had to petition them to be released from this—though I have little doubt you could cozen *them*. I suspect you have in the past."

"I stand ready to do as the Comyn have ordered," replied Leonie correctly, as a dutiful daughter of the

Hasturs should. "But I shall miss you!" she exclaimed. "Really, really. Fiora, I shall miss you! You have been so much kinder to me than I deserved!"

Fiora smiled at Leonie with genuine warmth.

"And I you, *domna*; try and be a credit to us there," she said. "Now, you must go. Have your attendant pack your things—you know she will not be allowed to accompany you to Arilinn? There are no human servants there, for they cannot come within the Veil—the trap-matrix that protects you at Arilinn Tower."

Fiora well remembered the Veil, and the Tower inside it. But not with trepidation; for thanks to the Veil, Arilinn Tower was the only place in all the Domains where a telepath could be completely shielded from the "noise" of outside minds without having to erect his or her own shields. No stray thoughts ever penetrated the Veil. Marelie had said that at one time, all Towers had such protections. Fiora had sometimes wished that Dalereuth did still. There was something so peaceful about a Tower containing nothing but trained, well-ordered minds.

Well, I shall never have that again, so there is no use in pining after it.

That revelation seemed a little dismaying to Leonie, and Fiora was really not too surprised. She had never in all her life had to do without a servant. "Must I dress myself, then?" she asked, then sighed, thinking of her complicated dresses, with lacing up the back, or long rows of hooks or buttons, of bodices that must be put on just *so*, and layers of petticoats; hard to reach and harder to do up properly even with a servant to help. "Ah, well, if you did, I suppose I can learn to do whatever I must." She did have simpler clothing; perhaps if she packed only that, she would not fare so badly. But she did dislike looking untidy, and until she got used to dressing herself, she probably would.

Fiora chuckled. "No, dear, you will not have to go about looking like a half-dressed hoyden. There are servants there in plenty, but they are all *kyrri*—nonhumans. They will help look after you. But the robes of a matrix worker and a Keeper are simpler than your Court dresses. I have dressed myself all my life, and there will truly be times when you will not *want* any sentient creature near you. And you will not need as much clothing as you wear now, for Arilinn Tower is as warm as a day in high summer, at all seasons."

"Oh," Leonie said, surprised once again. No one had ever told her so much about Arilinn before—probably because few she knew had ever gone there and fewer still returned willing to talk about it.

"Now listen, for I must tell you what your life at Arilinn will be like," Fiora said, and Leonie sat down again, obediently.

It would have to be different, if Fiora was warning her about it. Harder, without a doubt. But with unequaled rewards.

"First, you will not be allowed any contact with those outside the Tower," Fiora said. "I mean that, Leonie. No contact at all. Not your father, not your brother, not your dearest friend, not even though your family were dying. You are supposed to be concentrating all your mind on what is going on within the Tower, and learning that what goes on outside it need not concern you until you are a Keeper and qualified to make decisions on your own."

"I know that," Leonie replied. "You have already told me. I can bear with that."

But she thought differently, although she would not have told Fiora that openly. They could not keep her imprisoned away from Lorill in thought unless she wished it. And he would be in contact with the rest of the world. *I shall not be so isolated as Fiora thinks.*

"You need not pack all that you brought," Fiora continued. "They have your measure, and you will be wearing robes like mine for the most part. Take a dress or two, and a few keepsakes that you will be allowed to have for the first few weeks or months. Later you will have to give up even those few tokens, and all you have owned of your previous life will be put into storage. It is part of the process of detachment."

"Detachment?" Leonie asked curiously. "What is that? You have never told me of anything like that."

"A Keeper must have no attachments to anything but her work and those she works with," Fiora replied calmly. "So you must give up those things to which you have become attached. First, your kin and friends, then your possessions. This is so that you will realize that possessions mean nothing, and the only *true* kin you have are those who work with you in the Tower. Your loyalty must first be to them, then to the Domains as a whole, and only then to your kinfolk. Even your twin—you may be permitted to see him no more than once a year, and even then, it will be a full year once you arrive at Arilinn before that first visit."

Leonie considered that, and Fiora smiled a little sadly; Leonie would not be easy to teach—but, oh, how rewarding the girl would be, a credit to her teachers.

Still, she posed a problem far beyond Fiora's own skill. Fiora was no novice as a teacher, and her skill was considerable, but Leonie was more than she could handle.

Not more than Marelie could deal with, however. Fiora had no doubt that the formidable Keeper of Arilinn could make a Keeper of a catman if she chose. *So*, Fiora thought, *like it or not, she will learn.*

"What of my brother?" Leonie asked. "Why is he coming here?"

The last that Leonie had heard, Lorill was still at

Caer Donn. He'd said nothing of coming home. How would she know what was happening with the star folk if he was at Dalereuth.

"Your father suggested that he needed more training," Fiora replied delicately. "He requires more seasoning before he takes on any more errands for the Council."

What the older Hastur had told her in dismay was that his "young whelp" had compromised himself with Kermiac Lord Aldaran's own sister.

Lord Stefan Hastur had been angry, as much with himself as his son. That much had been clear to Fiora.

"He needs to learn that every female that looks at him is not flirting with him. He needs to see that women are not to be treated as playthings. I think being under the discipline of a woman while he masters his *laran* will teach him that."

There had been some doubt in Hastur's mind whether his son had misused his *laran*, consciously or unconsciously, in bending the Aldaran girl to incline toward him. That was certainly possible; while Lorill did not have nearly the power his twin sister had, what he did have was more than enough to content any Comyn father.

That must be trained, and quickly, before misuse became habitual.

"Your father also said, and I agree, that Lorill needs to learn the full extent of his own *laran*." At Leonie's brief surge, quickly covered, of skepticism, Fiora continued, "I know he does not appear to have nearly as much as you do, Leonie, but he has more than enough to qualify as your father's Heir, and more than many young Comyn. After all, your powers are formidable enough for three; anyone's compared to yours would appear to be slight."

Leonie pondered that as well, and realized that it

was entirely true. Lorill *had* reached her all the way from Aldaran, and had wakened her from a sound sleep, too. So he could not be all that weak.

"I am glad to see that he is receiving training at last, then," she replied. "Will he be here long?"

"Not long; probably no more than two or three tendays," Fiora replied. "After all, he will soon have to take his place in the Cadet Guards at Thendara. He will probably have as little time to contact you when he's there as you will have to reach him when you're at Arilinn."

"So we are both bowing to duty." Leonie replied, and stood. "I must get to mine, then, if I am to leave in the morning. Thank you again, Fiora!"

This is good, Leonie told herself, as she took her leave of the Keeper and went to pack her things. *Lorill will still be in the thick of things, and I shall know what is going on. No matter what. For I do not think that even the Keeper of Arilinn Tower can keep me apart from my twin brother mind-to-mind if that is what we truly wish.*

Fiora smiled as Leonie's steps retreated. She had not yet met the formidable Marelie; and Fiora had not lied when she said that she thought Marelie would be more than a match for Leonie's pranks.

But the only way that child will learn is by hard experience, she thought. *Well, she will have that—and more than she wants of it, before Marelie is done with her.*

CHAPTER 17

*B*ring together two Vegans, and they start a religion. *Bring together two Deltans, and they form a political party. Bring together two Terrans, and they build a town.*

That was the saying, anyway, and in Elizabeth's experience, it was probably true. There was something about Terrans—or at least those in the Service—that seemed to make them eager to put their signature on a new world, to make a little piece of Terra in the midst of whatever strangeness might be.

As if we were territorial animals, and we were marking our territory with a town instead of scent, Elizabeth thought, amused. And this particular city had gone up in record time, just over a month.

In the center of the complex stood the Terran Headquarters, very similar to the Terran Headquarters of any other spaceport in the galaxy. Even the lighting inside the complex was the same; mounted on the highest point of all the Empire buildings and on stanchions and poles overhead were the familiar yellow lights of Terra. Wherever Terrans went in the galaxy, they would find familiar working conditions. Too many psychological problems had been linked to the unfamiliar, sometimes uncomfortable, light of other suns. And indeed, tempers did start to ease a bit, the day those lights were turned on. One of the crew had told Elizabeth that it was nice to see faces that didn't look as if they were flushed or bathed in blood.

Right now there was one difference between what had been built here and the usual HQ buildings. These were wood, not stone; that would have to wait until materials were available for the permanent replacements. Stone was in the process of being quarried and bricks being made for the more substantial buildings that would replace the temporary wooden structures as soon as possible. Work on the spaceport, however, had not gone according to plan.

Usually the Terrans were able to hire local skilled workers to build whatever was the planetary equivalent of good roads, and use them to construct the first landing fields for the spaceport. The first ships in didn't require much more than their own did, after all; a flat, stable place to land, one able to take the heavy weight of a ship, and a good, secure refueling depot. Even Bronze Age cultures had sufficient road-building capability; the Romans and ancient Chinese had created perfectly good roads, and could, if given the proper design and instruction, have laid out a serviceable spaceport. But here on Darkover, the spaceport engineer had hit an unexpected snag.

The inhabitants of Cottman IV—now dubbed "Darkover," the best approximation for the name the natives had for their world—did not construct very good roads. In point of fact, they didn't really construct roads at all, for the most part. Roads seemed to just happen. Someone needed to go somewhere, and they followed game trails or cut across country to get there. If enough people followed the same track to the same place, it became a road as their horses and *chervines* and feet beat down the vegetation. And if someone truly needed to get across an obstacle like a stream or a ravine, he might throw up a rough bridge, or create a ford, or even a ferry.

But there was no earth-moving equipment at all, not even the concept of it. No rock-crushing equipment. No paving equipment. No "construction" equipment of any kind. No skilled workers used to that kind of work and readily trainable.

So, the first requisition from the new settlement had gone out asking, not for specialists and their equipment, and a Trade delegation, but for heavy machinery and the personnel to run it. Meanwhile, the spaceport engineer was making do with a pool of completely unskilled labor, former farmers who at least knew how to level land, and whatever machinery could be jury-rigged to clear and flatten the first landing field. The engineer was beside himself; he was having to instruct everyone in everything.

The Captain had appointed himself the default supervisor of the project, since he was the closest to being qualified for the job.

It put him in a very odd position: it was Empire policy to hire local workers for this sort of thing; it helped to ease the transition period and made for good relations with the locals. Local labor could assume that, rather than taking jobs from the people, the Empire would be providing them. And indeed, they had been able to hire as many Darkovans as had presented themselves for unskilled and semi-skilled labor. But there was no skilled labor pool here; there was no labor pool of those with any experience with even the most primitive machinery. For once, on a world with Iron Age culture, the Terrans were going to have to import such laborers, and the Captain found himself sending urgent communiqués on a daily basis justifying this departure from Standard Operating Procedures.

He had begun consulting David for more creative

ways of wording these missives, hoping to make them sound more urgent.

"Who would have thought that there would be a planet with Iron Age culture that didn't have *some* kind of heavy dirt-moving equipment?" he asked rhetorically. "Even the Romans had horse-drawn dredges and scrapers!"

"Be fair," David admonished. "The surface and climate are such here that almost any heavy machinery would be land-destroying, anti-ecological. It's hard to believe how fragile the ecology here is; they're one thin root layer away from losing whole mountainsides to mud slides every year. That's one reason why a lot of this land has been given over to sheep farming, and the shepherds watch how closely their pastures have been grazed over." He looked out the window of the Captain's office, and thought about how quick the locals had been to transplant turf and seedlings to the raw earth of the complex, once all the buildings were in place. It wasn't anything that the Terrans had even thought of, but as soon as the barriers were down, the men who had been building each structure vanished, then returned with chunks of sod and seedlings from Aldaran's greenhouse, swarming the place, and leaving greenery behind them. "Think about it, Captain; under circumstances like that, heavy machinery, even horse-powered, would be superfluous and even dangerous. So they never even thought of trying to use it."

"But the castle—" Captain Gibbons protested. "Surely there was some use for equipment like that in building Aldaran's fortress! And that isn't the only large-scale building here."

"Lots of men with picks and shovels, lots of women and children with baskets to carry off the unwanted earth to some of their terrace-gardens," David replied calmly. "That process eliminates a lot of damage to the environment, and makes for less loss to erosion. Have you seen how they're insisting that the spaceport engineer work in sections no bigger than the castle, and pave each one before he goes on to the next one? Same thing, same thinking."

The Captain grimaced and shuffled some of the papers on his desk. "That's another thing that bothers me; people just don't think that way. No population *starts off* with that kind of ecological and planetary consciousness."

David shook his head ruefully. "Captain, you are indulging in faulty logic. These people obviously *have* arrived at something like that kind of consciousness, so it doesn't make sense to say that no one does."

"But where did they get it?" Gibbons asked in frustration. "That's what I'm asking."

David laughed, and made a note on one of the Captain's draft communiqués. "I hope you weren't asking me that, because I don't have any answers," he said. "No more of an idea, in fact, than you do."

Captain Gibbons sighed. "Pity. I'd hoped that wife of yours had dug something up in her folk songs, or you had, in talking to these people. I suppose I'll have to add it to the list of things our sociologists are supposed to be looking up."

"In their copious spare time," David added.

The Captain only grunted, and went back to formulating a plea for ecologically-sound bulldozers and environmentally-correct backhoes.

There was another "city" growing up at Caer Donn; this one like a ring around the compact center of the Terran Zone, outside the fences of the Enclave, but also outside the old village of Caer Donn itself. It was growing just as rapidly as the Trade City, and it was no different from any other "city" of its type from one end

of the Galaxy to the other. There was a universal name
for this kind of settlement; the Native Quarter.

Like the other "cities" of its kind, the Native
Quarter was devoted to those who provided services
for the Terran newcomers.

These so-named Native Quarters, no matter where
in the Galaxy they were located, tended to be very much
alike. First to move in were those who had been hired
to build the spaceport and the buildings of the Zone.
These were workers and artisans of all kinds; displaced
men from Aldaran's lands who were being trained in
construction and the use of heavy machinery. Their
quarters, spartan by most standards, were constructed
even before the Married and Unmarried Personnel
quarters. The Terrans could and did live in the ship;
these men had nowhere else to go, for there were not
enough beds in the village for all of them.

David glanced through the fence at the buildings of
the Native Quarter, and noted that one had just
sprouted a sign that had not been there this morning.
A tavern? It seemed likely.

And where there are taverns and men, David
thought, a little sadly, *the brothels will not be far behind*.

It was only a matter of time. And only a matter of
time before the Terrans—like the few construction
workers—were also using those native "facilities."

Those half-dozen Terran experts in construction
were quartered with the other Terrans, inside the fences
of the Enclave, but David had no doubt that they already knew about the tavern. They might even be inside
it right now.

Given Captain Gibbons' reactions this afternoon,
David thought it might be a good idea to stop at the
HQ building before going home.

Home . . . that had a good sound. Their house was
finished now, although half the rooms were unfur-

nished. It was the first time in five years—three on the
ship, two in training—that David had anything he could
think of as a home.

Ysaye, as he had expected, was with her computer.
She had supervised the setting-up and initial configuring
of the HQ computer; David rather hoped he could
somehow convince her to stay when the ship lifted.
Elizabeth had few enough friends, and it would hurt
her to lose Ysaye. The bond between them had only
strengthened in the face of the steadfast refusal of some
of the Terrans to believe that Elizabeth could speak
telepathically with the natives.

The black woman looked up at his footstep, and
smiled. "Do you need to get into the computer,
David?" she asked.

"I'd like to have it run a cross-reference on—ah—
'ecologically sound principles' and local mythology,"
he said. "I know that's vague, but—"

"But I can phrase it in a way the computer will
understand," Ysaye replied. "Don't get up your hopes,
though; it probably won't come up with much. We don't
have that much data on the locals yet."

"What are you doing here at this hour?" he asked
curiously, watching as she rephrased his question
and loaded it into the statistical/sociological cross-
referencing program.

"Oh—I thought something was likely to happen,
and I was trying some rough cross-references myself,"
she replied vaguely.

"I suppose the computer told you that something
was going to happen," David chuckled, leaning back
as Ysaye ordered the system to run. "Or did you have
another one of your premonitions?"

"Hmm. That would be telling." She glanced up at
him from the corner of her eye.

But that stray thought triggered another question

he had about Ysaye. "You *do* talk to the computer, though, don't you?" he persisted.

"What, as in having a conversation with it?" She frowned, but whether at his question, or at a thought of her own, he couldn't tell. "Well—I talk *at* it. I suppose that might sound as if I were talking to it. It's mostly verbalizing thoughts out loud; I suppose it might sound like a conversation to an innocent bystander."

"I thought once I was having a kind of conversation with it," he offered. "It was a very strange experience."

"Or one of the techs had programmed it to play Socrates with you, and ask you leading questions based on keywords," she pointed out dryly. "That was being done back in the twentieth century. But if you told it something like, 'Einstein says everything is relative,' it would say something like, 'So tell me more about your relative Mr. Einstein.' It was the imitation of intelligence, not intelligence itself."

"We still haven't cracked that barrier of artificial intelligence," David observed. "I can't remember the last time anyone really tried for AI."

Ysaye sat back in her chair and looked thoughtful. "That's true; it's been a dead issue for a long time. But I wonder, sometimes, if AI hasn't been developing under our noses. We can store so much information now—and the computers can process it so fast. Really, the computer *is* an intelligence of a sort now."

"So if it ever became self-aware, it should theoretically be capable of communicating with another intelligence?" David asked. "Well, assuming that the other intelligence can make contact with it—perhaps through a terminal."

"True, and there is no way of telling right now that they don't," Ysaye admitted. "Since we have them programmed not to respond except to a question, we have no way of knowing. Unless we could read its mind."

David raised an eyebrow. "Have you ever tried that? I know you tested positive for psi, just as Elizabeth and I did—and I have to tell you, since we got down here, I'm inclined to trust telepathy as often as real speech. Maybe more. . . ."

Ysaye let out a breath she had been holding in a sigh. "I thought maybe it was only me. I thought—I don't know what I thought. I didn't tell the Captain, I didn't tell anyone. I didn't want people to think I was crazy. But—I didn't bother with the corticator. I didn't have to. Why bother, when I could talk to Lorill Hastur and Kermiac Aldaran and Felicia without giving myself a headache and enduring the machine?"

David nodded slowly. "Elizabeth said something similar; I'm not that—adept. I learned the languages the hard way; I mostly get only a vague sense of what's being said. Elizabeth says that she has had the same kind of contact with Lord Kermiac, with Felicia, and with Raymon Kadarin."

"I can touch Kadarin sometimes," Ysaye replied hesitantly. "But I keep away from him."

David was surprised; Kadarin had never been anything other than cordial with him. "You don't like him?"

Ysaye hesitated again. "That's not entirely true," she said carefully, after a moment. "I don't dislike him. What's there to dislike? He's very amiable. He's never said or done anything out of line. But I'm a little afraid of him. I don't have the feeling that he's a good man, if that makes any sense."

David had felt himself becoming more and more closely attuned to Ysaye as they talked, and now he sensed what Ysaye would not say aloud—that for most of her life she'd had a sixth sense about some men, those who would seek her out as an exotic. And he thought that she had sensed something of that sort of behavior in Kadarin. And as if she were uncomfortable even with thinking about him, she changed the subject.

"Have you seen Felicia's baby?" she asked abruptly.

The baby had been the source of quiet speculation ever since it had been born a week ago. No one, to David's knowledge, had seen it yet.

"I haven't," he replied. Then, curiously, "It *is* Aldaran's child, isn't it? I gathered that happens often enough here—is she some kind of secondary wife or something? No one seems to be making much of a fuss over it, except that it seems to be a good thing that the baby was born healthy."

"I can tell you that Felicia and Aldaran aren't married in any form at all," Ysaye said dryly. "Apparently it isn't considered any kind of a disgrace here to be the acknowledged mistress of a prominent man. The disgrace comes only if no man can own to being the father of a child."

There was more underlying Ysaye's words; again, David caught the sense of what she didn't say. That she thought Aldaran should be ashamed of himself for being such a womanizer, rather than being proud of his conquests—and pitied Felicia, for being a kind of willing accomplice—or victim—to Kermiac's wishes.

"Maybe you hadn't heard," Ysaye continued. "It seems that we're all invited to the naming ceremony for the baby, at their Midwinter Festival—that's very nearly our Christmas Day."

"Well, is it a boy or a girl?" David asked. "Do you think they have pink gifts and blue gifts around here?"

He had meant it as a joke, to lighten Ysaye's mood, but she took it seriously. "I'm not sure, and there are some rumors that perhaps it's something else."

"Something other than a boy or a girl?" David felt his eyebrows climbing. "Hmm. Well, that *does* happen sometimes on Earth, too, but not very often. Fortunately. And it's usually correctable to a degree by surgery. Well, if we come to feel it's appropriate, we could make delicate inquiries in that direction when the time comes. Surely Aurora is qualified to do the operation. Or do you think they'd resent our intrusion? Rather hard on the child, if it's an—well, *it*."

"I don't quite know how to describe it." Ysaye said, with a puzzled frown. "There seems to be the feeling that it's another *normal* option here, and it's not considered to be all that unfortunate. They call it *emmasca*, and I gather it's both—and neither."

She had to know as well as he did what the roots of that word were, so David didn't bother to make the obvious comments.

"I gather that these *emmasca* are rather rare and they're considered fortunate. They're very long-lived, for one thing. One of their kings—a Hastur king, Lorill told me—was one. Most of them are sterile, though." She shrugged. "Lorill tried to explain something very complicated involving genetics and the *emmasca* to me, and I didn't get most of it. Apparently his family were up to their eyebrows way back, in trying to manipulate their bloodlines to fix certain traits, and *they* ended up with a fair number of *emmasca*. At any rate, Felicia's child may be *emmasca*. And I gather that *that* has something to do with Aldaran's genetic heritage, which, believe it or not, is supposed to have even stranger things in it than Felicia's does."

David shook his head. "Hard to imagine that, but with one Ship's-worth of people inbreeding for centuries, God only knows what you'd get. So if the poor little tyke is this *emmasca*, it'll also be sterile?"

"Most of them are, but not all," Ysaye replied. "I gather they won't know until the kid hits puberty, because some of them actually turn male or female then. At any rate, it will be a nice chance for a celebration

—and a priceless chance for you to make one of your precious culture tapes!"

As the conversation turned to the innocuous subject of the festival, and the gold mine of information such a festival would be, David forgot their earlier conversation.

The Midwinter Festival was held in the great hall where they had first been welcomed. What had then seemed primitive and alien now seemed familiar and, in its own way, comfortable. The Terrans had learned to adapt to the climate, and if some of them breathed a sigh of relief now and again because they had their own centrally heated quarters to return to at day's end, no one mentioned it openly.

Lord and Lady Aldaran (she heavily pregnant, and making a rare public appearance) greeted all the visitors personally and bade them welcome.

"It's like Christmas," Elizabeth said with delight. "Even to the evergreens, and the smell of something like—like gingerbread!"

"Spicebread," Lady Aldaran said, with a warm smile. She was a classic, fragile redhead, pale-skinned and painfully thin despite the pregnancy, with masses of auburn curls that had been carefully arranged in an elaborate coiffure that looked as if a breath would disarrange it. It looked too heavy for her delicate neck. "You have this festival, too?"

"Something very like it," Elizabeth replied. "To tell you the truth, every planet I've ever heard of has a midwinter festival of some sort. It seems to be human nature to want some kind of celebration when the sun is at its dimmest and the world is at its darkest and coldest. It's almost always a kind of affirmation of hope or something like that."

"And what is the occasion?" Lady Aldaran asked,

curiously. "Here it is based about the winter solstice."

"Usually it's the birthday of some god or other—" Elizabeth began, and then blushed. "I beg your pardon. I hope you don't take that as irreligious."

"Hardly," the lady smiled. "For the most part, we Comyn are not a particularly devout lot. Personally, I have as much religion as the cat. We make a point to enjoy our festivals as heartily as possible, for whatever reason we are celebrating, and even the *cristoforos* have a saying; *the workman is entitled to his wage and his holiday*."

Elizabeth chuckled. "We have a saying like that, too; *the laborer is worthy of his hire*."

David would enjoy adding this little saying to his data bank. It was interesting that there seemed to be several languages current here, although only the one continent was habitable, at least so far as the satellite photos showed. Unless there were people living somewhere under the snow, leaving no traces, this was all there was.

"We must trade proverbs later," Lady Aldaran said, with a regretful smile that told Elizabeth how much she wished she had the leisure to do so now. "But I must see to my guests. The naming ceremony will be shortly." Her expression softened. "Such a sweet child. Felicia has been very fortunate."

"We christen—name—our children immediately," Elizabeth observed. "It seems a little strange to wait so long. It's been six weeks, hasn't it?"

"We usually do not name a child until we are certain that it will live," Lady Aldaran said, with a sad look in her eyes that made Elizabeth wonder if she had buried one or more little unnamed children herself. Or was she secretly fearful that her own child would not live so long? "This one seems healthy enough, though; generally if a child lives to this age, it lives at least to the

onset of *laran*. This one is likely to do well, by everything we can judge. And such a little dear, never crying
for more than a moment."

It seemed strange to Elizabeth that Lady Aldaran
should speak in such a friendly way about the child her
husband had fathered on someone else. Stranger still
that the lady should consider her erstwhile rival as a
friend. But of course she could not say anything about
it; she made a graceful remark about how fortunate it
was that the child was thriving, and withdrew to join
Ysaye. Lady Aldaran went to welcome a newly-arriving
group of people with snow liberally decorating their
outer clothes and boots.

Elizabeth noted that these newcomers seemed to be
from another branch of the Aldaran clan; from a place
called "Scathfell." Lady Aldaran greeted them warmly
as they removed their snow-covered wraps and handed
them over to be taken away by servants.

Then, at some signal Elizabeth could not detect, the
musicians ceased playing and everyone present gathered around the mother and child.

Lord Aldaran waited until he was the focus of all
eyes, from the curious ones of the Terrans, to the ap-
proving ones of his own spouse. Then he lifted the well-
wrapped baby from Felicia's arms.

"I acknowledge this child Thyra as mine," he said,
quietly but firmly. "And I pledge to assume responsibility for its support and care until it arrives at maturity."

Then came the real surprise, at least so far as Elizabeth was concerned. Lady Aldaran took Felicia's child
in her own arms.

"I acknowledge that this child Thyra, of my dear
friend Felicia, is the true and acknowledged child of my
husband Kermiac," she said, gazing fondly down at the
child's tiny face. "And as such, I assume responsibility

for its nurture and care under its father's roof, until it shall arrive at maturity."

"Lady Aldaran is a saint," someone muttered within Elizabeth's hearing, "since she above anyone must know that an *emmasca* child may not arrive at maturity until it is thirty, or even more. The 'child' may even outlive her as a child still."

Elizabeth did her best not to show that she had overheard this, but that was a startling revelation. It reminded her of something a friend of her mother's, a great bird lover, had once said; *Never buy a parrot unless you have someone to will him to.* Would Lady Aldaran have to "will" the care of this child to her own offspring?

But Lady Aldaran was continuing, after laying the child again in its mother's arms. "I, Margali of Aldaran, in acknowledgement of this, present Felicia with this token of my affection."

She reached out and placed a beautiful necklace of silver and the gems called "firestones" around Felicia's throat. There was some generalized clapping, during which the baby began to cry. Felicia opened her dress, with complete unselfconsciousness, and laid the child to her breast.

The baby began to suckle greedily, making little grunting noises like a happy piglet, and everyone began laughing and talking.

Elizabeth could not take her eyes off the perfect little thing, like a pink and white doll. She watched the little mite nurse with mingled wonder and pleasure. Next Midwinter *she* might have a child of her own— hers and David's. It would be greeted with no such ritual as this, but it would be born under this strange sun, and it would be no less a native of this world than Felicia's child.

She might name it, if it were a son, after the Captain. . . .

She drifted off into reverie; Zeb Scott came and sat by Felicia, talking to her softly.

"Oh, dear," Ysaye said in her ear, waking her out of her daydreams. "This looks like more than just a friendly chat."

Elizabeth took better note of the way Zeb was leaning toward Felicia and nodded, a little troubled. "This could be a complication . . . I think you're right, Ysaye. If Zeb isn't already involved with Felicia, it looks to me as if he could become very serious, in a very short time. If he does—it could be very good for Felicia, Zeb Scott is a wonderful man. But it could mean some danger to our good relationship with Lord Aldaran."

Ysaye seemed surprised. "How could it? Felicia isn't married to Lord Aldaran—or to anyone else as far as I know. Margali is due soon, and it seems to me that Felicia could be an embarrassment, then. Won't he be expected to pay more attention to his wife and his legitimate child? Wouldn't Margali and her relatives expect that much? I should think he'd be glad to have someone else take her—ah—off his hands."

"I don't think so," Elizabeth said warningly. "It doesn't seem to work that way here. Customs are awfully different."

Ysaye looked skeptical. "I don't know if human nature is likely to change that much," she said. "After all, if there's one thing we can take for granted in human cultures, it's that there is a certain degree of possessiveness about 'my man' and 'my woman.' And relatives take a dim view of a relationship that might threaten the 'true wife.' Somehow, I don't think this world is all that different."

"Probably not," said a familiar, but unwelcome voice. "I've never seen a lot of difference in human nature across cultures. And isn't it a shame, since human nature isn't all that admirable."

Even at a festival, Ryan Evans couldn't keep his sarcastic and caustic wit from coloring everything he came into contact with. Invited or not.

Elizabeth turned and put on a mask of politeness. "Why, Ryan," she said coolly. "I didn't know you were back from—what was it—the Dry Towns?"

"*Dry* Towns is right," Evans answered. "Nothing but desert, and a more inhospitable set of settlements I hope never to see. Rotten climate, barbarians one step up from cave-dwelling—it's enough to make me lose what little faith in human nature I have."

David showed up in time to rescue her from having to make a polite response. "Well, the fact that they'd settle in such a place at all says something for human nature," David responded cheerfully. "At least about undiscouragable optimism."

"Optimism." Evans snorted. "Well, you can have them, optimism and all. I must say though, Kadarin seems to have been born to be an agent. He speaks several of the languages, and he already knew a lot of the people, so at least they didn't murder us on sight. Most of them even took him for one of their own kind."

David lit up. "I wanted to talk with you about that; do you have some tapes of their languages?"

"Some," Evans replied. "Probably not anywhere near as much as you and your computers want. They were damned hard to get—you wouldn't believe how difficult it was to get people to talk to us. Curiosity seems to be at a low ebb out there; they're the most insular lot I've ever seen."

David didn't seem to be surprised. "I suppose that's to be expected of a desert culture," he pointed out. "Just surviving takes almost all of your resources, and a stranger may represent a real threat. Certainly a stranger is a drain on *your* resources, and hospitality could be deadly to you. Clannishness is only a part of it."

"Good point," said the Captain, joining them. "Glad to see you back, Evans; I'll want to see your report first thing tomorrow."

"I can give you the gist of it in a few words," Evans replied. "Very damn few. I gather that trade with the Dry Towns from the rest of the world is pretty minimal. Mostly what comes out is a few plants and botanicals and mostly medicinal. Precious metals, nil; *ordinary* metals, nil. Same as the rest of the planet, I gather. In fact, sir, damn-all to report. I could just as well have stayed here in—hmm, not exactly comfort, but I could have spared myself a few saddle-sores."

The Captain grunted, clearly disappointed. "Nothing for the Empire, then?"

"Apart as I said, from some possible medicinal plants, not a thing. Unless you're interested in exotic drugs." Evans grinned. The Captain frowned.

"You know how I feel about that. Drugs should stay where they originated."

The laws governing the import and export of potentially addictive substances were varied. In general, they were interdicted, with the laws of individual governments taking precedence within their sovereign space. For the most part, they were unbelievably harsh. Every local government had the right to prosecute the shipper who brought interdicted drugs into their sovereign space, which made it an extremely expensive proposition for anyone smuggling them in. Not only could the smuggler himself be punished, but the ship owner as well—often by the loss of the ship itself.

So within sovereign space, it was possible for extreme restriction, but outside it was another story. Some people would have liked to outlaw every single mood-altering substance no matter how mild, right down to caffeine and chocolate, but the difficulties of enforcing that were overwhelming, especially in the face of places like Keef and Vainwal, which had no laws to speak of on that subject.

Empire policy was that laws in interstellar space should be minimally restrictive; prohibitions were kept to an absolute minimum and were narrowly and harshly enforced. The few prohibited drugs were limited to those on the harmfulness index that were several degrees above mild feelings of well-being.

The Captain had his own feeling about how much harm that kind of minimal "supervision" did; Elizabeth and Ysaye shared his feelings. Evans, however, obviously didn't.

He was an open proponent of the kind of *laissez-faire* attitude found on Keef and Vainwal. True, these planets attracted a certain kind of tourist. True, those tourists were warned and informed of the risks. And for the most part—at least, officially—there was no one forcing those drugs into anyone's unwilling body. There were rumors, of course, of addicts made against their will, and forced to pay with their bodies for the feeding of their habits, but those were only rumors, and no one had ever been able to prove the truth of them. That was Evans' justification for his attitude. He was scornful of what he called "authoritarianism" and "paternalism." He claimed that there was no harm being done; whatever was going on, he said, was limited to consenting residents and visitors, and would not go off-planet.

For once, however, Evans didn't seem prepared to make his usual speech. "I know the rules," he replied, surprising Elizabeth, "And there's no point in debating theories. You know how I feel; the less control a government has over us, the better."

"Well, I don't agree with you any more than I ever did," the Captain replied. "We can debate principles some other time."

"Fine," Elizabeth said wearily, and turned away. Ryan was David's friend, and there were times that she liked him, too—but there were times when she disliked everything he stood for. This was supposed to be a celebration, and she really didn't want to get into an argument that could only provoke bad feeling. But at the same time, she did have some very strong feelings on the subject!

She had never, in her admittedly short life, ever seen a case where drugs did "no" harm. Even alcohol destroyed brain cells; even something as relatively harmless as chocolate and caffeine induced cravings which, if satisfied, might lead to harm in some individuals. If an informed and otherwise well-adjusted individual chose to use them, that was one thing—but to unleash a flood of exotic drugs on people who had probably never had the chance to think the problem such things posed all the way through—*that* could not and should not be permitted.

The havoc that alcohol had wrought in the Native American and Polynesian cultures on Terra was only one example of what could happen. Evans' waving of the "freedom flag" was superficially very attractive to people who didn't know any better. That he was highly intelligent only made his position more attractive to people who didn't realize he did not have the scruples or ethics to match it.

People with that high an intellect always ought to be targeted for serious ethics tutoring in early childhood, she thought, stifling a sigh.

But nothing could be done about Ryan Evans, certainly not at this late a date. He was unlikely to experience a crisis of conscience at his age.

The baby slept in Felicia's arms; the musicians began a dancing tune, and the natives began to gather for a circle dance. A few of the more adventurous Terrans, Zeb Scott included, allowed themselves to be persuaded into the circle. Elizabeth, who did not care for dancing, drifted over to the musicians. She passed by a table laden with refreshments and took a glass of the white mountain wine. The first sip was pleasant, but it had a strange aftertaste of bitterness.

Strangely like her conversation with Evans. . . .

CHAPTER
18

"Well?" asked Jessica Duval, a lieutenant with the ship's crew. Her catlike face was alive with curiosity. "Is it or isn't it?"

Ysaye made a face. She had never much cared for Jessica's insatiable appetite for gossip, and now that interest seemed even more distasteful. "I don't know, and I don't particularly care," she said, hoping that Jessica would stick a sock on her nosiness.

"But Ryan Evans says that the baby is some kind of mutant," Jessica persisted. "He told Ensign Rogers when he dropped his things off before he came to the festival, he said Kadarin told him. It's all over the ship."

"I heard the same thing, and I didn't bother to investigate the claims," Ysaye said dryly, hoping that no one standing nearby among the natives was either fluent in Terran Standard or adept at telepathy. "Just because *Rogers says that Evans says that Kadarin says*, that doesn't mean it's the truth or even close. I wasn't really interested in finding out the details. If it doesn't matter to these people, it shouldn't matter to us. Some things ought to be left in a little obscurity." She leveled what she hoped was a quelling look at Jessica, who shrugged, but didn't look the least intimidated or ashamed of herself.

"That's hardly an attitude worthy of a scientist,"

David teased. "Where would a scientist be if he didn't ask the questions that no one else would ask?"

Ysaye frowned at him; making it as clear as she could that she didn't consider this a subject for teasing. "There are a few things I wouldn't do even in the name of science, and violating someone's privacy is one of them. If you really want to know, you can either ask Felicia herself, or ask the child when it grows up." Her frown deepened. "You just might bother to take Felicia's feelings into consideration before you do. It seems to me that her position is difficult enough, but if you want to take the chance of making her uncomfortable, that's something you'll have to live with."

"Heaven forbid," David replied, sobering. "I must admit that I'm curious, but I'm not that curious, and I wouldn't make Felicia uncomfortable for the world. She's been extraordinarily helpful any time I needed to ask her something. That would be no way to repay that graciousness."

"That's what I like about you," Ysaye said affectionately, her stiff attitude melting away with her disapproval. "You agree that there are limits to investigation in the name of science."

"Well," David replied, with an ingenuous smile, "I think that anyone—even a hard scientist—would have to admit that. Really, even though there are questions a scientist should ask when no one else will, there are ethical limits to what a scientist can do. Some of those old experiments in genetic recombination, for instance, just before we got any kind of interstellar capability, resulted in some pretty tragic and bizarre accidents."

"Wait a moment," Jessica put in, suddenly losing her air of carelessness, "You can't be doctrinaire about that! Those *accidents* were the results of bad science—people doing things they weren't qualified to do, with inadequate protections! Some of those same experiments properly performed were all that allowed us to colonize Mars—and *that* let us terraform and colonize a lot of other planets without a proper atmosphere!"

Ysaye shook her head; that was one more thing that she and Jessica would never agree on. No matter how much good had come of it—what would have happened if Terrans hadn't interfered? "I'm not so sure they should have been colonized," she said doubtfully. "Maybe if we'd let them alone, they would have evolved along their own path someday."

This was such an old argument that David didn't even bother to get involved. He knew how Ysaye felt; she had talked about it fairly often with Elizabeth. Odd that someone involved in science should so often take an anti-scientific position. Apparently though, this went back to things she had been taught as a small child—a peculiar "thou shalt not interfere with nature" doctrine. Which made no sense, since Ysaye interfered with nature every time she took an anti-allergy shot, or was given a vaccine booster. Well, no matter; this argument would come to the same end it always did. No one ever converted anyone else. Instead, he waited for a lull and asked, "So, what did you think of the ceremony, Jessica?"

She seemed relieved at the change of subject. "I liked it," she said.

The expressions of everyone else in the group showed a similar relief, and David was sorry he hadn't intervened sooner. "Really, rather touching. It's too bad that people aren't that civilized about similar situations in our own culture—there wouldn't be any paternity suits or messy litigation. It didn't seem alien at all; it's the kind of thing you'd expect from Terrans if we were a little more worried about the welfare of our children than of our own pride and convenience."

"This place doesn't seem all that alien, really,"

someone else agreed. "Between this festival and the naming, this could have been a combined Christmas party and christening."

David laughed. "Well, Darkover isn't alien—at least the customs shouldn't be. These people are mostly of Terran stock, and Northern European at that."

Jessica's face turned thoughtful. "Does that make you feel too out-of-place, Ysaye?" she asked. "It never occurred to me that you might not find all this as familiar as some of the rest of us do. If anyone would feel alien here, I should think you would."

"Oddly enough, no," Ysaye replied, "Not really. I was brought up on the North American continent, in the New York-Baltimore megaplex, and it isn't as if I were from—oh—Nigeria. And after all, when it really comes down to it all, I'm a human, and so are they. We have a great deal more in common than we have of differences that make us alien."

She thought of her contacts, mind-to-mind, with Lorill Hastur and Kermiac Aldaran; their thoughts had hardly been those of aliens. Lorill, in fact, had been more courteous than many of her own shipmates, taking care that he didn't trouble or disturb her.

But what of that other, nebulous contact she had felt—the one she had sensed hovering in the back of her thoughts when she played her synthesized flute, or searched the archives for music for Elizabeth? It was as if there were someone else out there—one with fewer scruples than Lorill—trying to "eavesdrop" on her thoughts. She hadn't been *certain* of what she had sensed, so she hadn't said or done anything about it. But if there were folk here who were telepathic, did it follow that all of them could be counted upon to play by the rules?

Well, even if the "presence" hadn't been anything more than her overactive imagination, it hadn't felt particularly alien—at least, no more so than some of her own crewmates. The few clues she had picked up indicated someone very—apart. Not reclusive, exactly, but someone who felt herself distanced from others. Not entirely unlike the way she often felt, in fact. In some ways, as she had just demonstrated with Jessica, Ysaye often found her own shipmates more alien than any native of Darkover.

David interrupted her thoughts. "Have you seen Kadarin? I assume he must be back from the Dry Towns. Evans showed up just before the ceremony, and Jessica said Kadarin arrived back an hour or so before that."

"No," she replied, indifferently. Kadarin's presence or absence was not something that mattered much to her, when it all came down to it. "Should I have?"

David was about to reply, when there was a stir at the entrance to the hall. There was a certain commotion, then a silence dropped over that end of the room, a silence that seemed somewhat ominous. Ysaye sensed the sudden tenseness, and turned—

So did everyone else in the room. The dancers stopped in the middle of the set; the music died in a flurry of confused notes.

Ysaye, along with everyone else in the room, craned her neck to see what the cause of the disturbance could be. The crowd of dancers suddenly parted, noiselessly, making a corridor of silent, staring onlookers from the door to the dais where Lord and Lady Aldaran and Felicia still sat. And to her surprise, Lorill Hastur, with a small entourage, made his way through the dancers, heading for Kermiac Aldaran and his Lady.

Never before had Ysaye been so struck by an illustration of the phrase "a deafening silence."

The only sound was that of footsteps on the wooden floor; the boots of Lorill and his men.

On either side of the Hastur party was a crowd of folk with closed or hostile expressions. Lorill did not pretend not to notice, but Ysaye saw that his own expression was determined and earnest. He did not strike her as a young man about to make trouble.

She only hoped that trouble was not about to happen anyway, despite his good intentions.

Kermiac stood straight and cold; his face so set that it could have been carved in stone. Lady Aldaran was absolutely rigid, and even Felicia seemed frozen in place. And it was not her imagination; many of the men had placed their hands on the hilts of daggers that no longer seemed like such amusing ornaments. Ysaye could not for a moment imagine what was about to happen, but the tension in the room did not bode well for Lorill Hastur.

The young man stopped a few paces away from Lord Aldaran, and bowed stiffly. Kermiac returned his bow with a slight nod of his own—not the full bow that Lorill had granted him. His posture challenged Lorill; saying *this is my land; these are my people. Here you are not my equal.* Lorill reddened very slightly, but did not seem daunted.

"Lord Aldaran," said the Hastur heir, carefully and clearly, "I have come to apologize. I have been instructed by my father and the Keeper of Dalereuth Tower to tell you that I am an exceedingly foolish young man, who overstepped the bounds of proper guest-behavior and compounded his error by speaking and acting as only a fool would."

Kermiac's posture softened, just a bit. "Oh?" he replied. "And what do *you* say of that, Lorill Hastur?"

"That my father was being generous—sir," Lorill replied forthrightly. "I was not only foolish, I was exceedingly arrogant and stupid. I pledge to you that I meant no harm to your sister, but since I have never been outside of Domain lands, I—mistook what is custom among your people for what is considered boldness among mine. Your lady sister," he bowed gracefully in Mariel's direction," was simply being kind to a stranger. I am sorry if my reaction led her to expect more of me. The Keeper of Dalereuth made the error of my assumptions very clear to me, in—several ways. All of them quite eloquent."

By Lorill's reddening ears and the careful phrasing he used, Ysaye guessed that he had gotten a thorough dressing-down from this "Keeper," whomever she was.

"I came to apologize personally, for it did not seem that an apology brought by a messenger would be appropriate or sufficient under the circumstances. I hope that you will accept my apologies, sir," Lorill concluded, "and that with them, you will accept my father's naming-gifts for your child, the mother, and your lady."

Three of the men with Lorill held out small colorfully wrapped packages, and Ysaye held her breath, hoping that Aldaran would not refuse them.

For a fraction of a second, he hesitated, then he nodded, and the three men placed their packages in the ladies' hands, with Felicia accepting for the baby.

"Your apologies are accepted, young Hastur," he said. "Truly, it is often said in these mountains that 'If stupidity were a crime, half the human race would be hanged at every crossroads.' And I will be the first to tell you that I have earned such a fate twenty or thirty times over in my lifetime."

"What, Kermiac?" asked an old man who stood just behind him, dryly, "Only *thirty?*"

That brought a laugh, if only a nervous one, and the tension in the atmosphere eased, then drained completely away as Kermiac joined the laughter.

Aldaran shook his head and clapped the old man on the back. "You have seen me eat the fruit of my own folly far too often for me to dispute you, old friend," he said. "Be welcome, then, Lorill Hastur. This is the season when one should forgive, or so the *cristoforos* would tell us. Let us begin our acquaintance again."

At that, the postures of everyone in the room relaxed; servants came to take the newcomers' capes, and the music and dancing resumed. Lorill spent some time speaking with Lady Aldaran and Felicia, leaving both of them smiling with comments Ysaye could not hear, then he made his way across the room to where the Terrans stood clustered by the refreshment table. He seemed very relieved to find them here, as well he might be, Ysaye supposed. They gave him a set of "neutral" acquaintances with whom he could speak without worrying about hierarchy or offense.

He greeted the Terrans, slowly and carefully, and smiled with delight when David replied in *casta*. They spoke for a moment, and Ysaye let her mind relax so that she could follow the conversation by picking up Lorill's thoughts. After a few commonplace comments about the weather between here and his home, and the difficulty of the journey, David asked how Lorill's people had taken the news of the Terrans' arrival.

"Well, I suppose you must know that your arrival has set all astir in the Domains," the young man told David. "It will be worse when spring comes, and all those remote from Thendara and out of reach of the Towers learn what has come to pass."

"I suppose it would have to," David replied. "The influx of metal tools alone has probably upset the local balance of trade—or will when spring comes and trade starts up again, and those tools end up down in your land."

"Indeed," Lorill told him, "And it is those tools and the things you gave me alone that have convinced some of the members of the Comyn Council that you are not some kind of fable, something created by Lord Aldaran to confound us—or creatures from beyond the Wall Around the World. Some of your small gifts to me were things that only too clearly could not have come from any source on our world. Now they are arguing about further contact with you. Some say that you should not stay here—that, in fact, we should avoid you star folk at all costs. Your coming represents too much threat to our way of life.''

Ysaye nodded to herself; she could understand that. She wondered if she should tell Lorill about some of the none-too-subtle requests that Kermiac had made for weaponry. But—no, that would only increase the strain, and since the Terrans had no intention of granting any of those requests, it would make no difference anyway. The "Restricted" status of Darkover meant that there would be an Empire ship stationed at the hyperspatial exit point at all times, and any incoming ships would have to pass inspection before they were allowed to land—then pass a second inspection of cargo off-loaded. There would likely be some smuggling, but nothing larger than a hand weapon would ever get through. And how could a few hand weapons make any difference, even to a culture this primitive?

"I can see that," David replied. "But if anyone asks your opinion, you might point out that we are already here, and already an influence. They aren't going to keep the influence out; they'd be better off trying to control it in other ways. We'll cooperate if we can, but we can't cooperate if we can't participate. Try to shut us out, and you'll only end up with problems we can't help to control because you won't let us help with controlling them."

Lorill nodded as if he agreed. "That, if they ask me, is precisely what I hoped you would say. I will tell them if I get the chance. But," he shrugged, "they must have their arguments first, and dance the political dance as always before they will be ready to hear anything new. While that happens, my father thought I should come here, and mend what I inadvertently marred. You see me, David, a sadder and wiser man."

He smiled weakly. David chuckled. "You have my sympathy. I did something just about as stupid when I was your age, and my maiden aunt let me have it right between the eyes. In public. And then my *grandmother* took up where she left off."

Lorill shuddered. "I had rather face armed and enraged Dry Towners," he vowed, "than elderly ladies with sharp tongues and the right on their side. The Keeper of Dalereuth was one such as your grandmother, I imagine. I wonder I have any skin left."

Ysaye kept her mouth shut as David commiserated. Personally, she felt that whatever Lorill had endured, he'd deserved. The young man's attitude toward Kermiac's sister had been too cavalier, and he had been, she thought, quite arrogant in his assurance that there was no way that Kermiac could hold him to account for his actions. Evidently he had learned better.

After a while, the conversation turned to more neutral subjects. Lorill and David exchanged a few more pleasantries, and then the young Hastur lord turned to Ysaye, who had been feeling rather invisible. She had wondered if either Lorill or David had even remembered that she was there.

"So, lady," he asked, with a nod of his bright head, "have you learned our tongue yet?"

She shook her head. *Not very well*, she replied, in thought, since she knew that he would "hear" her.

"Ah," he said, and then continued mind-to-mind. *Shall we go a little apart then, so that people have the impression that we are speaking aloud? I sense that you are not comfortable with the notion that your fellow star folk know we can speak this way.*

"I should like to practice on you," she said openly, in fumbling and awkward Darkovan, "if you do not mind." And answered him, *That would make me feel a little better, if you would. You are right. There are those among my superiors who think that we who claim to speak this way are trying to practice some deception on them.*

Deceiving them, or yourselves? he asked wryly.

Both. Elizabeth—some folk think she is—unstable. Ysaye was unable to come up with an adequate description of the attitude of those of the crew who still thought Elizabeth's claims of telepathic contact were either the words of a fool or a charlatan. Fortunately Lorill seemed to understand.

In the country of the blind, the man who can see will be thought mad, he offered. *Come, let us go a little apart.*

Graciously, he took her arm and led her to an alcove, near enough to the musicians to be in full view of everyone—and so, by local standards, within the bounds of propriety—but shadowed enough that no one would be able to tell that their lips weren't moving. Ysaye wondered what he wanted. He had certainly been eager enough to get her to himself!

By your leave, lady, he said. *I hope you will indulge me in this, but I have been most strictly charged by my sister to ask you several hundred questions.* His expression was wry. *I have told her all I can of you star folk, and it is you by whom she is the most fascinated. My sister is very strong-willed, and even my father thinks twice before denying her!*

Ysaye chuckled. *I think most sisters are that way,* she told him. *Ask what you wish.*

After all, this could do no harm—and might do a great deal of good. If indulging Lorill's sister's questions would crack open the barriers to the rest of this planet, Ysaye would answer them until even Lorill was tired of talking.

Elizabeth had held her breath with the rest when Lorill Hastur put in his appearance, and had sighed with relief when Kermiac Aldaran accepted his gifts and his apologies. She scarcely noticed that Ryan Evans had appeared at her elbow until the man spoke up.

"Well, there's a little border war neatly averted," he said, startling her.

She jumped. "What?" she said, willing her heart down out of her throat. "What do you mean?"

Evans shrugged. "Well, the boy basically left here with a lot of bad feeling following him. He insulted Kermiac's sister, and that just isn't done here. By 'insulted,' I mean that he managed to cast aspersions on the girl's honor. Aldaran could have used his behavior as an excuse to declare war on the rest of the Domains; I gather it's been done before, more than once. This little pocket kingdom and the rest of them have some grievances of long standing, something I doubt Kermiac bothered to tell any of the rest of you. Kadarin was a lot more forthcoming—at least with me."

Elizabeth's eyes went back to Aldaran, who was talking with one of Lorrill's entourage as if there had never been anything other than cordial feelings between himself and the young Hastur. "Is that why he was hinting he'd like weapons from us?" she asked.

"Could be," Ryan replied carelessly. "He won't get them, though. I'm one of the biggest libertarians in the world, but even *I* don't believe in putting weapons of mass destruction into the hands of primitives. Anyway, that's academic; the boy made a nice apology, it's been accepted, and everything's peaches and cream again."

"One hopes so anyway," Elizabeth said, a little

doubtfully. "At least until that youngster puts his foot in his mouth again. . . ."

"He won't," Evans said positively. "I learned a few things from Kadarin out there. He couldn't exactly explain what these 'Keepers' are, but they have a lot of power. If one of them and his father put the fear of god into the kid, he's not likely to mess up again. Look, he's paying no attention to the local women at all; he's gone straight for Ysaye. Aldaran isn't going to fret about the reputation of one of *our* women, not for a minute."

"I suppose you're right," she sighed. Evans was going out of his way to be charming, she noticed; perhaps as a kind of tacit apology for his near-argument about drugs earlier.

"Oh, Kadarin taught me a fair bit about the local cultural morés around here," he said. "I'm probably better versed than most of us, now, since he made me live by them."

"Really?" That got her interest. "David and I have gotten permission for a field trip together. I'm horribly afraid that I'm going to make some kind of dreadful error."

Evans laughed, but it didn't sound like his usual sarcastic tone. "Why, Elizabeth—if I didn't know you better, I'd say that sounded like a plea for help!"

"Well," she admitted reluctantly, "it is, actually."

He seemed to think things over for a moment, then nodded. "Look, I'll tell you what—I'd rather not talk here, because you can't tell who of these natives has managed to pick up enough Terran Standard to get offended by something I say. Why don't you come meet me somewhere in about fifteen minutes? You can ask me all the questions you want then."

Elizabeth hesitated. There was something about him

that made her a little uneasy—and why couldn't this be done during working hours?

Then she chided herself. This was David's friend! There was no reason to think of him as some kind of a—a threat. And during working hours, they were both busy; this might be the only chance they'd get to discuss things uninterrupted.

"Where?" she asked.

"Oh—someplace quiet," he replied casually. "Somewhere neutral. Hmm—your house is too far away, and so is the ship. How about—how about my greenhouse? You know where it is, don't you? In the Science building? I left some experiments running— native plants I was trying to grow, and I haven't had a chance to check on them. We can talk while I look them over."

She could have chuckled with relief; obviously she had misread him. If he were intending something improper, surely the last place he'd choose for it would be his greenhouse in the lab complex!

"It sounds perfect," she said. "Thanks, Ryan. I don't know how I'll ever manage to repay you."

He grinned. "Oh, don't worry, I'll think of something you can do," he said, and turned to head for the door.

She tried to find David in the fifteen minutes Evans had stipulated, to tell him where she was going, but her husband had vanished somewhere.

Finally she ran into Jessica Duval who at least knew who he was with. "That Kadarin fellow showed up," she replied, in answer to Elizabeth's question, "And David went off with him." She wrinkled her perfect nose a little in distaste. "I can't imagine why; that man gives me the shivers."

"Well, would you tell him I've gone off to look at some of Ryan's new plants if he comes looking for me?"

she said, exasperated by David's disappearance. "Honestly, every time I want him, he's gone and wandered off and stays away for hours."

Jessica just laughed. "You knew what he was like when you married him, Liz," she replied. "Oh, I'll tell him, but you'll probably see him before I do."

"Probably," Elizabeth sighed. Well, she had tried.

No one seemed to be paying any attention to her, and it didn't look as if anyone in particular was going to miss her, so she slipped out without bothering to tell anyone else where she was going, collecting her coat from one of the servants and stepping out into the snowstorm.

Fortunately, it wasn't all that far a walk to the Science building once she got to the Caer Donn complex. And the computerized Directory at the front entrance told her exactly where Ryan Evans' labs were, even though she had never been in that part of the building before. He had a set of labs on the top floor.

The "greenhouse" was up on the roof; appropriate, she supposed, since he was trying to grow native plants. The door to the roof stood open, and when he heard her footsteps below, he called down the stairs, "Is that you?"

"Yes," she replied.

"Well, come on up! The plants I started before I left are doing just fine. I think you'll like them."

She climbed the narrow wooden staircase—more like a ladder than a stair—carefully. When she poked her head up into the greenhouse itself, she was struck by a faint, sweet perfume. She climbed all the way— up into the greenhouse and looked around curiously. Evans had enhanced the lighting and added warmth, so that it was as much like a day in summer as possible, and the plants had responded with riotous growth. "Where are you?" she called softly.

"This way," came Evans' voice, giving her direction. "At the back. Wait until you see these flowers, Liz. You won't believe they came from around here."

She pushed her way past luxuriant branches, noting as she drew near the back of the greenhouse that the faint scent grew stronger. Finally, she found Evans, bent over a growing-table with its own little clear plastic domed and hinged cover. Beneath it, she caught sight of what Evans was talking about—pots of beautifully delicate, five-petaled blue flowers.

"Oh, my," she exclaimed, coming closer and joining him. "Ryan, they're lovely! What are they called?"

"Kadarin calls them 'starflowers,' I can't remember the local name for them," Evans said, his eyes glittering as he patted the protective dome. "They require some pretty specific conditions to bloom, and I was hoping my timing was right, getting back when I did."

"I don't suppose they have a lovely scent to match, do they?" Elizabeth asked wistfully, unable to take her eyes from them. A gold pollen coated the inside of each blue bell, making them seem to glow. "I can't begin to tell you how much I miss scented flowers—roses, lilacs, hyacinth. . . ."

Evans shrugged, but his mouth twitched a little. "Kadarin said so, but you know me—I couldn't smell my upper lip. Why don't I crack the case, and let you find out for yourself?"

He broke the seals holding the dome in place, and Elizabeth leaned down to take a deep breath.

CHAPTER
19

"Ysaye," Jessica Duval interrupted, tapping her apologetically on the shoulder—fortunately, while she and Lorill were both sipping their drinks. "I hate to interrupt you, but have you seen David?"

Ysaye turned away from Lorill Hastur, and blinked. Jessica's question seemed a little odd. "No, not since just after the naming and Lord Hastur's arrival. I think he went off with Kadarin, but I don't know where. Why?"

"I'm trying to find him, and I thought you might know where he went," Jessica replied. "Well, if you see him, tell him Elizabeth went off to Ryan's greenhouse to look at some plants or something, all right? You know David; if he can't find her, he'll start worrying. I'm going back to the ship, so you'll probably see him before I do."

A thin line of cold ran down Ysaye's back, and a warning shiver of premonition crept over her. Plants? Why would Elizabeth want to look at *plants?* And why not go to look at them during the day?

There were more questions, questions she could not ask Jessica. Why would Evans want to get Elizabeth alone? There would be no one in the Science complex; everyone was here, at the party. So far as Ysaye knew, even the lowliest of techs had made arrangements to keep today and tomorrow free, either by scheduling what needed to be done so as to leave those two days free, or by having her set up the computer to monitor experiments.

Ryan Evans could not possibly have contrived a more private arrangement if he'd been the Captain. And Ysaye had a dreadful premonition of what Evans planned for that privacy.

Perhaps she was being paranoid; if so, she would apologize. But she would rather apologize than try to explain to David why his wife had been assaulted by his best friend.

"Thanks, Jessica, I'll tell him," she said absently, trying to think what, if anything, she could do immediately. If she could just get some time—Elizabeth hadn't been gone that long. Evans surely could not have gained much headway yet, and if she could interrupt him, she might be able to get to the greenhouse before anything actually happened. How could she arrange for an interruption?

Then she remembered. Evans had specifically said he hadn't given his report yet. The Captain knew he was here, and had given tacit approval to wait until tomorrow—but that *wasn't* according to regulations, and the computer was not aware that Evans was officially back in Caer Donn. According to regs, he *had* to at least log in, and the computer was the one in charge of making sure he did just that. All she had to do was tell it he was within paging distance, and the computer would do the rest.

She activated her communicator—even here, at a party, no member of the Terran crew was without one—and tapped into the computer. In a few moments she had logged his presence in Caer Donn, which would prompt the computer to page Evans and continue paging him until he answered. There was no way to escape that insistent beeping, which would sound both in his lab and from his wrist-com.

That would hold him for a little while, at least—long enough for Ysaye to get to the greenhouse and find an excuse to get Elizabeth away.

Lady Ysaye, Lorill Hastur said into her mind. *You are concerned for your friend, and you seem to think she is threatened. Can I help in any way?*

She didn't think he had picked up on her suspicions, only her concern, but she was touched and grateful for the offer. Well, the boy wasn't so bad a sort after all!

Find David and tell him—tell him that Elizabeth needs him, she said, telling him the minimum she could. *Then come to the Science building and Ryan Evans' greenhouse—look, I'll show you where it is.*

She wasn't sure why she added that; perhaps out of a sense of needing someone—a male, however young, someone that Evans wasn't going to be able to over-power—to back her up. Now she regretted all those lost opportunities to learn self-defense. Jessica Duval wouldn't have to look for a man to back her up—nor would Aurora. She didn't want to involve any of the other Terrans just at the moment, either. How would she explain her sudden dread of what Evans might do to Elizabeth? They would only laugh or argue; both wasting time. He was a Terran, one of their crewmates, and the best friend of Elizabeth's husband. Why would he try to molest her? By the time she got one of them to cooperate, it might be too late. Evans wasn't exactly popular, but no one had ever accused him of rape or the intention of rape. Lorill wasn't arguing; he took her premonition at face value. He was the best she had.

This mind-to-mind communication had an advantage she had not dreamed of until this moment; she was able to *show* Lorill exactly how to find the greenhouse. He nodded, and before he could do anything else, she had whirled and was running toward the door, ignoring the puzzled looks of those around her.

Elizabeth leaned down to breathe in the heady, intoxicating scent of the flowers—just as Ryan's pager went off.

He swore, and punched it to turn off the insistent beeping, but it wouldn't stop.

"Damn computer overrides," he muttered. "Stay right here, I'll be back."

He ran to the front of the greenhouse, then down the stairs to his office, leaving Elizabeth alone.

The scent of the flowers was heavy and resinous, like gardenias mingled with pine, and just as momentarily overpowering. But a fraction of a second later, Elizabeth wondered how she could have thought the perfume to be so overwhelming—it wasn't heavy at all, it was light and delicate. So light, in fact, that it buoyed her up and made her feel as if she were floating.

The wine had given her a trace of a headache; now that was gone, and she was filled with an incredible sense of well-being. Was this why people liked to get drunk? She sat down beside the tray of flowers and looked up at the glass roof of the greenhouse, watching the light break into splinters and shards of crystal above her.

She felt, for the first time, the sense of *one-ness* with nature, with the world, even with the flowers beside her, that so many mystics had described. It was incredible. Why, she could even feel what the flowers were feeling, how they reached upward for light and downward for nourishment. How they yearned for summer breezes, the way she yearned for David—

She wanted him then, as she had never wanted anything else, her body on fire with need for him.

At just that moment, she heard footsteps; thinking

it would be David, come to answer her longing for him, she rose giddily to her feet and turned—

Only it wasn't David, it was Ysaye.

She frowned with confusion. Why was it Ysaye? She wanted David! "Where is he?" she asked, then giggled to see the words come floating out of her mouth and hang in the air, like the words of the Caterpillar in a picture of one of the Alice books. "Where's David?"

"He's coming, Elizabeth," Ysaye replied instantly, and Elizabeth frowned again to see her thoughts. Why would Ysaye think that Ryan meant any harm to her? How silly—Ryan had simply brought her to see these lovely flowers. . . .

Ysaye set her jaw at the sight of her friend's face; there was no doubt whatsoever that Elizabeth was in a state of extreme intoxication, and probably hallucinating as well, given the way her eyes kept flicking from side to side, as if she saw something. Not surprising, given Ryan Evans' little hobby. So it wouldn't—technically—have been rape. Elizabeth probably wouldn't have known what was happening. Only God and Elizabeth knew how he'd gotten the drugs into her, though. Something at the party, perhaps?

Well, it didn't matter; what *did* matter was getting her out of here before Evans came back.

"Come on, Elizabeth," she coaxed. "David's waiting for you." Elizabeth was wavering on her feet, and Ysaye moved closer, getting an arm around her shoulders to support her, and inadvertently moving farther into the cloud of scent and pollen rising above a tray of blue flowers. The golden pollen settled on her clothing and seemed to stick to her. She sneezed a couple of times, then clenched her jaw and tried to breathe as little as possible. Damn Evans and his stupid plants! On top of everything else, she was going to need an allergen booster when all this was over! As soon as she got back to her quarters, she'd better stick this uniform in the cleaning chute, or better yet, the disposal.

She'd see that Aurora took the allergen booster out of Evans' pay. That would serve him right.

She guided her friend's uncertain steps out of the greenhouse, down the stairs and actually out into the hall before the sound of running feet—coming from the corridor, and not from the lab and office—made her look up.

It was Lorill Hastur, and David with him. She had never been so overjoyed to see two humans in her life.

I told him Elizabeth was ill, Lorill said in her mind, and she gave him a wordless burst of thanks for thinking of something so quickly.

"David, Elizabeth is reacting to something in the refreshments, I think," Ysaye called as they ran up. "She's acting kind of irrationally, and you'd better take her home."

"If anyone would know an allergic reaction, you would," David replied gratefully. "Bless you, Ysaye! Anyone else would have thought she was—"

"Intoxicated or worse, and ignored it," Lorill said gracefully. "It may have been some of the delicacies at the feast; Aldaran should have anticipated that you star folk might become ill with such unfamiliar spices and the like. A night in the safety of her bed should cure her."

David just nodded his thanks; for at that moment, Elizabeth's knees gave, and she nearly fell, dragging Ysaye to the ground with her. David caught them both, and picked Elizabeth up like a small child.

"I think that's just where I'd better put her," he said with an anxious glance at his wife's face, as Elizabeth giggled dreamily. "Looks like all those years of weight-lifting finally paid off."

Ysaye was beginning to feel dizzy herself, but she

kept herself in tight control until David was out of sight. But Lorill was not as callow as he appeared; nor as insensitive as she had thought. Before she swayed and lost her balance, he was at her elbow.

Ysaye, I think you are ill, yourself. Can I help?

I—I hate to ask—

Lorill smiled. *Let it be thanks for patience with my sister's questions. Can I help you to your quarters?*

The ship—the ship was so far away—she didn't think she'd be able to make it there, even with Lorill's help. This was no ordinary allergic reaction; everything had rainbows around it, and she felt as if she had drunk an entire bottle of wine by herself.

But wait—she had a room in the Singles quarters that she hardly ever used, except when she was working double-shifts on something here in the Science building.

I will take you there, Lorill said, following her thoughts with an ease she envied. And a moment later, he had picked her up as easily as David had picked up Elizabeth.

She closed her eyes as the corridor swung about her; the snow on her face as they passed between the buildings revived her a bit, but as soon as they were back in the warmth of the living quarters, she felt euphoria overcoming her again.

It must have been something in the food, or the wine—something he slipped to both of us. Could he have slipped it to more of the women? To all of us?

But it hardly seemed to matter, for she had rarely felt such an enormous sense of well-being. As Lorill opened the door of her room, and closed it behind him, the lights came on automatically. He looked startled for a moment, and she giggled.

That is hardly polite, lady, he chided her, with a grin. *After all, these star folk wonders are things I have never seen before.*

His grin widened as she giggled more, then he began to chuckle. As he placed her down on the bed, he glanced up at the walls, and something struck him as so hilarious that he collapsed beside her in gales of laughter.

She couldn't read his thoughts, exactly, but she caught the flavor of them—something about how her room resembled the cells of some kind of monastic order.

And for some reason, that set her off as well. They collapsed against each other, helpless with laughter, clinging to each other to stay upright. Anyone less like a monk than Lorill—

Then suddenly, they were clinging to each other for another reason entirely, and Ysaye felt afire with longing for his touch on her skin. It did not matter that she had never touched a man like this in her life—it did not matter that Lorill was years younger than she. None of that mattered, except that he was male and she was female and they were both caught in a storm that neither could control.

In a frenzy, they tore the clothing from each other, each so intimately within the other's mind that alien fastenings were no hindrance. As they tumbled back onto the bed, there was nothing left of reason. Only passion remained.

Lorill woke first, to find himself in a strangely barren room—and after a moment, he remembered where he was.

And what he had just done. He had seduced—and been seduced by—a virgin of the star folk, a woman as alien in her color and her thoughts as any *chieri* could be.

But why? He had acted like—like a beast in rut! Or

a poor fool caught in a Ghost Wind. And so had Ysaye. But they had been indoors!

He frowned at the thought. For that matter—so had Elizabeth.

Gingerly, carefully, he picked up Ysaye's garments. And yes, there was a faint, resinous scent of *kireseth* about them!

Quickly he thrust them away from himself. No, he would not be caught by *that* twice in a row! But what could he do with them?

Ysaye's memories, inadvertently shared, gave him the answer. He picked up her clothing, taking care not to shake loose the *kireseth* pollen still clinging to it, and stuffed the garments down a hatch. Her memories told him that the hatch led directly to some kind of laundry, where the garments would be cleansed and sterilized by machines, then returned to her. There would be no further chance of contamination.

But what of the past few hours? What would her folk do if they learned what he had done to Ysaye? Would they learn? She had been a virgin; was she pledged to be so for her work? Obviously she did not have the conditioning of a Darkovan Keeper, or he, at least, would be dead. But would the loss of her virginity endanger her health? Would it be obvious to her superiors when she returned to work? And what if she got with child by him?

He thought of his father's—and Fiora's—comments about his lack of self-control and his entanglements with women, and he cringed. He did not wish even to consider what they would say about this—*kireseth* or no *kireseth!*

Perhaps, if no one found him here and there were no physical consequences, Ysaye might suppose it was all a dream. Perhaps that would be the best, after all —even if it were the coward's way out. Of course, should she be with child, his honor would require him to acknowledge it.

He donned his clothing quickly, and opened his mind to the stray thoughts of others nearby. If he could manage to get away without anyone's seeing him, that would be all to the good, for her sake as well as his. He was not sure what was considered proper behavior for an unmarried woman of her people, but he was not at all sure that this qualified.

He waited until there was no one in the corridors outside, and slipped out of the door, shutting it behind him, thinking as he did so what story he must tell to explain his absence from the festival.

Perhaps—a visit to the tavern. He should go there to make it less a lie. And it was not far from here, which would help matters.

He reached the door to the outside world safely enough, and slipped out into the snow-spangled darkness.

When Ysaye woke, she had more to worry about than the confused memories of some strange—and rather embarrassing—dreams about Lorill Hastur. Her stomach was in knots, her sinuses felt as if someone had stuffed bowling balls under her cheekbones, and she was dizzy and weak. She fumbled her way to the shower and turned the hot water on herself at full force; it did nothing for her head, but it eased the cramps in her stomach somewhat.

Maybe those cramps explained the blood on her sheets. She'd always been irregular, but she had never trusted birth control medication to regulate her periods. There were so many things she had to do to her body that she rebelled at subjecting it to one more medication, to which she would probably be allergic anyway. And she certainly didn't need birth control medication

for birth control; celibacy had fewer failures and no side
effects.

She found a clean uniform in the closet and pulled
it on, resolutely blotting out those dreams of Lorill
Hastur. Those awful hallucinations probably had something to do with the drug Ryan Evans had slipped to
her and Elizabeth last night. At least she had made sure
that Elizabeth was with her own husband, not with
Evans.

Well, if she could *prove* he had done so, his career
would be finished. The Service might put up with a lot,
but it wouldn't tolerate drugging and seducing female
personnel.

But first, before anything else, she had to get to
Aurora for an allergen booster, before she got too sick
to do anything at all.

She bundled her coat on, and turned the light in her
room out behind her.

Room? It's like a cell of the penitents at Nevarsin!

She jerked her head up. Where had *that* thought
come from? For that matter, where and what was
Nevarsin?

Then she shook her head to clear it, as she ventured
out into the snow, heading—or rather, staggering—in
the direction of the ship, and Aurora's excellent sickbay. It was probably something she'd heard last night.
And right now, given how dizzy she felt, she probably
shouldn't trust anything her mind came up with. She
really wasn't rational during these attacks.

The ship seemed a million miles away, and she was
having trouble putting one foot in front of the other.
Fortunately, just as she got to the ramp, one of her
techs came trotting past, took a second look at her, and
stopped her.

The next thing she knew, she was looking up at
Aurora through a haze of pain from her head.

"—looks like another one of her allergy attacks to me," the young tech was saying. "I was there the last time."

"I think you're right, Tandy," Aurora said briskly. "Thanks for getting a medic team down to the ramp. The shape she's in now, she might have collapsed before she got up here."

Aurora leaned over Ysaye and tried to look encouraging. "You should be all right in a few days, Ysaye, but right now you're pretty sick." Ysaye heard a faint hiss as someone administered her allergen booster, but everything seemed fuzzy and far away.

She ought to tell them about Evans, but it was too much effort to talk.

She heard Aurora's voice fading out into the distance ". . . hook up those monitors and start running scans. See if you can find out what triggered this . . ."

"Ysaye?" Aurora's voice was fading back in again. "Ysaye! Can you hear me?"

Ysaye opened her eyes to see Aurora's face inches from her own. She felt oxygen tubing running across her cheeks into her nostrils. She tried to speak, but her mouth was dry and her voice came out midway between a croak and a groan. The end of a length of flexible tubing was slipped between her lips. "Here, sip on this—it's all right, Ysaye, it's just water. You've been mostly out of it for four days, so you probably feel pretty thirsty and weak.

The water moistened her mouth, but when it hit her stomach, her stomach rebelled instantly. Years of habit enabled Ysaye to roll sideways and grab the basin that was always kept next to each bed in sickbay. Aurora helped support her and the basin, and a pair of hands from behind her retrieved the tube she had dropped and held her braids out of the way. But even when her stomach was totally empty, she still felt sick. She fought dry heaves by force of will as Aurora gently laid her back against the pillow.

"Can you tell us *anything*, Ysaye? This isn't following your usual pattern. After the first booster it looked as though you were going to sleep it off and recover, but you didn't wake up after twenty hours, so we gave you a second booster. When you didn't respond to that, we started IV fluids—nothing we haven't given you before—to counter the dehydration that was starting, but whatever triggered this attack must still be in your body somehow." She looked dubiously around the room, and Ysaye saw that she was in the isolation chamber. There was definitely nothing in this room to which she was allergic. So it wasn't the room, it wasn't the air (in here it came through special filters), it wasn't the IV fluids or the water.

"Try to remember, Ysaye," Aurora said urgently. "You were at the banquet at Aldaran—did you eat anything that seemed strange?"

Ysaye's memory started to return. "Elizabeth . . . is Elizabeth all right?"

Aurora looked startled. "As far as I know, she's fine. She hasn't been in lately that I know of." She looked over at the tech on Ysaye's other side. "Check the log for the past week, Tandy."

Tandy's voice came back a minute later. "Negative. She hasn't been in."

The oxygen was clearing Ysaye's head a little, enough for her to hold a train of thought if she tried hard enough. "The banquet . . . Evans' greenhouse . . . the pollen—is there still pollen in my hair?"

"We'll find out," Aurora said. "Get a suction hood, Tandy."

Ysaye felt a partial vacuum around the top of her head, and then heard Tandy's voice. "There does seem to be traces of some sort of yellow dust here," she said.

"It was yellow—golden, really," Ysaye murmured.

"Take it to the lab for analysis," Aurora ordered.

After Tandy left the room, she looked at Ysaye's hair and sighed. "How do you feel about having your head shaved?"

"In this climate?" Ysaye shot back.

"You do have a point—not that you aren't going to be stuck right here for a while, but I hope it won't be long enough for your hair to grow back!" Aurora started digging equipment out of various cupboards. "I'll put a full face mask on you and cover your skin up to your neck. Then it should only take me a couple of hours to undo each and every one of those braids you wear and wash this whatever-it-is out of your hair. The things I do for my friends!"

"Thank you, Aurora," Ysaye said softly. "I really do appreciate it. I'm sorry to be such a nuisance."

"Don't worry about it," Aurora said lightly. "I don't have anything else planned for the rest of the day. And it's really a relief to have you awake again. I wonder what the devil that stuff is?"

Ysaye woke up the next morning certified pollen-free; Aurora told her that the last traces had passed out of her bloodstream during the night. But as soon as Ysaye tried to sit up, she was overwhelmed by nausea.

"Lie flat, and don't move," Aurora said. She dashed into the next room and returned a moment later with a package of salted crackers. "Nibble on these and see if they help."

Oddly enough, they did. Five minutes later Ysaye was able to sit up. It was then that she noticed how heavy and sore her breasts felt. "Aurora, are you sure you didn't overdo it on the IV fluid? I feel positively bloated."

Aurora laughed. "With any other woman, I'd test for pregnancy if she reported symptoms like that."

Ysaye sat very still, memories of herself and Lorill Hastur running through her head. "Test for it."

Aurora looked at her in astonishment, then closed her mouth and silently took a blood sample and left the room.

A few minutes later she returned.

"You're right. You're pregnant. Do you want to talk about it?"

Ysaye shook her head, cradling her hands protectively over her flat abdomen. She couldn't even think, much less talk.

Aurora sighed. "Well, if you decide you do want to talk, I'm here. But meanwhile, like it or not, we're going to have to report this to the Captain."

Leonie gasped at the doctor's words, and quickly ran her own sort of confirmation of them. And she was right. This star woman called Ysaye was with child, a tiny speck of a thing that had hardly been in existence for more than a few hours.

Lorill's child.

She had managed to escape from her duties long enough to follow Lorill as he brought his apologies to Kermiac Aldaran. She had felt a sense of premonition about that mission of repentance; and afraid that something would happen to him in Aldaran's hands, she had watched over the entire proceedings.

But nothing at all happened, other than Lorill humbling himself. That rankled, but she admitted that after all he had deserved to be humbled—and that her father was right in convincing him to make the apology in person. The Domains could not risk a conflict with Aldaran, especially not with these strangers among his people.

Besides, she was still curious about the star folk. The few things she had gleaned from her contact's mind were frustratingly incomplete. She wanted more specific information, and with Lorill there, she had a way to get it without revealing herself.

So she had stayed with him until he went to speak —as she had asked him—with the strange dark woman, Ysaye. Then she had transferred herself to the star woman's mind, lurking undetected where she could watch Ysaye's surface thoughts, as she answered Lorill's questions, questions she had directed him to ask. Leonie was fascinated by the strange world she glimpsed in those thoughts—a world where there seemed to be so much luxury, and yet so little that was luxurious. A world bounded by a strange sort of austerity, but one in which the individuals had so much wealth. Ysaye herself had so much freedom—and yet had so few choices. In that way, perhaps, and in their love of music, they were very alike.

It was confusing, and yet intriguing.

She lost Ysaye, though, in the woman's fear for her friend's well-being—and when she touched Ysaye's mind again, she shrank back from the strange and sensual images she found there. She had withdrawn so quickly that it had not even occurred to her that the man Ysaye had been with might have been her brother.

Until Lorill himself had called her, confessed what had happened, and begged her to see that all was well, that his seduction—however *kireseth*-inspired and controlled—had not been discovered. He had the feeling that the star folk, unfamiliar with the powers of the pollen, might not take that as an excuse.

Alarmed by the precarious position in which he had put himself, she had complied. As Ysaye rose from her bed and staggered to the ship and the healers there,

Leonie saw that she thought the encounter with Lorill was only a dream—something inspired by illness.

She breathed a sigh of relief, but dutifully stayed within Ysaye's mind until the healer helped the star woman, convinced that all would be well.

Until *those* words.

She withdrew hastily.

Lorill's child. First Hastur child of this generation; infinitely precious, the more so as Ysaye was obviously gifted with *laran* in abundance, and so the child would likely be gifted as well. She, Leonie, would certainly never bear a child; it was up to Lorill to continue the Hastur line. By *nedestro* children, if necessary, although many children by a proper *di catenas* bride from the Domains would be preferable. But any child of Hastur blood was to be nurtured and welcomed; doubly so in these days, when so few had *laran* in full measure.

She bent her will on Lorill, waking him from where he slumbered in his bed in the guest quarters of Castle Aldaran. He tried to shove her sleepily away, but her words shocked him to full wakefulness.

Your folly with the star woman has resulted in a child, she said shortly. *It cannot be ignored now, not by them, nor by us. You must go to Father and tell him, then return to Aldaran and confess your part in the situation.*

He gathered his scattered thoughts, and tried to marshal them. *How? How can they know it was—*

Don't be foolish, Leonie snapped at him, feeling horribly older and wiser than he, her twin. *This child is a Hastur; we can't ignore it and pretend it doesn't exist! Besides, she remembers some of what happened. When she becomes sensible, she'll realize that it wasn't a* kireseth *dream, it was you after all. And where did she get the pollen all over her, anyway?*

I don't know; somewhere in that building, I think. When she got the other woman—Elizabeth was acting like she'd been standing in a Ghost Wind, too. Lorill seemed dazed. *What am I supposed to do?*

Claim the child, of course! Leonie replied impatiently. *How can you not? It's a Hastur, we must take it and rear it properly—perhaps we can foster it with—*

But what if Ysaye wants to keep it? Lorill replied unexpectedly.

*She has no right—*Leonie began.

They're not our people, Lorill reminded her sharply. *They don't follow our laws. Even a Hastur could not order the girl-child of a Renunciate into his keeping; their laws could say that disposition of the child is only the mother's right. If she wishes to keep it and raise it herself, there is nothing we can do about it. She can even take it away into the stars if she chooses—in fact, that's probably what she will choose. She doesn't like it here, much.*

The very idea shocked Leonie to the core. That the woman might *take* a child of Hastur blood, not only to keep it from its father, but to take it away where it could not be properly reared and educated—

There was only one thing to do. She would have to reveal herself to Ysaye; to make friends with the woman, and then convince her to give over the child when it was born. It would mean close contact with the alien's mind. It might mean witnessing some uncomfortable—perhaps even frightening—things. Thoughts that were as alien to her as any nonhuman's. And she would have to make a special effort to learn to like Ysaye as much as if the woman were her best friend— you could not lie mind-to-mind, and she sensed that Ysaye would only release something as precious as her child into the hands of someone she liked and trusted.

None of that mattered. There was a Hastur child at stake.

She steeled herself, broke off contact with her

stricken brother, and prepared to touch Ysaye's mind again.

The doctor had done something to improve her condition somewhat; Ysaye was agitated, but much more coherent, and no longer so disoriented. The doctor had left her for a moment.

Now, if ever, was the time to reveal herself.

Ysaye? Leonie said carefully, as Ysaye jumped, startled by the voice in her mind. *You don't know me, but I am Lorill's twin, and there is much we have to talk about. . . .*

CHAPTER
20

"**I** can't believe it," Elizabeth said dazedly. "*Ysaye?* Pregnant? But how? By whom?"

"Believe it," Aurora said grimly. "She's just as pregnant as you are; according to the computer, you probably conceived within a few hours of each other. As for how and with whom—we were hoping you'd be able to tell us that. She is your best friend, after all."

Aurora at least had the courtesy not to say what Elizabeth herself was thinking; that if Ysaye hadn't refused the birth control implant "for religious reasons" none of this would be happening.

Aurora's colleague, Doctor Darwin Mettier, was not so charitable, or tactful.

"If Space Services would make birth control implants mandatory for both sexes until couples had permission from the Service to start a family, this could never happen," he said coldly. "And if this woman had thought about her safety and her duty first, instead of her religious scruples—"

"Hasn't she told you anything?" Elizabeth interrupted, still bewildered by the news, and feeling increasingly uncomfortable during the angry tirade.

"Nothing coherent." That was Darwin again, who was the specialist in internal medicine. "She keeps talking to someone named 'Leonie,' and all we know for certain is that she is adamant about taking this pregnancy to term." He obviously did not approve. "That's all very well for someone—you, for instance—prepared to start a family and stay in one place for a while. But she's needed on this ship, here and now. Her duty is to *us*, not to some whim of passion."

"That insistence doesn't surprise me, given her psychological profile," Aurora added. "And her background. Frankly, I was expecting her to ask us to sew a big red 'A' to all of her uniforms."

"That would only be applicable if she'd been married," Elizabeth pointed out absently, so bewildered by the situation that her mind whirled with trivialities. "I can't believe it. What is she going to do with a child? The Service is a hard place for a single mother."

"Make that 'impossible,' " Aurora snapped.

Elizabeth was already wondering if she and David should offer to adopt the baby. She knew Ysaye disliked this place as much as she liked it; and the baby would keep Ysaye bound to the planet for two years or more. Darwin obviously disapproved of the fact that Ysaye would not be leaving with the ship . . . how could two babies be that much more trouble than one? Ysaye would be planet-bound for the nine months of the pregnancy, but if negotiations and construction bogged down, the ship could be delayed here for that long anyway.

"That's going to be the least of our worries," Darwin replied harshly. "I'm far more worried about keeping her alive. Do you have any idea how badly allergic she is? Even if we do get quick orders to terminate this pregnancy, she might not live through it."

Elizabeth blanched. "Is it that bad?" she asked in a trembling voice.

Darwin, a muscular blond who would have looked more at home on the stevedore's dock, shrugged. "She's in a full allergic attack, and there is only so much we can do for her without killing the embryo, or malforming it. Frankly, in my opinion—which Aurora doesn't yet share—I think she's reacting allergically to the flood of hormones nurturing the embryo as well as whatever triggered the attack in the first place."

"I can't see how she could be," Aurora argued. "It's not in any of the literature—how could she be having a reaction to hormones which exist in her body all the time in smaller amounts? Women have been having children for millennia without having allergic reactions to the natural chemicals which enable us to bear them!"

"Aurora, you know how sick she gets every month, don't you see—it seems obvious there could be a connection—oh, never mind." Darwin shrugged, and turned back to Elizabeth. "You're sure you can't tell us anything? The father, whoever he is, should at least know what's going on."

Unspoken, but his thought that Elizabeth picked up clearly and she couldn't help but agree with—*The father should be brought to account for this. It's his responsibility, too*.

"Positive," Elizabeth replied. "Other than that I'm not too clear on that evening either." She flushed, remembering her intoxication and the incredible sexual arousal that had followed it. "There must have been something in the wine—"

"There's something else. You went off with Ryan Evans, didn't you?" Aurora asked sharply. "Did he slip you anything? Give you anything to eat or drink?"

"Why, no!" Elizabeth replied, shocked, and unable to fathom why Aurora should ask that question. "No, he was just going to give me some tips on dealing with the natives—we met at his greenhouse, and he showed me some flowers, and that was when his beeper went off. I hardly spent any time with him at all. Why?"

Aurora just shrugged and wouldn't answer the question. "Never mind. I doubt it was anything other than a hallucination. Maybe there was something you and Ysaye reacted to that the rest of us didn't. With her touchy allergies, I can well imagine that. And for you, the attack could have taken the form of euphoria."

Again, there were thoughts that Elizabeth read coming from Aurora; not as clearly this time, however. Something about Ysaye insisting that Ryan Evans had drugged—her! With the intent to seduce her!

Clearly that must be a hallucination. Ryan was David's friend. Ysaye didn't like or trust him, though—that was probably why she had imagined such a thing. It was easy, if a person was hallucinating, for mild suspicions to turn into horrid certainties.

"Can I see her?" Elizabeth asked timidly. Even though Aurora was her friend outside the medical facilities, inside the sickbay the doctor was nothing but a professional authority. And Darwin was just as aloof, if not more so.

Aurora shook her head. "I don't know. It might not be a good idea." She looked over to Darwin for confirmation.

He shook his head in a firm negative. "We want her isolated. She's hallucinating about talking to this imaginary Leonie, and about hearing a baby crying in pain. You people with your telepathic nonsense are only going to encourage her in that set of delusions. We need to calm her hallucinations, not reinforce them."

"But what if she—" Elizabeth stopped before she finished that sentence. What if Ysaye *was* speaking telepathically with a "Leonie?" Wasn't that what Lorill Hastur, who had left for the Domains this morning, had said his sister was called? Lorill and Ysaye had been talking quite a bit at the party; perhaps that had made a kind of bridge for Leonie to contact Ysaye directly. He'd also told Elizabeth that his sister was a much stronger telepath than he was, how could it be so out-landish to think that Leonie and Ysaye might have con-tacted each other, especially if Leonie was curious about the star-faring Terrans? And what had begun as curi-osity might have continued out of compassion; sym-pathy for Ysaye's plight, and a wish to figuratively "hold her hand," since the doctors were keeping her isolated from her friends.

And as for hearing her unborn child—there were countless instances of mothers-to-be communicating with their children in the womb. Of course, those were all subjective experiences, however well-documented, and Elizabeth feared that the so-logical Doctor Darwin would hardly find them convincing. How would a Dar-kovan feel? She wished she knew.

Darwin and Aurora were looking at her as if they expected her to finish her question. So she asked the first thing that came into her mind.

"What if she doesn't get better?"

"Then we'll have to terminate," Aurora said un-happily.

Elizabeth made a small motion of protest with her left hand, as her right cupped her still-flat stomach protectively.

"There won't be a choice, Elizabeth," Darwin added. "It's a choice between a productive member of the Service and a bit of protoplasm that isn't more than potential yet. It's Service regs. When you signed on with the Service, you made the Service your *de facto* next-of-kin and legal guardian in cases like this; it's in the contract. For the good of the Service, and for Ysaye's good, if the decision has to be made, *we* will make it, never mind what Ysaye wants. She's not in her right mind, anyway."

And with that, they dismissed Ysaye, and anything Ysaye might wish. Elizabeth left the sickbay with pro-

foundly mixed feelings. Fear for Ysaye, resentment at
the way her decisions were being made for her—

Frustration, at the realization that they were right.
There was no choice.

Not for any of them.

Leonie could have wept with frustration. She had
so little of healer training; if she'd had more, or at least
more time to work on the problem, perhaps she could
have done something about Ysaye's condition. Ysaye's
entire body was reacting to the physical changes of the
pregnancy as if Ysaye had been invaded by some kind
of disease.

But the demands of her training as Keeper were
taking most of her time, and the little she could spend
with Ysaye only showed her that the star woman's condition was worsening with every passing moment.

Leonie had never felt helpless before; there had
always been something she could do in any situation to
improve it—or at least, to change it to something more
her liking. But she was helpless now. Ysaye was as
determined to carry her child to term as Leonie was
that she do so; more so, perhaps. Leonie sensed that
she was communicating with it already, which meant
that it was already showing a spark of powerful *laran*.
But there were multiple problems she must face even
if this child was brought to term. Somehow she needed
to convince Ysaye that she must have Lorill—or at
least, a powerful telepath—with her when she gave
birth, or the child might kill both of them with its fear
and the pain of being born. And she needed to convince
Ysaye that only the Hasturs could properly rear it.

Neither of those was very likely, as Ysaye spent
more and more time drifting in hallucination. And as
her own duties kept her from contact with the star woman's mind.

At least she had convinced Ysaye that *she* was real, and not a hallucination.

She could not give less than her full attention to her teachers; firstly, because they would notice and she would receive just punishment for her inattention, and secondly, because that would cause them to ask just what she was so worried about. And *that* would reveal her forbidden delving into the star folks' minds, and her continued communication with Lorill, also forbidden. She was in isolation in this first year; *nothing* from the outside world was to take her attention away from her studies. Nothing from the outside world could be permitted to touch her in any way. When her studies were over, she would be a Keeper of Arilinn, and she could not be allowed to be anything but impartial, impassive, unemotional. She would hold too much power to be anything else.

Her teachers had branded those lessons on her flesh already. She had no intention of learning that particular lesson over again.

So, she must tuck Lorill, Lorill's child, and the star woman into a locked corner of her mind, and all her concern for them as well. She must keep her serene face, and her serene inner mask as well. She did not know what the Keeper of Arilinn would do if she discovered Leonie's double-dealing, but Leonie was quite certain it would not be pleasant, and would only add further problems to the ones she already had.

Finally, at the end of the day, she was able to seek the sanctuary of her rooms (now purged of every memento she had brought with her) and force her exhausted mind to contact Ysaye's.

There was nothing there.

Or rather, there was a fog of drugged sleep where Ysaye's mind had been; a sleep so profound that Ysaye did not dream and was not in the overworld. There

were no drugs that her people possessed that could
induce such a profound slumber. Ysaye was not even
aware of what was going on around her, a state even a
trained healer had difficulty in inducing. The mind was
a powerful thing, and fought its extinction, even in so
small a thing as sleep.

Leonie quickly sought for a mind physically near to
Ysaye, one that she could jump to in order to see what
was happening. She found one; not as sensitive as
Ysaye's, and one which did not accept its own *laran*.

But that made him all the more suitable. He would
not notice Leonie's presence in his mind, because he
could not.

She caught a name from the healer at his right hand;
Darwin. She recognized Darwin's companion as the
healer Ysaye trusted, the one called Aurora. His concentration was incredible; his mind was set on one thing
and one thing only; the task at hand. A Keeper might
envy such a fierce and all-exclusive concentration.

Then she realized what they were to do; and shrank
back in horror. She could only watch, frozen, as they
prepared to take Ysaye's child—and make her *emmasca*.

She was horrified; revolted. It was too soon to be
angry. She would be angry with these people later,
now—she was too shocked.

This man, Darwin; he had reasons in plenty why
this should be done. That Ysaye could not live to carry
the child to term; that if she tried they would both die.
That it would be thus if she ever became pregnant again,
and therefore would not only be a kindness to make
her *emmasca*, but medically advisable.

There were other reasons why he must do this. He
had been *ordered* to do so, by the Captain who was to
Ysaye as the King was to the Domains. And by people
beyond the Captain, who ranked beyond him, and could

give orders that no one of the star folk would dare to disobey.

Whether or not Ysaye agreed.

She would have fled—but something, some stirring of premonition, warned her. *Watch*, it breathed. *Listen. You will need this some day.*

The ancient operation that made a woman *emmasca* was both forbidden and lost. Oh, the Keeper of Arilinn, some priestesses of Avarra, and a few others *might* have the knowledge of it, but Leonie doubted that she would ever impart that knowledge to her successor. There were reasons why it should be forbidden—and yet, there could be reasons, compelling reasons, why the forbidden must be done. Perhaps, when Leonie recovered from her rage and outrage at this violation of Ysaye's will and her own, she would see those reasons.

Perhaps, someday, some woman might come to Leonie, and Leonie would see that it was necessary to give her this terrible gift. To her, maybe, this would not be violation, but freedom. . . .

So she stayed, imposing on herself the icy and uncaring calm of the Keeper, and of this healer.

And when it was over, she fled.

Ysaye woke, clear-headed, and aching. She knew what had happened before anyone told her. She knew not only because of the soreness where they had cut into her body, but because she was alone.

From the moment that she had been told she was with child, she had been aware of the presence inside her. Not a person, but a presence, a spark of life, something that could, one day, become the little girl she had seen in her dreams. A lovely child, in whom her genes and Lorill's combined to form a beauty that united the best of both their peoples. She was in pain, from the pain of her mother, but willing to bear that pain.

Now she was gone, and Ysaye was left alone and empty, her sense of that new life gone completely, aching with a sorrow too new and raw for tears. *My baby. She didn't want to die—where is she now?*

The door to her room opened. "Ysaye, how are you feeling?"

It was Aurora, of course, and with just enough concern tempered by professionalism that Ysaye could not be angry with her.

Assuming that she could have mustered so active an emotion as anger. She tried to, but she was too tired, too empty.

"All right, I suppose," she replied dispiritedly. "You took the baby, didn't you?"

"We terminated a life-threatening condition," Aurora corrected. "If we hadn't, you would have died, no question at all, and the baby with you. The choice was death for both of you, or just for the baby; and I followed my orders from the Captain and the Service."

A brief, weak anger managed to flare for a moment. "That's a lie, Aurora. We can regenerate limbs, there is no reason why—"

"A sophisticated medical facility can regenerate a limb, Ysaye," Aurora replied, matching anger with coldness. "A sophisticated *off-planet* medical facility. The kind we don't have here. You would not have survived the trip to one—assuming that the Captain was willing to abandon a new settlement and all the important negotiations to ferry one illegally-pregnant woman—without permission—at incredible expense— to one of those off-planet facilities. You are a valuable crew member, and subject to orders that you have to obey, orders you technically violated with your condition. The Service has a considerable interest in keeping you alive and functioning."

Ysaye shrank back in her bed, feeling both at fault and put-upon. Her brief anger died. Aurora had rightfully reminded her of her responsibilities, her duties, her place in the Service and in the crew. She had no right to dispute their orders.

"You're right," Ysaye said dully. "I'm sorry, Aurora. I—" She stopped, unable to continue, tears making a thickness and an ache in the back of her throat.

Aurora softened. "I'm sorry, too, Ysaye. I'm sorry we had to do this to you, but none of us had a choice. It was either lose you or— Ysaye, I have to tell you something else. I'm sorry, but—you were in such bad shape that we had to do a complete hysterectomy. Whatever triggered this made you severely allergic to estrogen."

That was nothing compared with the loss of the child, oddly enough. She had never thought of herself as a *female*, much, anyway—more as a kind of extension of the computer. Neutral, and neuter.

In a way, it was appropriate. A fitting sacrifice for the life that was never to be, now.

She closed her eyes, as her tears threatened to rise up and drown her; she fought them back, with the only thing that had ever brought her any sense of self, and of worth. Her identity as *female*, as *mother* was gone, before she had ever had a chance to experience either of them. There was only one identity left to her, the only one that had any value or meaning to the Service that gave and took, whether or not she wanted it.

"When can I go back to work?" she asked, each word an ache. "There must be a lot of it piled up by now."

Aurora raised a surprised eyebrow. "Well, now that

we have your allergies under control again, there's no reason why you can't work from your bed. I want you to get up and walk around a little every couple of hours. Otherwise stay off your feet for a week or so, but working shouldn't interfere with that. If you want to—I thought you'd want to rest."

Ysaye shook her head. "I'd rather work," she replied. "I've made enough of a nuisance of myself; I'd better take care of what I can."

Aurora helped her to sit up, supported with inflatable cushions. She ignored the ache in her stomach as she sat up, the dull stabs of pain from the area of the incision. There was less pain than she had thought there would be; Aurora must have given her a partial spinal block.

When at last she was in place and the terminal, on a movable shelf, had been lowered into place so she could reach it, Aurora left her alone.

She worked steadily, losing herself and her pain in the work, even though after a while she became impatient with the number of things tagged for her attention that could easily have been taken care of by the junior techs. What was the matter with these people? As Aurora had pointed out, Ysaye was not indispensable! What would they do if she'd been so sick that she couldn't have tended to these things for weeks or even months?

Before, she would have simply taken care of the problems herself. Now she was annoyed; she redirected every bit of silly nonsense to her junior technicians, distributing the load equally among all of them. When she had dealt with the few things that were beyond their abilities, she leaned back in her pillows, restless and discontented.

After a moment, she felt that Leonie was seeking her. For a moment she was as inclined to ignore the girl as she had been to see the last of Aurora. She did not want to hear any more "I'm sorrys," and she did not want to have to explain to Leonie why her brother's precious child had been destroyed. But in spite of her own feelings, she felt that the young Darkovan girl had come to depend on her; that somehow or other—perhaps through that brief bond of flesh, or even through the love of music they shared—the young Keeper-in-training had come to reach out to Ysaye as she could not to anyone nearer to her physically or by relationship. Whether this dependence was a fault in Leonie or not—or whether it was due entirely to loneliness—Ysaye did not bother to wonder.

With a sigh, she opened her mind to the girl, feeling ancient and worn with pain.

Hello, Leonie. What do you want?

The girl "felt" troubled. *It would do no good to say I am sorry, Ysaye, but it is true. And I know it was not your fault.*

Big of her, Ysaye thought ironically—but then again, it probably was. Given her culture, and her own pride, that might have been quite an admission. It was entirely possible that most Darkovans might have considered her entirely at fault for what had been done against her will.

Thank you, she replied instead. *I'm sorry, too*. She did not have to say how sorry; it was there like a gaping wound for Leonie to see. *Is there anything I can do for you?*

A moment of hesitation. *Could I hear some of your music?* the girl asked carefully. *I cannot sleep—do you remember that I told you that I used to listen to your music through you? Maybe music would be a good rest for your mind also.*

That was a good thought, and an amazingly kind one on Leonie's part.

But perhaps—with this much disquiet, you would not feel much like listening to music.

Once again, Ysaye was surprised; it was almost the first time that she had felt Leonie voice any concern for anything but what *she* cared about. Even the child had been an issue because Leonie felt strongly about a child of the Hastur blood.

I know, Leonie said, answering the thought. *You must have thought me very selfish.*

Ysaye was as touched by this as she had not been by Aurora's casual concern. *If I did*, she replied quietly, *it was only that young people are always a little selfish. That's partly a matter of survival, I suppose, if they are going to hold their own against the stronger and stronger-willed adults. They have to think first of themselves and their own needs and desires—which just might conflict with those of the adults.* She actually found herself feeling a little lightening of spirit. *As for music, I think it will be good to have something else to think about.*

Leonie seemed pleased out of all proportion for the favor. *You are so good to me—and I'm such a selfish little beast.* Behind the thought were others; Leonie had really been *with* Ysaye every step of the way, every moment of suffering, and what had been done with and to her had left Leonie very much aware of how privileged her own life was.

No, Leonie, Ysaye said gently. *I don't think you're selfish. Only young.*

Leonie dropped out of rapport for a moment, evidently thinking about Ysaye's words and her reactions. When she came back, her thoughts had a shading of a new humility. *This is what my teachers have been trying to tell me. And I have been foolishly thinking that all at once, I should be perfect and know everything.*

Ysaye was oddly touched, and found herself thinking that if circumstances had been different, she could have had a young girl much like Leonie for her daughter.

No. That was in the past, and irrevocable. Enough that this most arrogant of young women was thinking of something other than her own wishes. And enough that she had somehow assumed a place as Leonie's mentor. It would do neither of them any good to keep on flaying themselves with unhealthy introspection.

What music would you like, Leonie? Wagner?

Leonie's thoughts brightened; she seemed to have a taste for *heldenmusik*, huge orchestras, with everything larger than life. *If you would be so kind*, she replied.

Ysaye could control the music played in this room from the computer terminal. She called up the music program, and keyed in "The Ride of the Valkyries," directing the computer to play a random selection after that.

What are "Valkyries," Ysaye?

Warrior maidens, Ysaye replied, giving her a mental picture of Brunnhilde in full-dress, braids, winged helm, and all. *They come from the German legends that formed the basis for this opera.*

Leonie returned a picture, of a capable, well-muscled woman with short-cropped hair (the first indication of short hair among women that Ysaye had seen in this culture) and a short sword; dressed in something like a divided skirt and a red tunic.

Like our Renunciates, she supplied. *Brave and dependent on no one else. Sometimes I wish I was one of them.*

Sometimes I do, too, Ysaye replied wistfully. Warrior maidens, untouched—armored angels that the world could not affect.

The computer selected Berlioz, and Leonie's plea-

sure showed clearly. Then came one of the Bach cho-
rales, as if the computer was attempting to comfort her
by selecting her favorite pieces, and then the last movement of the Beethoven *Ninth*, with its "Hymn to Joy."
Prodded by Leonie's bewilderment at the German, she
supplied a modern translation of words she herself had
sung in college.

The words were trite doggerel even by Ysaye's not-
very-elevated standards, but the magic of Beethoven's
music had endowed them in her mind with a very real
inspiration. There was a pang of loss as she recalled the
young idealist who had sung those words—yet how far
removed was the trite from the archetypal? There were
tears on her face as the music continued into the finale.
Tears she had not been able, or willing to shed, until
now.

Perhaps the techs were right; perhaps the computer
was aware of her in a primitive way, and was trying to
comfort her as best it could. Certainly her tears were
a release she had denied herself until the music the
computer had chosen had forced them on her.

She wept quietly, but no longer ashamed or afraid,
for everything she had lost in the past few days—everything, in fact, from her innocence to her womanhood.
And all of it gone past retrieval.

She finally regained control of herself as the music
faded, leaving behind only silence.

Silence both physical and mental.

Leonie? she called. Surely the girl would not have
left her so abruptly . . . without bidding farewell.

Ysaye? the mental voice sounded faint and panicked. *Ysaye! I was following the music, I wanted to
make the computer choose something that would cheer
you!*

What? What on Earth could the girl mean?

Then suddenly, she realized what she meant—

Leonie, evidently picking up on Ysaye's "personalization" of the computer, thought it had a real mind.

Somehow, she had transferred herself into the great computer.

And now, if the level of Leonie's panic was any indication, she was trapped within the computer!

CHAPTER
21

At first Leonie had no idea what had happened to her.

To Ysaye, the computer was just another sort of person; one that even seemed to be able to read her mind at times. Leonie wanted it to stop playing music that saddened Ysaye and to choose something which would lighten her spirits. So rather than intrude on Ysaye's grief, she had sought to touch the computer directly, mind to mind.

She had moved her "self" toward it, as if she were entering the relays. It had seized her, abruptly and without warning.

It *was* an intelligence, though of a kind she had never encountered before, and very powerful. Powerful enough, in fact, to terrify her. She felt like a scorpion-ant looking up at the sole of a boot.

But after a moment, she managed to control her panic, as the computer ignored her presence even though it had pulled her in. She looked about her, finding it relatively easy to maintain herself and her sense of identity after all her training as a Keeper and her hours of practice in the relays and in the overworld.

But even for Leonie this place that *wasn't* a place was strange and disconcerting. It seemed to Leonie that she stood in a vast and deserted emptiness, with a sense of currents of power humming all about her, and invisible landscapes, layer upon layer of them, just out of reach.

This was nothing like the overworld. The overworld was to this place as a travel shelter was to Castle Hastur.

She tried to visualize herself moving. In the overworld, she would have seen where she was and where she was going. She felt as if she *were* moving, but she seemed to be moving through grayness with no visual clues at all. And she had no control over her speed, either; she slowed and speeded up with no warning. That made her feel even more disoriented and a little sick. She tried to will herself to stop, and it seemed to work, but she had no idea where she had begun nor where she had landed.

Darkness smothered her; there was no way to get her bearings.

Clearly, this was not even like being within a matrix.

She took hold of herself, and quelled her panic; she tried to center her mind and project a very clear picture of herself—Leonie Hastur, what she wanted and where she wanted to go. Which was, obviously, *out of here*.

Wherever "here" was.

She told herself that there was no reason to panic, this was no more than a very unpleasant experience. She was, after all, not here bodily; her body was safely behind the Veil at Arilinn, and the only thing here was her consciousness, her awareness. No matter how unpleasant it was, she had only to wait, and eventually she would return—or be returned—to her body.

Wouldn't she?

If this computer was an intelligence, as she had thought, perhaps she ought to deal with it as an intelligence. She should be able to communicate with it.

She marshaled all of her will, and formed her thought into a very specific question.

Who are you?

After a long time, out of the grayness, an answer arrived.

TE Model S14C, Multi-purpose Multitasker.

The answer made no sense, but at least it had answered her. *Help me!* she demanded.

State nature of problem, it droned.

Nature of the problem? *I want to get out of here!* Leonie replied.

Request not properly formulated.

Well, that was getting her nowhere! She looked around again; in the dimness she thought she saw glimmering lines and having nothing better to lead her, she decided to follow one of them.

Perhaps it would guide her out.

No sooner had she thought of doing so, then she was traveling at some tremendous speed along one of the lines. Then, she felt herself slammed—there was no other word for it—into an enormous grid.

It felt metallic, somehow; cold and hot at the same time, and it threw her back off of the track she had been following. She had once gotten an overflow of energy from the relays; she had felt then as she felt now, tingling, with every hair on end, and briefly dazed.

And what sounded like the same voice, a characterless buzz, repeated tonelessly, *State nature of problem*.

That again? Leonie repeated, with a growing sense of helplessness, *I said I wanted to get out of here! Please, show me the way out!*

There was a buzzing sound this time, but the voice repeated, *Request not formulated properly*.

Then, out of the darkness, far in the distance, a sense that someone was looking for her. Ysaye!

Panicked, she called out to her friend, and the voice in the darkness strengthened. *Leonie? Leonie? Where are you?* The voice was nearer now.

Ysaye was trying to help her! Leonie formed all her frustration into a single cry. *Ysaye! Help me! I'm lost, I want to get out of here!*

Even though she had not addressed it, the ruler of this place—whatever it was—cut between Leonie and Ysaye like a great wall.

State nature of problem, it droned.

Go away! she shouted at it. *I'm lost, I need to find a way out of here!*

Request not formulated properly, came the instant answer.

In fury and frustration, Leonie cried out for her friend. *Ysaye! I'm here in the computer and I can't find the way out!*

Once again, she had a sense of rapidly traveling along some invisible line and ramming with sufficient impact to make her dizzy, against something that felt for all intents and purposes like a wall. As Leonie rebounded off it, stunned and shocked, and without the strength to formulate her thoughts, again that droning passionless voice, completely emotionless, imposed itself between her and Ysaye.

State nature of request.

At this point Leonie had lost any sense of adventure, and the last of her bravery.

Help! she screamed in a state of complete panic. *Help me! Ysaye! Anybody! Help me out of here, I'm lost! Please! Get me out of here!*

And once again: *Request not properly formulated.*

Leonie felt a great surge of fury and despair, and through it, she heard Ysaye's mental voice again.

Leonie, ask it who you are.

That made no sense. *But I know who I am*, she protested, *and it knows. I've told it a dozen times!*

Leonie, it doesn't understand, or rather, it sees you

in a different way than you see yourself, Ysaye said patiently. *Ask it who it thinks you are.*

It made no sense, but Ysaye knew this thing; she must know something that prompted the strange order.

All right, then, thought Leonie in exhaustion. She turned all of her attention to the gray formlessness around her, trying to personify it so that she could address it.

Call it, "computer," Ysaye prompted. *Say "Computer, who am I?"*

Computer? Leonie said, hesitantly, feeling frustrated and helpless. *Computer, who am I?*

The answer was prompt and made no more sense than the identity it had given itself. *Process 392397642.*

Leonie only felt despair and hopelessness at this jumble of letters and numbers, but Ysaye exclaimed with jubilation.

Wonderful! Got it. Hang on, Leonie!

Something flashed past; something that had a flavor of Ysaye about it, mingled with the grayness of the computer. *Delete Process 392397642.*

Process deleted, replied the computer.

Abruptly, Leonie found herself flung free of the machine—and back into her prone body at Arilinn.

She opened her eyes, aching all over, and terrified. Her head pounded, hard enough to explode, and her stomach churned.

Dimly, distantly, she felt Ysaye's pleasure that all was well, and far more distantly, she felt Lorill—confused, knowing that something had threatened his twin, and wondering what in the world—any world—had happened.

She shivered and cried a little, feeling that if she moved or spoke she might start screaming and never stop. Finally, both fear and reaction gave way to complete exhaustion; she pulled the covers over herself, and with it pulled together such tattered remnants of dignity and discipline as she could still summon, and let herself fall into sleep—or unconsciousness.

But even through her sleep, she formed a firm and unshakable conviction.

Never again.

She would not seek out the strange "technologies" of these star folk. She would advise strongly against others doing so—and when she had the power to enforce her will, she would enforce this edict.

Terran technologies must be left to Terrans. They may have much that is good, but it is all—all of it—too dangerous for us to touch. No one else must dare this.

Life went on, whether they wished it to or not; Ysaye recovered from the surgery and immersed herself in her work, finding little solace there, but enough to keep her mind busy. At night, when she was unable to sleep, she put on the corticator to learn the languages of Darkover. It gave her a headache, but it kept her from having to think. And for as long as she wore the corticator, dreams did not trouble her either.

She avoided Elizabeth; her friend glowed with happiness over her pregnancy, her new home, and her work, and Ysaye could not bear to be the skeleton at the feast. She lost weight, and Aurora scolded her, finally ordering her on a special diet that had her shipmates staring with envy at her meal trays, laden as they were with fresh fruit, choice cuts of meat, and calorie-crammed, rich deserts.

No one made any reference to her terminated pregnancy; the only time anyone ever spoke of her surgery was to commiserate on the hysterectomy, then say lightly, "But then, you never were the sort to settle down and have children." One or two of the women

even said they were envious of her—no longer subject
to the tyranny of hormones.

The first time it happened, she was shocked speechless at their callous lack of tact. But then someone else
made a similar remark, one that would have been
thoughtless at best and cruel at worst if they had known
of the lost child. And at first, Ysaye thought they were
all simply avoiding the subject of her pregnancy to the
point of pretending it had never happened, but grad-
ually she came to realize that they simply didn't know
about what had really happened to her. So far as they
were concerned, she'd had a life-threatening allergy
attack, one that had somehow caused problems that
required the hysterectomy. If anyone knew how unlikely that was, they weren't talking. And the few people who did know about the child were either native
Darkovans, or friends who wouldn't mention it unless
she brought it up—or the medical staff, who would
never mention it at all and had locked it in sealed records.

When she figured it all out, she was nearly as an-
gered as relieved. In a way, she felt cheated; she ought
to be able to mourn and have people understand why
she was in mourning; now they would simply think her
behavior was some kind of silly female reaction to the
loss of an organ she could perfectly well do without.

Surgery, even major surgery, no longer required the
long recovery periods it had in eras long gone. Within
a week, she was on her feet in her daily routine and
there was very little pain; within two, there was nothing
but a narrow red scar to remind her that anything had
ever happened.

That made her feel cheated, too—something had
been taken from her, something vital, and there was
nothing to show it had ever happened. There should
have been pain, as a kind of penance. Yet she did have

her work, and that work often required mobility, and it was her duty to heal as quickly as she could. Just as it was the medical staff's duty to see that she healed quickly.

Leonie contacted her only to say that she was tired, and hoped Ysaye was all right. She said she was very busy with something—at first, Ysaye had thought that the girl was staying away from her because she was still angry about losing the child. Then she thought it might be because she had been so terrified by the incident with the computer. But when Leonie finally appeared one night and indicated she was ready to talk again, it was with no sign of fear—and if anything, the bond between Ysaye and the girl was stronger than ever.

Where have you been keeping yourself? Ysaye asked, adding lightly, *besides behind this "Veil of Arilinn,"* that is.

Oh, Ysaye, that is truer than you know, the girl said, as weary as Ysaye had ever heard her. *I have been taking special training only a Keeper receives. Now that I have it—well, no man will ever be able to force me to give up my virginity.*

That's a trick a lot of women could use, Ysaye commented.

Leonie sighed. *It is not that easy. And I doubt that most women would want it, when they knew what the training required. But Keepers must be able to guard themselves, for there are so few of us.*

Sounds like the old tale that a witch had to be a virgin to work magic.

She sensed Leonie nodding. *Very like. There is a long tradition behind it, but it is—is very hard on a person. It means that energy must be transmitted through the physical body, and everything must be in perfect balance. That is why Keepers are virgin, always. And*

*why we must be able to defend that virginity. I could not
meet with you until that defense had become reflex.*

Ysaye couldn't see the connection between transmitting energy through the body and being virgin, but she didn't say anything. *Sounds like more than I'd care to do.*

I have also been learning how to channel my family's particular Gift. The Hasturs are like living matrixes—we can do without a matrix what most people can only do with one. I did not know I had that Gift until last week. Ysaye caught the background of the thought and realized that this "matrix" was some sort of amplifier of psi powers. If she could work without one, Leonie must be powerful indeed. No wonder she was being trained so strictly!

Leonie seemed much older than she had a mere few weeks ago, as if all this training had aged her and given her the experience of a much older woman.

Sounds to me as if you could use some music. That was all Ysaye could give her, though she would dearly have liked to offer the girl better sympathy than that. Why, the poor thing was having her childhood stolen from her! Matrixes, energons—none of this meant much of anything to Ysaye, except that it seemed that the more responsibility was laid on the girl, the less girl-like she became. She was—what? Fifteen? And she was taking on tasks at which an adult would quail, making sacrifices about which even an adult would have serious second thoughts. It hardly seemed fair.

I should like some music, Leonie agreed. *Are you still dreaming badly?*

Ysaye cued up music—Ralph Vaughan Williams—and took a moment before replying. She had thought that when the child was gone, she would no longer have dreams about it—but now, if anything, they were worse. Ysaye slept, often only to find herself in a kind of vague, dreamlike landscape covered with mist. And the baby was there. No longer a child, but an infant, a little girl barely old enough to walk, who cried and cried in the dim distance—but when Ysaye tried to approach her, she receded and moved out of sight, leaving only the heartbreaking weeping. And Ysaye would wake up to find herself also weeping as if her heart would break.

Yes, she said, finally. *Unless I wear the corticator.* She showed Leonie some of what the dreams had been like, and added, wryly, *I am likely to be very good at a number of languages before this is over.*

Leonie was silent for a moment, and Ysaye sensed that she was thinking. *I can only guess at this*, she said, after a long moment, *But I think there is a reason why you have these dreams. You wanted her, you wanted to bear her into life, and so she is still bound to you.*

Mystical nonsense? Ysaye didn't think so. Too many things dismissed as "mystical nonsense" turned out to be very real on this world. *If I—if I let her go, emotionally, will she stop haunting me?*

Leonie's answer was hesitant. *I don't know, Ysaye. You may be so bound that she will not leave you until you join her.*

Not an encouraging thought, but—in its own way —a comforting one. Ysaye had wanted the child, and in a way that made no rational sense at all and was hard for her to understand, she still did.

Her mother would have blamed her for what had happened—her mother would doubtless disinherit her if she ever found out; Ysaye was still baffled by why she had acted the way she had. It made no sense. It was as if something had turned off everything except her lowest instincts, and that same something had inflamed those instincts.

And there was still something missing about this whole situation; the unresolved question of why she had become so intoxicated—and why Elizabeth had been just as intoxicated, although there had been no nightmare ending to her intoxication. Ryan Evans had played a part in it, and not a small one. Ysaye was certain he had somehow drugged Elizabeth, and might have drugged her as well. If she could prove that, she might have a *reason* for all this. A reason that did not include totally taking leave of her senses. She wished there were some way to make Evans pay for all the pain he had caused—preferably out of his own hide.

Perhaps when she had a reason, had a cause, and someone to charge with that cause, she would be able to sleep at night.

Perhaps then her daughter would stop crying.

A few days later, she was on her way down to one of the lower levels of the ship, when she saw a very familiar back.

"Kadarin!" she called in surprise, as she recognized the lanky figure. "Whatever are you doing on the ship?" She was glad to be able to speak to him in *casta*; in this much, at least, the hours under the corticator were bearing fruit. Being able to speak to him so that her mind did not have to touch his made it possible for her to feel a bit more friendly toward him.

Kadarin stopped, turned, and smiled when he saw who had addressed him in his own tongue. Then his smile faded, as quickly as it had come. He inclined his head to her. "*S'dia shaya, domna,*" he said, and paused. "I was sorry to hear about your baby," he continued softly. "Children are very precious to us. Very precious."

"Thank you," Ysaye murmured automatically, then added, startled, "but where did you hear about my child?"

Kadarin looked embarrassed, but Ysaye guessed it

before he could speak. The only people who had known besides the medics and the Lornes were the natives. And one native in particular. "Don't tell me; Lorill spread the news all over Caer Donn." She sighed. "There goes my reputation."

"Not at all, *domna*," Kadarin protested. "He only told Kermiac and Felicia because they were concerned that you were ill, and none of the *Terranan* would tell us of what. Felicia told me, and further said to send her sympathies. That is all." He shook his head. "And you must know, it is not shameful to us to bear any child whose parentage is known. The only disgrace is for a woman not to be able to say who fathered her child—or to have the father deny that he did."

Ysaye bit her tongue to keep from saying something bitter, but that did not prevent a waspish comment from escaping. "And I'm sure that Lorill thinks any woman would be honored to bear him a child, so telling people what happened should make me happy."

"Any woman on Darkover," Kadarin pointed out quietly, "would be honored to bear a Hastur child. And both of them would be cared for and given privileges for the rest of their lives. You could have demanded anything of Lorill that he was empowered to give. You still could; you risked your life."

Well, she couldn't argue with that. But it was their custom, not hers, and he obviously didn't understand why being talked about made her feel badly. "Where I come from," Ysaye said sadly, hoping she could explain, "A woman is not supposed to—what's the word?—*accandir* with any man except her husband."

Kadarin blinked in surprise. "Does your language have no word for the lying down of man with woman, that you use ours? Do you have matings with machines, then?"

Ysaye shook her head. "The words I know for it

are either vague euphemisms that wouldn't translate properly, or are terms not usable in polite company," she admitted, "which probably shows you how we regard someone who engages in that kind of behavior." She shrugged helplessly. "Even I feel that way, Kadarin. I feel like—like a woman who could not tell who fathered her child. Or one who took a child into her bed, since Lorill *is* just a child by the standards of our Empire."

He looked at her attentively, and suddenly she realized that she had been feeling the lack of having someone *adult* that she could talk to about it all. Aurora encouraged her to "put it behind her," Elizabeth didn't understand, and Leonie was another child, Lorill's twin.

"I don't even remember *why* I did it," she admitted. "It was crazy behavior; I just don't fling myself at men years my junior as if I were some kind of—female animal in season. But my mind goes all fuzzy when I try to remember why it happened, and what I was thinking." She shivered. "Sometimes I think there may be something wrong with my mind, and that—incident— with Lorill is only one symptom."

"I doubt that there's anything wrong with your mind," Kadarin said reassuringly. "I was caught in a Ghost Wind once, and my memories of that time are quite hazy indeed. Lorill said something about *kireseth* pollen upon your clothing, and that pollen was probably the cause of everything."

Ysaye looked at him as if *he* had gone crazy. "Ghost Wind?" she asked. "Pollen?"

"Ah, I forget," he shook his head. "I have spoken to a few others of this, but not to you; only the ones who were to go with me out into the lands beyond Caer Donn. Sometimes, when the weather gets hot—that is, relatively speaking—bringing a kind of short summer out-of-season, the pollen of the *kireseth* flowers is blown about on the wind. It happens in the lowlands and valleys more often than in mountains, such as Caer Donn, of course. The pollen is quite intoxicating, makes one see visions, and—ah—stimulates mating. Anyone caught by a Ghost Wind tends to go a bit mad—and there are generally quite a few babies born seven months later."

"Oh," she said, many inexplicable things coming together to form a nasty picture.

"No one seeks to be caught in a Ghost Wind," he continued, "Because the visions can make a person do things he would never do in his right mind. Because of that, there are prohibitions about the handling of the flowers that no one I know would flout."

"Never?" she asked sarcastically.

"Never. Only the *leroni* can handle the flowers safely; that is the word from the Towers. Truly, *domna*," he added earnestly. "If you were caught in pollen, what happened is no disgrace, no one will blame you for any of it, and it is no reflection on your normal behavior."

"*Kireseth.*" Ysaye stood quietly, as the pattern settled into place. She closed her eyes briefly against the red haze of anger that crossed her vision, and forced herself to speak softly and carefully. "Are those the flowers that Evans was growing in the greenhouse at his lab? The ones with the little blue bell-shaped flowers?"

"Yes, those are the ones," Kadarin confirmed. "I have warned him about how the pollen carries and he had them under glass when last I saw them; that may even be where you were exposed to it, if they bloomed before he expected them to. He has quite an impressive crop of them; it is amazing how well they do in an artificial environment."

"Of course," Ysaye said as casually as she could

manage, "if they got too warm, they would all die."
The fires of hell would not be warm enough for Evans,
she thought grimly.

Kadarin shrugged. "I don't know, I am not a grower
of plants. Probably. But that is not ever likely to be a
problem upon this world."

"No," Ysaye replied automatically. "Of course
not."

"Kadarin?" Zeb Scott appeared at the end of the
corridor. "There you are! Come on, the shuttle is this
way. If you want a chance to go up before you take
Elizabeth and David into the field, you'd better catch
this one."

He rushed up, took Kadarin by the arm, and started
to tow him down the corridor. Ysaye looked after them
for a moment, then headed for the outside, the Science
building, and the xenobotany lab.

Ysaye stood looking down at the lovely blue flowers
beneath their sealed cover—a cover she had last seen
standing open, with Elizabeth on the floor next to the
plant bench. A locked cover; one that would need a
specific fingerprint to unlock. Kadarin had spoken the
truth; it was an impressive crop.

The monstrous little things were positively thriving,
Ysaye thought.

But not for long.

There wasn't a computer in this complex that she
couldn't override—or lock up, once she had put in the
override commands. Every bench in this greenhouse
was controlled from the lab computer, and the greenhouse itself was completely controlled by the computer
as well. She returned to the lab, and ordered the computer to put quarantine seals on the greenhouse. Above
her, the door swung shut with an audible *thud*, and the
hiss of the seals clamping in place made her smile.

Ysaye, what are you doing? Leonie demanded in her mind. *Your anger reached me even through the Veil!*

Briefly, Ysaye explained, and felt Leonie's startlement and her answering anger.

That is sacrilege! the girl exclaimed. *Only the Tower workers can touch* kireseth *flowers safely! So that is what happened to you and Lorill! Why, that filthy beast—*

Will be taken care of by the Captain as soon as I finish here, Ysaye told her grimly. The scent of the blossoms filled the air throughout the lab, even after the greenhouse had been sealed, so Ysaye told the computer to seal off the lab from the rest of the complex and set the air recycler to run at maximum, with full detoxification protocols.

That should make sure he hasn't contaminated the whole building, she told Leonie, *And that will make sure there are no more pregnant crew members*.

She coded in the last of the tasks—to elevate the temperature in the greenhouse to well over the highest recorded temperature of the most arid of Terra's deserts, and to run the dehumidifier as well. That should kill every flower in there, and yet preserve the evidence she needed to convict Ryan Evans of some very specific charges. Intoxication without consent, cultivation of a controlled substance, administration of an unknown drug without prior approval, assault by pharmaceutical, and attempted rape. He wasn't going to get out of this one. Just to make certain, she set all the cameras in the lab to record what happened there. When Evans discovered what had happened, he might say or do something to incriminate himself further.

She sensed Leonie's approval as she put in the lockdown code. Now the only people who would be able to enter the greenhouse section of the lab were herself and the Captain. And she was the only person who could unlock the lab computer. She started to turn to go find the Captain, feeling a little like one of the Valkyries of legend.

Then the lab door slid open and Evans entered.

He looked surprised. "What are you doing in here?" he asked.

She didn't—quite—snarl at him.

"Sterilizing your unauthorized experiment," she replied through clenched teeth.

"No!" Evans dove across the room and shoved her away from the terminal and into the opposite wall. He began punching frantically at the keys. "You can't do that! Do you have any idea what these plants are worth? They have properties you can't even imagine!"

He does not know you were here that night? Leonie said in surprise.

Evidently not, Ysaye replied, and answered him grimly, "Oh, I think I have a pretty good idea."

She rubbed her shoulder, which had absorbed most of the force of the collision with the wall. But she remembered the watching cameras, and asked, "Just what did you plan to do with those—plants?"

She couldn't for a moment imagine how he had managed to work in the lab without being affected by the flowers—or had his brains been so scrambled by everything else he'd indulged in that he didn't even notice?

Evans was still trying to override her lockdowns, talking rapidly about the commercial possibilities for the pollen on Keef, in the brothels and drug-dens. "The Madams are going to pay through the nose for this!" he said, frantically. "It'll lower their training and spoilage costs, and the girls and boys could start working earlier, which would increase their useful lives—Ysaye, what did you do here? How can I turn it off?"

Useful lives? Leonie said, puzzled. *What does he mean? How can there be such a thing as a useless life?*

Ysaye thought that Evans' own life might well qualify in that category, but she said only, *Believe me, Leonie, you don't want to know what he means.*

Aloud, she said to Evans for the benefit of the cameras, "Did you really expect Captain Gibbons to hold still for any of this?"

Evans gave up trying to get into the computer, and turned big, mock-innocent eyes on her. "Why do you think this experiment isn't in the computer? Be a sport, Ysaye," his tone turned wheedling, "I'll make it worth your while. How about five percent of the profits and eight grams for your own use." He leered at her. "It would even make a cast-iron virgin like you loosen up and enjoy life. Just get over here and cancel what you did."

Was this supposed to convince her? She was still linked with Leonie who was shocked into speechlessness by this attitude.

"Only over my dead body do you get your damned drugs. In fact, just thinking about this makes me want to kill you," Ysaye said flatly. She wasn't sure how much of the anger was hers and how much Leonie's; both of them were outraged.

Evans blinked, taken aback by this unexpected show of aggression, particularly from such an unexpected source. Then he took a bullying stance. "Don't be a stupid bitch, Ysaye. You couldn't hurt anyone. You're a tech, not a killer."

"Not a killer?" Anger burned all of the sense out of her. "You bastard. Thanks to you and your damned drugs, that's exactly what I am! Didn't you ever wonder how Elizabeth found her way out of your greenhouse the night of the Festival? I was the one that got Elizabeth out of here when you drugged her and planned to rape her! And I'm going to make damned sure that

you end up in a prison for the rest of your unnatural
life!"

"The hell you are!" Evans screamed, and lunged at
her, grabbing her by the throat.

Ysaye found herself blacking out as she tried un-
successfully to throw him off.

How dare *you lay hands on us?* Leonie's voice
screamed in fury, as her Keeper's reflexes took over
Ysaye's mind and body.

Fire crackled along their nerves and into the body
of the man holding them. The three of them dropped,
convulsing, to the floor, thrashing about on the cold
vinylite.

Evans screamed as he burned—Ysaye screamed as
power surged through her overloaded nerves, meeting
resistance and burning it away. Leonie screamed with
the pain of Ysaye's body. They were nose-to-nose with
a charred corpse, and still the power scorched Ysaye's
soul, as fire alarms sounded, and emergency fans
pumped air through the decontamination filters at the
maximum possible speed.

The mingled scents of burned flesh and *kireseth* pollen faded away as the Tower monitor bent over their
twitching body, and they sank thankfully into darkness.

CHAPTER
22

"I wish we could have made that shuttle," Zeb Scott said wistfully, urging his horse up a rise as only a born rider could. Elizabeth envied him that; she still felt she sat her horse like a sack of grain. "It's going to be a while until we can get another pair of seats up to the observation station on that moon."

"Ah, well, all things in their time," Kadarin replied philosophically as his horse mirrored Zeb's. "And our loss is the Lornes' gain, is it not?"

He grinned wickedly at David and Elizabeth. David just grinned in return, but Elizabeth found herself wishing that she could have been alone with David. After all, they both knew how to ride, they had the best maps that Survey could provide, they were as good at *casta* and *cahuenga* as Ryan Evans, and they were only going to one of Lord Aldaran's remote villages. They really didn't need a guide.

Given that the Captain had not permitted them any kind of leave for a real honeymoon, this would have made a good opportunity for them to be alone together. You just couldn't be "alone" for long when someone was always activating your beeper for something or other. She'd even been beeped twice the night of the Festival—or so David said. She didn't really remember that, and since no one had thought it important enough to leave a message, she didn't have any record of it.

Well, at least, they had this little trek, with only two others with them instead of the whole crew. So she contented herself with what little she had, instead of fretting for more.

David smiled over at her, as if he had sensed her thoughts.

Kadarin rode a little ahead of them. He had said so little thus far that she might as *well* have been alone with David. Perhaps he, too, had sensed her wish for some privacy, and was giving the newly-married couple the best illusion of it that he could. Kadarin could be amazingly sensitive that way.

And Zeb, while not a *good* friend, was someone they both knew and trusted. So in a sense, it was nearer than she had thought possible to the honeymoon she had wanted.

But despite the pleasant way the journey had begun, by late afternoon, she was plagued with a growing sense of disquiet. They camped without any incident—and Zeb and Kadarin pitched their travel shelter far enough away to give her an illusion of privacy. Yet throughout that evening and night, she continued to feel restless and somehow afraid, as if something horrible was going to happen. Her dreams were full of nightmares, and she woke up once during the night with her heart pounding with terror.

The morning dawned clear and relatively warm, and it seemed that her disquiet was nothing more than night-fear. They packed up and returned to the trail. But halfway through this, their second day, an odd wind began to rise.

Elizabeth sniffed, as an odd perfume, resinous and faintly familiar, wreathed around her.

"Ah, now this is likely to cause some delay," Kadarin said at the same moment, his strange eyes lighting with some kind of emotion Elizabeth couldn't put a name to. Amusement? "This is a winter blooming; we must take care to be within walls before the wind can reach us."

"Wind?" Zeb Scott laughed. "Kadarin, I'm an Arkansas boy, I've been through tornadoes there and sandstorms in the Arizona desert, and I've never been afraid of a wind yet!"

Kadarin smiled, a little scornfully. "You would do well to fear this wind, even if you are one of the Terrans whose technology can overcome all difficulties. Even your Captain should learn to fear the wind of a winter blooming."

But Kadarin's scorn was for Zeb's belief, not for Zeb himself. And that made Elizabeth think about something she had been wondering about since the beginning of this trip. And interestingly, although she did not make any attempt to get Kadarin's attention, he seemed to be aware of her thought, and reined in his horse to come alongside hers.

"Yes, *domna*?" he said. "You have a question?"

She smiled shyly. "More of a curiosity, if you don't mind. I wondered why you were always so deferential to Zeb—or, for that matter, to me. Ryan Evans has a much higher rank in the Terran Service, and you show him just bare politeness."

Kadarin seemed startled; he reflected silently for a moment, then replied to her mind-to-mind, rather than vocally. And he seemed amused. *Thank you for bringing that to my attention; I must be careful of that. It is, I think, a purely automatic reaction on my part. Zeb is very like one of the Comyn, the mighty Hastur-kin. Does red hair signify nothing of caste with your people?*

She was a little surprised at that; the Service was completely "color-blind," and it had never occurred to her that something like a physical attribute could denote rank. *Indeed, it does not*, she told him. *The only rank*

*among us is one of a person's earned status within the
Service. In fact, Captain Gibbons is the highest in rank
of all of us.*

Kadarin nodded, slowly. *So it is something like—
oh, the Thendara City Guards. I had wondered at that,
I could not see what it was that made you all defer to
such a funny little old man. So Zeb is not highly regarded
among you?*

She smiled. *Only by virtue of being a trustworthy
man; so far as real rank goes, he's one of the lowest.
Even David and I outrank him by quite a bit.*

Kadarin nodded. *And what of Ryan Evans?*

*Ysaye outranks him; he is about the same as David,
and I am slightly lower in rank.*

He raised an eyebrow. *Strange. I must consider this.*

He urged his horse forward again, back to ride knee-
to-knee with Zeb Scott. "Well, friend," he said to Scott,
"you may not believe in ghosts, but you would do well
to believe in what we call the Ghost Wind. The winds
at this season bear the *kireseth* pollen—and whether
you call it drug, as some do, or poison, as the *cristoforos*
think, it does not matter. It is very dangerous, even to
you *Terranan*."

Was it Elizabeth's imagination, or had he cast an
odd and significant look back at her?

Zeb looked fascinated. "Ghost Wind? *Kireseth?* Kadarin, you can't just leave it at that. Is it a drug, or a
poison? Is it deadly, or not?"

Kadarin pursed his lips thoughtfully. "That would
depend on definitions," he said. "It *is* used in the Towers, only not as the pure resin, but rather as a distillation
of one fraction. In that form, it is a liqueur, called
kirian, and it is a useful drug to diminish resistance
against telepathy. The pure pollen and all other frac-
tions of the pollen are banned here. The Towers think
that some of the side effects are entirely too dangerous,

and although I do not entirely agree with them, I tend to think that it is not for the unwary. Under the influence of the pollen and the other distillations, men can go mad, so the Towers say—and certainly, these things have the effect of making the beasts lose their minds. Only *kirian* seems to be safe, because all that it does is to diminish resistance to telepathic contact. In those with no telepathy, it only makes them sleepy."

Zeb looked skeptical. "Telepathy?" he said. "I don't know—I mean, I'm just an ordinary guy, but I've never seen anything to make me believe telepathy is even possible." He grinned ruefully back at David and Elizabeth. "Sorry, folks, I know you two are supposed to be really high-powered mind-readers, but there it is. Before I believed in it, I'd have to see some really solid evidence."

Kadarin shrugged, and said, "Stay out in the Ghost Wind, then, and I guarantee your skepticism will end. Felicia will be pleased."

Zeb nodded, and Elizabeth had the sinking feeling that Kadarin had been taunting him with this—or goading him, perhaps, into something he would not have thought of on his own. "So—maybe I'll do just that!"

"On your head be it, I take no responsibility." Kadarin then grinned wickedly. "There are other side effects, and those may not please you as much. You may find yourself sharing pleasure with a catman or a *cralmac*, or even a sheep!"

When David and Zeb laughed, he shook his head. "Oh, laugh if you will," he said, "I am older than I look, and I have seen many strange things in these hills."

And now he refused to meet Elizabeth's eyes, as if he knew something that he did not want her to know.

"I just might risk it anyway," Zeb said. "Hey, I'm a spaceman, and I've been known to wake up next to quite a few strange things after a night on the town!"

Now Kadarin laughed aloud, an edged laughter that made Elizabeth very uneasy. "Perhaps, but I wonder what you will have to say afterward if you dare? And I wonder what you will think when you find you hear voices in your head. But I think we must at least have the courtesy to get the Lornes to shelter."

David protested. "Wait a minute, here—Elizabeth has always been more of a telepath than I have, and frankly, I wish I were as good as she is. I'd kind of like to get downwind of something that would give me a little more in that department than I've got already. Liz, what do you think? Couldn't you use something that would give you a telepathic boost?"

Something about the sweet, resinous scent in the air disturbed Elizabeth deeply, but before she could reply, Kadarin did so for her.

"I think this would be a mistake, a grave one," he said. "Elizabeth, it is no secret that you are with child—"

"I won't risk my baby to some strange drug," she said firmly, and turned a pleading face toward David. "And I don't want to be alone, if this stuff makes the local wildlife act in strange ways."

"Bravo!" Kadarin laughed again, and it seemed to her that while part of him approved, part of him was mocking her for some reason. "Zeb, you can, if you wish, make the experiment, but I must tell you that *I* do not recommend it. You must do this on your own responsibility."

"Oh, but now you've challenged me, and I never refuse a challenge," Scott replied. As Elizabeth had feared, he had responded to Kadarin's dare without thinking of anything but that he'd been given a challenge. "But where can we find shelter for the others against your Ghost Wind?"

Kadarin looked at the horizon, his brow creased with thought. "On your map, the one you made with pictures from the air, there is a ruined building. The roof was taken off, by the owner, I think, so that he did not have to pay taxes upon it. If you set up the tents there, and stay inside the walls and your tents, Elizabeth would be safe from the pollen. And if you wish to experience the Ghost Wind, you can simply stand outside the walls. If you change your mind, the tents will still be there to shelter you."

Elizabeth sniffed again; the wind was definitely stronger, and so was the resinous scent in the air. "If that's the best we can do for shelter, we had better get into it pretty quickly," she said. "And Zeb—I really don't think you should do this."

He laughed, and it seemed to her that some of the wildness in Kadarin's laughter had crept into his. "Oh, no, fair lady," he mocked. "It would hardly be the *manly* thing to resist a challenge like this!"

She couldn't find any sensible answer for that, and doubted that he would listen to one, anyway. She concentrated on urging her horse after Kadarin's, off the road and onto a barely visible track. Several times during the next hour, she wondered how on earth he was finding his way—meanwhile the scent kept getting stronger, and she began to feel just a little light-headed. She sighed with relief as they topped a rise, and she saw the walls of the ruined manor.

"Here is where we leave you, then," Kadarin said. "Zeb and I will go up there."

He pointed off to their right, deeper into the hills.

"There is a meadow there where I think I recall the *kireseth* flowers often bloom. That is probably the source of this Ghost Wind, or one source at any rate." He grinned, and turned his horse's head on the designated path, as Zeb Scott followed his lead.

"Go straight to the source, hmm?" Zeb said, his eyes glowing with anticipation.

"I wish you wouldn't—" Elizabeth said once more, but they waved farewell to her and continued on the new path.

"We will come back for you," Kadarin called over his shoulder. "Or at least—I will," he added teasingly.

Then they disappeared over the crest of a hill, leaving Elizabeth and David on their original path. David shrugged as Elizabeth looked at him with reproach.

"He's his own man, Liz," David said. "We'll be all right."

She sighed. "I suppose you're right—"

"And this gives us a real chance to be alone," he added mischievously. "That might be half the reason they went off like that!"

"I don't think that little-boy I-dare-you nonsense had anything to do with us," she replied sourly. "But you're right; it does give us a chance to be alone. I suppose I shouldn't complain."

They continued following the path that led to the ruined manor, and Elizabeth noticed that the weather was warming more and more by the minute. Already the horses were hock-deep in melting snow and mud, and leaves and even flowers were unfolding all around them. They were having too much trouble controlling their horses, who were becoming quite restive and inclined to fight the bit, to exchange any more conversation. But even though Elizabeth was fighting her horse every step of the way—it was showing a lot of interest in David's mare, and it was a *gelding!*—she caught glimpses of birds and normally-shy animals—rabbits of some sort, she thought—cavorting about as if they were drunk.

So Kadarin had been right about this pollen! She

only hoped they could reach shelter before it affected her and David, too.

The horse kept fighting her, and there was no doubt that, gelded or not, the beast had only one thing on his mind, and it had nothing to do with reaching shelter. So she really didn't pay any attention to their goal until she actually turned the recalcitrant beast in through what was left of the gate.

Then she looked up—and inside the ruined walls, she saw a cluster of tents.

What?

Who would camp here, so far from Caer Donn, trying to hide their camp in a deserted building?

Who else—except a lawbreaker, an outlaw?

Sudden fear overtook her, as she realized that she had seen these tents before, in her dreams of last night. And terrible things had followed that first glimpse of tents. She tried to wheel her horse, crying out to David in terror, "David! Let's get out of here fast!"

David reined in his horse, his eyes wide—but before they could do anything, wild and barbaric figures appeared from every direction, surrounding them and seizing their bridles. Elizabeth was stunned; like a frightened animal, she huddled in on herself, hardly able to think.

They were human, but not like any humans Elizabeth had ever seen before; roughly and poorly clad, bearded, hair straggling and unwashed.

Exactly, she thought dazedly, as you would imagine a bandit would look.

As one of them, marginally better dressed than the others, forced her horse's head down, he cried out something in a language she could not understand. She suddenly wondered if Kadarin had set this up. He had certainly seemed amused.

But why would he do this? And how could he have

predicted that this "Ghost Wind" thing would have come up? There would have been no reason otherwise for them to come anywhere near this manor. Leading them into an ambush would destroy his standing with the Terrans—perhaps he didn't care. Perhaps he had intended something like this all along. They could be worth a fortune in ransom to—to just about anyone.

Yet until that moment, she had not thought that Kadarin ever meant her any worse harm than a bit of teasing. And she had never had one of her intuitions about someone be so completely wrong before.

The man who had seized her bridle was repeating something in a sharply interrogative tone in which she heard the word *Comyn* repeated several times. That was the only word she recognized; the one that meant the ruling caste of Darkover. Other than that, she didn't recognize anything he said; he simply wasn't speaking any of the Darkovan languages she knew.

But David answered the man in the same language, so David obviously understood. "Liz, they seem to think we're some kin of Aldaran—and he's not a big fan of Kermiac, apparently. They want to know what we're doing here, without an escort."

"What?" she said, baffled and confused. Had Kadarin known nothing about these people? Was this just a monstrous, horrible accident?

David replied shortly. The man gabbled something else; David listened to him, frowning. "I told him we were only guests of Lord Aldaran. So now he's accusing us of being kin to Lorill Hastur, and spies for the Hasturs."

At the sound of Lorill's name, the man holding her bridle grimaced furiously, and repeated "Hastur," shaking his fist. Elizabeth shrank away from him, for he was a tall man, with clothing a little cleaner and less ragged than the others, and with the fierce and wild look of a hawk. He looked as if he could do a great deal of damage with that huge knife at his side, and what was worse, he looked as if he might enjoy doing it, too.

"Oh, God, David—he doesn't seem to like that, either!" Fear seized her heart and made it beat faster. "Tell him—tell him we don't know any Hasturs! Tell him we just wanted shelter from the wind! Try and get him to let us go!"

"I'll try," David said grimly. "But I don't think anything I tell him is going to make much of an impression."

She closed her eyes, as another breath of that resinous air washed over her and made her head spin for a moment. And in the wake of that dizziness, she was suddenly inside David's mind, as she had been—that night her baby had been conceived.

But she had no chance to think about that; she concentrated on David's questions, and the man's reply.

"What do you want with us?" David asked. "We came in here for shelter from the wind. We meant no intrusion, and if you wish, we will leave."

"I don't think so," the man answered shortly. "You are wealthy, whoever you are, with your horses and your fine clothes and packs. We will have ransom from you, before you depart from here."

David shook his head. Without speaking, Elizabeth understood what he was thinking, that they had somehow gotten involved in Darkovan politics.

But no, she thought, shivering so from fear that she could not have spoken if she wanted to. It wasn't politics—it was greed. These men were nothing but robbers; they wanted money. And when they had it, there was no guarantee that these bandits would let her and David go.

But David persisted in his assumption. "I beg your

pardon, sir, but you don't understand. We are not associated with Aldaran, nor do we have any relationship with the Hasturs. My wife and I have no quarrel with you or your people."

The man laughed, harshly. "That may or may not be true, stranger—but whoever your kin is, your red hair and your *laran* proclaim you to be allied to the Hastur-kin. And we have you. The agreement is plain; we will have the customary ransom. Your people may not come beyond the river—when you do, you break the old agreement, and you cannot escape without just payment."

David grimaced. "Liz, I'm going to try the truth. Surely these people must have heard about us by now." He turned back to the bandit leader. "I fear that your trap is missprung, for I pledge you, we are neither folk of Aldaran nor of what you call the Hastur-kin. We are visitors here, and surely you have heard of us—we come from a world which circles one of the stars in the sky—"

The man interrupted with a gesture of disgust. "What do you think I am, a fool? Do you think to dazzle me with some fantastic tale? Do you truly expect me to believe such nonsense? Even I know that the stars are no more than distant balls of fire!"

David tried to reply, but the man cut him off with an impatient gesture.

"I can see I waste time with you," the man spat. "You must certainly think I am a drooling idiot, to try to fool me with such stable-sweepings. You will go to our leader, and you may try, if you like, to think up some more believable story for him." He grinned wolfishly. "But don't try that fool's drivel about being from some other world on him. He is a *laranzu*, and he will know at once if you are trying to make a fool of him."

Laranzu? David's linguistic mind made short work

of the unfamiliar word—it obviously had something to do with *laran*, which should mean that the man had telepathic powers, like Felicia and Kermiac.

"He says their leader is a telepath," David replied, "At least there's this much, there's no way to lie to someone with *laran*. He'll have to believe that we're telling the truth."

"Let's just hope he not only believes that, but he'll believe it when we tell him that it's Terran policy to pay no ransom," she replied, still shivering. "If he understands that there's no benefit in holding us, maybe he'll let us go."

David subsided into silence while they rode, the bandits' hands keeping firm hold of their bridles, into one of the half-ruined buildings inside the walls. Elizabeth rode silently in David's wake, with a growing feeling of certainty that their troubles were only beginning, and that it would not be that simple.

Her premonition was right. Their guide stopped their horses before a tent, and made it very clear that if they did not dismount on their own, they would be "aided" to do so. The horses and gear were taken away—probably never to be seen again—and they were "escorted" into the tent. There was a young man there, clothed much like their talkative guide, seated cross-legged on a stack of folded blankets. His hair was almost as red as David's and he had the same fierce grin as their captor.

"Well, cousin, what have we here?" he asked the first man.

"A jester," the man replied, "for when he knew he was caught, he tried to tell me some tale of having been dropped here from one of the stars in the sky. I told him that he might try that tale upon you, and that if he insists on it, you will know of what to make of it."

"Christ," David swore under his breath. Aloud, he

said, "If you are truly a *laranzu*, you will know from
my mind that I speak the truth. We are visitors from
another world, we are no kin to any man on this world,
and we are of no worth to anyone."

The man stared fixedly at David for several seconds,
then spat. He turned to the first bandit, ignoring David
and Elizabeth. "One of two things is true; either he is
a poor madman who believes what he is saying, or else
Aldaran and his *laranzu'in* have found some way to
shield the mind, and this is one of his *laranzu*, a man
with such surpassing skill he thinks to make us believe
this nonsense."

"Or else to believe that he is mad, and worthless,"
the first man said. "For who would ever care to ransom
a madman? Rather, they would be glad that such an
embarrassment was gone."

The second one snorted. "Well, he did not reckon
to find me too old and wily a fox to see through his
tales." He gestured abruptly. "Take them to the prisoner's tent, and put a damper on it so that they cannot
reach their fellows at Aldaran. Let them think over their
tale in solitude for a little time, and perhaps they will
think better of telling us where they come from."

Before either of them could move, several men had
David prisoner, and two men had taken Elizabeth's
arms as well. David began to swear and struggle, but
without avail. A few moments later, they had thrown
David ungently down inside another tent, and Elizabeth
had been deposited beside him. The men left, then, but
Elizabeth had no doubt that several of them were waiting outside, guarding them. She kept feeling a dull kind
of vibration that gave her a headache; she guessed that
it might be the "telepathic damper" the bandit chief
spoke of. After a moment, she realized that she had
real proof of this, for she no longer sensed anything of
David's thoughts.

"Well," David said at last, pulling himself up into a sitting position. "We've certainly gotten into a mess now. I thought that when Kadarin and Zeb went off and left us that we were in trouble—but now we're *really* in trouble. Got any ideas?"

Elizabeth shook her head, helplessly, and began to cry. David moved to hold her in his arms to give her the little comfort he could. She had taken for granted, since they had landed on this world, that if she were ever in trouble she could always call on Ysaye—or even one of the natives—with her telepathy. Now she couldn't. They were on their own, in the hands of men who were probably so steeped in violence and hatred that they would certainly stoop to anything to get what they wanted—men of the sort she had only encountered in books and records, never in person. She had no idea what, if anything, she could do to appeal to them. Nor, clearly, did David; his life of shelter and privilege, and all his scholastic and scientific training, had left him as unable to deal with criminals as was she.

And she was terrified.

CHAPTER 23

Leonie floated in a warm and comforting darkness, as if she were lying in a deep featherbed. Yet there were voices disturbing the darkness. *I cannot save them both*, Leonie heard, as from a vast distance. *I do not think I can do much for the other except to hold off death for a little longer, and while I do that, she drains the youngster. Yet if she dies, her death will affect Leonie. It will shock her, and leave her weak and unable to continue her training for some time, a tenday or so, at least.*

Leonie considered that, in an oddly detached state of mind. A little rest might not be such a bad thing. . . .

Then save Leonie, cushion her as best you can, and let the other die, replied a voice sharp-edged with impatience and heavy with authority. *So long as she can continue her training eventually. She is too valuable—and the other is nothing to us.*

Leonie was confused; it seemed she was listening to the Terranan doctors discussing the fates of Ysaye and her child.

If her own people cannot save her life, why should you even try? Leonie knew that voice; it was Marelie, the Keeper of Arilinn Tower. And with that recognition, memory returned, and she knew who the "other" must be.

Ysaye!

When the man called Ryan Evans had seized Ysaye, they had been so tightly linked that Leonie had reacted to the attack as if it had been to herself. And reflex provided the response that had been drilled into her for the past several weeks.

For no Keeper could continue to work after she had lost her virginity—or at least, not without a long time of reconditioning and cleansing of her channels. So the Towers decreed that any man who dared to lay hands on one must serve as an immediate and horrifying example to anyone else who contemplated such violence. Every Keeper was taught the defense that Leonie unleashed on Evans, a defense that literally called fire up within the man, and charred him to the bone in a matter of moments.

But Ysaye was no longer virgin—and had never been properly trained to allow the energies of *laran* flow through her channels anyway. So the power had backlashed on Ysaye as well, and Leonie had shared her agony as she burned with Ryan Evans.

And it must be that Ysaye still clung to life only through that link they shared.

As Leonie realized this, she also felt it, draining away her energy, leechlike—and felt the Arilinn chief healer and the best monitor, working together, slowly severing that bond.

"No—" she whispered to herself, but she was given no more choice than Ysaye had been. The last thread holding them together snapped, whiplashing back into Leonie, and flinging her out of the strange darkness into which she had awakened, and out into the overworld.

She knew it for what it was immediately; the restless gray mist, the vague hints of Arilinn Tower where her body lay, and other Towers farther away—Neskaya,

Dalereuth, Corandolis, Thendara. But she was not alone here. Another woman stood before her, a very thin, tall, dark-skinned woman with features never seen on a Darkovan.

With a shock, she recognized Ysaye from the few glimpses she had gotten when the star woman looked in a mirror. And beside Ysaye, clinging to her hand, was a very young girl, in whose face Leonie read both Ysaye's heritage and Hastur blood. Both Ysaye and the child were slightly transparent, and the far-off bulk of Neskaya Tower could be seen through Ysaye's insubstantial body.

Well, Leonie, the apparition said. *You were right.*

Leonie shook her head, still trying to recover from the shock of being suddenly snapped into the overworld. *Right about what?* she asked.

That my child wouldn't stop crying until I joined her. Ysaye seemed very calm, very detached—inhumanly so. As if human concerns no longer mattered to her. *You owe me a blood-debt, you know. If it hadn't been for you . . . Lorill never would have come to Aldaran in the first place, he never would have returned, and when I confronted Ryan Evans, it would have been with someone from Security at my back.*

Leonie shivered, realizing what she faced could command almost any blood-debt from her that Ysaye cared to name. For it was very true that Leonie was as guilty of Ysaye's blood as Ryan Evans was. Perhaps more so; if Lorill had never played a part in this tragedy, it all might have ended very differently. And Lorill had gone to Aldaran only because Leonie wanted him to do so.

What do you want from me? she asked, shivering and submissive. This was not the Ysaye she knew; it was an Ysaye stripped of all the things that made her human. There was no telling what she wanted.

My friends Elizabeth and David have been taken prisoner, by bandits living in the old keep of Scorpion Point, Ysaye replied dispassionately. *You must see that someone learns this, someone who can tell it to my people.*

Who? Leonie cried out, relieved to have gotten off so easily. *The Keeper of Arilinn? The Keeper at Aldaran?*

Ysaye shook her head, but was already looking off into the distance, as if she were impatient to be somewhere else. *Most of the Terrans don't believe in* laran *at all. They will not believe a source like that. No— Kadarin and Zeb Scott are somewhere near where David and Elizabeth are being held, and with a Ghost Wind blowing, they are as open to a sending as any worker in the relays. They can determine the truth of the matter, and go for help.* She looked directly into Leonie's eyes, and Leonie shivered again at the cold light she saw there. *Enough,* Ysaye said. *We must go.*

And with that, she picked up her child, turned, and walked away, covering incredible spans of distance with each seemingly-ordinary step, until she dwindled into the distance, and was gone into the mist. Leonie stood where she had been all along, too frozen to follow, even if she could have found the courage.

Then, abruptly, there was another feeling of something snapping back on her, and she found herself back in her body in the Tower, with the motherly face of Ysabet, Arilinn's best healer, bending over her.

She tried to talk, and couldn't; her voice was nothing more than a rasp, and she was tired, so incredibly tired, as utterly drained as if she had tried to hold the relays open for a tenday by herself.

"Don't talk, *chiya,*" Ysabet said quietly. "Here, let me help you drink this—the things you need now are rest and sleep—"

Leonie shook her head, turning her face away from the cup of some potion that Ysabet offered her, until finally, with a grimace of exasperation, Ysabet put it down. *All right, then,* the woman said, mind-to-mind. *What is it that is so urgent it cannot wait?*

There is a debt I must pay—an obligation. Leonie told her as much as she could without revealing how her unauthorized contact with Ysaye had taken place since she arrived at Arilinn. And while she could not lie mind-to-mind, she left out enough that Ysabet made the conclusion that Ysaye, an untrained and therefore unpredictable telepath, had seized on Leonie's mind as she was attacked, not the other way around; and Leonie had reacted to the unexpected double-attack as she had been trained. Leonie, raw and open as she was, saw Ysabet come to all the conclusions she had hoped the woman would, and felt a weary relief. She said nothing of the blood-debt that Ysaye had laid on her; she only made it seem as if she feared to sleep with this debt unpaid.

That, at least, was not feigned; sleep would bring dreams, and those dreams would certainly be nightmares. Leonie did not want to face those dreams just yet.

Reluctantly, Ysabet agreed to let her rest without the medicine for a little while, so long as she simply lay in her bed, quietly. *I shall bring you some fruit juice in a moment,* Ysabet said. *I must go and lay this tale at the feet of the Keeper and she will make of it what she will. Let us hope that this star-woman was the only one of her people with so much* laran.

With that, Ysabet let her down upon her pillows again, and Leonie, obedient in appearance, at least, closed her eyes.

But the moment the woman had left her room, she marshaled the last of her weary strength, and sent out a thought-probe in the direction of Aldaran, seeking two minds now drifting on a Ghost Wind.

When Elizabeth and David were lost behind the rim of the hill they had topped, Zeb realized that he had probably done something pretty stupid, letting himself be goaded into this little expedition. He was alone, completely alone, with an unpredictable alien—and about to experience the effects of some kind of hallucinogenic drug. He knew better, from his years spent growing up in Arizona, to think that any "natural" hallucinogen must be weaker than a synthetic. Try and tell that to the peyote-chewers!

Once again, as if he sensed Zeb's growing unease, Kadarin asked, "Are you sure you wouldn't rather seek shelter against the Ghost Wind?" There was a hint of mockery in that voice that made all his Terran-engendered macho instinct rise up on its hind legs and beat its chest.

"Not a chance, friend," Zeb replied. "I'm not afraid of any wind that ever blew, or ghosts, or any drug that's ever been."

But out of the back of his mind, he thought he heard his grandfather saying *There ain't a hoss that cain't be rode, but there ain't a* man *that cain't be* throwed. *So you better remember before you aim to fork a bronc that you may not be the man that kin ride that hoss.*

Well, it was too late to back out now; as they topped the next ridge, dismounted, and tethered their horses, the wind blew straight into their faces. The smell of the pollen was heavy and resinous, and for a moment, Zeb felt as if he were fighting to take a breath.

He'd done his share of experimenting, on Keef and in the spaceport towns of a dozen other worlds; there was no doubt in his mind that this was a very powerful drug, both psychedelic and intoxicating. It took effect almost immediately.

At first, the main effect was one of euphoria, an incredibly uplifting sense of well-being. He sat right down on the soft, long grass, and watched the sky break up into splinters and shards of light above him. Kadarin perched beside him, and he could feel the watchful, amused regard of the alien.

Kadarin did not seem to be as strongly affected as Zeb. And that only reminded him of something that had occurred to him a few days ago. Strange, how much Kadarin looked like a human, when everything he said and did showed that he obviously wasn't.

Zeb had lived and worked with nonhumans all across the Terran Empire; sometimes he was the only human on a Survey crew when personnel got stretched thin. He was well known for being a man who was as near to being without prejudice as any human could be, which made him a prime candidate for such assignments. What struck him at this moment was how little the other crew members had realized how *very* alien Kadarin was.

It wasn't anything that showed on the surface, although in general a native species either was fully human, or obviously was something else. And you only had to look at Felicia to know that some of these— whatevers—were cross-fertile with humans, which just wasn't supposed to happen according to the biology Zeb knew. And on top of that Felicia had given birth to Aldaran's child, which showed that the hybrids were cross-fertile, too. . . .

Though the baby had six fingers on either hand, and a pair of eyes like butter-amber. Not exactly the kind of traits that cropped up all that often in human families.

That led to another question. Funny, how his mind kept running on with questions, while his body was

perfectly content to sit here and breathe in this
pollen. Was *Kadarin* cross-fertile with humans?

I'm not sure. Kadarin said, without opening his
mouth. *I have no children—and it's not for lack of
trying.* He laughed then, wryly, which did require opening his mouth. *I am far older than I look, believe me;
all my kind are. Did you know I was a good deal older
than Kermiac? I was born—you may believe this or
not, as you like—in the same year as Kermiac's great-
grandfather. I suppose I am like a mule of sorts; any
horse-breeder will tell you that a mule is sterile.*

Zeb nodded at that; his grandfather had bred mules
for the tourist trade.

*And now and again in a zoo, you will see other
species interbreed. Lion and tiger, for instance. Not
often—but sometimes those species are close enough for
the offspring to be fertile. So I may be a mule, and Felicia
may be a tigron. She is a normal female—but she is much
younger than I am.*

It suddenly occurred to him that either this was a
hallucination, or it was telepathy. But if it was a hallucination, where had Kadarin gotten the concept of
"tigrons" from? Those were Terran animals; he could
only have plucked it from Zeb's mind.

So this must be telepathy. Maybe Elizabeth wasn't
as gullible as Zeb had thought. He covered his eyes for
a moment with his hands, to shut off the light-play and
think better. How after this could he manage not to
believe in telepathy?

No—a lifetime of skepticism could not be left behind. It still didn't make sense. This could still be a
hallucination. It didn't take telepathy to make him *think*
that Kadarin was talking to him.

"How can you manage still to disbelieve?" Kadarin
asked, and this time it was with real words. Zeb took
his hands away to make sure the man's mouth was

moving. "Or is there nothing that would prove it to you beyond a shadow of doubt?"

Was *that* the reason for all this dare-double-dare machismo? To put him into a position where he'd supposedly get evidence that would make him a believer? "Not that I can think of," Zeb replied.

"Then I suppose I will simply have to wait until circumstances prove it to you," Kadarin said. "But I have to tell you, Zeb, it truly troubles me to be thought dishonest. I do not lie; none of my people lie. We are, most of us, gifted with at least enough telepathy that we know when we are being lied to."

He fell silent, and once again, Zeb heard that voice in his head. *I suppose I should not be surprised that these head-blind men do not believe in anything they cannot see or touch.*

The air was still filled with the heavy scent of *kireseth* blossoms. Around them, Zeb watched the little creatures that lived in the grass and the trees as they, too, were affected by the pollen. A squirrel—or rather, something that was almost like a squirrel—ran lightly down a tree at the edge of the grove in front of him. He found himself feeling what the little beast felt.

Now that was distinctly odd, for it *was* all feeling, with no real thinking, and it wasn't something he would have been able to make up for himself. It was enjoying the warm day, and the heavy, aphrodisiac scent of the blossoms on the air; the heavy resins worked differently on the little creature's brain than on his. It had lost every trace of fear, the euphoria and disorientation that should have bothered it mattered not at all, and its only quest at the moment was to find a female. And even that was not so important; if no female of the right size—let alone the right species—wandered near, it would simply roll in the grass and play like a kit with the sunbeams. . . .

This was a lovely world. At first, Zeb hadn't much for it, too cold, too windy, too mountain There was a streak of what his grandfather used to laughingly call "an eco-freak" in him, a streak that his grandfather shared, and he just hadn't been able to warm up to this planet.

But now it was sharing itself with him, and he realized how much he liked it. He'd almost forgotten this other part of himself, being in space for so long. But now, this pollen had made it all wake up again; had put him in touch with his truest mind, his innermost self. And he wanted to be a part of this world, as he had never wanted to be part of any world, even long-gone Terra. When he'd had to sell his grandfather's ranch to pay the back taxes, it had just about broken his heart, and he'd turned his back on Terra and headed straight into space. But now this place had just opened up for him, and he felt as if it was offering itself in place of his long lost love.

And there were people who needed him here, too. Felicia, and baby Thyra. Kermiac Aldaran wouldn't be around forever, and neither would his lady—and besides, little Thyra needed a daddy, and Felicia was one of those gentle creatures that needed a husband-protector. Not every woman did, and that was fine with Zeb; he liked seeing a proud and independent woman in operation in the same way he liked to see a mustang running free, without seeing the need to break either one to bridle and saddle. But for him—well, he needed to be the protector. And sweet Felicia needed someone like him.

Was that why Kadarin had goaded him into this? He acted like Felicia's big brother sometimes; was he trying to get Zeb to see the whole picture going on here? Maybe so; surely if he hadn't, there was a real likelihood Zeb would have finished his work here, and drifted on, just as he had on every other world he'd put down on.

But now—this time, he'd put down roots; he'd stay. And it seemed to him as if the world about him sensed his acceptance, and accepted him in turn. . . .

Yes, he'd stay; he'd stay just like Elizabeth and David, and his kids (and Felicia's) would grow up to play with their kids, all Darkovans together.

The meadow in front of him wavered, and vanished, and in its place he suddenly saw the walls of the ruined castle the Lornes had been heading for. Only it wasn't deserted. It was full of men, and he knew as well as he knew his own name that these men were the same kind of lawless varmints that had made parts of the Old West impossible for honest men to live in. Bandits, that was what they were—

And then, he saw to his absolute horror, that they had David and Elizabeth prisoner.

They had to get back. They had to get help! And they had to do it before it was too late. "Bob," he said decisively, "I've got to get back!"

Kadarin rose lazily to his feet. "Any time."

Zeb listened to Commander MacAran's briefing, with no sign that he was short on sleep and long on adrenaline. Now that something was being done, the pre-mission calm that always settled over him had flung its cushioning over his nerves. It was out of his hands now, and into the hands of his superiors. Now he no longer had to make decisions; just take orders.

It was dark now; they would attack at dawn.

"All right, so far as we can tell, there's no back way into this place, and no hidden entrances," muttered Ralph MacAran, who had been made chief of the rescue team. "Just to be sure, though—I want the flier to come in right on top of them, so nobody's going to be able

to pull a fast one on us and sneak the Lornes out ~~~
back."

He was already in shock—they all were—from the grisly deaths of Ysaye and Ryan Evans. And then, Zeb and that native, Kadarin, had come pounding over the horizon, having ridden their horses to collapse, with this. One horrible disaster after another.

Zeb Scott, who would be the pilot, nodded tersely, and headed for the craft. Within moments it was airborne, and the plan was to have it come over the horizon at tree-top level as soon as MacAran gave the attack signal.

"The rest of you, fan out and cover the entrance; Kelly, you've been working with Lorne and you speak the language better than anyone else, so once we're in place, take the bullhorn and tell them they're surrounded. Tell them to surrender, give them a few minutes, and if they don't walk out under a white flag within five minutes, back off. Then I'll be putting a few smoke-bombs over the walls, just as a warning. If that doesn't work—well, then it'll be up to Zeb and the SWAT team. And to keep them from getting out the back, I'll lob a few incendiary grenades into the woods."

He patted the side of the hand-missile launcher, and Commander Britton frowned.

"Do you really think that's a good idea?" he asked. "What if they threaten to kill the Lornes?"

MacAran shrugged. "Empire policy; we pay no ransoms, make no negotiation with terrorists and kidnappers, and if they kill the hostages, we kill them."

Britton grimaced, but said nothing.

Aurora Lakshman made a gesture of protest. "Ralph—I don't like the idea of hitting these people who know nothing of explosives with a barrage of grenades. That's the kind of thing people on Earth in ages past did all too often to underdeveloped nations—we have a reputation for it. Do we really want to do that here and now?"

"It's just a bang and a lot of smoke, it's only to scare them, and if they have any brains, they'll surrender right off," MacAran replied, "And I wouldn't do it if we had any other options. But we don't and I have my orders."

"And what if they still don't surrender?" Aurora demanded. "What if they *do* kill David and Elizabeth? Are you going to incinerate them from above? Why not just ignore the demands—pretend that we don't care? Surely, sooner or later, these men will let the Lornes go!"

"If you abandon them," Kadarin put in, "the bandits will almost certainly kill them, once no one seems interested in paying a ransom. It is not in their interest to let someone go who knows where they are."

MacAran frowned at the unsolicited comment; if he'd had his way, Kadarin wouldn't be along at all. *He* still wasn't sure Kadarin had nothing to do with this— after all, it had been the Darkovan who'd picked the place for the Lornes to shelter from the "Ghost Wind" in. Though why they needed to take shelter from a wind . . . well, it didn't matter, what did matter was that Kadarin's involvement in this seemed a little too pat. He could not get over the idea that somewhere behind that imperturbable facade, Kadarin was laughing at him.

He looked at the rest of his troops; tough men, many of whom had been in police forces or other combat-organizations on different worlds before they joined the Service.

"All right, people," he said, finally. "Move out, and get into place. With luck, they'll believe us and turn the Lornes loose, and all this will just impress the natives that we don't play footsie with terrorists."

And if luck isn't with us, he thought, *I hope to God they don't call our bluff. And I hope they're still alive.*

Elizabeth was very cold without the Terran sleeping bag which the bandits had confiscated; it took her a long time every night to drop off, and even then she slept fitfully and restlessly. Each night she had nightmares. And each morning, as the red sun just cleared the mountain tops and rose out of a sea of heavy, grayish-pink clouds, she woke again with her stomach heaving.

This morning, the fourth of their captivity, was no different.

She pushed open the tent flap, and went past the sleepy-eyed guard to the crude and barely-adequate lean-to in one corner of the roofless room that served as an equally crude bathroom. As she bent over the pot there, cramped with nausea, she could only think how unfair it was for her first bouts with morning sickness to begin here and now. At one point in the benighted past, there had been a medical theory that women who suffered from morning sickness had a only psychological problem, that secretly they did not wish to be pregnant.

A theory put forth by male doctors, she thought. Just like the one that women who suffered PMS and other similar problems secretly did not want to be women. Or that they wanted attention.

Well, this had to be the worst way of getting attention that she had ever seen.

This was their fourth day of imprisonment, and she only hoped that Zeb and Kadarin had not gone crazy, or walked off a cliff, or been caught by some other set of bandits. She was certain that if this particular lot had gotten hold of the other two, their leader would have lost no chance to gloat.

When her stomach finally settled, she wiped her

mouth and wrapped her down jacket about her shoulders, and staggered past the smirking guard back to their tent, shivering. Although the bandits had fed them, after a fashion, she felt perpetually hungry and cold. And dirty; her hair felt ready to crawl off her scalp. She felt she would have given her right hand for a good soak in a hot bath.

David had awakened as she'd lurched out to the primitive privy. "Are you all right, love?" he asked in concern as she pushed her way back through the flap of the tent.

"Nothing that won't correct itself in a few months," she sighed, reaching for the cup of water he handed to her to rinse the sour taste from her mouth. "That's the one good thing about pregnancy; it's going to end in its own time."

"It could be worse," he said, trying to cheer her up. "Imagine having morning sickness in zero-gee."

She shuddered. "You imagine it; I'd rather not."

He held her closer, and she snuggled into his arms, trying to get a little warmer. "Are you sure you're all right?" he persisted. "I don't like it that you're sick, and we don't have any medical care for you. This is the third day in a row that you've lost your breakfast."

"No, it isn't," she replied. "I haven't *had* breakfast yet. And women have been having babies and morning sickness for thousands of years without medical help. I'll be all right."

He tightened his arms around her. "I wish they'd just let us go—or something. But since you're out of contact with Ysaye—I'm not holding my breath waiting."

"Surely by now at least Ysaye is raising a ruckus. I've never been out of contact with her for this long before."

But David shook his head. "We've gotten used to

having that constant contact, but before we landed here, that telepathic link was a pretty hit-or-miss thing. And we don't know how distance affects it, so she might well assume that you're just too far away to reach. Or too busy."

Elizabeth bit her lip, and tried not to think how right he was. "Look, there's Kadarin and Zeb Scott, too—"

"And Kadarin could have set this up," David interrupted. "Even if he didn't, I'm not inclined to put too much faith in him. He has an entirely too peculiar a sense of humor for my taste. He might think this situation is all very amusing."

That was so true that Elizabeth didn't even bother to agree. She fell glumly silent. After a while—a long while—one of their captors entered with what passed for their breakfast; some kind of stale bread and dried meat, and a couple of lukewarm cups of whatever that local equivalent of coffee was.

It was just as unappetizing as all the rest of their meals had been, and Elizabeth picked up a round of the bread and began to gnaw on it, dispiritedly. "I wish they'd tell us something," she said, breaking the silence.

"Like what?" David wrestled with a scrap of the meat.

"Anything," she said passionately. "Whether or not they've at least been in touch with Lord Aldaran. What if they go to him, and he counts noses and just tells them that he isn't missing anyone? Where does that leave us?"

"Maybe they'll figure out that we were telling the truth," David offered, and sighed. "But God only knows how long that would take."

But something had caught Elizabeth's attention—a sound that hadn't been there before. She cocked her

head sideways, frowning. "David, do you hear anything?"

He stopped chewing and listened a moment. "Is
that—no, that's not the wind, is it?" he said in wonder.
"It sounds like a plane! There can't be a plane on the
planet that isn't ours. Liz, they're coming for us!"

His voice was drowned out by the roar of a flier
making a low pass over the walls and returning.

"This is Captain Gibbons of the starship Minnesota!" roared an amplified voice from somewhere outside the walls.

"No it's not. it's Grant Kelly—" David said, but
Elizabeth hushed him.

*"We have you surrounded. You are holding two
members of the crew of the starship* Minnesota. *You
have five minutes to release them. We do not negotiate;
we do not pay ransom. If you release them, we will
withdraw. If you do not, we will use weapons on you.
If you harm or kill them, we will kill you. Your time
starts now."*

"Yes!" David shouted, jumping to his feet. "That's
telling them!"

Elizabeth was terrified. "No!" she cried. "They
can't! They don't know he's serious!"

"Then they'll have to learn," David replied heart-
lessly. "For all our people know, we're already dead."

The minutes dragged; then came the unmistakable
sound of a portable missile-launcher, and a pervasive,
creeping smell of smoke, followed by the roar of the
flier coming in again at tree-top level, and the sound of
weapons' fire.

Smoke poured into the tent, obscuring everything.
Elizabeth coughed and choked, and David turned stark
white. There were shouts, and the tent walls shook.

Elizabeth flung herself to the floor of the tent; David
threw himself on top of her to protect her. The next

few moments were sheer chaos; filled with the screams of men and animals, the choking stench of burning, and shouts of "Fire! The woods are on fire!"

Then one of their captors tore open the tent flap and dragged them both out into the open, his face a mask of terror. He shoved them before him, through the haze of smoke, out into what had been the great hall of the place.

And Elizabeth saw, over the ragged tops of the walls, the wall of flames where ages-old trees had been.

Elizabeth coughed and choked from the smoke as the bandits shoved them out past the walls and into the open. She staggered forward, David at her side, even though she couldn't see a thing through the thick smoke that made her eyes water and burn. In a moment, she was in Aurora Lakshman's arms.

The bandit held onto David's arm a moment longer. The linguist was astonished by the depth of anger and bitterness in the man's face.

"You think of *us* as barbarians," he said. "But you are the ones who do not observe the Compact. You cannot be civilized. A brute animal has more morals and ethics than you people."

Then he shoved David after his wife, and vanished into the smoke.

He goes to fight the fire, David heard in his mind, and turned to find Kadarin waiting to escort him to the flier. *Even a bandit will fight a fire in these forests. And only a madman would set one.*

Kadarin nodded at David's look of surprise, and turned grimly to lead him through the smoke.

EPILOGUE

Lorill Hastur faced the Comyn Council with more of a sense of weariness than anything else. He probably should have been trembling with fear at the idea of facing so many important people; instead, he was only tired. He still did not know how so many things could have gone wrong, and had no idea of how to right them. Perhaps there was no way to do so, ever. He had only spent days fighting the forest fire, but he felt years older.

"To sum it all up," he concluded, "Even though I am not very old, nor very wise, and even though the will of Hastur is no more the law of the land than that of any other Comyn lord, if you were to ask me, I would say to have as little to do with these Terrans as possible. They are still in the back pocket of Aldaran, and we all know that the wishes of Aldaran are often at violent odds with the best interests of the rest of the Domains. They are not evil people, yet Aldaran is all they know—and what Aldaran has told them of us. Their customs are so far from ours that it often seemed to me that they could hardly be considered human. But that is not the worst of it. The worst is the weapons that they hold."

He closed his eyes for a moment, trying to forget the things he had seen. He had gone to help fight the fire, as had every man, woman and child in the area.

It had been a nightmare, and the memories would be slow to fade.

"They have terrible weapons," he said. "Weapons that work at a distance, in violation of the Compact. And they seem ready to use them with very little provocation, even when other choices are available. I cannot see how they can possibly be made to give those weapons up."

At the murmur of disbelief, he opened his eyes and glared at the mutterers. "I tell you, I have seen those weapons at work! I watched how they accidentally set a fire in the forest, a fire it took three days and nights to stop, and which destroyed two dozen leagues of forest in that time! I fought that fire myself—and from there, I came straight here. Although the Terrans used special machines and liquids to help quell the fire which they started, without which we surely would have been fighting the blaze for weeks, I say to you, we must leave these people to themselves, for they are too perilous to have in our midst."

"What of your sister, Leonie?" called one man. "She urged contact with these people—what has she to say of this?"

"Nothing," Lorill replied shortly. "She is in seclusion; she has begun her training at Arilinn as a Keeper, and she is not permitted to communicate with her kin. And at any rate, it would seem to me, sirs, that the wishes of a young girl are not to be weighed against the violence of men who would break the Compact."

He took his seat, and the debate began. And as he sat there, he knew how it would end. He would have his way—for now. But not forever.

Leonie had been right; not all the will of the Comyn could hold these Terrans back forever. And he longed, with a longing that was an ache, that he *could* talk to her. A few days ago, he had believed that nothing in

the world could cut Leonie off from him—not all the
will of all the Keepers in the world.

He had been speaking with her right up until the
moment he left Aldaran to return home; two days later,
he had been held to shelter by a storm. He had tried
to contact her then, and had been met only by a complete barrier.

Then had come men looking for help to fight a great
fire, and before he left, he had heard that *Terranan*
weapons had started that fire. He had heard first-hand
the tale of the distance-weapons that they used. And
when he expressed disbelief, they courteously demonstrated those weapons for him.

He knew then that he needed to speak with Leonie,
desperately, to find out how the *Terranan* could do such
things. He had continued to try to reach her, thinking
that the barrier between them was some construct of
the Keepers, and that she would soon get around it,
but after a day or so he had realized that it was not
something created to wall him out by the Keeper of
Arilinn, but was a barrier built of some great and terrible shock Leonie had endured.

And when he returned home, he found a message
waiting for him there—saying only that for the rest of
her training at Arilinn she could not be allowed to communicate with any of her kin. He would have taken
oath that nothing short of death or catastrophe could
have cut Leonie off from him. And now he feared that
it was catastrophe which had.

He rubbed his weary eyes, and looked up, to see
the last of the lords of the Domain registering their
votes.

He had won. The youngest man in the Council, and
his will had prevailed. There would be no contact with
the *Terranan*. They would remain in involuntary iso-

lation in the Hellers. He should have been thrilled, that so many older, more powerful men had bent to his will, unprompted by any word from his father.

But the taste of victory was dust and ashes in his mouth.

DAW

MARION ZIMMER BRADLEY

THE DARKOVER NOVELS

The Founding

☐ DARKOVER LANDFALL   UE2234—$3.99

The Ages of Chaos

☐ HAWKMISTRESS!   UE2239—$4.99
☐ STORMQUEEN!   UE2310—$4.50

The Hundred Kingdoms

☐ TWO TO CONQUER   UE2174—$4.99
☐ THE HEIRS OF HAMMERFELL   UE2451—$4.99
☐ THE HEIRS OF HAMMERFELL (hardcover)   UE2395—$18.95

The Renunciates (Free Amazons)

☐ THE SHATTERED CHAIN   UE2308—$4.50
☐ THENDARA HOUSE   UE2240—$4.99
☐ CITY OF SORCERY   UE2332—$4.99

Against the Terrans: The First Age

☐ REDISCOVERY   UE2529—$4.99
☐ REDISCOVERY (hardcover)*   UE2561—$18.00
☐ THE SPELL SWORD   UE2237—$3.99
☐ THE FORBIDDEN TOWER   UE2373—$4.99
☐ STAR OF DANGER   UE2607—$4.99

Against the Terrans: The Second Age

☐ THE BLOODY SUN   UE2603—$4.99
☐ THE HERITAGE OF HASTUR   UE2413—$4.99
☐ SHARRA'S EXILE   UE2309—$4.99

*with Mercedes Lackey

Buy them at your local bookstore or use this convenient coupon for ordering.

PENGUIN USA P.O. Box 999—Dept. #17109, Bergenfield, New Jersey 07621

Please send me the DAW BOOKS I have checked above, for which I am enclosing
$_____ (please add $2.00 per order to cover postage and handling). Send check
or money order (no cash or C.O.D.'s) or charge by Mastercard or Visa (with a
$15.00 minimum.) Prices and numbers are subject to change without notice.

Card #_____ Exp. Date _____
Signature_____
Name_____
Address_____
City _____ State _____ Zip _____

For faster service when ordering by credit card call **1-800-253-6476**

Please allow a minimum of 4 to 6 weeks for delivery.

A note concerning:

MARION ZIMMER BRADLEY'S
FANTASY MAGAZINE

Fans of Marion Zimmer Bradley will be pleased to hear that she is now publishing her own fantasy magazine. If you're interested in subscribing and/or would like to submit material to it, write her at:

P.O. Box 249
Berkeley, CA 94701

(If you're interested in writing for the magazine, please enclose a SASE for her free Writer's Guidelines *before* submitting material.)

THE FRIENDS OF DARKOVER

So popular have been the novels of the planet Darkover that an organization of readers and fans has come into being, virtually spontaneously. The Friends of Darkover is purely an amateur and voluntary group. It has no paid officers and has not established any formal membership dues. Thendara Council serves as a central point for information on Darkover-oriented newsletters ad maintains a chronological list of Marion Zimmer Bradley's books.   Contact may be made by writing to the Friends of Darkover, Thendara Council, PO Box 72, Berkeley, CA 94701 and enclosing a SASE (Self-Addressed Stamped Envelope) for information.

(These notices are inserted gratis as a service to readers. DAW Books is in no way connected with these organizations professionally or commercially.)

DAW

MARION ZIMMER BRADLEY
NON-DARKOVER NOVELS

- [ ] **HUNTERS OF THE RED MOON**　　UE1968—$3.99
- [ ] **THE SURVIVORS**　　UE1861—$3.99
- [ ] **WARRIOR WOMAN**　　UE2253—$3.50

NON-DARKOVER ANTHOLOGIES

- [ ] **SWORD AND SORCERESS I**　　UE2359—$4.50
- [ ] **SWORD AND SORCERESS II**　　UE2360—$3.95
- [ ] **SWORD AND SORCERESS III**　　UE2302—$4.50
- [ ] **SWORD AND SORCERESS IV**　　UE2412—$4.50
- [ ] **SWORD AND SORCERESS V**　　UE2288—$3.50
- [ ] **SWORD AND SORCERESS VI**　　UE2423—$3.95
- [ ] **SWORD AND SORCERESS VII**　　UE2457—$4.50
- [ ] **SWORD AND SORCERESS VIII**　　UE2486—$4.50
- [ ] **SWORD AND SORCERESS IX**　　UE2509—$4.50
- [ ] **SWORD AND SORCERESS X**　　UE2552—$4.99

COLLECTIONS

- [ ] **LYTHANDE** (with Vonda N. McIntyre)　　UE2291—$3.95
- [ ] **THE BEST OF MARION ZIMMER BRADLEY** edited by Martin H. Greenberg　　UE2268—$3.95

DAW

MARION ZIMMER BRADLEY, Editor
THE DARKOVER ANTHOLOGIES

Mercedes Lackey

The Novels of Valdemar

THE MAGE WARS (with Larry Dixon)
☐ **THE BLACK GRYPHON (hardcover)**   UE2577—$22.00

THE LAST HERALD-MAGE
☐ **MAGIC'S PAWN: Book 1**   UE2352—$4.99
☐ **MAGIC'S PROMISE: Book 2**   UE2401—$4.99
☐ **MAGIC'S PRICE: Book 3**   UE2426—$4.99

VOWS AND HONOR
☐ **THE OATHBOUND: Book 1**   UE2285—$4.99
☐ **OATHBREAKERS: Book 2**   UE2319—$4.99

KEROWYN'S TALE
☐ **BY THE SWORD**   UE2463—$5.99

THE HERALDS OF VALDEMAR
☐ **ARROWS OF THE QUEEN: Book 1**   UE2378—$4.99
☐ **ARROW'S FLIGHT: Book 2**   UE2377—$4.99
☐ **ARROW'S FALL: Book 3**   UE2400—$4.99

THE MAGE WINDS
☐ **WINDS OF FATE: Book 1 (hardcover)**   UE2489—$18.95
☐ **WINDS OF FATE: Book 1 (paperback)**   UE2516—$4.99
☐ **WINDS OF CHANGE: Book 2 (hardcover)**   UE2534—$20.00
☐ **WINDS OF CHANGE: Book 2 (paperback)**   UE2563—$4.99
☐ **WINDS OF FURY: Book 3 (hardcover)**   UE2562—$20.00

Buy them at your local bookstore or use this convenient coupon for ordering.

PENGUIN USA   P.O. Box 999, Dept. #17109, Bergenfield, New Jersey 07621

Please send me the DAW BOOKS I have checked above, for which I am enclosing
$_____ (please add $2.00 per order to cover postage and handling.) Send check
or money order (no cash or C.O.D.'s) or charge by Mastercard or Visa (with a
$15.00 minimum.) Prices and numbers are subject to change without notice.

Card #_____ Exp. Date _____
Signature_____
Name_____
Address_____
City _____ State _____ Zip _____

For faster service when ordering by credit card call **1-800-253-6476**

Please allow a minimum of 4 to 6 weeks for delivery.

DAW

A note from the publishers concerning:

QUEEN'S OWN

You are invited to join "Queen's Own," an organization of readers and fans of the works of Mercedes (Misty) Lackey. This appreciation society has a worldwide membership of all ages. Nominal dues are charged.

"Queen's Own" publishes a newsletter 9 times a year, providing information about Mercedes Lackey's upcoming books, tapes, convention appearances, and more. A network of pen friends is also available for those who wish to share their enjoyment of her work.

For more information, please send a business-size SASE (self-addressed stamped envelope) to:

"Queen's Own"
P.O. Box 132
Shiloh, NJ 08353

(This notice is inserted gratis as a service to readers. DAW Books is in no way connected with this organization professionally or commercially.)